Return To You

A Small Town, Second Chance Romance

BELLA RIVERS

ebook ISBN: 978-1-962627-04-7
print ISBN (couple cover): 978-1-962627-14-6
print ISBN (discreet cover): 978-1-962627-08-5

v5

Developmental editing: Angela James

Copyediting/Proofreading: Grace Wynter, The Writer's Station

Final Review: Teresa Beeman, Next Chapter Editing

Cover design: Echo Grayce, Wildheart Graphics

Contents

CHAPTER ONE

Ethan

"Ethan? Holy fuck, man!" The voice jolts me, and I nearly spill gas on the bike's tank. It was bound to happen. I just didn't think I'd be recognized as soon as I rolled into Emerald Creek.

I'm technically not even there yet. I stopped for gas on the side of the road when the village was in sight. I need a minute to gather myself.

I hang the dispenser back and turn to face whoever it is calling my name. Long, assured steps. A big smile on someone's face that used to sport a frown.

"Colton, man." I extend my hand, but he grabs me in a bear hug and slaps my back.

"Fuck! It's been what? Five, six years?"

"Ten."

He pauses, starts to say something, then stops.

I *was* here, five, six years ago. Not gonna forget that. I just spent the short time drunk so it would go by faster.

But now is different.

I'm different.

"What brings you back?" He glances at my bike. "Visiting your old digs?"

"It's Ma's birthday."

"Oh nice. I didn't know. When is it?"

"Sunday."

"I didn't know," he repeats himself. "Ten years, wow."

"I see 'em now and then," I say, feeling the need to justify myself. To explain that I'm not a complete piece of shit who walked out on his family and never saw them again.

"Yeah-yeah-yeah. Craig—uh, your dad—he likes to brag. 'Bout where they went to visit you." He lets out a short, kind laugh. "What was it...uh... Greece? Turkey? Germany?"

Yup, ten years in the Air Force, you get to see some pretty awesome places. Some not so great, too, or less exotic.

I see my siblings, too, but less often. I always find myself on a mission on Christmas and Thanksgiving, and I never complain about it. I've been known to volunteer a lot.

But I need to put an end to that.

The reasons I ran away? They're making less and less sense to me now, and that's why I'm able to come back.

I blamed myself for the accident that badly injured my brother and took his passenger's life. I wasn't driving, I wasn't at the scene, but at the time I thought, for sure, if I'd done something different that night, said something different, it wouldn't have happened.

Now that I've seen combat and operations, I can tell you: shit goes wrong all the time, and there's fuck nothing you can do about it, even with the best planning, even when you anticipate all that shit. There's more shit coming at you. And there's nothing else you can do than do your best.

So, running scared from a little town in Vermont because you think you messed up? Not worth it. We only have one life to live.

Hey, even the girl who broke my heart is gone. Married, lives in Texas. There's no chance I'll run into her. Hell, running into her brother first thing is the closest I'll get to a past that's way behind me now.

"It's good to see you, Colt. This your place now?" It's a rhetorical question. Colton used to work here, but he's clearly the owner now, judging by the name painted on the facade. Funny how things change.

The garage I'm looking at is nothing like I remember. Gone is the junk in the front. In its place, a vintage baby blue Chevy. The gas pumps are still old as dirt, but they seem in good working order. They're clean, and there's rags and stuff to clean the windshields. Hell, the small office even has potted flowers that someone seems to water.

"Nice bay you got there." The main improvement is in the garage, and Colton straightens proudly at my words.

"Thanks, man." Colton was never a talker.

My tank full, I place the pump back and pocket my credit card. "Business is good?"

"Doin' good. How 'bout you? Where'd you live now?"

"Right now, the back of my bike. Next up, hoping for somewhere warm."

Colton doesn't ask questions. Just lifts his chin and pats my bike. "Two thousand eighteen?" He crouches to take a look at the exhaust.

I nod. "Been giving me a little rattle, but other'n that, she runs smooth."

"Bet she does. Drop her off whenever, I'll take a look at that rattle."

"Careful, might take you up on that."

He unfolds his frame and lays an unsettling gaze on me. "Yeah. Hope you do." He takes a step back, and I straddle my bike, grab my helmet. "Never took you as a bike guy," he drops.

"Never thought I'd be one. Just wanna make sure I don't settle in a place with six months of winter," I say with a grin. "No offense."

He gives me a full smile. "None taken. I get it, man. No risk of that with a ride like this."

Yeah, that's partly why I bought it.

We're saved from the awkward moment between us by a teenage girl wearing blue coveralls, her hair in a bun on top of her head, calling from the mouth of the bay. "Yo, Colt! I'm all done here. What next?"

"Just a sec," Colton calls back to her.

She walks toward us, wiping her hands in a greasy rag, and eyes me top to bottom, a frown on her face, like she's trying to place me. She does look vaguely familiar. "Hey."

"Hey," I answer.

Colton tips his chin at me. "You know who this is?"

She tilts her head. "Maybe?"

"Surprised a hockey girl doesn't know her legends."

The girl's mouth gapes. "Hold on. *Ethan King*?" she asks tentatively.

Colton nods. "Taught me blocking like no coach ever has."

I look at him in surprise, but he's still looking at her. "No way," she says, her eyes like saucers on me. "*The* Ethan King who took us to Nationals?"

"The one and only," Colton answers.

"Coach will be stoked to know you're in town. Can I tell him?"

"Coach Randall?" I can't believe he's still around. Ten years is a lifetime for me. I suppose at his age, it's nothing. "He must be what—a hundred years old?"

The girl laughs. "I won't tell him you said that."

"Yeah, I wouldn't either."

"He'd have me benched. But hey, you'll come to the Arena, right? Do some training with us? We have preseason camp soon."

Being pulled into my hometown's life is exactly what I don't want. Just as I bought a bike to prevent me from settling in the Yankee part of the country if I can help it, I gave myself a hard rule of not sticking around too long. Not getting sucked in.

"I'll probably be gone, but if I can, I'll stop by." I don't want to crush her hopes.

"Cool. I'll tell Coach," the girl says as she saunters back to the bay, pulling her phone from her pocket.

Ah shit. I guess there's no getting around saying hello to the old man. And what's wrong with that, anyway? Except that I was hoping to make my stay here painless. Absent of memories. I'm not big on nostalgic reunions.

The girl comes back running to us. "Mister K, can I get a selfie?" She nudges herself against me, holding her phone at arm's length.

Colton frowns. "You don't have to, man."

I smile toward the phone while the girl takes several pictures. I'm not used to fake-smiling—or smiling—and my cheeks kinda hurt.

"Thanks!" The girl runs back to the bay and shouts out to Colton. "Boss, gonna start on the Bronco!"

"Not without me you're not. Be just a sec."

"I should go," I say.

"It's okay. She's just messing with me. Funny girl."

"She looks familiar. Do I know her?"

Colton shrugs. "I doubt it—she's barely fifteen. Tracy Prescott. Big family. They live above Chandler's Knoll. Dad's with Fish and Game."

I suppose I know the family. That's what life in a small town is like. Everyone's linked one way or another. You can't step foot anywhere without meeting someone you know.

The feeling sits uncomfortably in the pit of my stomach. On base, people come and go all the time. You quickly learn to make new friends or risk having no friends at all. You're also free to feed them whatever backstory you make up for your own sorry life, and no one cares if you're pretending to be who you're not, as long as you do an honest job and buy a round of beers every once in a while.

Here, there's no escaping who you are. Your past. Your present actions. People's opinions on what your future should look like. Who you're with, who you should be with, and especially—*especially*—who you *shouldn't* be with.

I roll out of Colton's garage on an empty promise of a beer together, feeling a little bit like a jerk. Why did I need to tell him about not wanting to settle here? And why did I agree to a beer at my brother's pub, when I know darn well I'm going to find an excuse to get out of it? The last thing I want is to hear about his sister, and she's bound to come up in conversation if we share a drink.

I take the long way alongside the river, down Deweys' Hollow. I thought this would be a fun bike ride—and it is—but *fuck*. So many memories suddenly resurfacing.

Heading back into the village through the covered bridge, I notice how the downtown looks busier than I expected. There's a banner across main street announcing the town fair this Saturday, and another one congratulating Christopher Wright for being New England's Best Baker. *Shit, Chris won New England's Best Baker? That's huge. Colton must be proud of his cousin.*

Main street is crawling with stop-and-go traffic and jaywalkers. A car pulls out of a parking spot in front of a flower shop where the video store used to be.

I slide in and minutes later, I'm walking out with a gorgeous bouquet that set me back... a lot. But hey. I've missed so many of Mom's birthdays, I can splurge a little.

"Well if it isn't Ethan King in the flesh!"

I look down to the petite woman in a modest flowery dress. "Ms. Angela!" I bend down to hug her, the instinct strong, then hesitate. Is it appropriate to hug your third-grade teacher?

"Come here, you big goof!" She takes me in a strong hug that surprises me. "Are these for me? Why, you shouldn't have," she says, laughing.

I laugh with her. "They're for Ma."

She frowns. "She didn't mention you were coming."

"It's a surprise," I confirm.

She rolls her eyes and looks around, at the line in front of the ice cream place—now expanded to cover the corner of the block—at the patrons going in and out of the general store—looking spiffy with fresh paint and overflowing window boxes—at the people sifting through boxes of books on sale in front of the bookshop. "Well, if you want to keep this a surprise, you should get there before she hears it from someone else." She gives me a friendly tap on the arm. "I'll see you later!"

By the time I get to the farm, I've seen a new coffee shop, a sign for the hotel I didn't even know we had, the bookshop with a new, weird name, my brother Justin's pub, packed with patrons at their outdoor seating, and a restaurant right next to it that I don't remember. There are signs for a hot dog shack, the local history museum, an art exhibit, a summer fair, numerous kids' camps.

The town is hopping and nothing like I remember it. It makes me happy and vaguely unsettled at the same time. Like there's something important that I'm missing.

After the covered bridge, it's a familiar ride up to the farm on a winding road that's fucking fun on a bike. King Knoll's Farm soon spreads ahead, and a gentle hum takes ahold of me.

It's about time I'm able to come back here and visit.

Even if I'll never live here, it'll be nice to feel normal when I come.

Although I never wanted to work on the farm, even if I've been gone too long, I still want to be part of the family again. I'm done being a loner. I have three brothers and a sister who all but idolize me. A mom and dad who adore me.

I have no business staying away any longer.

Case in point. I hear Mom's shrieks of pure happiness the minute I take my helmet off. She runs to me and lunges into my arms, and I twirl her around.

You'd think I'd gone to war or something.

"Awww..." she says, at a loss for words, pinching my cheeks. She searches my eyes, and I know she's wondering. She's wondering if I'm here by accident, or if I remembered her birthday.

She still thinks I'm disconnected from the family. From her.

I grab the flowers from the saddle pocket and shove them into her hands. "Happy Birthday, Mom." Then I step back, prepared to memorize her look of disbelief and bliss and gratefulness all mixed together as she goes through the different stages a mother, I suppose, experiences at the return of the prodigal son.

"Bir...?" She looks at the flowers. At me. Squints. Tucks her nose in the flowers. "Mmm. They smell good. Why, thank you!" Then she tucks her arm under mine and takes us up the front porch. "Craig, guess who's here!" she says, shoving the flowers in a dark corner of the kitchen.

"Well, looks who's here," Dad echoes, taking me into a brief hug and slapping my back. "Why didn't you call? What brings you here?" His eyes are dancing. At least he's happy.

"Ma's birthday," I proudly announce.

"Who wants lemonade?" Ma butts in.

"Your Ma's birthday, huh? Which one?"

Oh fuck. This isn't good. Maybe it's a test? "Her...big one?" I'm pretty sure Mom is turning fifty this year. Does she not want to celebrate? Shit.

Dad chuckles, crosses his arms, and bounces on his heels. "You missed it."

"Oh f—darn." I glance at Mom, who's arranging the flowers in a vase now. "Sorry—was it last week?"

Dad is having a field day. "It was last *winter. January.* But since you're here, you could stay 'til her next birthday."

Mom looks up, hopeful.

"Next January?" I ask stupidly.

"That's typically how birthdays work. Come back like clockwork on the same day every year."

Mom sets the vase on the dining table, then hugs me. "I don't care, honey. Long's you're here, I'm happy." She tilts her head back, her eyes brimming with true joy.

I hug her tighter. "Well, Happy Wednesday," I say and feel her laugh against my chest.

Her voice returns muffled. "Happiest Wednesday ever."

Minutes later, we're seated on the front porch, sipping lemonade in stem glasses—"because it's my birthday," Mom said. "Now, tell us all about what you been up to," she adds.

And I do. I catch them up from our last long phone call, up to now, when I'm between assignments.

"So what's next?" Dad asks.

"I requested orders for a billet at Hulbert Field." I don't tell them that's my second choice. My first choice, I don't get to request it. I'd be tapped on the shoulder. I'd be fucking great at it, but the brass will think I'm too young. Mom frowns. "Hulbert Field?"

I nod. "Florida."

"Florida?!" she beams. "Why that's closer than Germany! Still the crypto thingy?"

"Yep. Cryptanalysis and SINGINT."

"I bet you're great at it."

I nod. "I am." I'm fucking great at it. No reason not to say it.

I'm proud of what I'm doing. I've always wanted to do the right thing. To have an impact. That's why I joined the Air Force.

"No way you could do that with the Green Mountain Boys, huh?' she asks, referring to the Air National Guard in Burlington.

Dad does the chin lift.

"Nah, they specialize in combat. Look, end of the day, I'll go where I'm needed. I can tell you as much, I won't be needed here." My last words ring awkwardly, at least to me. I don't know if Mom and Dad ever fully understood why I left, back in the day. How I felt I had let my family down, messed up so spectacularly I had no other option than to leave and enlist in order to finally do something useful. I've come around since then.

Mom stands and gathers our empty glasses. "Well, Hulbert would be stupid not to hire you," she says before going back inside.

The landline trills, then Mom's distant voice reaches us.

Dad crosses his arms and squints at me. "Proud of ya. Even if Florida is... kinda far."

"Same time zone. And I'd have a guest room."

"Yeah, that'd be nice. Florida. For your mother's birthday."

I tilt my head and smile. "Florida in January. You gotta admit. Better'n Vermont."

"Warmer," Dad concedes.

That afternoon, I join my siblings—Justin, Haley, Logan, and Hunter—at Clark's Meadow, where the town fair is being held this upcoming weekend. Everyone who can is helping to set up tents. My brothers and sister throw themselves at me, and before I can get too emotional, I ask them what to do.

We end up erecting tents for hours, setting up a base for bleachers that haven't been delivered yet, and lining up porta-potties.

I make it sound like it was a pain in the neck, but honestly? Best fun I've had in years.

We get home just in time for my brothers to take care of a few chores while Mom makes a fuss about settling me in the new guest room they arranged in the finished basement.

My childhood bedroom has been turned into an office. The pine shelf running across the small end of the room where I had my trophies and my favorite books is now stacked with accounting binders. With the way I left, I'm not going to ask where my stuff is.

When I get out of the shower, the waft of pot roast hits a tender spot. I surprise Mom in the kitchen, grab her from behind and give her a quick hug. "You remembered that's my favorite dish, or is that your Wednesday night special?"

"It is *not* a Wednesday night special." She turns to face me, her eyes misty. She opens her mouth to say something, then closes it.

"I'll set the table," I say to clear the moment. I need to occupy myself or else stuff is going to start choking me. Stuff like missing books and pot roast and how some things change—like people—and others never do—like feelings.

Haley joins us, followed by Justin. His huge dog, Moose, sprawls with a sigh on the porch as we take our seats around the farmhouse table. The whole King family is around the table for the first time in a very long time.

"So," Justin says once we start digging in our heaping plates, "How long you here for this time?"

I finish my mouth, wipe my lips, rinse the pot roast with beer. "It's kinda open right now. Don't have a timeline yet."

Mom gasps, Haley freezes with her glass of wine midair, and my three brothers stop their chewing.

Dad rubs his nose. "You can stay here as long as you like. I'll keep you busy."

I know what he means. He's disappointed I never considered working on the farm, but I think—I hope—deep down he understands where I'm coming from. The need to be useful in a grand way.

Mom shrieks and drops her fork. "Ohmygod, my baby is staying!" she says and for some reason, everyone laughs.

"Mom—I just said, I didn't know how long I was staying."

Mom waves my comment away. "That's a good start. A very good start."

Seeing the need to redirect the general conversation, Dad turns to Haley to discuss some wine making production of some sort that she wants to start on the farm. Turns out, she has a whole business plan, with projections and market research. She also works on the farm and at my brother Justin's pub in town. I'm impressed by her drive.

Once dinner is over, I stand to clear dishes alongside my siblings. "Thanks for dinner, Ma."

Mom and Dad follow us into the kitchen. With seven of us, we're done cleaning in no time. "That was fast. You finally got everyone trained," I joke, my memory pulling up endless arguments over who was supposed to do what, ended by Dad's threats that whoever didn't help wouldn't get fed the next meal. My joke falls flat, my siblings clearly having no idea what I'm talking about. Or choosing to ignore it entirely.

"I forgot how the days were so long here in the summer," I say to change the conversation but really end up pointing out how much I've forgotten about my hometown. And I'm sorry if it hurts their feelings, I didn't mean it that way, but I still stand by my choice of living my life on different terms.

Dad stores the broom away. "Makes up for the short season. More hours in the day to fit in the work."

"Let's go to the Growler," Logan declares, maybe to change the conversation, but more probably because he does have an itch to go out. He and Hunter are men now. They were the babies in the family, but now they're almost as tall as me and just as strong, if not stronger, judging by the work they did on the fairgrounds today. At dinner, they asked me a dozen questions about my job, life on base, and my next steps, before giving Mom and Dad a full recap of everything that should be done differently for the fair and could Mom just talk to the Events Committee about having axe throwing next year?

"I'm out," Haley says. "You guys have fun."

"Aww come on, Haley," Hunter insists. "Let's go and find you a *decent* boyfriend."

"With you as my sidekicks? No thank you."

I follow up with Dad's last comment before chiming in. "Need me to do something?"

"Nah. Workday's over. You go have a beer with your brothers. It's not like they see you that often." He doesn't mean it like it's a bad thing. He just says it as it is. And he's right.

"Where's that place you wanted to go?" I ask Logan.

"The Growler. It's up in the hills. We can take Justin's truck."

"Why don't we go to Lazy's?" I'm anxious to see my brother's pub, but I'd understand if that's the last place he wants to go tonight. He took the night off, after all. Still, I add, "I wanna check it out."

"Sure," Justin says, holding in a smile, while Hunter and Logan shrug their okays.

"You okay, man?" I ask as we climb into his truck. Justin is the closest to me in age—four years younger. He's also been mostly quiet all evening, except for a couple of questions for me.

He looks at me with a quick smile and shrugs. "Course. Why?"

I wonder if Dad's insinuations about working on the farm got to him too. After all, he also bailed out of the family business to open the only pub in town, the Lazy Salamander. But I don't want to get into that conversation with him. It seems useless. "Nothin'," I answer, and he leaves it at that.

We park on The Green and push the large doors open when we get to the pub. The clatter of dozens of patrons eating and chatting mixed with background music pulls us in. Moose follows us and trots right to the office beyond the bar while Justin guides us to a booth.

Lazy's is busy for a Wednesday night in small town America, but nothing that Justin's staff can't handle. His place is large, with high ceilings and dark wood paneling, yet it feels comfortable and homey. It could be the black-and-white photos of locals on the walls, or maybe the dim lighting from the small lamps next to each table. More probably, because of the easy banter that greets us when we walk in.

As soon as we're seated, a round of beers appears on our table, and our server leaves immediately. We sprawl on the comfortable seats, just happy to be together.

"Wow, that's a rare sight." I look up to the soft-spoken man about my age standing at the top of our table.

Shit! "Noah, man!" I stand and we back slap each other. He tilts his chin at my brothers. Memories of AP Math and cramming together in high school mingle with earlier ones of sharing candy in the back of his family's general store.

"Saw you roll into town earlier, and I couldn't believe it. Figured I'd come here to find out." He pushes his glasses up his nose, and warmth spreads through me at the familiar gesture. Noah was the self-assured nerd among us, but being in Emerald Creek, he was outdoorsy, too, and from the looks of him, he still is. "I'll let you catch up with your brothers, but before you leave, you better come in to the store and tell me all about your life, yeah?"

I nod. "I will."

"Cryptanalysis," he adds with a huge smile. "Damn you."

I laugh. "I'll catch up with you, promise."

The rest of the evening goes by quickly, with people stopping by to greet me and comment about the four King brothers being together.

We get back to the farm around midnight. Hunter and Logan crash right away. Justin lingers, not leaving yet. I take two bottles of beer out of the fridge, making a mental note to go to the store tomorrow and stock up. I'll have to borrow a car.

Didn't think about that when I bought the bike.

We sit on the porch, his big-ass dog at our feet. "So fucking proud of you," I finally tell him after a long silence.

He turns his head to me, bottle midair. "Proud of what?"

I state the obvious. "The way you rebuilt your life. The way you created something for this whole town."

He stares at me. "Anybody did something good with his life, it's you, man. I just sell beer."

He takes a long pull on his beer, then looks away to the dark fields. "Aren't you tired of running away?" he asks softly. With compassion, not accusation. I know what he's talking about. That night that changed everything. When he almost died because of something I did, and the next morning I still left.

But I've learned to forgive myself. And I know Justin carries guilt for that night too. He was wounded, but someone died. "What about you?" I ask him. It was hard not to notice, even from a distance, the electricity coursing between him and a pretty brunette on the fairgrounds. Yet he didn't introduce her to me, and no one brought her up at dinner.

"What about me?"

Maybe I shouldn't broach that topic now. I don't know where he is, mentally. I just got back. "You ever think of settling down?"

"Settling down?"

"Yeah. Having what Mom and Dad have. That sounds pretty awesome to me. You?"

"I—I can't do that. Not after what happened. Not after what I did to you. It's just not gonna happen."

I reel back in shock. "Fuck man, what are you talking about?" I look at him, not sure where to even start. "I ran away like a fucking coward when you were in the hospital. I barely knew if you were gonna make it. I can't believe you never said anything about that. *I* failed *you*." Moose sets his big head on my lap. "But you know what? I forgave myself. I was just a kid. I was scared. I messed up. People mess up, bro. The only thing to do is pick up the pieces and keep going."

"Yeah, except not everyone got to do that."

He's talking about the girl who died in the car crash. The one I pushed away, and he picked up. I was selfishly focusing on other stuff, and I did feel guilty, at the time. All the what-ifs. But not anymore. "It wasn't your fault. You almost died to save her. You did everything you could, and more."

"It doesn't matter. I shouldn't have... driven her home."

Fuck. I barely got here, and I have to talk about that night again. And of course I do. It was the night Justin almost died, *and the next morning I still left.*

Mom and Dad made it clear that I shouldn't thwart my own plans because of the accident. I was scheduled to start officer training at Maxwell Air Force Base in the next few days. It was enough they had one son whose life was on hold; they didn't want me to give up on my dream career. And so after some negotiating, I left once we knew for sure Justin was out of the woods and it was all about a long, painful recovery for him. *"It's so unfair to him,"* I'd told Mom.

"That's why I need you to go and have the life he won't have. You owe it to him."

And fuck, but my mother telling me these words to help me cope, nearly killed me with guilt. And anger. And powerlessness. All these emotions fighting to bring me down. The guilt was the strongest, and in my young mind, it felt as if my mother couldn't stand the sight of me. As if she knew that if I'd acted differently, Justin wouldn't be lying in a hospital bed. As if it was painted all over my face.

I tried to tell her, tell them—Mom and Dad—I said, *"I should've—"* but Dad cut me off. *"Don't go there, son,"* he'd simply stated, and he never elaborated, so I drew my own conclusions.

Don't go there, or your mother won't stand the sight of you.

Don't go there, or you'll carry the burden of your brother's injuries.

Don't go there, it's too late to do anything now.

Don't go there, but don't stay here either.

Just go. Leave.

Leave us.

They never said any of that, of course, and possibly they didn't think this way either. But in my young mind, that's how it went.

It didn't help that it was also the night the only girl I ever loved broke my heart. In a way, it made it easier to leave Emerald Creek. I could hide my guilt and forget my pain.

I'd make myself as scarce as possible to my family so they didn't have to stare in the eye the person who could have, should have, prevented Justin's accident. And I was never going to see her again.

I never talked about my breakup to anyone in the years that followed, because it would seem so trivial compared to the drama they've all endured. But tonight, even that pain, as petty as it is, digs acutely in my chest. It *is* so petty, and I *am* over it, but reliving that night makes the pain raw again, these two wounds of unequal importance hurting me almost equally.

But I'm here with my brother, and I can do something for him. "We were kids, Justin. You were a baby. But if you want to go down that road, then—you... you did right by her. She came to the party to find me. I should have been looking out for her." The truth is, she came to the party to cause trouble. I took care of it. Who could predict the chain of events that would unfold?

"What do you mean? She was your girlfriend. I hit on your girlfriend. I took her home to get lucky and—"

"She wasn't my girlfriend. I didn't even know where she lived. We'd hooked up once before, and I'd called it off. Then she came onto me a little strong at the party, and I told her off a little strong too. There was nothing between us."

Justin seems lost. "I thought... I thought... I thought that's why you never came back."

"Nah, she wasn't the one," I feel necessary to say, handing him another beer. Trying not to think about the girl who broke my heart. We sit for a while, talking about the girl who died in the crash—who he almost gave his life for, trying to save her. We talk about her parents too. And about the guy who crashed his car into theirs.

I try to dole out a little bit of wisdom without acting like an older brother know-it-all, which I definitely am not. I might feel like I'm in an okay place right now, but I could be wrong. But hey, I'll do anything for my brother. For the little time that I'm here, the least I can do is fix some of the stuff I broke.

We talk a little longer about the accident, and then we call it a night, Justin sleeping on the couch on account of too many beers.

The next couple of days, I stay at the farm, helping Dad fix fences and adjust a wobbly barn door.

Then Saturday, I go to the fair, thinking it's going to be just another day in small town America. Which, in a way, it is.

And in another way, it rocks me to my core.

Chapter Two

Grace

Rituals help. At the beginning, there were days when their predictability seemed to amplify the emptiness of my life. But now, there's a comfort to them. A healthy dependency on a good thing to come. Now, I hardly ever think of them as rituals—crutches. Now, they're part of the life I designed for myself. They're my healthy habits.

Since I've been back in Emerald Creek, a day in my hometown starts with coffee at Easy Monday and ends with a drink at Lazy's. If I'm being honest, at the beginning, whatever happened in between was just filler. I worked at the resort, in their spa. It was a job.

Now, I'm proud of my business. Employing four beauticians and one receptionist at A Touch Of Grace makes me feel good about myself. Pampering clients is meaningful and fulfilling, especially now that I'll also be offering massages.

It's not what I expected my life would be. But who's lucky enough to see their teenage dreams come true? Yeah, I don't see many hands up.

My rituals helped me. Mainly in forcing me to have a social life, and ultimately, to find deep joy in trivial delights.

And this morning as I enter the best coffee shop in town, before I even hear the voices calling me, a smile forms on my lips, the warmth in my core increases.

I'm in a good place.

"Grace! Over here!" Two of my girlfriends, Alex and Haley, are sitting on a deep couch, nudged between the wooden sculpture of a siren and a tower of romance books, lattes in hand.

Millie, the young woman who owns Easy Monday, smiles as she hands me a Maple Chill without my needing to ask her. "Have an awesome day, sweetheart."

It's summer in Emerald Creek. Even the weather is eerily perfect. Today is our summer fair, and I'll be giving free massages to grow my business.

It'll be awesome. There's no reason why it wouldn't.

I return Millie's smile. "You too." As I make my way across the crowded room, I'm greeted by friendly faces.

Coming back was the right choice.

I plop on a low armchair across from my friends. "What's up?"

Haley rolls her eyes. "Ugh. I don't even know where to start."

Alex stops taking pictures of her latte in its locally made pottery mug, and gives me a tentative smile. "Are you okay?" She glances with alarm at Haley.

"Sure, why?" I answer Alex, ignoring Haley for now. Her sense for drama and suspense hasn't subsided since we were kids.

Alex is new to Emerald Creek. She still doesn't know how to read us all. She's also a straight shooter, and her asking me if I'm okay raises an alarm.

"Yeah, she doesn't care anymore," Haley butts in.

Alex frowns at her, then turns to me. "I saw the listing... just... are you sure you're gonna be okay?"

"What listing?"

"Shit," she whispers, narrowing her eyes on me. "Maybe we should talk about this somewhere else."

I grab my to-go mug and stand. "I have to open in ten minutes anyway, but I can drop you off at Clark's Meadow." Seeing Alex's puzzlement, I add, "Where the fair will be. You don't need to go that early, though. I just want to get situated and have a parking spot that's not miles away from my tent."

"Oh I'm totally coming," Alex says. "I need content for our socials. Get the hype up. And maybe we can talk?"

Why is she being so cagey?

"It's gonna be so hot today," Haley moans as she climbs in, shotgun. "We should go to Mayer's Hole tonight," she adds as I pull out of my parking spot and head out of town.

Alex clears her throat and leans in between us. "Guys, in a minute you'll tell me all about Mayer's Hole, but first I need to know that Grace is alright with her building being on the market."

I jerk my head to her and nearly knock off one of the flower baskets adorning the covered bridge. Once we're safely on the other side of the narrow passage, Haley says, "What the fuck?"

Yeah, *what the fuck* sounds right.

"The spa building is for sale. I know because we're looking for a location for our new headquarters. And our realtor sent us the link to your place."

"Who's the listing agent?" Haley asks, tapping on her phone.

"I can find out," Alex answers.

"On it," Haley mumbles.

"You didn't know?" Alex asks me.

My head is spinning, and my mouth is dry. Thank god the Jeep knows its way around here, because I don't feel like I'm behind the wheel anymore. Why didn't my landlord tell me?

"I didn't. Tell me everything," I say as we wind through the country road.

"It's priced to sell... and the thing is, the listing states that it can be bought rented out or empty."

My body feels cold. The car bobs up and down the uneven field as I make my way like a robot to a parking spot. Then I shut the engine down, and we sit in silence. "Shit." I open my door to let some air in. "I can't really talk about all that right now. Shit," I say again. Which seems to be the only reaction I can muster at the moment.

Too many thoughts are fighting for my attention. How fast do I need to move? What happens to all the investments I made? The paint, the new bathrooms, the refurbished floors? Where will I move? Again, how soon do I need to move? Not to mention, this location is—was—*perfect*. The Georgian house is ideally located downtown, with ample parking space, room to expand the business upstairs, a deck for events, and a unique inside architecture that makes women feel so pampered. "It's going to cost me a fortune to recreate that atmosphere," I whisper. I step out the car. "I'll think of something."

Alex stands next to me and pulls me in a hug. "I'm here for you. Let me know what I can do."

I'm pretty sure Alex is loaded now. She could do anything. But I don't want that. "I'll need help, not pity."

"Of course, honey. Didn't even cross my mind."

"Liar."

She gives me a squeeze. "You've always been an inspiration to me. You can do this. And we'll help you."

"I gotta say, that beats my shitty news," Haley says. She gives me a quick hug. "What she said. Lemme know how I can help. Hey, come to Sunday dinner tomorrow with your folks. Mom and Dad would love to see them, and we'll brainstorm new places for the spa." Haley's parents host an informal dinner at their farm once a month, and everyone they know has an open invitation. "You'll come too, Alex?"

"Sure. By the way, what happened to you?"

She rolls her eyes. "Oh, nothing important. Ethan rolled into town and get this—"

Ethan? My stomach bottoms.

The rest of her words are lost on me. Something about their mother's birthday, a motorcycle, and flowers, all covered by the sound of blood whooshing in my ears to the rhythm of my heartbeat.

Oh god, it was so long ago. *Ten years.* So much has happened since, that he was not a part of.

They both laugh when Haley is done talking.

"You okay?" Haley asks me. "You look pale." Haley knows what happened between her brother and me, but only the watered-down version I served her after everything was over.

I focus my eyes back on her. Mouth dry, I manage to say, "Yeah, yeah. Just uh... that whole lease business." *Liar.* "How—how long is he staying?" I ask, trying to look disinterested and merely polite.

She looks at me, eyes widening. "Oh, honey. He's probably already packing to leave."

"Don't—" I start, making a sweeping motion toward my face. "It's just—it's the lease problem making me like this. Not-not-not Ethan."

She nods, unconvinced.

"Tell him I said hi," I add because that's what someone who doesn't care would say. And I don't care. I really don't. Well, I don't *not* care, but I only care in a childhood-friend kind of way. The sort of care where you just say, *"Tell him I said hi."* And frankly? It *is* the lease issue making me emotional. I'm about to maybe fucking lose my business, for Chrissakes! Of course I'm unhinged, emotional, hypersensitive.

"You know, about tomorrow—" Haley starts. I can tell she's reading my emotions right now, pulling back the invite to the farm to protect me.

I don't need this. I'm not this emotionally unstable girl who would cry for any little thing.

I'm *not* depressed anymore.

I just need to stay focused.

I squeeze her hand. "I'll come. You're right. Someone might know someone who knows someone. That's how these things get sorted out. I'll need all the help possible to find a new location." I purposely avoid bringing up her brother. She needs to know I'm totally, absolutely over him. I mean, it was ten years ago. And I am totally over him. Totally.

We part ways and I hurry to my tent, planning on hiding in there the whole day. What does he look like now? Is he happy in his life? For all the pain I've suffered because of him, I can't bring myself to hate him.

Hating him would have helped.

But I never could.

I take a few deep breaths and try to focus on the here and now. In my enclosed space, I should feel safe. I should feel elsewhere. Autumn, a friend of mine who is a decorator, turned my tent into a Thousand-And-One-Nights scene. It's dreamy and awesome and a complete contrast to the bright outdoors. It's an escape from the real world.

For the next few hours, I'm safe from him. He won't see me; I won't run into him.

For the next few hours, only my clients need to matter.

Yet all I can think about is Ethan.

Ethan is here.

And because I'm weird like that, I make a mountain out of it when really, I shouldn't. What happened between Ethan and me was blown out of proportion by my teenage projections.

I need to let the past go, for my own sanity. I've done it once before; I've built myself back up. I'm not going down the rabbit hole of what-ifs again.

Nope.

Massage after massage, I focus on my clients' concerns, on the knots that bother them, that reappear when they're stressed out. When they expect it the least.

I provide them a short respite and convince them to try a longer treatment at the spa. I talk about the benefits of monthly massages.

Focusing on others is what I need for myself. I was just caught off guard when Haley said he was back. Frazzled by the challenges my business is facing, I overreacted to this piece of news.

And it's fine and understandable I'd be somewhat affected by the fact that I might see my first love again. You'd have to be very insensitive to not care about seeing someone again who had such an impact on you.

But this is all in the past. None of this has any bearing on my present life. On my present happiness. I am living my best life, and it's all thanks to me. And nothing will jeopardize it. Not even a broken lease. Or Ethan coming back to Emerald Creek.

Once I finish Ms. Angela's massage, my thoughts are back under control, my emotions in check. So while she gets dressed, I text my brother, Colton. He's a little bit of a hermit. Not too much, but just really quiet. I like to call him every day, even if he rarely picks up. I still leave him a message, tell him I'm just checking in on him and that I love him, that sort of thing. I just like to let him know.

I know, I'm a little different like that, and I wear my emotions on my sleeve a lot. Well, most of them. Today, because I don't want to interrupt people's quiet time, I text him.

Me

> What's up? <3 u

Colton

Everything okay?

Why is he asking that?

> If this is about the listing, yes, I'll figure it out.

Colton

What listing?

> Why are you asking me if I'm okay?

Colton

Nothing.

Bubbles float under Colt's name for a beat. Then nothing again. Then bubbles.

Colton

What's up?

There must be something he wants to talk about.

Me

> What's going on?

Colton

Nothin

You're weird.

Colton

You're weirder

You weirdo

Colton

gtg

Wait

Can you take Dad to the fair today?

Our father has congestive heart failure, and with Mom working a lot, we help take care of him.

Colton

I thought you were at the fair

I'm working

When Ms. Angela came in, there were three or four people lined up. There might be more now.

Colton

me 2

Can you take half hour for Dad

Colton

> I have some asshole breaking my balls about his Porsche Carrera. Take u 10 minutes.

It'll be more than ten minutes. By the time I get to my car, get to Mom and Dad's, get him to the bathroom, get his shoes on, get him in the car, find a spot mid-day when it'll be packed...

> A Porsche Carrera? on our dirt roads?

Colton liked a message.

I sigh.

> Take Dad in the Porsche. <happy emoji>

"Everything okay?" Ms. Angela asks as she ties her sneakers.

"We're trying to figure out how to bring Dad to the fair. Colton is working and I…"

Ms. Angela pokes her head out the tent, ducks back in, and says, "I'm sending in the next client and then you go on and enjoy some family time."

"Thanks, that's sweet of you."

Colton

> Kay I'll bring him

"Oh well, looks like Colt got it."

"Even better. More time for you," she says as she exits my tent.

While I change the sheet on the massage table, I hear voices outside the thin fabric of the tent. Ms. Angela and…

Another voice, in particular, that makes my heart…

Stop.

That voice?

There's no mistaking it.

That voice?

I'd recognize it *anywhere*.

I barely have time to rush to the back of the tent, silently curse Ms. Angela for being not so sweet after all, turn my back to the entrance, and try to compose myself.

CHAPTER THREE

Ethan

A few hours earlier

*

I've been volunteered to go help with the last odds and ends of set up. Turns out, there's still a lot to do. Not just odds and ends. For one, delivery of the bleachers for the ox pulling was delayed until last night, so at the first sign of dawn—4 a.m. in Northern Vermont in the summer—a bunch of us get on that.

Someone already set down plywood sheets on the flattest surface of the field, and we tackle assembly of the bleachers right away.

"Ah, fuck." My brother Logan throws a plank meant for seating to the side and grabs another. "Fuck! This one's splintered too!"

"Lemme see?"

"It's splintered, Ethan. We can't use it."

"Maybe we can fix it."

He grumbles and walks to the pile of planks. "There's no extra! That means we'll be missing two benches."

I pick up the two planks he's shoved aside and go to a small shack where I noticed the guys were getting tools from. There's a couple metal boxes with people's names painted on them. I rummage through the largest one and find what I'm looking for.

"You wanna use this one," someone behind me says, pointing over my shoulder to a big brand carpenter glue wax.

Owen Parker. Figures. "Hey, Owen. Yeah, that's gonna take too long to cure and set." I grab the one I'm looking for. It doesn't specifically mention 'wood' on the labeling, but I know for a fact that's the one we need to use if we want those bleachers to be ready in just a few hours. "That super glue gel will set in just a few seconds."

"It doesn't say wood on it," he insists.

"I know. Wanna help me? I'm gonna make a Dutchman patch." Looking through the shed, I take a piece of scrap wood that's the thickness of the seat, a saw, and a chisel, set myself right out the shed and get to work while Parker walks away.

Some things never change.

I'm almost done when I hear footsteps behind me. "Dude named Owen Parker said you might need help, but it looks like you're all set."

I glance at the guy talking to me and tighten the clamp on the second repair. "Yeah. Hope it's okay I helped myself."

He shakes his head, a small smile on his face. "That's what it's for. Not everyone knows what they're doing, though, but you—you a carpenter?"

I shrug. "Nah. Just... always liked working with wood." The first seat is dry, so I sand it down.

"You're Ethan, right? Ethan King."

I straighten and extend my hand. "Yeah."

"Lucas Hunt. We're new in town."

I nod. "I'd say welcome, but I'm not really from here anymore." Then I start sanding the other plank.

"See you around," Lucas says as a goodbye.

I tidy my workstation, put the tools and glue back, then grab both planks and haul them to the bleachers.

I'm not from here anymore. Shit.

Parker hollers, "No need, King, we just closed those down." He points to the top bleachers, where there's yellow tape across the gaping hole.

I smirk. "Gotcha."

He looks at me. I know it's useless telling him his setup is dangerous, and even more asking him to give me a hand with the planks. Everyone else is gone, so I climb the bleachers two by two.

Fuck.

I should have warmed up this morning.

My back is tight, and I feel the pain radiating down my spine to my leg.

Am I actually getting old, or is this from riding the bike? I set the planks nice and snug, admire my handiwork, then straighten, a hand on my lumbar region like that's gonna help.

"Jeez, man, you look just like Dad," Logan jokes.

"You got any Advil, smartass?"

"Nope. I think they have an emergency tent somewhere, though."

Yeah, I don't need that.

I wobble down the bleachers and walk around to see if anyone else needs help.

Cassandra, a woman I remember from way back when, stops me. I'm ashamed to say, my friends and I used to lurk around her lingerie shop, trying to get a glimpse at whatever she was selling inside. Her windows were always PG 13, showing only modest nightwear and photos of white wolves in snow-capped landscapes.

But somehow, we knew what was inside and we were insanely curious.

She asks me with genuine interest what I've been up to, then tells me, "you know, if your back is hurting, there's someone over there giving free massages." She points me to a tent where a few people are lined up. "You should try it."

A *massage,* me? Not a chance. "Sure, thanks."

I go toward the enclosures where the pigs are kept. Several people recognize me. "Hey man, you're back! What's with the limp?" someone I went to school with asks.

"Nothin'. Just my back. Carried too much shit."

"Tell me about it. Some mornings I feel like I'm a hundred." He waves toward the tent where the line is growing. "I just went there. She did a pretty good job. Plus it's free. What's her name again? She was a few years behind us... Anyway—Give it a try. I'll see you around, I gotta catch up with someone."

I turn around to look at the piglets then figure, what the hell. My back isn't getting any better. Might as well get a massage sooner than later.

There's a line of people waiting in front of the tent, next to a small table where the high school girl working at Colton's—Tracy?— is scribbling notes.

I limp to the tent. "My back is tight, and people said you could help?"

She flashes a bright smile. "Aww! Mister K! Sure thing! There's a thirty-minute wait."

"Can I put my name down and come back in thirty?"

A burly man at the head of the line cuts into our conversation. "You go on right ahead." The people behind him nod. "Saw you help with all those tents the other day. And the bleachers now."

The line shifts and someone says, "Thank you for your service."

I nod to the man who said that. He looks vaguely familiar. I don't want preferential treatment. It's not right. It's just a pulled muscle. It's not like I got wounded in combat. "Nah, I'll wait. Thank you, though."

Ms. Angela comes out of the tent, patting her hair down, and stops when she sees me. "Massage table is ready. You're up next." Her tone accepts no discussion, and I'm her four-foot tall, obedient student again.

So I nod and go in.

It's dark inside the tent, and my eyes strain to adjust. A sweet and relaxing scent fills the atmosphere. Oriental-type carpets cover the ground, giving the space a sense of being elsewhere. There's a chair next to the entrance and a massage table in the center.

To the back, there's the silhouette of a woman busying herself at a small console with lotions. My heart ba-booms at the shape of her shoulders, the tilt of her head. Jesus fucking Christ, she's thousands of miles away. Not here. And even if she was here, what does it matter? Shake it off, man.

But her dark, curly hair stirs something deep inside me, and I hold my breath.

Am I hallucinating? It *can't* be her, dammit.

It's a trick of my imagination.

Shit.

It's been so long.

But then she turns around, and my heart hammers in my chest.

The last time I saw this woman, she didn't even have *one* word for me.

After everything we'd shared. After everything she'd told me.

She was walking down the aisle, holding some idiot's arm, a stiff smile fooling only herself, her gaze glazing over me.

And she didn't have one word for me.

Not one explanation.

Didn't even bother trying to be my friend.

It was like I'd never existed.

I'd been on leave, decided four years without coming back to my hometown was enough. I had one week off, and god played a trick on me. It was the weekend she was marrying someone else.

She was supposed to be mine.

Always was.

She said so herself. So many times.

But after her wedding, didn't she move to Texas? She's not supposed to *be* here.

She does a double take. Her eyes round, her mouth gapes, her breath catches.

"Why are you here?" I ask right as she says, "What brings you here?"

I clear my throat. "I'm—I'm just visiting." I should add something generic and half-assed polite, like *It's nice to see you*, or *How have you been*, but the words stay stuck in my throat.

She's supposed to be in fucking Texas.

She blinks several times, takes a small breath, shows me a list of services calligraphed on an elegant paper and framed in gold. "I mean, what type of massage would you like?"

Oh, really? Not even *Hey, Ethan*. Not even *Wow, it's been a while*.

Granted, I'm not good at small talk either.

But really? "I dunno. My back is tight. It hurts down to my leg."

I can't believe we're talking like we're two fucking strangers.

I glance at the tent opening. I never should have come here. I should just go. It's only gonna get weirder and weirder.

Her voice is melodious with a touch of coldness. Professional. "Strip down to your underwear and get under the sheet. Face down." She turns around. "Let me know when you're ready."

Yeah, that's not gonna work. "I-I... maybe I should just go."

She whips around. Her eyes are shiny, her bottom lip trembles until she pulls herself together and snaps her mouth in a fine line. Her voice catches when she says, "Yeah, maybe you should."

What the hell? *I don't think so.* I pull my T-shirt off my back. Her eyes narrow on my torso, slide down to my abs, and even in the dimness of the tent I can see her cheeks turning a deep red. She catches herself and turns her back to me just as I unbuckle my jeans.

I fold my clothes neatly and place them on a stool. My hands don't shake. My heartbeat doesn't rattle the tent. Nothing betrays the anger boiling inside me. Then I slide under the cool sheet.

Face down. I turn on my belly. I wish I could look at her. Make her squirm under my gaze. Ask her to her face what the hell happened to her.

To us.

"Ready," I grunt.

CHAPTER FOUR

Grace

Of course he doesn't care. He never has. I tell him it'd be better if he left, and he decides to stay? Why? To spite me? Rub in my face that we're just two strangers? That I'm a nobody giving him a massage?

The last time I saw him, really saw him, he betrayed me.

So seeing him here without warning? I don't know that I can handle it.

"Ready." His voice is emotionless. Like I said, I'm a stranger to him.

I'm used to this now. I'm used to being just a side note in people's lives.

It's okay. Tonight, I'll go through my memory box. Imagine what could have been. If I imagine it hard enough, I can believe it's true. At least for a minute or two. That's all I need.

I know I shouldn't be doing that. I know I'm stronger than that. And I am. I really am. Just now and then, I need a little pick-me-up.

That's all it is. I know it's not reality. Doesn't mean I don't like the fantasy.

Don't judge me. If you like to read romances where the guy is hot and young and a billionaire and he only wants little old you, you're doing the same. If you go to gaming conventions dressed as your favorite hero, you're doing the same.

We all have our ways of getting through shit.

I have my memory box, my fantasy world. That gets me through.

Meanwhile, Mr. Hotshot here needs his massage.

He breaks my heart, shatters it to pieces, sees how distressed I am, knows it's because of him, offers to leave to let me live my sad little life in peace, and when I say yes please (or something close to that) he taunts me by staying here to torture me some more?

I pull the sheet down and get started.

"Ow!"

Yep, that'll hurt all right. Man, he's a bundle of tightness. Okay, I should go easier now. After all, he's just a client now, and I have a reputation to uphold. I don't want him walking out of the tent cussing and complaining about what a bad experience he had.

It's enough that I'm losing my space. I can't afford to lose my clients.

I ease up, use the heel of my hands instead of my knuckles, feel the deep tissue loosening under my touch, then graduate him to a deep massage using my elbows. "We only have ten minutes, so I'll focus on the pain point. Get you walking normally again."

Without him looking at me, it's easier.

He doesn't answer.

I do need to get to his quads, though. I wish there was another way, but there isn't. "Now turn around." I cover his body with the sheet, step away to oil my hands again and to give him privacy as he gets situated on the table.

"No."

"'Scuse me?"

"I ain't turning 'round."

I blink several times.

He pushes himself up on his forearms and speaks to the table. "Matter of fact, the massage is over, and I need you to step out so I can get dressed."

So he thinks he can boss me around and tell me how to do my job? "The treatment isn't over. It's already just a mini massage. Cut it in half and it's a waste of time."

"Nope." He doesn't move, though.

Was it something I did? Was it too hard? "I can adjust the pressure..." And then I get it. "It's a normal physical reaction in men. I see it all the time. There's no need to—"

"You see it *all the time*?" he blurts.

What's he all worked up about? "It's a sign of relaxation. Nothing to be self-conscious about." I hand him a pillow to cover his midsection. "Here."

"No."

"If you walk out of here limping, I'll lose business. I need to get to your quad. Now get on your back. You're holding up other people."

He huffs. "Turn around first."

Fine. The ruffling of the sheet sends a shiver down my spine. What is happening to me? It can't be because of how he's changed.

And he has changed.

Ethan was always athletic. He was Emerald Creek's golden boy. The hockey star. The football captain. It drove all the other boys crazy.

They could never measure up to him. But he was such a good guy, no one that I know was ever jealous of him.

Everybody liked him. He was that kind of person.

When he walked into my tent earlier, I was taken aback by the mass of muscle he'd become.

That was after I registered and dealt with the shock of being so close to Ethan King.

He was supposed to be the love of my life.

Or so I thought, growing up.

"Ready," he grunts.

He has one arm thrown over his face, hiding his eyes, while the other hand holds onto the pillow for dear life. In the process of him turning around and focusing solely on hiding his privates, the sheet slipped off, revealing a torso that I'm intimately familiar with.

I rub my hands with oil, lean over his hairy thigh, and get to work. Starting from right above the knee, I identify the knot and work my way up, kneading and stretching. I close my eyes to focus. All I need is to feel the muscles under my hands. To let his body guide me.

"That's enough," he snaps and sits up.

My eyes fly open. I was almost there. Almost got that pesky knot untangled. I lift my face to meet his, then quickly look down. "Not quite." I run my hands higher up, dig deep with my knuckles up to his hip area, which is connected to his back. *There.* "That should do it. For now." I straighten, avoiding his gaze by focusing on his naked shoulder. That seems like a safe place to look at.

It's not.

I remember crying on this shoulder.

I remember laughing so hard I bumped my forehead on this shoulder.

I remember the way his shoulder would curve around me to make me feel safe.

Everything about him is a painful memory.

Whipping around, I prepare a sample of arnica and CBD ointment while he gets dressed. "That'll help," I tell him, turning around just in time to catch his gaze drilling into me. He blinks several times. His jaw clenches as he pockets the small box. "How much is it? And the… massage?"

That's it, huh. Just a transaction. "It's free. Says on the tent."

He narrows his eyes on me and frowns. "Why?"

We're really not talking about us, then? Nothing about the past? Wow. "I'm launching my massage business. This is advertising. How's your back feel?"

He straightens. "It—it feels like new… Grace."

My name coming out of his mouth pierces me. It's been ten years since I've heard it, and it breaks me to pieces. I bite the inside of my cheeks to keep my lips from trembling. "That's great," I chirp. "Use the cream. It'll help." He could use more work, but I'm certainly not giving him the brochure to my spa in town.

Anyway, he's probably just staying a couple of days. If that. And thank god.

There's no way I can be in the same town as Ethan King.

I think he's saying thank you or something like that, but I can't take it anymore. I turn my back to him, pretending to occupy myself with a fresh sheet and oils and lighting a new candle.

I let the tears fall freely, careful not to sniffle, not to wipe them, not to breathe. Careful not to show any emotion.

Until light invades the tent, indicating he's leaving.

And then I'm alone for a moment in the silent and empty tent, and peace slowly returns to me.

I silently thank Ms. Angela for sending people away on the pretext of me picking Dad up. Then I text Colton to take good care of our father, because I certainly can't.

I can't even take care of myself in this moment.

But I'm not letting this state of mind take root. I'll get over this bump in the road like I always do. I'll get back to my happy normal. I just have a handful of hours to get over myself, and I'm going to focus on that. I'm going to focus on being perfectly okay by the time I get to the farm tomorrow.

Because I have bigger problems than Ethan King.

CHAPTER FIVE

Ethan

I get that she's over me. That she's married to someone else now. But we had something, didn't we? Forget how things ended. Let's set that aside for a minute.

As far as I can remember, Grace was in my life. She's my sister Haley's age, and they were best friends. She was constantly at the farm, playing or helping with chores. Our mothers were and still are best friends.

We were close.

Not like siblings, though.

Different.

It was always different with Grace.

I felt the need to protect her. With four years on her, I took my role seriously. First, I felt the need to protect her from my brother Justin's wild ideas. Like jumping from the roof into the above-ground pool. He wanted the girls to go first—"you're lighter, you'll get less water out of the pool." Haley told him to get lost, but Grace was already halfway up the ladder. "Okay, I'll go," she said in her little voice, her wholesome innocence striking me. I jumped on the ladder and brought her, giggling, down.

"You're a sissy, Grace," Justin said.

"And you're an idiot!" I replied as he jumped, hit the bottom, broke his leg.

I was blamed for that, by the way. For letting him get hurt. Didn't really care, at the time. I thought he needed to learn his own lessons.

Grace never annoyed me the way Haley sometimes did—especially when I was with my friends. Haley was the consummate little sister, making fun of me, pulling my stinky socks out of the hamper whenever girls came to the farm.

Grace? She was gentle and helpful. She grew up to be funny, real funny, but never at the expense of others. She'd make fun of herself, or of a situation. She'd come up with games and ideas for a fun evening.

And then she became a woman, and I was lost to her.

She was the epitome of what I thought a woman should be. Sexy and kind, soft and tough, smart and active. She was going to take the world by storm. She wanted to leave Emerald Creek as soon as possible, travel the world, see places. And so did I.

We fell in love—at least I thought we did. It wasn't without complications, and I was ready to tackle those.

But then, just like that, we were over. Before we really even began.

Her decision.

I respected it.

I just never stopped loving her.

I'd had a taste of Grace, and no one else would do.

So yeah, the way she treated me just now? I don't get it. How could she be so cold? How could she act like I was just another rando getting a massage?

I guess I've been a fool all along. Maybe she never loved me the way she said she did.

Maybe I should stop thinking about the past.

My steps take me to Justin's food tent. The line is long, but he and the pretty brunette work in sync and it moves fast.

Coming out of nowhere, Haley slides in front of me in line. "It's on me." She pulls her wallet out and orders two sandwiches with fancy names, some mac 'n cheese balls, a cup of gazpacho, and two sodas.

"Aren't you working at the pub today?" I ask.

"I'm on a break. It's still early." She walks ahead of me, seeming to know where she's going. "Let's go test the bleachers. I heard some out-of-towner helped." She glances at me with a devious smile. "Not sure how I feel about that. Does he even know what he's doing?"

Carrying the food in one hand, I grab her in a playful headlock with my free arm as we walk away, eventually letting her wiggle her way out. She punches my bicep. I pull her hair. She screams and kicks, laughing all the while.

Some things haven't changed.

We settle on the bleachers—I guide us toward the planks I repaired without telling Haley, and she doesn't make a comment, which means she doesn't even notice. Good.

From here, we have a vantage point of the massage tent, and my gaze keeps drifting there. I take the wrap Haley is handing me. "So. Fill me in on the gossip. What's new in town?"

"Justin is secretly in love with Chloe, while pretending he's only working with her to please the town's events committee."

"Figured that."

"Mom and Dad have an Angus cow that's driving everyone insane. She's called Daisy."

"Good to know. What's insane about it?"

"*Her*. Daisy keeps escaping and eats everyone's flowers."

"Why don't they just make burgers out of it—her?"

"Shut up! We love her."

"Gotcha. We love Daisy. What else?"

"There's a new couple in town, started their construction company. Thalia and Lucas. And Autumn is setting herself up as a decorator."

"I met Lucas. There's enough work here?"

"You wouldn't believe it. So many second homeowners now. They all want their little slice of heaven, and well, we have the space. You can hardly tell they're here, except during festivals, and judging by how you need a reservation now to get a table pretty much everywhere. And did you see all the new fancy shops in town? Second-home owners shop there."

True. I'd noticed them but didn't stop to wonder how they made a living. Seems like my baby sister has a solid head on her shoulders.

"I heard you talk with Dad about a new project you want to start?"

"The fermentory. I like the farm," she says a little defensively, "but I want to put my mark on it."

"That's great." I hope she hears the admiration in my tone. Even though I've kept in touch with my family, they're the ones who have been visiting me. While abroad, our conversations focused more on the place I was living than on their life in Vermont.

"How's the leg?" someone shouts from a distance.

"Better, thanks!"

"You go see Grace?" the guy shouts.

Feeling Haley straighten next to me, I give him a thumbs up. "Yup."

"In't she som'thin?"

I nod. "Sure is."

He gives me a wave and leaves me with my sister's gaze piercing hot through my skull while I focus hard on the last of my wrap.

Haley doesn't say anything for a while, and I start to believe I made her reaction all up, but then she drops innocently, "So, how *was* Grace?"

I take a long pull on my soda. "Great massage."

"Cool! But how was *Grace?*"

I shrug. "Graceful?"

"Ouch."

"Whaddayamean, *ouch*? Nothin' wrong with being graceful. You should try it sometime."

Haley punches my bicep. Again. "Idiot."

"Yep, definitely should try it."

"You wanna go to Mayer's Hole tonight?" she asks, seemingly out of the blue. But I know better. Haley always has an agenda.

"I don't think so. But thanks."

She rolls her eyes. "The girls want to go skinny dipping. Obviously, if you're coming, that kills the skinny part, but hey... So? You'll come?"

I pretend to walk into her trap. "What girls?"

"Whoever. Alex, me, Kiara..." She trails off, obviously leaving a name out. *Grace.* Waiting for me to ask, maybe. "I'll post it on Echoes. We can have a whole group going. How's that?"

There's no chance in hell I'm going to Mayer's Hole, or the river, or the lake. Too many memories there. But I can't tell her that. "I'll pass and just stay home with Mom and Dad."

"You always were a party pooper. I almost forgot."

"I sure am. Worse than ever."

"Seriously, Ethan. What'd you think of Grace? Honestly."

I stay poker-faced, my gaze fixed on the bleachers across from us. "She's... an awesome masseuse. Very professional." The way she addressed my embarrassing moment alone said so.

She tears thin strips off the wax paper around her wrap. "You mean you guys didn't catch up on... anything?"

"Um. Like what? It's been years since I've seen her."

She bumps her knee against mine. "Exactly. Lots to catch up on."

I grunt. "We weren't that close." An image jumps at me, punishing my lie: Grace's naked body under mine, her legs pulling me inside her, her nails raking my back.

Haley doesn't bother swallowing before saying, "Huh. I always thought she had something for you."

Shit, so Grace never even told Haley? Or is Haley fishing for information? I don't have time for this high school chick shit. "All your friends had something for me," I say to play into her hand while deflecting her focus.

"Ooooh, I don't know about that."

I laugh, partially glad we're off the topic of Grace. But still wanting to know more about her. "Hard to catch up on a whole lifetime in fifteen minutes."

"Well, she's coming to the farm tomorrow. You'll have all the time in the world to catch up."

Shit. So there's no escaping it. I want to see her, and at the same I really don't want to fucking see her. "When did they move back?" I need at least some context.

"They?"

"Grace and her... husband." The word grates my mouth.

She does a double take. "Oh—no. She's divorced. That didn't last long. Maybe a few months?"

My blood runs cold. She was married *only a few months*, and *no one thought to tell me*? What the fuck? I want to punch something.

Haley continues. "She um... she went through some tough shit for a while..."

I whip my face to her. "What happened?"

Haley squints, then shrugs. "Long time ago. 'ts all good now." She dips a mac'n cheese ball in the gazpacho and slurps it.

"What kind of tough shit? You sure she's okay?"

"You saw her. She rocks. She's doing great."

I'm teetering between a stupid relief that she's divorced and the knowledge that she went through hard times. Not knowing more kills me. "Was the marriage that bad?" My fists reflexively ball at the number of scenarios going through my head right now.

Haley squints her eyes at me. "You know, you're awful nosy for someone who *supposedly* wasn't that close to her."

CHAPTER SIX

Grace

The rest of the day goes by in a haze, as I give massage after massage until my hands hurt and the sun sets. I try to empty my mind so I can focus on my clients and the needs of their bodies and souls. That alone roots me. Finding the connection, appeasing their pain, their stress. Feeling relief flood through them as my hands instinctively find their way to their knots and untie them.

For a few hours, I lose myself in bringing relief to others, and it brings me temporary peace.

Only temporary.

"Ms. Grace? Everyone is gone," Tracy says. She stands at the opening of the tent, eyes shiny. "Everyone was so happy! I'm so excited for you."

"How are you feeling, Trace? Did you remember to stretch?" I take the booklet she hands me, where she's been gathering people's information—mainly name and email—on a voluntary basis. That was Alex's idea.

"Sorta."

I wave her in. "Get on the table, sweetie."

"Are you sure? It's super late."

"Come on." Tracy is one of the high school's best athletes, and I know she's counting on her skills for a college scholarship. She injured her thigh recently, and she's shared her concerns with me. "It's the least I can do." The high schoolers helping at the fair earn Community Service hours, but she went above and beyond.

While I work on her, my thoughts drift to Ethan, when really, all I should be worrying about right now is where to transport my business and how much it's going to cost me. "I got a selfie with Mister K the other day. Isn't he so hot?"

"Mister K?" Who is that?

She sighs. "Ethan King. He's too old for me." She shakes her head in a serious manner, and I can't help but laugh.

"Yes—he is too old for you."

"I need someone like him, except, like, *fifteen years* younger." She rolls her eyes. "Looks aren't everything. You can tell he's a super nice guy." She sighs. "Supposedly my cousin dated him in high school, but I don't believe her. She's too mean for someone like him."

Ethan was a heartbreaker in high school. I resist the urge to ask who her cousin is. Tracy comes from a large family, and I sometimes get lost in the family trees—not just hers. I know everyone Ethan dated, at least the girls from Emerald Creek High, but I do *not* want to go down that memory lane. It would bring up the more painful memory. Ethan's college years.

Besides, I have more important things to worry about.

"How do you feel?" I ask Tracy.

She shakes her legs and stands up. "Ohmygod! Like new. Not gonna lie, Ms. Grace, you have magic in your hands."

"Awww, thank you, Tracy."

"Hey, your spa is called A Touch Of Grace for a reason."

I smile and dump the sheet in the hamper. Tracy helps me pack up my accessories. "Would you—would you consider giving me massages after training? I have pre-season camp next week."

Oh wow. I guess my massage really helped her. "At the Arena?" I hadn't thought of the young athletes in town, but that would be great exposure.

She nods.

"Sure. Have your mom call me." We fold the table and roll the carpet. Autumn insisted I leave everything, and she'd pick it up tomorrow.

Tracy helps me carry all my massage stuff to the car, and while we're carrying the table, her mom shows up to pick her up. After a quick chat, we agree on a daily massage for Tracy after training. I priced it a little on the high end because of the convenience of me going to the Arena every day, and she didn't even seem to think it was pricey.

My phone rings as I get in my car. *Haley.* I let it go to voicemail, telling myself I need to focus on my lease issues, when really I'm terrified she'll bring up Ethan in the conversation.

I can't right now.

Just like I won't be going to Lazy's for a beer and a chat with Justin because he's Ethan's brother.

Too risky.

Back to the safe problem at hand. The one I can solve. My lease.

I run through my options as I drive back into town. Looking at the worst-case scenario—the one where I have to vacate and can't find another place—I suppose that for a while I could keep A Touch Of Grace afloat by having my staff give in-house facials and mani-pedis, while I continue developing the massage business by going to people's home with my portable table. But God—it would *kill* me to leave my place. I've put so much of my heart and soul into creating the haven that it is now.

As I enter the spa, I take in the soft luxury of the space I've created. The leather armchairs and their soft throws, the velvet wingback, the pine accent furniture, the side tables with magazines—I would take all this with me. And the sound system and my scented candles and all the minute details that contribute to the atmosphere of relaxation. All this I would keep.

But could I recreate the same welcoming sophistication without the waxed hardwood floors I paid a fortune to bring back to life? Without the painted moldings that are now the right hue of cream? Without the warm copper accents on the mantle that reflect so perfectly in the mirrored panels?

Moving somewhere else would mean so much more than just moving furniture and equipment.

How much time do I have left here? Alex said it was *priced to sell*.

And where would my team go if I have nowhere to offer services? My house is way too small, and I can't think of any available space in town. Cheyenne, Hope, Shanice, Fabrizio, Claudia—they're all counting on me, on A Touch Of Grace, for their livelihoods.

Ignoring my phone dinging with text messages, I unlock the filing cabinet hidden behind a discreet wood paneling and sift through it until I find the lease. Flicking on the desk lamp, I read through it carefully.

And there it is.

I thought so.

A right of first refusal.

Okay. Okay. Maybe this can work. Could I actually buy this place? It sounds crazy, but... I look up a realtor site on my phone, type in the spa's address and bring up the listing. There it is. The photos are... *from my website.* Not cool at all. And the price...

The price is... it's not cheap, but it's not over the top either. It will sell, for sure. Just not to me. I barely have ten percent of that price set aside. No bank will lend me the balance, and even then, it would leave me with no cash reserves.

It's okay.

It's not the end of the world.

I just need to move.

Shit.

I let my friends' calls go to voicemail, and message them that my day went really well, but I'm beat and taking a rain check on the river swim. I drag myself home, running scenarios through my head.

I'm not greeted by the habitual rubbing of my cat on my legs. "Damian?" I call out, expecting him to run to me like the good little dog he's not.

He doesn't. I leave my shoes at the entrance and get to my bedroom. "Damian?"

Muffled meows sound from behind my closet door. "What are you doing in there?" I turn the handle, but the door stays stuck, and it takes several tugs and shoves to unstuck it.

Damian darts out and runs to the kitchen, then turns around to look at me with reproach in his gaze. "How'd you get in there?" I ask, following him to get his kibble ready.

The sound of his food being prepared improves his mood, and he loops around my legs, meowing with need until I feed him. I pet his head, the fur soft against my reddened skin. "Who's a good boy? Who got stuck in the closet?"

He ignores me.

I return to my room, ready to put this day behind me. As I'm getting ready to jump in the shower, my phone rings with the tone set for Mom.

I'll answer later.

I need a moment to myself.

The piping hot water barely warms my insides. Though it's sweltering outside, I feel chilled to the bone. Literally exhausted—there's nothing left inside me.

And although I know what's drained my energy is the massages I gave all day, the image that keeps imposing itself on my closed eyes is Ethan—his gaze drilling into me. The way he whipped his shirt off as if he knew the effect it would have on me. How his muscles rolled on his back and his biceps bulged when he plopped himself on his forearms and told me to stop the massage.

Those arms that used to make me feel safe. That gaze that used to worship me.

Or so I thought.

The memories assault me. He's the same and yet he's different. His voice is deeper. His resolve, stronger. His presence, more impactful than ever.

I've always been helpless in the presence of Ethan King. But now is not the time for teenage angst. Now I'm a grown-ass woman with grown-ass problems and no time or energy for the Ethan Kings of this world.

I pat myself dry and call Mom back.

She picks up immediately. "We need to talk."

"I'm toast."

"I know. Don't matter."

"Is this about the lease?" I don't want them worrying about my business.

"What lease?"

I sigh. She's best friends with Lynn, Ethan's mom. She has to know I saw him. She may even know the exact circumstances. That's why she's not taking no for an answer.

"The Hallmark channel is having their Christmas in July marathon. Been a while we haven't watched those. C'mon." I can almost feel her bite her tongue, not adding *'It'll be like good old days.'*

"Okay." There's no point arguing, or she'll come here. It wasn't good old days, but when I came back from Texas, little things like watching TV with Mom did help pull me out of the hole.

"Bring Damian," she declares, knowing my cat is also a sucker for sweet, sappy movies.

After another fight with my closet door, I put on some comfy clothes and haul my ass to my parents'.

Mom sets the lasagna on the table. "You sure took your sweet time. It's almost burned," she says.

"Why didn't you turn the oven off?" Dad says in my defense.

"My closet door keeps getting stuck," I semi-lie. "I don't know what's wrong with it."

"I could try and take a look," Dad says half-heartedly. He's exhausted just thinking about it. "I'd tell you to ask your brother, but—"

"Yeah, no." Colton is a magician with cars. Old houses? Not his thing. He doesn't see the point in maintaining the delicate details of centuries-old homes. He'd just as quickly knock down my intricately carved door and its period hinges and replace it with a faux barn door on a railing.

"Why don't you call these lovely new people—Thalia and Lucas?"

"Maybe."

After dinner, Mom insists on cleaning up on her own, so I take Dad to the living room and massage his shoulders, hands, and feet.

"How's baby Skye?" Dad asks.

"Not a baby anymore," I answer, and somehow that thought makes me sad. Skye may not have been the reason I came back to Emerald Creek, but when my cousin, Chris, got full custody of her when she was a newborn, I jumped in to help.

She gave me a purpose. A reason to get out of bed in the morning. Now I'm out of that funk, thank god, but I'm finding any little change affects me. "She loves Alex."

Dad pats my hand. "You miss taking care of her. Taking her to school, babysitting..."

"It's summer," I counter, not wanting to talk about that. But I'm not getting rid of her car seat, and I haven't had the heart to clean up the scrunchies or even the candy wrappers she left there last time. It seems too final. "And Chris and Alex still need me for babysitting."

"Chris did good," Dad says. "I hope you find that too, some day."

I don't want to answer that. There's nothing to say, nothing we could agree on.

I'm perfectly content alone, with Damian, and Skye, every now and then. What else could I possibly want?

"Gracie bear, you're tired. Time to go watch TV with Mom."

"I'm not tired."

"Your hands are shaking."

He can feel that? I look into his eyes tenderly. He doesn't look good today. "Right back atcha, Dad. You need some rest."

He nods. "I'll be watching the game. You and Mom need your girl time." He leans back in his recliner, remote control on his lap, and narrows his eyes on the screen, the glare flickering in bluish hues over his ashen face.

Mom is done in the kitchen, so we settle on their bed upstairs, a bowl of maple popcorn between us, Damian purring at our feet, the window open to the outside breeze from the lake.

With a deep sigh, I proceed to tell her about the building possibly being sold and A Touch Of Grace needing to move. That should keep her off my case about Ethan. Surely she'll see I have something *important* to actually worry about.

"You won't tell Dad about the lease, right?" I whisper as she selects the Hallmark Channel.

"Course not." We have this tacit agreement to not worry Dad. "What are you going to do?" She pauses the movie.

"I don't know yet. The landlord hasn't even notified me yet."

"Isn't that weird?"

"I have no idea. I'll look into it next week. Can we just watch movies now?"

"Sure." As the opening credits roll, she fusses with the popcorn, the remote, Damian. Then she can't handle it anymore. "Your tent looked busy, honey." Her opening doesn't fool me. "I couldn't even sneak in to say hello. You did good."

I keep my eyes on the screen. "Yeah. Hopefully people were happy, and they'll book at the salon. Wherever that may be."

"It'll take time, like everything else."

Right. And I might need to move.

Unable to hold it any further, she blurts, "I heard you saw Ethan."

"I did."

"And?" Her fingers hover over the remote, but she doesn't pause the movie. Not yet.

I throw a piece of popcorn in my mouth. "And what?"

"How's he doing?"

I shrug. "He pulled a muscle. I massaged his thigh. He should be fine. Gave him some arni—"

"I'm not talking about his thigh, Grace, although I've heard he's... spectacular."

"Ew, Mom!" I grab a handful of popcorn this time.

"Is he?"

"Is he what?"

"Spectacular."

"Mom! Gross."

She turns the sound off. "And why is it gross?"

"He could be your son?" As the words leave my lips, a little twist of pain unfurls in the depths of my fantasies. He *could* have been her son, in a way.

"I know he could be my son. I have a son. A very handsome son. Spectacular in his own way. I also have a gorgeous daughter. What's gross about stating the obvious?"

I grab the remote from her and turn the sound back up.

She sighs in an exaggerated manner. Pretends to watch. Then, "You could at least tell me how it went, you know. It'd be nice for me to know."

"It—it went... normal. He came in, got his massage, and left."

"That's it?"

I indulge her. "He came in limping and walked out totally normal. Next thing you know, Echoes is going to report your daughter performs miracles." Echoes is Emerald Creek's own social media platform, and lots of gossip gets spread there alongside useful information.

She reaches to pat my hand. "Don't be so closed off, Gracie Bear. Let it out, sweetheart. You're usually good with that."

What am I going to let out? That tonight, I'll fall asleep imagining how perfect life would be if Ethan had turned out to be who I imagined he would? I'm different. I'm weird. And that's okay. Mom knows it. It doesn't mean I have to openly disclose my bizarre ways of coping with life.

I'll get over it.

I've gotten over way worse than Ethan pretending we were mere acquaintances.

This isn't going to kill me.

I squeeze her hand back. "He *is* spectacular, and he doesn't care about me. You see? Nothing new. It's like it always was."

She pulls me against her, but our eyes stay glued to the screen where commercials are now running. "Oh, honey, I don't believe for one second that he doesn't care about you."

I close my eyes to try and keep it all in, but tears spill over. I brush them off with the back of my hand. Mom doesn't notice, or if she does, she stays silent as the TV cuts back to the now happy couple skating in Central Park.

"Where'd you go, honey?" Mom brings me back to the present.

"Thinking about my lease."

She sees right through my lie. "You used to be an open book. Talk to me."

"I still am, Mom."

She plays with the ties of her hoodie. "When you came back from Texas..." she starts, then takes a shaky breath. "I thought I was going to lose you. I thought you might die of heartbreak."

I snuggle against her. "Oh, Mom, don't," I whisper. "Please." I don't want to go back there. To revisit those days.

"But it took you weeks to tell me how you felt. It took you weeks to open up again. You weren't talking to me about it, and I didn't know how to help you. Please don't do this again. Talk to me."

I peck her cheek. I'm going to have to work on suppressing the flow of memories that surged when I saw Ethan again. But that's a normal reaction. And not one I need to worry Mom about.

"It was... a surprise to see him," I say. "I'm not gonna lie. But it was so long ago, Mom. We were kids. I'm a different person now, and so is he. We've each been through a lot. We came out on the other side of it totally changed. We've got nothing in common now."

Only memories. I have mine, and I cherish them. I don't know what his are like. It's irrelevant. As far as I know, none of his memories involve me.

I was always a child to him, and when I wasn't anymore?

I was a mistake.

That's what he'd said. His final words to me. *"This was a mistake."*

CHAPTER SEVEN

Ethan

I manage to stop asking questions about Grace. Mainly because it turns out, Mom and Dad have become quite social since I last lived in Emerald Creek, and now, they host Sunday dinners. I'd heard of those. I didn't know what it meant.

What it means, is that once a month, everyone they know—and they know almost everyone—has an open invitation to the King farm.

And like Haley told me, this includes Grace.

Which was also explicitly confirmed when Mom called her best friend, in front of me, to confirm that she and Dennis and Grace and maybe even Colton were coming.

I acted like I wasn't listening. I focused on keeping my breathing even. On pretending this didn't mean anything to me.

Now I'm outside with a beer and offer to take over the barbecue since Justin called to say he "couldn't make it," and it seems that this is his primary function at Sunday dinner. Manning the barbecue.

I don't have his cooking expertise, and I don't care. I just need a vantage point from which to observe the dynamics. Specifically, what the hell is going on with Grace.

She's wearing a white summer dress that shows her shoulders and cascades down to her calves on one side, a little higher on the other. Her hair is pulled back loosely, with a bright pink flower pinned in it. She moves around with ease, smiling at everyone, holding a little girl's hand. She looks like she could be her daughter, though, so I pay double attention. And *what if* she had a child? God the kid is cute. I get all soft at the thought of Grace having a daughter who would look just like her.

Lucky father.

But she calls her Grace, and weirdly enough, I breathe easier.

She's Skye, her cousin Chris's daughter.

She and Haley sit next to each other at the end of a long trestle table. I can't hear what they're saying, but I see Haley pointing from her plate to me. Grace's gaze follows and gets lost somewhere over my head, like she couldn't be less interested.

Like I'm a total stranger.

She eats salad.

When everyone's seated, I load a plate with burgers, hot dogs, and chargrilled marinated chicken and squeeze on a bench across from them.

I set the plate in front of her. "Help yourself."

"Oh thanks," she says in a crisp, airy voice. She looks everywhere except at me. She doesn't help herself.

As I stare at her, her cheekbones color, and the skin above her breasts turns reddish in places.

"Massage was great," I say, still staring at Grace, feeling Haley's eyes drilling daggers in my skull again.

"The lotion help?"

"I dunno. Didn't try it yet."

She blinks a few times like it's a stupid thing to say, but she has no comeback. No advice.

And above all, she still. Doesn't. Meet. My. Gaze.

I can't confront her here, right? I can't come back, ten years later, and make a scene in front of the whole village because a girl I thought loved me seems to think I'm some piece of shit now.

Just because I didn't get closure at the time doesn't mean I can get it now.

We're on different timelines. I should have confronted her ten years ago. Now's too late.

Now, it doesn't matter. She moved on, got married. Got divorced. I'm a blip in her life. I can't expect her to feel anything about me.

"Who's that little cutie?" I ask, looking at Skye who has climbed onto Grace's lap and looks just like her.

"I'm Skye," the mini Grace answers. "Who are you?" She reaches to the platter, takes a hotdog, bites it, then sets it on the side of Grace's plate.

"I'm Ethan."

She widens her eyes at me. "Uncle Justin's big brother?"

That gets me a chuckle. So sweet that she calls him Uncle. "That's me."

"Wow." She takes another bite of her hotdog.

Wow what? I don't know much about kids, so I have no idea if this is good or bad.

"Did you kill a lot of bad people?"

Um. Again, not sure what to make of that question. "Not a lot."

She looks disappointed. Then her eyes brighten, and she straightens with excitement. "Did you take them as prisoners?"

"No prisoners."

"That's okay," she says in a comforting tone. "I'm sure you did your best."

Haley, Grace, and I share a brief laugh, and Grace's gaze finally meets mine, setting a burning path from my irises down to a place right below my ribcage. The feeling stays there as Grace visibly relaxes.

"Hey, man." Chris walks up to us, his arm around the shoulders of a pretty young woman. Shit. I haven't seen him in ten years. He's changed. He's... a man now. I remember a skinny, angsty teenager. He's nothing like that. Looking at him, I measure how much time has passed. How we all must have changed.

"Daddy! This is Uncle Justin's brother!" Skye squeals as I stand up to greet him.

I go to shake his hand, but he pulls me into a back-slapping hug just like Colton had. "Missed you," he mumbles. Pulling away, he adds, "This is Alexandra."

"Alek-zandra is Daddy's girlfriend," Skye pipes as I shake her hand.

Grace starts to scoot over on the bench. "Why don't you guys join us?"

"Daddy, you promised I could ride Sunshine," Skye cuts in, sliding off Grace's lap and running toward the barn.

"That's—yup—actually why we came—to get Skye," Chris says as an apology. "I'll catch up with you later."

Haley stands up. "I'll go saddle her for you."

I'm not left alone with Grace, not even for a minute. A young woman slides next to her. "Hey, I heard. Sorry."

What did she hear? What is she sorry about? Is it about her father's declining health? Grace gives the woman a small smile and a shrug. "Thanks. I'll figure it out."

Not her dad, I guess.

"If you need us, just holler. We're wrapping up at the resort and after that, we could have time for small projects."

Definitely not her dad.

Grace's face lights up. "Thanks!"

"There you are." Lucas, the guy I briefly met during the fair setup, sits next to me, slaps my back, and takes the woman's hand in his, twining their fingers. "This is the guy I told you about," he tells her. "Ethan."

"You're the carpenter? I'm Thalia."

Grace frowns, her inquisitive gaze going between the three of us.

"I'm hardly a carpenter," I tell Thalia. "It's just a hobby I picked up."

"In case you want to turn it into more," Thalia says, pulling out a business card. "We're looking to hire." Is it me or does Grace look panicked right now?

I take the card out of politeness. "I'm leaving in a few days, but thanks. You never know," I add with a chuckle.

"Ethan is with the Air Force," Grace volunteers, her cheeks tinting. "He hardly ever comes to Emerald Creek."

"Oh, sorry," Thalia chuckles. "I don't know why I thought—never mind."

"It's my fault," Lucas interrupts. "I've been telling her non-stop what a great job you did at the fair and how I could use a guy like you."

"He's always been good with his hands," Grace drops, then blushes as she realizes what she just said. "You know, carving things and stuff," she adds quickly.

Carving things? A vague childhood memory pops up. Little wooden figurines. I pocket their business card with a smile. "Thanks. Something to fall back on if all else fails."

Thalia shrugs, "Or if you ever get bored while you're here. We always have small jobs lined up."

"Let's get some food," Lucas says, maybe reading my eagerness to be alone with Grace, maybe simply hungry. He stands and pulls Thalia to him.

"So... What's going on with you? What Thalia said," I ask Grace the minute they're gone, for now putting aside her comment about me being good with my hands.

She furrows her eyebrows at me, picking at the half-eaten hot-dog Skye left on her plate.

"Thalia asked if you were okay. Offered her help." I know it's none of my business. But Thalia and Lucas are new in town, he said so himself. Thalia can't be that close of a friend to Grace. So if she knows something's bothering Grace, why shouldn't I? "She said *she heard* and she was sorry," I insist. Grace can't possibly pretend she doesn't know what I'm talking about now.

"Oh—nothing," Grace waves her hand. "My uh—my lease. I might lose my lease. For the spa." She tears a piece of bread from the hotdog and pops it in her mouth.

"Oh, shit. That doesn't sound good. How come?" I push my plate to the side and prop my arms on the table, leaning closer to Grace.

Her eyes fleetingly meet my gaze, then narrow back down on her plate where she's destroying the hotdog bun with her fingers. "The building is for sale, so whoever buys it can break the lease. It's-it's-it'll be fine."

It doesn't seem like it's going to be fine *at all*. "How can Thalia help?"

She shakes her head slowly. "Um—if or when I have to move elsewhere, I'd probably need some work done."

I don't know anything about spas. But I can imagine there's got to be electrical and plumbing needed, and that's always costly. And then décor. Paint. Floors. "That sucks. I'm sorry."

She takes a shaky breath that nearly does me in. "Life of a small business owner." She smiles with her lips sealed tightly to each other, then deepens her inhale. As she exhales, her gaze falls on mine. "It'll figure itself out. It always does. How about you? How's your job treating you?"

I blink. "I uh—I wanted to apologize."

Her eyes widen and she straightens on the bench.

"The other day, at the fair, I was rude to you."

Her face softens.

I continue. "I was taken aback. I wasn't prepared to see you again, and it was—it was..." What was it? Surprising? Earth-shattering? "I just wasn't prepared, and I was a jerk. I'm sorry."

"Yeah," she chuckles. "Same here. I didn't handle it too well. I'm glad we're past that, though."

Past what exactly? "Yeah... About that..."

She looks at me with alarm, stacking her cutlery on her plate. "I should probably check on Dad." She stands slowly. Deliberately. Not like someone who retreats in haste. More like someone who's made the conscious decision they're not going to engage. For whatever reason.

"Any chance you'd want to talk? About what happened back then."

She lays a thoughtful and deep gaze on me. "We were different people back then. Dwelling on the past doesn't help. Never does." She picks up her plate. "Have a nice stay, Ethan," she adds and until then, until then I was going along with her story, but the way she says my name, Ethan, the way it rolls in her mouth and on her tongue, the way she drags it out a little... nope.

"Let's have coffee."

"I don't think that's a good idea."

And why not? Friends have coffee together. Ex-lovers? Generally not. What am I to her? "Just two old friends."

She smiles softly, almost sadly. "Bye, Ethan."

I knew it.

She swerves back to the porch, climbs the steps, stops to talk to someone, disappears inside the house. We have unresolved matters, and I need to clear them, if only so I can move forward. She said herself we're different people now, and she's right.

What does she think of me? Does she think I fled Emerald Creek to avoid facing my responsibilities? Which I did. Is that how she sees me?

Of course she doesn't see anything else in me than the guy who bailed on everyone when things got tough.

Why would she see anything else? What have I done with my life that means something here? I didn't try to build a family. I didn't try to build a business. I didn't try to build a house. I could have tried all of these things.

I might have succeeded. I might have failed.

Chris, Justin, Grace. They all tried. They succeeded. You could say Grace failed at her marriage. But was it really a failure? At least she tried.

They all built something with their lives. They faced challenges that they overcame. They have something to show for the past ten years.

All I did was run away. And sure, that *communication thingy*, like Mom says. That holds value for me. Outside of Emerald Creek, with the Air Force, I'm someone. Here? Not much.

Later in the evening, anyone still here is marveling at how beautiful the witching hour is. How the air brims with fragrance and the sounds of the meadow.

But Grace is long gone, and the air feels empty to me.

The wraparound porch where we've retreated offers me a front row seat to the scene of my childhood and early adulthood. It feels intimately close and yet remote, like something I broke and shouldn't come near. It's almost painful in its beauty. *I should think about this more often when I'm away. Remember this beauty is always here.*

Even if to some extent, I'm eager to leave already.

I'm lost in my thoughts when Mom comes out of the house, handing me the cordless landline phone. "It's for you. Coach Randall."

I stand, feeling awkward to take this phone call sitting down, and step away. "Coach!"

"King. How'ya doin, son?"

"Good! Great. I was actually planning on swinging by the Arena and catching up. How's tomorrow?" I glance at Dad. For approval, and maybe there's something planned? Something they need me for?

"Another time, son, I'm afraid. My sister passed away—"

"Oh, I'm sorry to hear that."

"Yeah, well, a blessing. She had Alzheimer's. Been mourning her for years now." He clears his throat. "Anyhoo. I gotta leave town. Memorial is next week. Haven't seen my other siblings in way too long... you know how it is."

"Yeah." Why is he telling me this?

"So I have this Varsity Preseason camp next week."

Oh hell no. Feeling what's coming, I step off the porch completely, away from company.

"Was hopin' you could jump in and take over."

Hell. No.

"Whole plan is typed up, schedule, all that. You'd just have to follow along my notes. Nothing to improvise."

"Uhh. Jeez, coach, I don't know. I—I actually might have to leave town next week," I lie. There is no way in hell I am coaching a bunch of kids in hockey.

"You still play, right?"

"Y-yeah, course, but like I said—"

"It's just kids, King. They don't bite. And they need you."

I kick the dirt with the tip of my sneaker. "Coach, I dunno."

"I guess I could ask Owen to jump in. We're close to getting to Nationals this year, but they need a lot of work."

Fuck. "Owen Parker?" He's got to be kidding.

"He's all I got. 'Cept you. So—whaddayasay?"

I look up to the sky, then close my eyes when all I hear is his silence, heavy with expectation.

"I heard you already met our Tracy," he drops. "Wait 'til you see her on the ice. She's quite something. So—what should I tell the kids?"

I take a deep breath. "What time tomorrow?"

❦

As I walk into the Arena the next morning at eight, I curse this small town for making me do something I did not want to do, while at the same time, my eyes dampen, my chest tightens.

The sharp, crisp air of the rink hits my nostrils, and from memory, I can almost taste the cold on my tongue. On the ice, two players are already practicing, their skates scraping the ice, their sticks slapping the puck. A rush of adrenaline fills me, remembering these quiet moments of warming up, of focus before a game, before the place filled with the cheers of the crowd, the flash of team colors, the thud of colliding bodies.

This used to be my life. My home away from home. My refuge.

And it'll be my refuge from Grace. No chance I'll run into her here now.

She used to be on the bleachers. Not anymore.

Fuck.

I school myself into being in the moment.

"Ethan!" A woman about Mom's age is beaming at me.

"Mrs. Parker! How are you?" Owen's mom was always on the bleachers, cheering us on.

"I missed you!" she answers with a huge smile, hands on her hips. "Why—do you look handsome. Coach tells me you're filling in for him this week," she says as she goes into the glassed office off the entrance. "Come over here!" she calls over her shoulder as she grabs a three-ring binder. "I work here now," she explains. "Well, I'm not paid, so technically I *volunteer*, but if you ask me, some people who volunteer think they're at a buffet or something. Do whatever they please, come whenever they want. Not me." She straightens and leafs through the binder. "Lessee. Yup. It's all there." She hands me the binder. "You bring your skates and helmet?"

"Nah." They're with my move from Germany, somewhere in a container. "Figured I'd borrow some. Just like a rookie. You gonna have my size?" If all else fails, I'll coach from the sidelines, but I'm not gonna lie—being at the Arena just woke up an itch in me. I skated in Germany, but this is different. Here, I feel a buzz of excitement coursing through my veins that I wish would die down. *Must be a Pavlovian response*, I tell myself to make it go away.

"Well, lessee," she answers.

We do find skates that fit me, and a helmet. The stick isn't an issue. And to assuage her concerns, I put on Dad's jacket and gloves that I've been carrying bunched in my fist.

She makes a funny face.

I can't really move my shoulders, and the sleeves end several inches above my wrists. She insists on rummaging through the lost and found until she finds a jacket and gloves more to my size.

"Thanks, Mrs. Parker."

She folds back the jackets that didn't fit me. "Suzy, please. Mrs. Parker makes me feel old."

I smile at her. "I'll try."

She straightens from the lost-and-found chest, her face flustered from leaning down. "You know," she says, blowing hair off her forehead, "you were one of Owen's best friends. I bet he'll be happy to know you're here."

Best friend? "We actually bumped into each other the other day. He seems good. We were busy, didn't have time to catch up."

She frowns at me. "Huh. He was always a knucklehead, you know. But you... you set a good example for him." She seems lost in contemplation, and honestly, I don't know what to tell her. "Anyhoo, you know the place, so I'll let you get on with it."

Twenty minutes later, all the kids are here.

"Listen up!" I semi shout to get their attention right at nine o'clock.

Something stirs inside me as they quiet and look at me expectantly. After a quick and—it turns out—unnecessary introduction of who I am, I take attendance, trying to memorize their names. Lots of familiar last names. It's odd and comforting at the same time. Like slipping into jeans again after months of wearing fatigues. Then I ask them what their goal is this year for the team. As the answers roll in, I push them into their whys and hows. "Coach! Can we go train now?" one of the boys asks.

"We *are* training. Know your why." They're impatient, though, and I get it. "Alright, let's hit it." We head back outside for dynamic stretching, then agility ladders, and finally light jogging. "Alright, let's hit the ice."

They run like a pack of puppies to get changed. Man! their enthusiasm is incredible. This is going to be fun.

The day goes by super fast, with a quick lunch break where we go over strengths and points to improve. I check the schedule again to see how Coach Randall structures the afternoons, and something catches my eye. "Is someone getting a massage?"

Tracy, the girl who I met at Colton's the day I got to Emerald Creek, raises her hand shyly. "Me. I got injured earlier this summer."

I'd noticed she wasn't engaging much. I didn't say anything yet, was just trying to figure out their strengths and weaknesses, see how they worked as a group before tackling them individually. "That's great. Good for you. I take it your PT cleared you for training, yeah?"

"Yes, Coach."

"Lemme know if anything bothers you. Don't push yourself."

She nods.

"Kay, let's hit it."

Three hours later, we wrap up. The clatter of pucks against sticks recedes and the air fills with chatter as we file toward the locker rooms.

I glance toward the bleachers absentmindedly, looking for someone who hasn't been there for me in over a decade.

And I freeze as she slowly steps down.

And looks over my shoulder.

"Ready, Tracy?" Grace smiles.

CHAPTER EIGHT

Grace

H e *is* spectacular. He's all I fantasized about, except better. Saying that he takes my breath away doesn't even begin to describe it. My heart threatens to fly out of my ribcage, my legs refuse to function, my hands are clammy and my vision blurred.

What is Ethan doing here? Am I hallucinating?

I mean, it's not entirely impossible. I've been fantasizing so much about Ethan, I wouldn't be surprised if my crazy brain made him up entirely. I don't even know how I went through a normal conversation with him yesterday at the farm. It was like I was watching myself act like a perfectly sane person.

"Is this Coach Randall's camp?" I asked Suzy Parker at the reception, when I got here a few minutes ago.

She smiled. "Coach had an emergency, but he found a replacement. Are you here for Tracy? Her mom said you'd come."

I nodded.

"Go right in!" she said. "Quite some training he's doing there."

I usually try to stay away from the Arena. Chris plays here, so I do go on occasion, but not if I can avoid it.

So many memories of Ethan are tied to this place. To hockey. We didn't always have an Arena, or a team. We got one thanks to Ethan. He was spotted by a rich tourist skating on the lake, and one thing leading to another, a year later we had a brand spanking new arena. The first game, Ethan racked up several key assists and scored three goals.

After the game, he gave me his puck.

I treasured it like anything that came from Ethan. Three years later, Ethan took us to Nationals. We traveled to Massachusetts for that. It seemed the whole town was there. When he came out in all his glory—he was already glorious back then—he pulled out the puck he'd scored the first goal with and gave it to me.

I saw stars. Felt butterflies in my belly. My stupid grin didn't leave me for the next twenty-four hours.

Ethan had given me his puck. Again.

That had to mean something, right?

It didn't matter that he'd ruffled my hair like I was a little kid (I *was* still a little kid, at the time). It didn't matter that he didn't sign it (what did I need *that* for?). What mattered, was that he'd said, "You're my good luck charm, Gracie Bear."

And I believed him.

He was only being nice; I see that now. It took me a long time to peel apart this crazy attraction—infatuation, call it what you want—I'd had for Ethan.

It was my fault I fell so hard for him and hurt so bad when he broke my heart.

I'd been building up to him throughout my entire life, without anyone or anything to tell me to stop making shit up.

He'd done nothing but treat me like a family friend, his sister's bestie. Well, for most of the time. Then, things took another turn. At least in my mind they did. In his? I didn't mean a thing to him.

I should have known that.

I *did* know it.

I should have *understood* the consequences.

I see it now. I can't hold him accountable for what happened.

"Hey, Coach!" I say, hoping to feel detached. "How's it going?"

He frowns at me, looking puzzled.

Look. I don't know. I just said hi. Why is he being weird like that? I'm trying to be normal! Can't he just say *hi* back or am I always, always misunderstanding this man?

"Grace..." he says.

Oh—I get it. He's wondering why I'm here. He might think I'm ambushing him like some puck bunny. I laugh. It *is* kinda funny. On the other hand, he wanted to have coffee together. Like old friends. Those two words still sting, but I have to shove my feelings aside. "Oh—I'm just here for Tracy." I lift my duffel bag, like that's gonna help him understand. "Massage?"

Several things seem to pass across his face, like a whole storm. Rain. Sunshine. Thunder. Why is this man so complicated? Tracy is behind him, and as I descend the bleachers as fast as my cottony legs allow, I motion her to follow me to a private room. "Let's go," I say in a whisper, my vocal cords going on strike the moment I reach the bottom and Ethan is there.

He's occupying the whole space, his scent of clean sweat, leather and rubber slapping me like the best and the worst memory, a surge of happiness and despair so intrinsically linked together, this might signal the end of my existence on Earth, and if it does, it won't matter because I will have lived all the emotions I care to ever experience.

How I perform the massage, and how I get home—I do not know.

I do know that I wake up the next day with the dread of what awaits me that evening.

Another massage at the Arena, another few minutes in the inevitable presence of Ethan King, who makes me feel both alive and dead in the same breath.

But this time I'm mentally prepared. I know what's coming. I will handle the situation like a grown-up. And so, in the car, I rehearse.

"Coach! How did the teams do today?"

I should call him Ethan, right? Not Coach. Oh god, I don't know if I can even *say* his name. *"Guys! Aren't you lucky to have Coach Ethan this week?"* Okay, maybe if I talk *about* him, it'll go smoother. Still, I need to try the direct address.

Okay. Here we go. What could I tell him? Oh, I know. *"Ethan! Do you know if Coach Randall will be back before you leave? I bet he'd love to see you."* Okay, that went well. Voice working and everything. I just need to practice.

"Ethan! Ethan! Ethan!"

By the time I pull into the parking lot, I've said his name a hundred times. It might seem crazy. But I'm just being prepared.

Also, today, I get to the Arena right on time. None of this being early and watching my childhood crush possess the ice like a god nonsense.

By the time I'm out of my car, I'm two minutes late. Good.

Even better, Millie is coming out of the Arena. I walk up to her, hoping to kill a few more minutes with a little chat, but she inexplicably waves at me from afar and dashes to her car.

I wave back at her, smiling, counting to ten.

Perfect.

He'll be in the men's locker room.

He's not.

He's in the middle of a wide circle of teenagers drinking sports drinks and munching on snacks that are way too healthy for kids their age (What will they be eating when they start having health issues? You gotta live, guys, you gotta live), and he says—no—he exclaims, "There she is!" like they've all been waiting for me to make my grand entrance.

I freeze at the door, a deer caught in the headlights of the man who always shone too bright for me. He walks toward me. Gives me his killer smile, the one that tips his mouth up on one side only, the one that creates that dimple that I very distinctly remember licking. And he hands me a to-go cup from Easy Monday with *my* name on it in *his* handwriting, not Millie's. I know Millie's handwriting, and this is not hers. And I used to know Ethan's, and this is *exactly* like his. "Extra spicy chai with almond milk and maple syrup."

"Oh..."

"It's called a... I dunno. Something fancy."

A Harvest Hug. My favorite. Harvest Hug.

"I got it delivered and hot... because it's cold in here."

"Oh..."

He shoves the cup in my hands, and thankfully, our fingers don't touch, because that would have led to disaster. "And I had her use two cups because her sleeves are shit."

Her sleeves *are* shit. "She has insulated cups..." I start saying, stupidly, and stop myself. She *sells* insulated cups (real cute ones, for what it's worth). *What am I doing?* "Thanks," I say, looking up to meet his gaze.

Mistake.

My lady parts applaud.

Big mistake.

I take a sip of the tea. It's divine—everything Millie sells is divine—and it's my favorite. I wonder if he asked her what I liked? Did he mention me? Or did he just say, "Hey, get me something hot. Not coffee 'cause it's too late." Or something like that.

I wonder.

I take another sip of tea because it helps me focus on staying sane, and not asking him silly questions like *How did you know this was my favorite?* But mainly because it explains why I'm not looking at him when I'm dying to and when I still feel his eyes on me.

God he feels good.

I store that feeling for a later time, when I'll need it.

And again that day, the massage comes and goes without a hitch, and I get home and do what I need to do, and I'm back the next day.

This time, I don't know why—I swear, I didn't plan it—I'm early. Just a little bit. Like maybe fifteen minutes. "Don't you want to go out there and watch the training?" Suzy Parker asks me.

I can't decently say, *No, watching Ethan King on the ice coaching kids with care and attention is not something I should do.* "I guess I should check how Tracy is doing."

See? That's why I'm early. To see how my client is faring. What I'll need to pay attention to during the massage.

I place myself away from the entrance, so I'm not in the danger zone when practice ends, the red zone of Ethan coming out, the zone where my body parts start betraying me.

I sit off to the side and try to focus only on my client. I force myself to keep my eyes off Ethan as he glides on the ice. Tracy leans into a power turn, and I notice the trembling in her thigh. She'll need effleurage and petrissage, as well as passive stretching.

Good, I'm doing good.

Ethan's voice guiding his team makes it hard to forget he's here, though, so when he leaves the ice—it's hard not to notice—I breathe easier. This is what it's supposed to be. A private gig at the end of the day. Another way to spread the word. To build my business.

Not a full-on assault on my sanity.

Then Ethan comes back, holding something in his hand. I strive not to look, and mostly, I succeed.

He glides effortlessly across the rink. Shouts a few instructions to the kids. Then locks eyes with me (okay, I might have cheated a little and taken a peek at him) and before you know it, he's jumping off the ice, into the bleachers, standing in front of me handing me an insulated mug from Easy Monday.

The ones you buy.

Not just any mug either, but Millie's cutest one. Light pink with gold bears and dark green trees. I was admiring it just the other day.

"Harvest Hug. That's what it's called. You like it, right?" That killer smile again. That dimple.

I grab the mug and hold onto it for dear life. "Oh gosh. I... you didn't need to do that." I take a deep breath to say thank you, but he's already gone, sliding on the ice, rallying the kids around him, a magnet for them too.

Eyes glued to him, I sip my tea.

Then I give Tracy her massage.

Before I leave, he swipes the mug from me. "For tomorrow," he says. Our eyes lock briefly, his gaze tender.

But he doesn't even wait for me to say anything. Just like that, he's gone. Poof.

Why doesn't he even try to talk to me? What happened to wanting to have coffee together?

Ugh. I've never understood him. Never will.

And now he's ruining The Harvest Hug for me. I'll never be able to order it and not think of him. "Selfish," I mutter under my breath.

On Thursday their training goes on forever. My cup is waiting for me on the bleachers, and I down it, quick little sips, then stand to exit and wait near the lockers.

Ethan slides up to me. "Where'you going?"

"I'm gonna wait inside."

"Why?"

Because I can't keep my eyes off you. Because I'm imprinting so much of the way your body moves, the way your voice sounds, even the way your scent carries in wafts when you walk past me, I can't sleep at night anymore. Because I need to stop the torture. "It's getting cold."

And before I know it, I'm wrapped in the jacket he was wearing, and he leans into me to tuck the hat he was wearing snug over my head, and this time, this time, I do think I'm going to faint because now his scent is all around me.

And I remember his scent.

I thought I was making it up but no, I wasn't.

His scent is unique, and it's been with me since I can remember having feelings for him that were beyond friendship.

And I definitely remember the smell that defined the best night of my life. It was his. His, mixed with sex, and nature all around us. I lock my hands around the mug he's brought me again. It's empty now, only a tether I use to avoid, literally, fainting.

And I feel my body relax, warm up, and melt into everything that is Ethan. Even if he's not really here, holding me in his arms, enclosing me in his being.

It's as close to him as I'll ever get now.

And it's divine.

And it won't last.

And so I savor it for the minutes that I can.

CHAPTER NINE

Grace

I don't know how I get home, but I do. Just one more day of this and it'll be over. What's one more day? It'll be fine. I'll be fine.

I really need to dial back into the reality of my life. Pay my bills, clean my house. Come up with a plan for the spa. Feed my cat. Where *is* Damian? I can hear him, but he's not rubbing himself in loops around my legs. His cries get louder as I go down the hallway and into my bedroom.

He's meowing furiously again from behind my closet door.

"You're a silly, silly cat, and you're paying for your silliness." I push the door in until it creaks open enough for Damian to come out. He looks at me, reproach in his eyes.

"What? Just stop going in there. How do you even get the door open?" I swear, I checked this morning, and the door *was* closed. Tight.

I struggle to push the door wide open. With a weird thump, it suddenly gives in, and I automatically look up, to the box.

The box, where my eyes always go each time I come in (twice a day at least) and at night, before I go to sleep. Because this stupid door stays stuck, so now I leave it open at night to avoid wasting time in the morning trying to get to my clothes.

This time I grab the old box and bring it to my bed. It started as a shoe box, and at some point I had to move its contents to the box that held my first cowboy boots. Damian jumps on the bed, sniffs through the box, and sits back like the sphinx, looking at me through squinted eyes.

He knows the ritual. He's giving me two and half minutes to go down memory lane, and then he's done. Then I'll have to put the box away.

"It's different this time, okay? I need a little more time. He's here, you see. It doesn't mean anything, but it's important to me. It means these things, here, they're not dead. Not really. Now do you believe me?"

Damian purrs, stands, and walks on the lid of the box.

It was—still is—an awesome-looking box, way more deserving of its precious contents than the blue sneakers box that was falling apart. Yet Damian sits on it, the lid caving in slightly.

It's okay. I'm not that cray-cray. It's just a box. "Damian, move," I finally say, shooing him away from the lid. I can't help it.

He squints at me and stays put. Not budging.

Okay, then. Whatever. It's not about the lid anyway.

I move my gaze to the contents of the box, two decades worth of memories that carry meaning only for me. Usually, it's a feel-good moment, this time alone, under the watchful eye of Damian. A moment when I relive the good times, the hopes, the dreams.

When I don't feel so alone.

When I rewrite the present. How things could have been, should have been. And for a few minutes, I'm in my fantasy life. And it feels *good*.

Tonight, however, it's hard.

These aren't memories anymore. These aren't dreams.

These are proof perfect that I live in my own universe that does not align with the real world.

And seeing Ethan, and him being everything I ever imagined he'd become and even better, but not being these things to me, with me—a best friend, a lover, a husband, the father of my children.

I'm not gonna lie, it's hard this time.

God I need to get out of this funk.

"What d'you think, Damian?" I contemplate the disposable mug that held the Harvest Hug Ethan brought me on Monday, with my name in his handwriting on it.

Damian meows.

"I agree." I stand, rinse the inside of the cup carefully one last time, and wipe it. Then I add it to the box. With the two pucks, the jersey, carved wooden figurines, the letters, the newspaper clippings, a tiny twine ring protected by a ziplock, a dried mistletoe turning to dust, and a carved tree bark.

Probably the last thing I'll add.

Although, not sure what I'll do with the travel mug, once he gives it back to me.

If he gives it back to me.

It's really pretty. If I used it every day, it would be like having Ethan with me. Like he might pop up at any time. Like he's not really gone and he might say, "Hey, Grace, gimme the mug back so I can get you a Harvest Hug tomorrow."

Like maybe we'd be as I wish we were, where I'd get *his* hugs.

And *his* kisses.

Damian meows loudly at me.

"Okay, okay, time's up, I know."

Damian stands from the lid and lifts it with his nuzzle. I place it back on the box, careful not to squoosh the mug, then slip it on the shelf right next to the door. Where I can see it every day.

Twice a day at least.

"What'cha say, Damian? It's Thursday." Thursday is Game Night in Emerald Creek. A women's-only gathering in the back of Cassandra's lingerie shop. We play games as an excuse to get together, gossip together, sometimes cry together, always laugh together.

Damian meows enthusiastically and runs to his bowl.

Sometimes I wonder if he has dog genes.

I refill his kibble, then make myself a sandwich and eat it standing above my sink so I don't get anything dirty. I drink a glass of water, and a second.

There'll be alcohol at Game Night, so I want to get there hydrated.

"Ready, Damian?"

He trots to his litter box.

Total dog vibes.

I brush my teeth, fix my makeup, then pick up Damian. "Let's have some girl time."

He meows.

"You're a cat. You're allowed."

Cassandra's shop is in a cute cape house twinkling with fairy lights. I park the jeep, pick up Damian, and round to the back where laughter and light spill out of the partly open windows. Pushing the door open, I'm taken in by warm hellos from everywhere.

Mom and Lynn are sprawled on the white sectionals in the back right corner, playing gin rummy with Suzy Parker and my receptionist,

Claudia Fletcher. Their bare feet rest on gold and pink pillows, and white bubblies occupy their free hands.

Ms. Angela and her posse are hunched over Emerald Creek's mystery game, an adaptation of Clue where intimate knowledge of the town's gossip is key to winning.

Haley brings them her variation of a Moscow mule, setting their drinks on off-white felt coasters, then returns behind a mirrored bar, pouring one of her new wine-like inventions into stem glasses.

Other women are gathered in small groups, chatting or playing games, munching and drinking.

My friends are sprawled on the left side of the room, soy candles softly flickering around them. Autumn, a newly established decorator, is there, and so is Kiara, a talented pastry chef. She jumps up when she sees me. "You brought Damian!" she shrieks and grabs my cat from my arms. "Come here you little scoundrel, you little rascal. Tickle tickle tickle."

Damian makes himself soft as a rag doll and lets her have her way with him.

I kick my shoes off and drop my offering of lotions and serum samples on a small table next to the door for the ladies to take on their way out, then settle in a pink bean bag next to my friends, letting the girly vibes of Cassandra's she-shed mellow me. Digging my toes in the faux fur throw rug, I inhale the subtle aroma of small bouquets spread throughout the room, admire her new golden trinkets, the mirrors reflecting tea light candles, making mental notes for my own spa.

Haley hands me a stem glass filled with a bubbly, purple beverage and takes a seat next to me.

Haley's experiments aren't always conclusive. "What's this one?" I'd rather be prepared.

"It's raspberry wine. What d'you think about it?"

The sharp yet floral notes hit my palate with a burst of bubbles. "Delicious. Wow. Raspberries?"

"I'm totally using that in my Christmas pastries this year," Kiara says, still holding Damian. "I don't know how yet. You have any ideas?" she asks Haley.

I strain to focus on the conversation that follows between the two, but my mind keeps wandering. To Christmas and secret Santas. To New Years and mistletoe. To swimming at the lake... to other things at the lake.

"Sorry I'm late! What did I miss?" Alex asks as she enters the room. "Oh good—you're here," she says to me. As she walks to the back of the room where the bar is, she's greeted by everyone, and it warms me to see how well loved she is in Emerald Creek, and how she's now part of our small-town family.

"Munchies," she announces as she sets a tray on the bar and snatches one of the glasses Haley poured and left on the bar for anyone to help themselves. Settling with us, she asks me, "So—what do we know? What are you doing?"

I haven't *done* anything since Saturday. Mainly, I've been going day-to-day like a zombie, unable to take action. "I still haven't heard from Richardson, but I know the price is out of my reach."

"Who's Richardson?" Alex asks.

"Georgie?" Ms. Angela chimes in from her station at the middle of the room. "He's the landlord."

"You were going to buy it?" Kiara says, petting Damian as he climbs up her shoulder.

"I have a right of first refusal, so I'll know when it sells. Not that I can afford it, so really... not that useful." The din of conversation dies down as everyone listens in.

Kiara sits cross-legged at my feet. "But you'll know ahead of time if you need to move, right?"

"I guess."

Cassandra, Ms. Angela, and the other women around don't ask questions or seem surprised.

They all know.

Their sympathetic murmurs confirm it. I glance at Mom and Lynn who looked up from their game but stay quiet, letting the rest of the women take the lead.

"We need to do something," Ms. Angela declares. "Can we sign a petition?"

"He's allowed to sell," someone points out.

"It's just not right that he didn't talk to her first."

"He was always a coward."

"Well hung, but a coward," another of the older ladies at Ms. Angela's table, Cheryl, chimes in.

"How d'you know he was well hung?" Kiara asks.

"That was his dad," Ms. Angela interjects. "George."

"Heh! Stuff happened... back in the day. We weren't as shy as you young people," Cheryl says.

"Ah... the sixties," Ms. Angela sighs dreamily. "Were you part of the calendar?" she adds.

"Oh yeah. That's how I know George Senior was—you know. Well endowed."

"I remember you mentioning that."

"Not that it did him any good," Cheryl volunteers. "Or me."

Ms. Angela giggles like this is a totally normal conversation.

"What calendar?" Haley asks.

"We did a naked calendar after the fire, to raise money."

"Naked?" Several of the young women ask.

My attention is diverted from my present problems. These old ladies naked on a calendar? That was sixty years ago? They would have been in their twenties...

"Totally naked?" I ask.

"We shot totally naked, but you can't see anything. Except for George. If you look closely at his month, his ding-dong shows between his legs. I think he was July. Or August. He's fly-fishing in the Emerald Creek."

Ms. Angela laughs loudly. "Oh my gosh! Yes. I remember now."

"He didn't know how to use it. Total waste," Cheryl doubles down, turning around in her seat to face us.

"Mom!" Suzy Parker cries, putting her hands on her ears. Lynn and Mom are trying not to laugh too hard. And failing.

"Oh, knock it off, Suze. It was before your dad," Cheryl chuckles. Then, turning to Ms. Angela, she asks, "What month were you?"

"I was January. I was in a bubble bath. We shot in the vintage tub that's upstairs in what's now the bakery. The tub was so deep you could only see my face, so someone brought some bricks for me to sit on. And then I had one leg out. We shot with and without nipples."

"What?!" several of us exclaim.

"Eventually they chose to publish the one where the nipples have suds on'em. We would have made more money with nipples, but they chickened out."

"I remember," Cheryl chuckles.

"Nipples, really?" Haley says.

"I had beautiful breasts," Cheryl declares.

"She did," Ms. Angela says.

"Still does," Cassandra corrects her. Suzy is now shaking her arms around her head like she's going to explode or something.

Cheryl laughs hysterically. "Except now the nipples are below the surface no matter what!"

Everyone is laughing so hard, Damian finds refuge behind the bar.

When the laughter dies down, Haley says, "I'll get naked to save the spa, but can we explore other options first?"

My heart swells at my friend's suggestion. Even if she is joking, and I'd never let her do that if she weren't, the fact that it crossed her mind and that she wants to help means the world to me.

"Can anyone talk to Georgie?" Cassandra interjects.

"Good luck with that," Autumn answers. "He's... not the most pleasant person."

Alex wets her lips. "You got that right. We need a different angle." I glance at Alex. *Did she try to talk to my landlord?* The way she's ignoring my gaze, she totally did.

"We'll think of something," Cassandra says. "Right now, let's give Grace some space to relax and think about other things." Murmurs of approval meet her suggestion, and the din of conversation resumes.

What am I going to do? Scenarios build in my mind, each one bleaker than the other.

"Grace! Gracie?" Ms. Angela is touching my arm gently. She's holding a small plate of appetizers Alex brought, and her friends are waiting for her to come back to their table.

"Sorry—you were saying?"

"I was asking about the massage business. How's it going, dear?"

"Oh... uh... Picking up. You know. Slow and steady. Thank you."

"I heard you have a young client?"

Um? "Oh—yes. Tracy."

"She's on the hockey team?"

"That's right. And she was injured. I'm treating her right after practice."

Kiara's eyes widen. "At the Arena?"

"Yep."

Haley eyes widen. "You never said!"

Kiara makes a show of whining and rolling her eyes. "Ohmygod, please don't break Ethan's heart again."

I know she's making a joke, but I don't know where the punch line is. "Pardon?" My tone comes out more curt than I intended. My gaze involuntarily flits to Lynn and Mom, but they're deep into their card game, and too far to hear us now that everyone is cackling again.

"Just kidding. Last time he was here he spent three days drunk. The running joke is it was because you got married."

"*What?*"

She nods enthusiastically. "He was so plastered he had to leave before the end of the ceremony." Plopping an appetizer in her mouth before Ms. Angela returns to her game, she lifts her shoulders, seeming to defy Haley to contradict her.

Haley glares daggers at Kiara but says nothing.

My heart bangs, yet my blood runs cold. "What are you talking about?" Ethan was not at my wedding. He couldn't have been. "Why would he care if I got married? Besides, Ethan was not at my wedding."

Kiara raises her hand. "Not that it matters, but he was. I was there. Me and Colton and Craig carried him out. Well, Craig and Colton carried him, and I drove the car back to the farm."

Ethan was at my *wedding*? And he didn't say *anything* to me? I'm about to say something like, *he certainly didn't get drunk because I was getting married*, when Ms. Angela leans her chair back toward us. Glancing at the card-playing team to make sure Mom and Lynn don't hear, she whispers, "Oh yes! I remember that. Young love! We were hoping he'd save the day and convince our Grace to stay in Emerald Creek and marry one of our own, but no such luck. She got whisked away to Texas!" She takes a loud gulp of her Moscow mule. "Luckily, that didn't last long. You came back," she adds, then straightens her chair to resume her mystery game.

My heart constricts at the circumstances that brought me back home.

I don't talk about it, and I don't want to think about it. As if feeling I need emotional support, Damian jumps on my lap and starts kneading my thighs. I hand my glass to Haley. "That wine is wicked good, Haley. Hit me up with another?"

She stands to pour me another drink, then hands it to me with a small smile. "Here you go, sister."

And her calling me that—sister—just about kills me. Kills me right there. My bottom lip shakes and tears overflow. Damian jumps off my lap while Kiara takes the glass from me before it shakes so hard I stain Cassandra's gorgeous off-white carpet.

"Oh-kay," Cassandra says. "Time for some retail therapy. Grace, honey, you're up!"

Kiara pulls me out of the bean bag. I take a deep breath and look bravely at Haley. "I'm good, I'm good," I assure my friends. "It's your wine," I add for Haley's benefit. "You should call it the Tearjerker. I don't know what happened to me."

"You're just tired, dear," Ms. Angela offers, her sideways glance to her friends telling a different story.

Damian rubs against my legs, but he doesn't follow me into Cass's boutique. That's the domain of her white angora, and he knows it instinctively.

"Get in the changing room and take your clothes off," Cass tells me. Every now and then she'll pull someone out of Game Nights without an explanation, and she'll give them a piece of lingerie of her choosing. Alex, who moved here last winter, told me she had gifted her a beautiful bodice. Now, Alex is having this torrid love story with Chris, so that makes sense. But me? "Cass, you know, I don't really need anything. I mean, I'm super thankful that you want to—"

"Tut-tut-tut." Cass hands me a two-piece swimsuit through the curtain. "Try this on."

I indulge her. The bikini top cups my breasts in the most alluring way, but it has enough coverage that it doesn't look like I'm trying out for the Sports Illustrated swimsuit issue. The bottom is cut high on the thighs, the back barely covering my ass, but I guess—covering it. The swimsuit is in hues of crimson with a sprinkling of gold. There's a gold charm at the back of the bottom that's repeated in the center of the bra.

"Does it fit?"

Not gonna lie, I look great. The best I've felt in a long time. "I think?"

She swipes the curtain open. "Holy mother of god. Turn around. Wowzer." She swipes the curtain closed. "That was easy. It's all yours."

"Cass, I... I want to pay for it. I can afford it." I slip back into my faded jeans and silk blouse and enter the shop, where Cass is wrapping the swimsuit in silk paper. "I appreciate what you're trying to do but—"

"Mmm, darling. You have no idea what I'm doing. All I'm asking you, is to choose wisely who you wear this for. 'Cause it'll do a number on them."

I smile inwardly. Cass has a bit of a reputation as a witch, and she's demonstrating that she feeds that legend. I point to her she-shed where I left my bag. "Lemme get my wallet."

"You don't get it, do you? It's a gift." She turns to a shelf behind her and pulls out a folded piece of fabric that matches the bikini. "I'm adding the matching wrap." She wraps it in a gold silk paper.

I open my mouth to protest.

She stares me down and grabs flip flops that jingle with the same charm and places them on top of the two wrapped items. "We can go all night. I have a whole shop."

My eyes widen. "Thank you."

She places her gifts in a purple bag with a golden owl as a logo. "The best way you can thank me is to be happy. Truly, deeply happy." She hands me the bag.

Baubles won't make me truly happy. Cass is a lovely woman, but she's wrong here. I'll indulge her for now, and then I'll talk her into allowing me to return the gift. Maybe donate it as an auction item for the Silver House.

Or for the spa.

I set her gift next to the door and return to my spot on the bean bag. The older generation is gone, and it's just a few of us left here now. Haley takes my hand. "You gonna be okay?"

I squeeze her hand back. "Yeah. I always am. Not like I have a choice."

She leans against me. "That bad?"

I take a deep breath. "It's just... I wasn't prepared. There's nothing between us, obviously."

"Right," she says. "Maybe—maybe you should talk it out with him. You know? Instead of him being this ghost from the past for you, if you got to know the new Ethan, it could sort of... exorcize it for you. Be done with him for good."

That makes sense. She's totally right. I need to exorcize the past. By making Ethan a part of my present life instead of trying to avoid him, I can put him back where he belongs. With my childhood friends. Nothing more. I probably won't even like him that much.

"Also," Haley continues, "you never had closure. You deserve closure."

And again, she's right. So right. I should have said yes to his offer of having coffee together. Instead of pushing him away at the farm the other day, I should have agreed to that conversation. Adult to adult.

None of this teen angst business. I'm better than that. "Thanks," I tell Haley, believing wholeheartedly that this is what I need to do.

I'll talk to him tomorrow.

CHAPTER TEN

Ethan

It's the last day of preseason camp, and last night, I had a sense of dread. Of loss. Of something good coming to an end that I didn't want to.

Sure, it was the kids. That's what I told myself. They're great kids.

But, really, who am I kidding?

It's Grace.

Of course it's her.

It was always Grace.

I'm about to, probably, never see her again. For real, this time.

I don't think I can ever come back to Emerald Creek.

Fuck me, but the pain is too sharp. Too real. Too present, even after all these years.

It's almost as if it's now condensed.

But before I go, before the curtain, really, really falls, I want to know.

I want her to talk to me. Tell me what happened, in her mind, that she could just drop me like that.

So, throughout the week, I came up with a plan.

Bring her to the crime scene.

Bring her to the lake.

And what better excuse than an end-of-camp barbecue? It's what everyone does. Hell, one of the parents even suggested it—with a tactful hint, on my part. They even ended up organizing it.

Before her massage, I take Tracy aside. "You make sure Grace comes, will ya? She works too hard."

"Gotcha, Coach. On it."

And then I hear them. On the other side of the wall. Grace and Tracy.

"Oh, I don't know. I need to get home to my cat."

Giggles. "Grace, don't tell me you're a cat lady!" She calls her Grace now? No more Ms. Grace.

(Grace, offended.) "I'm not a cat lady."

(Hilarious giggling.) "You so are. Wait 'til I tell coach K."

(Grace, slightly angry.) "Tell him what? That I have better things to do than go to his barbecue?"

This time it's Tracy who's offended. "It's not *his* barbecue, swear to god. It was all our idea! I don't even know if Coach K wants to come. He's so grumpy anyway."

"Oh. For real?"

"Yeah, totes. You're cool and all, but really, we're hoping to get rid of Coach K early so we can have some fun, if you see whaddimean."

"Tracy! No! No-no-no! What—okay, you win. I'll come."

"Are you sure? You don't *have* to."

What is she doing?

"Um, Tracy, after what you told me? Yeah, I kinda have to come."

Oh thank Christ.

A couple of hours later, the lake breeze barely tampers the scorching sun. We're all down to our swimsuits, goofing in the water.

Or most of us are.

Grace is sitting on the beach, still wearing a long summer dress, her arms wrapped around her knees, looking into emptiness. Is she thinking of us? Is her mind's eye taking her back to what happened between us here?

Or is her soul filled with other, more meaningful memories? She's had a whole life. I put mine on hold.

A couple of parents show up with the food and the dad starts the barbecue. I come out of the water to help, and as I set foot on the sand, Grace stands and leaves to chat with the mom, who's walking back to the cars.

Then the parents leave, and it's just the kids, me, and Grace. But she and I might as well be miles apart. She stands a little to the side. I can feel her observing me, but she averts her gaze every time I seek the connection. She's friendly with the kids though, open with them. They like her, and the girls seek her company.

It's just with me that I feel like she built a wall.

Insisting that she come was stupid. What was I hoping for? I just let it go and focus on the kids.

Later, as we're gathered around the fire pit roasting marshmallows, I feel it's time for a little wrap up chat.

"Wanna go around and tell me what your main takeaway for the camp was? Just one per person."

"Trust your teammate in power plays."

"Strengthen the line chemistry."

"Improve my endurance."

"The difference between impulse and instinct."

"Yeah, I didn't get that one," someone interjects.

I pull my marshmallow out of the fire and let it cool. "Impulse leads to mistakes. Instinct is what leads you to avoiding mistakes."

"But how can you tell the difference?"

That's a tough one. "Instinct is like your sixth sense. Like that voice telling you something is off, or your hair straightening on the back of your neck when something's not right. You gotta learn to listen to that. Impulse is action-reaction. We often act on impulse when we're angry, losing our footing. That's when we make mistakes. You'll learn with time. It's important to listen to yourselves and reflect on your actions often. Look back on why you did what you did and grow from that."

The group stays silent.

"Look, guys, you're gonna make mistakes, on the ice, in life. It's how it is. The question is—and you know this already—what do you learn from them?"

"So you don't repeat them," someone volunteers.

My gaze involuntarily slides to Grace, then back to the fire. "And sometimes, so you can fix them."

"What mistakes do you regret?" someone asks.

"Those I could have fixed and I didn't."

"Aww," one of the girls coos, while another asks, "Coach! Why aren't you married yet?"

"Maybe he was, you idiot!" another girl hisses.

"How old are you, five? You don't ask those questions," a third one says.

The girls keep pestering me with questions. The boys are watching the girls.

Grace is listening.

"Grace, is it true Coach K was super popular?"

Grace's deep brown gaze glides over me, her eyes reflecting the light of the embers. She turns her marshmallow, seeming to have to think about it. She twists her mouth. Bends her head this way and that. "You could say that, I suppose. He was really popular with some girls." Then she giggles like she's pulling my leg. Like there's this joke we're all in on. She even looks at me straight in the eye to drive that point home and fake-laughs harder.

Pretending this is so much fun.

I know she's pretending. Because I know how she looks when she's hurting and acting like she's not. I've seen that look on her.

I'll never forget it.

A whole group of us were here, at the lake, on this very beach. It was daytime. Hot and sunny, like today. It was the summer after my first year of college, and I hadn't been around a lot that year. I hadn't seen Grace in months.

She took my breath away. It was her, lovely, adorable Grace, with the confidence of her youth, the life-loving energy that had always been Grace.

But looking at me like a woman looks at a man.

Making me look away, she was so obvious.

That day, the girl I was dating noticed. What was her name again? Anna? Annie? Something like that. Anyway, she started teasing Grace. Not in a fun way. I could tell by Grace's reaction. Grace was always someone who could take a joke about herself. No, this girl was making fun of Grace in a mean-girl type of way. We were all on a large, flat stone jutting high over the lake, the water deep below us, and the girl just wouldn't stop picking on Grace.

"Leave her alone," I finally said, not adding, *she's just a kid,* because that would have been flat-out ridiculous. But really—how could she think it was okay to make fun of her that way?

Not-Annie said something else, and it made me angry. So angry. Why did I care? I'd probably say the same sort of stuff to my brothers or Haley.

But I saw Grace's shiny eyes on me—not on the girl—her gaze going from my face to my arm still wrapped around my sort-of girlfriend laughing wholeheartedly, and her lower lip trembling, and the way she bit on it to make it stop.

"It's not nice," I told the girl, and then I *did* add, but I thought it was to shut her up, and shame her a little, "she's just a kid."

What undid me, was the look in Grace's eyes as her gaze went back to me and the utter despair as she looked at the two of us.

And then the girl shouted something else, and Grace jumped into the water. She didn't dive. She jumped in and let herself sink like a stone and didn't resurface.

I jumped after her.

Opened my eyes under water—it hurt like hell—and didn't see her. Resurfaced, took a breath, and saw her there, looking at me, lip steady. Then she disappeared below the surface again, swimming away from the shore, and this time I followed her, promising myself I wouldn't lose her.

She dipped under water again, and I dipped with her. Her moving limbs touched mine at times and it was electric. I opened my eyes again, her hair flowed around her, her lush lips moved as if she was talking to me.

And she smiled.

The most beautiful smile a man has ever seen.

Then she swam up, and I followed her to the surface.

"What are you doing?" I asked, relieved she was okay.

"Shutting down the noise."

Then Not-Annie shrieked, and Grace plunged again, and I followed her.

That day I broke up with Not-Annie.

The following year, Grace kissed me in the projection room of the church basement, at youth nights, and as I pulled her softly away from me, my world began to change.

It wasn't so much the taste of her lips on mine, or the feel of her body fleetingly pressed against me, that affected me so deeply. No, it was the way she gave herself to me—wholeheartedly; the way she trusted me with her feelings; the fact that *she chose me*, that deeply moved me in a way that would prove life-altering.

I didn't kiss her back.

I had to push her gently away, explain I was too old for her, watch the pain on her features as she bit her trembling lip. I did everything I could not to hurt her too much.

Over the following months, knowing her feelings for me, I let myself fall more and more for her. The distance I kept between us didn't affect the depth of my feelings for her. It only strengthened them as I saw her mature.

Two years later, I was lost to her.

A couple of hours later, it's just Grace, me, and Tracy waiting on her ride home. "I can take you home," Grace offers.

"No, my cousin'll kill me."

"Can you call her?"

"She's not picking up. I'm so sorry I'm keeping you. She's such a pain."

"It's alright," I say. Then, because I feel I have to, I tell Grace, "You can go home if you need to."

Tracy snickers. "Take care of your kitty." Then she leans on Grace, giggling affectionately. "Ohmygod, I didn't mean it that way, swear I didn't!"

Grace laughs. "It's alright. I *am* a cat lady. Who cares?"

I turn my head to Grace, and catch her gaze on me. In the shining bright department, the stars have nothing on her eyes.

"Seriously, I don't mind," I tell Grace. And then, because I can't help myself, I add, "It's so beautiful here. Brings back a lot of memories." She whips her head around, but not before I see the color on her cheeks.

"I—you shouldn't stay alone with Tracy. It's..."

Tracy sighs. "It's cool."

"It's just not good protocol," Grace says.

"She's right," I concede.

"Ugh. I hate my cousin," Tracy says for the umpteenth time just as an engine roars down the dirt road. She jumps to her feet. "That'll be me! Bye guys!" I follow her, to make sure it is her cousin and she's all good.

A woman comes out the car and ambles my way. "Ethan! Ohmygod! Ethan!"

Oh fuck. *Please*. "Annie?"

CHAPTER ELEVEN

Grace

I gather my things and follow Tracy and Ethan from afar, planning on dashing to my car to avoid any awkward goodbyes.
The plan of having coffee with Ethan went out the door real
fast tonight. Because the truth is, there's no way talking things
through with Ethan will help put *anything* behind me.

The only way forward for me is to leave him where he belongs:
in the past. Not to pretend he wasn't anything to me, or that we
could be friends.

Lying to myself is never a good idea.

A car door slams, and then another.

And then voices, carried through the still summer night.

"Ethan! Ohmygod, Ethan!" This comes from a sultry female
voice.

"Annie?" Ethan's deep voice answers.

"It's me, Amy!" Laughter this time, light and playful, coming
from her.

Amy Keller. My blood runs cold. Amy Keller was Ethan's girl-friend at some point, and to say that I hated her at the time is an understatement. My physical reaction to her now underlines truth number one that I'm finally accepting. Ethan meant something to me, and that part of my past still affects me.

All the more reason to stay away from it.

"Hey!" Ethan's deep voice echoes. Silence, then lower, "It's good to see you."

I stop in my tracks. I can't walk in on them. I hold my breath.

"Same here, big boy." Under the merciless moonlight, I see her shapely arms wrap around Ethan in a full-body hug. He lets go of her, but she keeps one hand on his shoulder, the other on his chest, her head tilted back to take him all in.

My heart is thumping so hard, I can't hear myself think. They talk but I don't know what they're saying. Her melodious voice mixes with his raspy bass. I don't *want* to know what they're saying.

Oh god, please get me out of here.

I take a deep breath and announce my presence by stomping to the parking area, pretending I'm seeing them just now.

"Good night," I say as I pass them.

"Grace, hold on a sec!" Ethan says.

I have no choice but to stop and look at him. At *them.* "Hey, Amy."

He steps back, away from her, and she looks between us, mouth slightly agape.

"Of course you're together now. How cute."

"Oh no, we're not together," I say as it's the most outlandish idea ever. Why would she think that?

"Really?" she frowns, but still backs away from Ethan, plunging her hands in the pockets of her tight jeans. "Well, I'm back for good now.

Can you believe it? We should catch up." Her eyes are on Ethan the whole time.

Amy Keller and Ethan King catching up is not something I need to witness. Even if I know there's nothing between them, and probably was very little anyway back in the day, jealousy is rearing its ugly head and I need to smack it away right now. "'Night," I say with a small wave.

"Grace, hold up. I need to give you something." Ethan's commanding voice stops me, and I can't help but look, look at their bodies so close, at the way she claims him with her eyes, with a hand back on his arm.

Ethan steps away from her, his gaze drilling into me.

Amy squeezes Ethan's arm. "I'll be at the Growler tonight."

He looks down at her hand on his arm like he can't wait to flick it away. "Okay."

"See you there?"

"Probably not."

Even if his last words warm me, my whole being reels. Why can't I be more like her? Grabbing what I want? Going for it? Enjoying the little time we have together without a care for the future? I bet you *I* could be in his arms, right now, if I wanted.

I used to be that girl.

She glances at the passenger door, where Tracy is oblivious to her, headphones on, the silver glare of her screen lighting her face. "I hope you change your mind," she purrs. Her gaze travels around the parking space, glides over me, and stops on his motorcycle. "Ohmygod, is this yours?" She steps away from him, sashays to his bike, caresses the saddle, then whips around and strikes a suggestive pose. "Give me a ride?"

He glances toward the car where Tracy is waiting. "Not today."

She crosses her arms and walks to her car. Then turns around and says, "Growler, tonight. Yeah?"

"Doubt it."

She winks at him. "Can't wait."

Then she's gone and I can't help myself. "That should be fun." I hate the snarkiness in my tone. The pinch in my underbelly.

"What?"

"A night on the town with Amy Keller."

He huffs. "Right."

"Seriously, why not?"

"Not my idea of fun."

"She seems to still have feelings for you."

Disbelief paints his features. "Not my idea of feelings either." He lowers his gaze on me, a question in his eyes. Then it comes. He says it. "I really need to talk to you. About what happened back then. Between us. I need to understand."

Those few years come back to me in a whirlwind. The way he let me take his mouth the first time I kissed him in the church basement at youth night. How he didn't push me back right away, rather let me taste him. How his hands fell on my hips naturally. How his heartbeat was so strong I could feel it, and that's how I knew he loved me, even when he said, "I'm too old for you, Grace," and he gently broke the kiss. The way he said it, the way he acted, I knew—I thought I knew—he was just asking me for more time.

And two years later, there we were. He took control of our second first kiss, opened me to new sensations, sensations I had no idea could be so much better than in my fantasies. The way he later caressed my breasts, and teased the tips, and lowered his mouth to them, and trailed wet kisses down my navel, and unbuttoned my jeans, and the way his fingers felt oh so much better than mine and how was that even possible? I thought I knew how to pleasure myself, but my god—Ethan? Ethan created wants I didn't know I had, and he assuaged them and then created others and teased me endlessly until I begged and he growled and he let me come on his fingers, on his mouth, against his crotch.

Beyond and way deeper than that, he was my hero in so many ways. Standing up for my brother when he was being bullied. Helping his father on the farm from dusk to dawn. Volunteering for every cause Emerald Creek stood up for. And still making me feel like I was the most important thing in his life. Telling me as much.

"It's so long ago, I don't even remember any of it," I say.

"Really."

I scoff. "Ethan. We were kids, just fooling around. I mean—yeah, really."

He stays silent for a beat. "That's all it was to you?"

What am I supposed to say or do now? Getting closure means revisiting painful events I haven't thought about in years. It means reopening old wounds.

Why would I do that?

It was ten years ago. *Ten years!*

I need to live in the present so I can build my future. I need to be grounded.

Accept the past, enjoy the present, and embrace the future. That's all there is to it.

I won't get closure by revisiting the past. I'll get closure by walking away and never looking back, and that's what I've been doing. Been doing it with things more painful than my first heartbreak, and it works perfectly fine.

And if I need to lie to Ethan to protect myself, then I'll lie.

It's best for him too.

"Of course it's all it was. You know it."

"Right," he mumbles and turns away. His shoulders are hunched, and his stride powerful. I want to run after him. Tell him I'm full of shit. Tell him I still love him and it's killing me.

But that's the whole thing, right? I'm still in love with a shadow from the past—*that's* what's killing me.

So I'm doing the right thing by walking away. I'm looking out for myself. Which is what I need to do.

My vision blurred, I watch Ethan straddle his bike and disappear in a cloud of dirt, his red light dimming behind the branches, until there's nothing left of him.

Then I get in my car, wait for my heartbeat to slow down, wipe my tears, and drive home to Damian.

He's locked himself in the closet again, and this time I nearly lose it trying to pry the damn door open. But instead of giving into the temptation of a self-pity party—because, really, nothing is going right—I do the one, easy thing I can do to fix one thing in my life. I call Lucas and Thalia to have them send someone asap. I tell them where I hide the spare key, knowing I can trust them.

When my phone dings with messages from the girls, I don't even have the strength to check what they want. I put my phone on silent.

I can barely stand myself right now. I'd be a shit friend.

CHAPTER TWELVE

Ethan

I gun my bike, leaving Grace in my rearview mirror, a dark shape that's not even looking at me.

I don't mean anything to her. Nothing at all. I need to let it go, clear my brain, cleanse my heart.

What was I thinking, again? Oh yeah, that just bringing her to the lake would trigger something. Make her tell me why she dumped me there, yelling things that made no sense. That worked out well. Did I think she was going to apologize?

We were barely older than the kids on the Varsity team I trained this week.

It's not like no one told me that she was too young. Too young for me. Too young for love.

And I was too young too.

We were both unable to deal with the force of feelings we didn't understand. Feelings of trust, and friendship, that grew over the years, then, with hormones kicking in, morphed into something so powerful, we couldn't manage—or even understand—what was happening to us.

And so we failed. We crashed. I fled the scene, instead of trying to understand, mend, correct whatever had possessed her and build upon it.

I dip down Dewey's Hollow, then up Woodbury Knoll, where we'd... ah fuck, I can't do that.

There are too many memories, everywhere.

Even at the farm.

There's one place though that wasn't there back then.

My brother Justin's pub.

And that's where my wheels take me. To the Lazy Salamander, aka Lazy's, now the heart of Emerald Creek, with its cozy booths, slick bar, tall ceilings, comfort food, and a shitload of local beers on draft.

I sit my ass on a stool and watch with envy as Justin pours beers, chats up customers, checks his phone, and smiles like only someone in love can smile.

He has his shit together. He built something out of nothing. He created a hub for our hometown, something we needed desperately. In the time that I was gone, he and his best friend, Chris, became pillars of Emerald Creek.

Me? I have nothing to show for my ten years of hiding. Nothing that means anything here.

"You still around, man?" I turn to the deep voice and greet Colton. "Beer's on me," he tells Justin as he slides on a stool next to me.

"First was on the house," Justin answers. "What can I get you?"

"Switchback. Please." Then Colton turns to me. "What you been up to?"

I smile. "Believe it or not, I coached the Varsity preseason camp."

"No way. Good for you." He stays quiet for a couple of beats, watching Justin draft his beer. Doesn't bring up his young employee, Tracy. Or his sister. "D'you like it?" he finally asks.

I push my empty pint glass toward Justin so he gets me a refill. "Kids were great." *Your sister, not so much.* But I can't tell him that.

"How's Grace doing?" Justin asks Colton. "Haven't seen her here in a while."

Colton shakes his head. "No idea."

"Wasn't she giving massages to some kid at camp?" Justin's not gonna let go, is he?

Colton and he exchange a look. Colton gives him an *I dunno* shrug.

"Yup," I drop. "To Tracy. Got injured."

"I had no idea," Colton says, seeming genuinely surprised. "Grace tell you?" he asks Justin.

Justin gives me a pointed look. "Nope. Millie." His smirk drips to his whole body, and he leans back, crosses his arms, clearly enjoying the power he thinks he has over me. "Heard you got Grace a special order every day. Delivered too. How'd that work out for you?"

I look away and finish my beer. Slam it on the counter. "Another."

Justin glances outside. "Not if you're riding your bike tonight."

Colton wiggles his fingers at me. "Keys." Then, to Justin, "This one's on me."

I feel like getting into a good bar fight, the kind that'll send teeth flying and bodies slamming into solid furniture.

The kind that will knock the lights out of me for long enough that when I come to, I won't even remember why the hell I wanted that.

"Come on, man."

"What the hell, I'm too old for this shit." I hand him the keys, and we get lost in silence as more and more people fill the bar and some sort of karaoke starts.

"Too old, huh?" Colton says, picking up like we were just talking minutes ago. I'm on beer three or four. Colton switched to soft drinks a while back. I might move onto bourbon if the anger in my gut doesn't fucking go away.

My answer is slurred. "You happy with your life?"

"For the most part. My own boss. Decent money."

"What about the rest?"

He shrugs. "Get lucky when I need to."

I grunt—I can see the appeal. "I'll drink to that."

Colton stands, gets behind the bar, and fills two tall glasses with water. Pushes one in front of me and downs the other, standing. Taking his place back on the stool, he says, "You know, women, they want you to want them."

I eye him sideways.

"And they're not much into drunks." He downs his glass of water. "Come on, let's get you home." He stands, and I follow him.

"I'm not a drunk," I say as I slump into his passenger seat.

He pulls out. "You won't be. Not under my watch. Or under Justin's. Or under anyone else's who gives a shit."

We ride in silence, his headlights illuminating the trees bordering the dark road that leads to King Knoll's Farm.

"Coffees was a good start," he says.

I clench my jaw. He's just trying to help. But help what? What am I trying to accomplish here?

"It's only a start, though. Won't get you very far," he continues.

"We *are* talking about your sister, right?"

"Yeah," he says softly, turning onto the long driveway to the farm.

"That don't bother you?"

He turns his head briefly to me. "I love her. I want her to be happy. Lemme be straight with you. I think you're the only one who can give her that."

The *only* one? "Give her what?"

"The love she needs. You've always been it for her."

That's bullshit. That girl is gone. Look, he's her brother. What does he know? Take me—I know nothing about Haley. Colton's just trying to be nice. He was always a nice kid. I'm surprised he's into relationship advice. I wouldn't have pegged him for one of those. I need to let him down easy. "Naah. It was never that way."

"You know, this is getting a little old." He slows to a stop in front of the farm. "This driving you home drunk because you don't have the guts to do what you need to do with my sister."

I turn my head slowly and stare at him. "You guys let her marry some guy nobody heard about and was barely old enough to shave, and I wasn't good enough for her? You're *fucking* kidding me, right?"

In my drunken anger I do see the puzzlement and some degree of pain on his face. So I add, "Pardon my French."

"You were gone four years when she got married, man. You expect to roll into town and she'll be in your bed? I'll say it again. It's gonna take a little more work."

I stay in my seat, looking into nothingness. "Besides... I'm leaving soon. Be far away."

He looks at me with disappointment mixed with anger. "Then you better stay the fuck away from her while you're here.

"She's been through enough shit in her life. She's in a good place now. Don't mess it up." He looks out the window, and even in my drunkenness I can tell he's not done talking. "Look, man. I love you. Love you like a brother. Never forget what you did for me. But Grace?

She needs a break, and she's found it here. She's in a good place now. Don't fuck it up. If you can't give her what she needs, stay away."

Half of the stuff he says, I have no idea what he's talking about. The other half, I get him loud and clear.

Saturday, I wake up with a splitting headache and go for a long run in the hills. I come back to a message for me on the kitchen counter. Mom and Dad are out and about, and I am to call Thalia and Lucas back for a small favor they need. Their number is scribbled on the note.

"Thanks for the call back," Lucas says. "We have a small job, was hoping you could jump in for us and do it first thing today, if you're available. It's for someone who knows someone in town—you know how it goes. Anyhoo, they have a door that keeps getting stuck. A closet door in the bedroom. It's an old house, and the woman wants someone who knows what they're doing. Won't break anything, respects antiques, yadda yadda. You get the picture. I'd go, but I have this big job starting and—"

"I gotcha, man. Lemme shower and I'm on my way."

"Come and grab my truck, so you can use my tools."

"Cool. What's the address?"

CHAPTER THIRTEEN

Grace

Saturday morning, I go straight to the spa without stopping at Easy Monday. I'm taking no chances. I don't want to risk seeing Ethan. Or *Amy*. Or anyone.

The lights are on when I enter, door unlocked, classical guitar playing softly through hidden speakers, the soothing scent of beeswax candles and essential oils instantly calming my nerves.

Claudia is nervously arranging magazines on the small tables in the big room. "Grace. What are we going to *do*?"

"We'll figure something out. Coffee?"

"But—they're coming in thirty minutes! What are we going to do about the clients?"

I stop at the coffee machine. "Who? What are you talking about?"

She puts her fists on her hips. "You didn't listen to your messages."

My messages. My phone? No. No, I did not. I stupidly pull out my phone out and see I have twelve voicemails and fifteen unread text messages.

Weirdly, nothing from Mom.

Skimming through the text messages, I can tell they all have to do with the sale of the building.

A cold anger fills me. "Who's coming in thirty minutes?"

Claudia twists her hands. "A realtor. With a client."

A realtor has the nerve to come visit my spa on a *Saturday*? Without *asking me* politely first? "When's our first client?" I already know the answer, but since I already missed what amounts to the Apocalypse, checking with Claudia seems wise.

"At ten."

That gives us two hours.

I group text my friends.

Me

> ur needed ASAP. Bring ideas.

My phone rings immediately. *Alex*. "Finally," she says when I pick up. "I have bad news and more bad news. Which one do you want first?"

"Very funny. Are you in your car?"

"Yes. You said to come over and bring ammo, so I'm stopping at Easy Monday's."

Thank god. "You'll tell me the news here." I hang up and turn to Claudia.

"You know what's really weird? That no one was worried last night when I wasn't picking up."

Claudia reddens. "They um—we..." she clears her throat. "Word got around that maybe you and Ethan had gotten into a disagreement. And so the... the general consensus was to leave you be. For now. But then the realtor left a message on this phone," she says, pointing to her desk, "and we..."

"I could have been injured in my home! No one was worried?"

Claudia's redness is now bordering on crimson. "Your—your mom went by your place, and she assessed that you-you-you just needed a little time."

Great.

Did she actually look through the window?

Well, at least they were worried.

None of this dying alone at home business for me. Yet.

I pull out the lease agreement again, then put it back into the filing cabinet. There's no time for me to read over it at this point. I look around, at a loss as to what to do right now.

The front door chimes and Kiara comes in, carrying four huge pink boxes. She passes them to Claudia, dashes to her car and comes back with... what is she doing with my mug? How did she even get it?

"Maple Kiss for you, and double chocolate mousse brownies, chocolate eclairs, and chocolate tartlets, apple cinnamon donuts, and chocolate donuts for the Bitch Brigade."

The Bitch Brigade?

Claudia opens the pastry boxes next to the coffee station and sets a stack of flowery napkins next to the pastries. "That's a lot of chocolate," she says as she sets more napkins on the side tables.

"How did you get my mug?" I ask Kiara.

She fusses with her signature pink boxes, arranging them on the console, moving mugs around to make more space. "Dark chocolate is required in times of crisis. Helps with heart rate and mood and even cognitive—"

"How did you get my mug?" I repeat louder.

"Well they better not stain the armchairs," Claudia mumbles, setting more cocktail napkins throughout the spa.

"How did you get—"

"Colton," she says as if that's an answer. Then she hugs me and looks me in the eye. "Good to know it's still your mug and also that you're not throwing it in my face."

"Why would I do that?"

She lifts her shoulders. "Eh... the jury was out. After last night."

Can I please get a break? "I don't want to hear about Ethan and Amy at the Growler," I snap.

Claudia, out of napkins, grabs a dusting cloth and runs it haphazardly on perfectly clean surfaces.

Kiara frowns. "The fuck are you talking about?"

Oh.

"Your brother drove a weeping Ethan back home last night," Kiara continues. "From Lazy's. Where he was very much alone and totally getting on everyone's nerves."

"*Weeping*?"

"The dude version of weeping. Drunk and talking in circles about you."

I roll my eyes. "Oh please."

Kiara shrugs. "Who cares anyway?"

Claudia stops her dusting. "I'm with Kiara. We have bigger problems to solve than... men. And that's saying something."

"Agreed," I say. And still, holding the mug with Ethan's handwriting on it makes me... all fuzzy and warm. Close second to the knowledge that he spent the evening *and the night* alone.

"Girl, we're going to need you to focus," Kiara says, snapping me out of my dreamy state. "We do not want to lose the spa."

"You're going to have to tell us what to do," Claudia agrees, and checks her watch. "Fifteen minutes. Oops, here they come!"

I glance outside, expecting to see the realtor with one or two people. Instead, I see a line of cars pulling alongside the curb, my girlfriends coming out with cousins, sisters, mothers, daughters. Others are arriving by foot.

A loving mob is marching down on A Touch Of Grace, Alex leading them.

While Claudia holds the door open for them, Alex takes three steps up the staircase, then calls everyone to attention. Claudia closes the door and keeps an eye out for the realtor.

"Listen up!" Alex says. "We don't have time to brainstorm, so here's what we're going to do right now. You're to pretend this is an open house, you're serious buyers, but you've already either noticed or heard from reliable sources that this house has problems. Think leaking roof, black mold, ancient plumbing." She turns to me. "Any real problems we should throw in there?"

I point to my chest. "The tenant doesn't pay her rent on time." Total lie, like the rest.

Alex makes a sad face. "The bad news is, from my intel, the people visiting in... a few minutes, are looking for a place for them to move into. As a *home*."

Shit. That means they can break the lease. "There are rotten planks on the deck that broke three weeks ago?" That might not deter a buyer. "Makes the case for deferred maintenance," I venture.

"Good point, let's lean on that," Alex says, then claps her hands. "Alright everyone! Now please spread out and play the part. Remember that you do not know one another, and you do not know Grace. The buyers are flatlanders." She steps down to my level and adds for me, "We'll deal with the realtor later."

"I could sue you for this," he tells me once his buyers and my friends are gone. His face is red and sweaty.

"Me? Why?"

"You-you-you organized all this."

"All *what*? This is a small town. Word got around that you were showing the house this morning. They were kind enough to come before the spa was open—I even provided little cakes and stuff!"

He wags his finger at me. "I'll pay for a house inspection myself. This house will sell in no time once my buyers see the report. Start packing your lotions."

"Maybe if *you* tell the seller to repair the deck it'll get done? Be a shame if someone got hurt through their negligence."

He slams the door on his way out, looking furiously at all my friends who took refuge in their cars but didn't leave. He's barely around the corner when they all come back in.

Cassandra leads the charge. "We need a plan. Any ideas?"

Autumn takes a mini chocolate éclair from the box Kiara is passing around. "A fundraiser?"

Several women voice their approval.

"For what?" Kiara asks, handing me a double mousse chocolate brownie.

"To help Grace buy the building."

Oh *wow*. They would help me *buy* the building? That is not happening, but I'll take all the love and support from where that intention is coming from. "Guys, that's super generous, but no. I can't accept charity for my spa. All I need is help finding another location. Does anyone have leads?"

"The old schoolhouse up Hunger Hill?"

"Too small."

"The Chandler's barn next to Dewey's Brook? Heard someone was interested in buying it to move it to LA."

"No water or electric."

"There's some rental space on Allen Block, upstairs."

My heart sinks. An upstairs location on a busy street is not what I was hoping for, but if all else fails…

"We could always do pop-up spas at one another's homes for a while," Haley says. "I could see if Mom can offer up the farm for an afternoon to kick it off."

"I could coordinate," Claudia says.

"That could actually be fun," Autumn says. "I'd donate props and my time to decorate the space."

That's lovely and creative and thoughtful, but my friends don't realize how much equipment is actually involved in running a high-end spa like mine. Just the pedicure stations and the state of the art, all-in-one facial station I use can't be moved from place to place like I did with my portable massage table for the fair. Needing time to think on their ideas as well as absorb the love coming my way, I plop the whole brownie in my mouth.

Chloe, Justin's new girlfriend, steps up. "How about a subscription? You ask people to buy a monthly facial or mani-pedi or massage subscription, you give them a discount for committing for a year, and a deeper discount if they pay a year in advance."

Smart. "That would give me some cash," I say, my mouth still full.

Cassandra seems to think on that. "Nothing like what you'd need to buy the place outright, but…"

"Maybe enough to get a local bank to talk to you?" Haley offers.

Cassandra narrows her eyes on me. "You know, if you want to go for it, I'll contact my mailing list. You might get a lot of new clients too. I don't know why we haven't thought of that before!"

Cassandra's clientele is high end. They're from New York, Boston, and Montreal, and they come to Emerald Creek to have a private retreat... and do some quality shopping at places like Cassie's lingerie boutique. I squeeze her hand. "That would be fantastic."

Cassandra takes the stack of brochures Claudia is already handing her. "I'll hold onto these until you have your subscription figured out," she tells me.

"I'll start working on that," Claudia says.

"I'll help you," Alex tells her. Turning to me, she adds, "You should reach out to your clients and tell them what's going on. Reassure them that no matter what, A Touch Of Grace will always be available to them in Emerald Creek. You don't want false rumors to spread, and you never know—someone might come up with another idea."

They leave one by one, hugging me tight and reassuring me that all will be okay.

And it will.

I know it will.

Because with friends like them, how could it not?

The morning starts busier than usual. We have walk-ins of people eager to support the spa with a side of gossip, and I'll take it all. Luckily, all my staff is on deck. No last-minute childcare issue, breakup drama, uncooperating cars. Cheyenne is early, and she takes a walk-in for a simple manicure before her normal start time. Hope and Shanice brought chocolate maple candies to give to their guests after their facials. And Fabrizio, our hair and makeup artist, hugs me then declares, "After I get all these bitches ready for their wedding, you're mine. Clear your evening." Which doesn't mean what you might think—simply that he's decided I need the indulgence of the best hairdresser in the state (his claim to fame).

We have so much demand on Saturday, that I tell Claudia to open my scheduling for Sunday. A Touch Of Grace is open every day, but I let my staff decide if and which Sundays they want to work. As for me, I usually reserve my Sundays for my family, but right now? I can use all the business and all the distraction from the rest of my life.

Taking the last sip of coffee from the mug Ethan gave me, I take comfort in the knowledge that I'll always have Emerald Creek.

Even if I'll never have *him*.

When my phone rings and it's Lucas telling me the guy he sent to fix my closet door thinks Damian is sick and should see the vet, I see that as a sign that my small town and the universe will always have my back.

Then I rush home.

Chapter Fourteen

Ethan

L   ess than an hour later, I pull up to a cute little cape house, clean
     white siding, dark shutters, flowers in a hanging basket off the
front steps. The key is under the fake rock right where Lucas said it
would be.

The beauty of living in a small town, but also—seriously?

Whatever. I'm happy to have something to keep me busy.

The door opens without a creak. A cat jumps in front of me out of
nowhere, then jumps on the back of a light gray couch, watching me.

The small living room faces French doors that open on a deck overlooking a small and colorful garden, pastures and forests extending
beyond the rustic picket fence. I could see myself living in a place
like this, someday. When I settle down. There's something about the
coziness and peacefulness. It's unpretentious yet homey.

The cat hisses at me. "Easy there, tiger." Crouching at his level, I
extend my hand. He sniffs me hesitantly, then slits his eyes at me. I
decide against trying to pet him.

Besides, I have a door to fix. As I turn to go down the hallway and find the bedroom, my eye catches on a series of photos set on the mantle.

I know these people.

And it makes sense. Small town.

But no. It's more than that. There's a photo of Colton. A photo of Shannon and Dennis.

And a collage of photos of a pudgy baby, a toddler with huge brown eyes, a little girl with a thick mane of black curls sitting on the lap of a woman with the same hair, the same smile, the same eyes.

My heart pounds loudly. I whip around. This isn't Colton's house. Colton wouldn't have a pale gray couch, a white carpet... The Harpers? I know their house, and unless they've moved... I open the hallway closet. A woman's shoes and coats neatly lined. A faint perfume I've become addicted to.

Grace.

I'm in Grace's house.

I turn around and take in the rest of the space.

Small. Tidy. Apart from the pictures, totally impersonal.

It might as well be staged for an open house.

No books strewn haphazardly. No stack of mail. No glass in the sink. No cereal bowl left to dry. No shoes in the entrance. No wilted flowers. Not even a trace of chip crumbs on the sofa or on the floor.

What happened to you, Grace?

Colton's words to me echo. *"Maybe it's best you stay away from her while you're here."'*

Be best for me, too, to stay away from her.

I just need to get the job done and get out of here.

Kicking my shoes off, I trudge to the bedroom and pause at the entrance. This is where she sleeps. Under a bedspread that has a girly color—taupe? mauve? I never knew what these were. But suddenly it feels important.

My phone dings with a text. It's Lucas, checking if I found the place.

I shoot him a quick answer, shake my weird thoughts away, and wiggle the stuck closet door. After some careful give and take, it opens wide enough for me to step into the large walk-in closet and take a look at it from the inside.

Grace's scent assails me, creating a weird feeling that takes a hold of me somewhere deep in my gut, and I have to fight the urge to bury my face in her clothes.

What the fuck is wrong with me?

Under the watchful gaze of the cat, who's now on the bed, I unhinge the door. It'll need some sanding first. I carry the door outside, careful not to let the cat out, and using the basic tools I find in Lucas's truck, I sand it where it's been scraping against the frame. Once I'm back inside, I'll adjust the hinges to keep it from tilting.

Walking back into the house, I force myself not to look at the photos on the mantle. I want to do this job and get out of here asap. Truth is, I'm enjoying the job itself. It keeps me busy, and out of my head, which is not a fun place to be right now.

As I reach the bedroom, I stop in my tracks. There's a large box on the floor, the lid to the side with the cat sitting on it, watching me. Daring me, it seems.

"What the hell, fella? You wanna get me in trouble?"

"Meow."

I set the door against the wall. "I don't have time for this shit." I crouch to pick up the mess so I can do my job without stepping on it.

Is this garbage? There's a disposable coffee cup sticking out of the box. Why would Grace—or anyone—keep a disposable coffee cup when she's clearly a neat freak?

Resisting the urge to look through the box—could she be a closet hoarder? Is there such a thing as a closet hoarder?—I shove it back inside but my hand freezes. The cup has a name on it.

Grace.

In my handwriting.

What the fuck? Is that the cup I brought her on the first day of preseason camp? This time I take a good look at the contents of the box, my heart hammering in my chest.

A jersey takes up most of the space. I know this jersey. Still, I unfold it.

King.

How old is this thing?

Setting the jersey aside, I continue my exploration, blood roaring in my ears. There's a stack of letters in colorful envelopes, tied together with a twine. Are these love letters? Not from me. I never wrote Grace.

What the heck, I'm checking.

It's fucking Christmas cards... from Mom. In their envelopes. I open one, and it's folded to the paragraph where she gives news about me. I open another, and another, and it's the same. Each year, Mom sends a Christmas letter with news from all of us. We joke that she obviously tries to give each child the same space on the page, and so if one of us had nothing particular going on that year, it had a lot of filler.

Grace has each one unfolded and refolded so that when you open it, the first thing you see is the paragraph about me. With unsteady fingers, I stack the letters back together and don't bother reattaching the twine. I'm not letting this go.

She and I are going to have a little conversation. She'll know I went through that box.

Oh yeah, she'll know.

Setting the letters aside, I dig deeper into the box.

A puck.

And another puck.

A plastic sleeve with newspaper cutouts. Seeing the first one, I know what each will be about: me. Me and Hockey.

At the bottom, there's another small Ziplock bag with a tiny loop of twine. That brings up no memory at all.

Little figurines of wood roll around. I pick one up. It's a coarse doll carved in maple. There are others, some showing better craftsmanship than others. Did I carve these?

Maybe. Since they're in this box, I'll go for yes. I must have been... what? Twelve?

Jesus.

To the side, there's a piece of bark that feels fairly recent. The wood isn't decaying or turning to sand the way bark does after a few years. I pick it up and turn it around, revealing the carving I very distinctly remember.

A Heart Pranck Reign

My vision blurs as I trace the letters with my finger—the anagram of our names, carved into a majestic oak tree where I'd built a treehouse for us. We'd worked hours on finding an anagram that would mean something without giving our relationship away. No G + E for us. Not only did we want secrecy, we deserved more than what everyone else was doing.

We meant so much more than that.

We wanted to seal our relationship, and how better than by putting our imprint in the woods that sheltered our love?

That was when we'd decided we were it for each other.

Why did she carve out the tree trunk? I turn it in my hands and notice some burn marks. I put it back in the box.

The cat meows and jumps from the lid of the box to the bed and starts licking its paws.

I stand up and sift through the rest of her shelves. Just in case she keeps a box for any and all boyfriends? You can never be too sure.

I find nothing and feel ashamed I even considered that Grace might be... a psychopath?

She's not.

She's a liar. Not the bad kind, though.

Except when it comes to me.

Absentmindedly, I hook the door back up, fiddle with the hinges. Screw them the way they should be to stop the door from tilting. Satisfied with my work, I pick up the box and call Lucas.

"All good?" he asks.

"Yeah, all set. Wasn't much." I tell him what I did. "But uh... there's a problem with the cat."

"What cat?"

"The owner has a cat and uh... it's been puking and shitting everywhere. I mean, it's not a pretty sight. Thought you'd want to let the owner know. I don't know much about cats, but they might want to take it to the vet ASAP."

"Oh shit. Sorry you had to deal with that."

"That's alright. Just... thought they shouldn't wait."

"Definitely. I'll let her know right away."

"Great."

"I'm on another job, so whenever, no rush, just leave the truck at my house, keys under the seat."

"Gotcha."

I hang up and take the box and set myself on the gray couch, looking outside the cute little garden. The view extends far away, up a distant hill, and a thought strikes me. Pulling the map app up on my phone, I'm pretty sure I'm right. Just for the heck of it—not that it matters at this point—I'll check on that later. As I pocket my phone, the cat jumps onto my lap and purrs.

I give it a scratch between the ears.

"How long you think she's gonna be?" I ask as it starts kneading its paws on my thigh.

Maybe thirty seconds into that, the cat stretches, and then I hear the engine, and the door, and her voice.

"Damian? Oh my god Damian, baby, are you okay?"

Damian jumps off the couch and greets Grace with perfectly healthy and happy purrs.

That's my cue to stand and turn around, the box in my hands.

CHAPTER FIFTEEN

Grace

My mouth goes dry. "What are you doing here?" I pick up Damian. "Are you okay, baby?"

"He's fine," Ethan says, "but we need to talk." He drops my box on the kitchen counter. "Care to explain yourself?"

My heart beats hard, and I squeeze Damian for comfort. Protection. But the fiend jumps off me and runs away.

"How did you get in here, and how dare you snoop through my things?"

Ethan lifts his hands as if to plead innocent. He looks like nothing innocent right now. Tall and menacingly handsome, his eyes raking over my body like he could consume me right here and now, his breathing heavy with... desire?

Ohmygod, here I go again. Making stuff up. "Answer me," I snap.

"I came to do a job. Fix your closet door."

"I didn't ask you to!" I shriek.

He shakes his head and lowers his hands. "I know you didn't. Lucas did."

"Lucas?" I did see Lucas's truck outside. And it was Lucas who called me at the spa to tell me his "worker" had called about Damian.

"Look, the point is, I didn't snoop through your things. Your cat threw the box almost literally at my feet. I was picking it up and... well..."

He's at a loss for words and so am I. This is so embarrassing.

"You need to go," I say.

He crosses his arms. "That seems to be your go-to phrase when it comes to me."

What does that even mean? "Just leave," I snap.

"Nope." He reaches over, his heat and scent invading my space in a way that agrees way too much with my lady parts. "Not until we talk about *this*." He snatches the box.

I try to grab the box from him, but he lifts it over his head, holding it in just one hand. I jump to get it and only achieve bumping into his hard, wide, warm chest.

Screw this. "Give it to me," I hiss, and from the look on his face, I'm pretty sure he feels the anger coming at him the way I feel it seeping from me.

"Fuck, but you were always even more beautiful when you were angry. You haven't changed a bit where that's concerned."

My mouth gapes. What? What is he *doing*? "Give it to me!" I yell and punch his chest with a closed fist.

He backs up, the box still over his head. "Are you trying to turn me on? 'Cause it's working." He backs into the bedroom.

I storm after him, speechless.

"Now that I think about it, I'm always turned on by you."

"Ethan!" I seethe.

"But now, maybe more than usual." He circles the bed until he's on the other side of it.

"Give. Me. The. Box."

"Come and get it."

I jump on the bed to try and reach the box. Now two feet higher, I lunge at him. He grabs me by the waist with his free hand and turns me around, pinning me against the wall.

The feel of him against me is so good and so wrong at the same time. I want it to last forever, and I wish it had never happened. Closing my eyes, I lean my head against the wall.

His hand leaves my waist and takes my wrist, pinning it above my head, lifting my breasts until they graze his chest. "Look at me, Grace."

Flitting my eyes open, I trail my upward gaze to take in his corded neck, his stubble, the pulp of his bottom lip—

"Look me in the eye."

I exaggerate the tilt of my head back to reach his gaze. Round my eyes on him. Pretend I'm choking because he's so out of reach.

He nudges his knee between my legs, forcing my thighs apart. What is he doing? God it feels so good. I resist the urge to rub myself against him. *Ohmygod, Grace, get a grip*.

His knee reaches my clit, and he makes a soft stroking motion. I'm going to lose it. I swear, I'm losing it. Then he slowly lifts his knee higher...slowly...until my pubic bone is fully resting on it, the pressure making me throb, and *then he continues lifting,* slowly, slowly, my body straddling his thigh, my feet leaving the floor, lifting until my eyes are level with his.

He doesn't show sign of any effort. "Better?" he asks.

I swallow loudly.

A small smile plays through his beautiful blue eyes. He throws the box behind him, and it lands with a soft thump on the bed. He takes my other wrist in his free hand and places it next to my face. Both his thumbs stroke my palms. His smell of fresh sweat hits me right below the ribcage, making me pant.

My mouth is dry, my breathing labored. The itch between my legs is unbearable.

"So tell me," he says in a low rumble. "What's with the jersey?"

"The—the what?" Why is talking about his jersey? Did he not see everything else that's in the box? Did he *forget* what everything in the box means to us—to me?

"Why do you have a jersey from when I was a kid when I gave you... at least three more."

Now he's upset not to find other stuff? I'm so confused right now. "What?"

His eyes trail down to my neck, and he tilts his head slightly as if to kiss me right there. His breath tickles me to my core, making me squirm. "You know..." he starts, then interrupts himself, takes a deep breath that lifts me higher against him. "I got grounded a whole week for losing that jersey."

I blink. I don't know what to say about that. I'm sorry, I guess? I stole his jersey, okay? I was eleven. Can I get a pass? I remember that weekend vividly. There'd been a snowstorm, sudden, unpredicted. Lynn had called Mom and asked if her kids could crash at our place instead of making the uncertain trek back up the mountain to their farm. I'd had trouble falling asleep, my heart beating too hard at the thought of Ethan right on the other side of the wall. So when I'd found his jersey in the bathroom, I'd rolled it into my own clothes. "Do you want me to confess to your mom?" I say snarkily.

"Mmm..." he says, trailing his gaze down to my breasts, the rumbling of his voice almost making me come against his thigh. "No. What

I'd like to know is where are the other jerseys. Those I actually *gave* you."

I shut my eyes.

He tightens his grasp on my wrists and jerks his leg up, sliding me lower against him. "Answer me." His mouth caresses my hair. "What did you do with the other jerseys?"

I shut my eyes and focus on my erratic heartbeats and his ragged breathing.

Like that's going to calm me down.

"Lemme guess. There's one under your pillow?"

I gasp. "You did not. You did not look under my pillow."

He laughs softly. "Just a wild guess." He rubs his chin over my temple. "And the others? Where are the others, Grace?"

I rotate them. There's one in the wash and one with my lingerie. Jeez! We're quite the pair of pervs. "Does it matter?" I whisper.

"No. We'll get to that later."

Now he's sort of freaking me out. "What do you want?"

There's a little fantasy playing in my head where he answers, *you, Grace, I want you* and then he kisses me passionately and we make savage love and we walk into the sunset together, happy forever.

Instead, he lowers his knee, his heat ceding place to cold solitude. "I want answers," he says as he drops his hold on my wrists and steps away from me.

Now he's going to drop me? "You had no business snooping through my stuff!" I yell as he turns his back on me, leaving the bedroom.

"And you had no business pretending I mean nothing to you," he answers over his shoulder.

Oh no he didn't. After what he did to me? I stomp after him and stand in front of him when he reaches the kitchen counter. "There was a time when you meant *everything* to me." I poke his chest with my finger. "A long, long time ago. I would have done *anything* for you!"

He turns his gaze to the side, to my patio and beyond, looking utterly bored.

"Do you hear me?" I continue. "I would have followed you *any-where* you were stationed. But that was stupid me. That was before I realized you were just fooling around with me. And with other girls."

Now his attention is back on me. "What other girls?" he snaps.

"That poor girl who died. She was your college girlfriend, wasn't she? And I was your hometown side... whatever you guys call that."

"I wasn't—" he interrupts himself and frowns. "What did you say earlier about being a military wife?"

Of course! Let's not talk about the other girls. How convenient. "I never said I'd be your *wife*." *Liar! Liar liar liar.* How many times had I fantasized about being his, entirely his?

Hurt paints his face, and I almost hurl myself at him, kiss him, confess. But he'd only hurt me more. I always saw—projected—more with Ethan than what was really there, as far as he was concerned. "I said I would have followed you anywhere you were stationed."

Ethan trails his eyes on me, seeming to hesitate. He rakes his hand through his hair. Something seems to be tearing at him, and for the life of me, I don't get it.

"It's all in the past, Ethan," I plead. "So what if my cat threw an old box of forgotten childhood souvenirs on the floor? So what if Emerald Creek had the softest jerseys ever? Can't you see it doesn't mean *anything* now?"

He keeps looking past me, to the garden and beyond. "Hold that thought." He bends to pick his shoes up, doesn't even bother putting them on. Before walking out in just his socks, he adds, "This conversation is far from over."

The way he clicks the door softly behind him is what undoes me.

I know Ethan to the core. No matter how life, especially life in the military, may have toughened him and wizened him, to the core Ethan has passion within him. It may be tamed, but it's there for the stuff he cares about.

The fact that he can walk away from me so entirely calm?

I can't stand it.

I whip the front door open. He's settling in Lucas's truck, the door wide open, fumbling with his shoes. "Just take another ten years, you... agh!" I don't even know what to call him. I slam the door and the whole house shakes.

Then I throw myself on the couch and cry like a teenager.

When I'm calmer and Ethan is long gone, I pick up the phone.

"Hey honey." The deep voice settles me.

I sit back into my couch and tuck my legs under me. "Hey."

"Somethin' wrong?"

I take a deep breath. "He's back, Kyle," I breathe, tears filling my eyes again.

The line goes silent. A charged, heavy silence. Then, "Is that a good thing or a bad thing?"

I think back to what everything that is Ethan does to me. To the way I feel alive again. And fragile again.

To the way he makes me feel, the way he *does* look at me. Like I mean the world to him. And then like he hates me. Wishes I wasn't there.

To the way he pinned me against the wall like he was about to ravage me and then walked away without emotion. "I don't know yet," I whisper. My gaze turns outside my window to Woodbury Knoll.

Kyle clears his throat. "Want me to talk to him?" He chuckles, but I know he's only half joking. I know, if I asked him right now, he'd jump on a plane and be with me.

I sit upright, my spirits lifted by his half joke. "Tell me what you're doing right now."

And he does, without insisting, without asking how I'm feeling. He knows what I need. And what I need right now is to sit with my feelings but not dwell on them. Just let them be. And talk about other things.

When he's done talking, he says, "You should go out with the girls."

"You're right."

"I'm usually right, when it comes to you." He is.

"Love you."

I hang up, straighten my makeup and my hair, then get back to the spa right in time for my first appointment.

CHAPTER SIXTEEN

Ethan

I choose to walk on sharp rocks, the sharper the edge, the better. My mind focuses on the knife-like feeling of blade into soft tissue, sending the question of Grace to the back. For later. Once in Lucas's truck, I leave the pebbles stuck to my socks, and count slowly as I lace my shoes. Breathe in. Breathe out. My fingers don't shake. My heartbeat is under control.

The door opens, Grace yells something I don't quite understand, and then the door slams, making me blink.

I focus back on my breath.

I lost it just now. When she said it was all in the past? Fucking lost it. Managed to keep it under control.

Because really? If I'd never known Grace, if I'd just met her a few days ago? Pretty sure I'd be falling for her. But more importantly, I never got over her. Ever. Had her under my skin for over a decade, and I'm pretty sure I was under hers too.

So I'm going to check on this one last thing, and then yeah—she and I are having that conversation.

I pull out from her driveway, avoid looking in the rearview mirror, then drop off the truck at Lucas's and straddle my bike. To say that I ride aimlessly would be a lie.

I know where I'm going.

But I still make it a point to notice the road, to enjoy the ride, to feel every bump in the handles, every sunray on my skin through the partial shade of the canopy of trees, the cooling of the temperature when I dip toward the river, the pebbles in my shoe as I shift gears. I push my speed as I go uphill, angling in the curves, reeling in the feeling of the powerful engine under me, drunk on its noise.

Then I get to the fork in the road. I take the dirt road, until it turns into a path. And then the path ends, and I continue on foot.

And I find it.

The tree is still there. And in a way it's not.

It was hit by lightning. What remains of the trunk stands eight feet tall, the top part split in half. Charred limbs still lay on the ground in this remote part of the forest. There's no trace of the treehouse, of course. It's been over a decade. Although... as I trudge through the broken branches and undergrowth, there it is. The remnant of a pallet I'd used for the flooring.

The carpet and sheer curtains and the pillows are all gone, though I'm sure if I dug under the branches, I might find traces of the mirror Grace had insisted on bringing up. "Look how beautiful we are," she'd say when we lay naked, after sex.

Sometimes during. She was so daring. So beautiful. So fun.

So in love with me.

Turning around to face what's left of the tree again, I see it now. The spot on the trunk, at eye level, now carved out. The spot that held our phrase.

Tracing its contours, I imagine her coming here, using a chisel to save this small piece of what was once us. Did she often return here, after I was gone? Did she use the tree house for herself? Or did she only come when she could no longer see the tree from her house?

I figured that out, waiting for her with her cat on my lap. The couch faced Woodbury Knoll, and she would have had a vantage point on our tree, which stood so tall above the others. That was one of the reasons we'd chosen it. So we could see it from afar. Like a silent testimonial to our hidden love.

It was so tall, it attracted lightning. How ironic, I think. Just like our love—too big, too tall. It was meant to burn down.

Nimble limbs spurt from the broken trunk, making me pause. This tree hasn't been gone long. A year or two at most. Running my thumb on the scar from its missing piece, I come to the same conclusion. Grace has been here relatively recently. My guess is, right after lightning hit the tree and she could no longer see it from her window.

So—while I was thousands of miles away. While she hadn't seen me in years. While there was no plausible reason to believe she'd ever see me again, other than, possibly, in passing, she came here. To carve out our sign. To safekeep it. To have it closer to her.

I sit on the fallen trunk, take my shoes off, shake the pebbles off, put my shoes back on. My eyes are a little wet, I'm not gonna lie.

I'm calm... *er*. I just need to understand her. My heart is heavy. I don't know where to start. And I don't want this to be the end, either.

I swing by the farm to change into clean jeans and a T-shirt. Mom is reading in the sunroom and Dad headed out for some business with the neighboring farm. I look for the travel mug I bought for Grace and never had a chance to give back to her after the end of camp, so I can clean it and bring it back to her. But it's not in my saddle bags, where I could swear I put it.

Then it hits me. I gave it to Colton. What the fuck was I thinking? He probably threw it away. Sneaking into Mom's craft drawer, I take a gold permanent marker and drive my motorcycle to Easy Monday. There's a bright pink mug with cat silhouettes in various poses all around.

Perfect.

"A Harvest Hug?" the owner, Millie asks me. "Lemme rinse that for you first."

"Actually, it's still morning, so..."

She smiles at me. "Maple Kiss then."

She does the whole frothing thing and hands me the mug. "She's gonna love that one too," she says as I pay.

Once on my bike, I pull out Mom's gold permanent marker and write the words:

A Heart Pranck Reign

Then I secure the mug upright in a saddle bag and drive carefully downtown.

Grace's spa is in a house off The Green. With its white columns, steps to the front door, and girly decor inside—all golds and whites and light pink—it's a little intimidating for a guy like me. I feel like the proverbial bull in a China shop. "I'm here to see Grace—Miz Harper." Shit, is that still her last name? I know so little about her current life, it twists me.

The lady at the reception desk taps on a slick computer screen that seems to float above the antique desk. "Do you have an appointment?"

I round my eyes at her. An appointment, *me*? In a place *like this*?

"Uh... no, I'm just... I just need to talk to her."

Her eyebrows shoot up and a warm smile spreads over her face. She points to a fancy little white seat, the kind that's probably named after a French king. "Have a seat."

"Thanks," I say, as I park myself standing in the corner next to a window.

"She's going to be a while," the lady says. "Want me to refill this for you?" She's pointing to the mug I'm holding. Does she think this is *my* mug?

"How long?"

She checks her computer again. "About ninety more minutes."

Ninety? Ninety *more*? What is she doing in there? Fuck. "Could you just... could I just pop in? It's rather urgent." I stomp back to the reception desk, hovering over the computer. "Where is she?"

A man holding a comb backs up from a side room into the reception area, eyeing me top to bottom, a small smile forming on his lips. Before I can figure out what's going on with him, the lady blinks at me. "If you barge in there while she's doing a facial, someone will get fired. And that someone won't be you, since you don't work here."

"Really? She would do that?"

"Oh—she would," the man volunteers.

The lady crosses her arms. "Do I know you? You look familiar."

I can't lie to her. I can't bolt out. Small town and all that, Mom and Dad would know in less than an hour. If that. "I'm Ethan King, ma'am."

"Called it!" the man singsongs as he walks back into what must be a small hair salon. His voice comes out muffled. "He's even *more* handsome than you said..."

The lady nods. "M-hm. Well, Ethan King, did they drill your manners out of you in the service?"

I feel myself blush all the way to my hairline. "It looks like it."

She nods. "Ninety minutes."

"Right-oh."

She lifts her eyebrows.

"I mean, yes ma'am." I glance at the chair she wanted me to sit in. Then at Grace's mug.

A phone trills on the reception desk. She picks it up.

I step outside and take a power walk away from The Green, feeling awkward with my cute mug.

When I come back, the receptionist is on the phone again. Or maybe still. She looks flustered. "But we need the product now... No! It's on you. You need to fix this... what do you mean, a whole week? How are we supposed to..."

She lowers her voice as a woman wearing a black tunic with A Touch Of Grace embroidered in gold letters guides a client to the exit, thanking her and handing her a small bag of candies. She does a double take at me, then smiles and goes to a side room.

"To *you* it's not that far out!" the receptionist continues. "And why should we fix your mistake..." She hangs up with more anger than I would have thought her capable of. Picks up the phone again. Her voice is melodious when she asks, "Honey, where are you?... oh... no, never mind... No, it's fine... some mix-up with a delivery. Grace is going to be beside herself." She hangs up and makes another call. "Justin? Any chance you're around Morrisville? No? Never mind. No-no-no, I said never mind, dear." And she presses the button again. "Alex darling? Where are you, I hear noise.... Oh... I see... no, never mind. Sure, you go now!" When she hangs up this time, she looks anxiously down the hall.

I walk to her desk. "Anything I can help with?"

She looks at me top to bottom. "Well..." her eyes dart to the hallway again.

"I'm a family friend, you can tr—"

She rolls her eyes. "Oh, I know who you are. Trust me. Took me a minute, but I'm all caught up now."

What is that supposed to mean? I fiddle uneasily with the mug.

The hairdresser comes out of his room, and they have a silent eye exchange while his client hands her credit card over.

"Are you riding your sexy motorcycle?" she asks once the client is gone. "Because that's not going to help."

"I'm afraid so."

She sighs. "Good lord, I hope she doesn't fire me for this." She glances to the side door, where the woman in the black tunic—clearly a beautician—is now leaning against the door frame, arms crossed, seeming to enjoy the show.

It's hard for me to picture Grace as a boss firing people. "Tell me what I can do, and I'll do everything I can to keep you out of trouble."

"Ooooh—he fine," the beautician murmurs.

"Shanice!" the hairdresser scolds her, but his blush and glance my way tell a different story. "We appreciate the help, don't we, Claudia?" he says to the receptionist.

"Just sayin', Fabrizio. Nothin' wrong wid'at," Shanice says.

Claudia searches through a handbag she keeps in a drawer and hands me car keys. Then she scribbles an address on a sticky note. "There's been a mix-up in a delivery that we *absolutely* need. They sent it to another spa in another town, three counties over. Everyone is tied up all day, same thing each day. Now, we could either have them send it back and—"

"I got it. What car is that?"

"M-hm," Shanice voices.

Claudia looks at me top to bottom. "The red and white Mini coop. Hope you can fit in."

I scratch my head. Look outside. "How large is the delivery?"

Fabrizio joins me at the window. "Oh dear."

"Pardon?" Claudia asks.

"The stuff I'm supposed to bring back. Will there be enough space in the trunk? The back seat?"

"Oh my."

"I can see if there's a spare truck at the farm," I offer.

Claudia glances nervously at her watch, then down the hall. Then she opens the drawer again and hands me another set of keys.

"Just take Grace's car. You know which one it is, right?"

The 2010 forest green Wrangler with flowery fabric wrapped on the seats. "Uh-huh." I give her her keys back. "Alrighty." I set the mug on the reception desk. "Will you give her this?"

"You sure you don't want to give it to her yourself?"

"I want her to have it when she comes out. Of her... whatever she's doing."

Shanice snaps the mug up. "I'll make sure she gets it. You go now."

"That's a nice thought, Ethan," Claudia says. "I'm sure she'll appreciate it."

"Oooph," Fabrizio utters, his eyebrows shooting up in a comical expression of doubt.

I grunt and leave. I'm with Fabrizio on this one.

CHAPTER SEVENTEEN

Grace

My client, Cheryl, snores lightly as I run the gua sha stone right below her cheekbones, then smooth her oval, striving to sculpt her soft tissues into the youthful shape she seeks. Her skin is dry, soaking up all the product I apply. After her service, I'll have to remind her that a once-in-a-while facial can't replace daily care. Even a basic moisturizer would be better than nothing.

My thoughts drift to finding a new location. Nothing will replace the easy luxury this century-old house exudes, and that's reason to focus on growing my business. People should come to the spa for an overall experience.

No matter what happens here, I will continue interviewing new aestheticians so I can keep focus on growing my massage business. I'll look for a place where I can have a large gathering area for bachelorettes or GNO's. Maybe I could apply for a liquor license and serve cocktails? Now that's an idea. I'll ask Justin how that works. He'll know. He created the pub in town. Maybe I'll risk going to Lazy's tonight?

Or maybe not.

What if Ethan goes there? And he's bound to, right? He's his brother.

God I'm so angry at him. What he did this morning? How dare he?

"Ow!" Cheryl says.

"Oopsie, sorry there."

She opens one eye. "Are you okay?"

"Fine!" I exclaim. "Are you? Okay? I'm sorry I hurt you."

She closes her eyes and settles deeper on the cozy table. "I just detected... tension. No worries."

Tension. Right. I wonder why. Although the way he had me pinned against the wall... holy crap. I clench my teeth and set the jade stone down. Taking a deep breath, I give Cheryl her hand massage, the last part of my signature ninety-minute facial. I don't know if I'm more mortified that he found my secret box, or angry that he confronted me about it, or aroused by him.

God! He felt even better than I remembered.

His scent—pure, now that it wasn't from the jacket he'd been wearing—hit me right below the solar plexus, like something essential, primeval, something I needed like my own breath. I inhaled all of him like my life depended on it.

The feel of his skin seared through mine, warmed me, scorched me, and I swear I can still feel it, the way his muscles tightened, the delicious way his hands closed around my wrists, the way his stubble grated the side of my face.

To sleep next to Ethan just once more and absorb, breathe in everything that is him.

Now *that* would be a youth serum.

"Honey?"

Startled, I open my eyes. "Yep? Other hand now."

"We did the other hand already."

"Oh did we now?"

I glance at the small clock on the marble mantle of the treatment room. Oh, we are way past time. I mentally go over the treatments Grace's Signature Ninety Minute Facial includes, to make sure I haven't forgotten anything.

I might be a little cuckoo and a lot in my head, but I have a business to run and I'm not jeopardizing it over some leftover teenage fantasy of Mister Hotshot.

"How do you feel?" I ask Cheryl.

She stretches on the table. "Absolutely transformed."

And I can't believe he was arrogant enough to want to talk again. *"Hold that thought." "This conversation is not over."*

Yessir, it is over. Been over a looong time.

God I'm such a mess of conflicted feelings.

After Cheryl leaves, I rush back to the reception area. On the way, I notice Fabrizio glancing at me as he's cleaning up his space. Hope is giving someone a facial in our other room. Shanice comes out of the break room with a happy glint in her eye. Good. I just want alone time. "Did you locate our product?"

"I'm on it." Claudia's voice is assured enough that I actually relax.

"Great. I'm going to take five." I'm about to slouch on the small couch in the break room when my eyes catch on a mug. Another cutie from Millie's. It's set on the little round table where I left my phone and my rings. This one has kittens on it. Shanice must have forgotten it.

Stepping out of the break room, I call toward her. "Is this yours? It's the cutest." I raise the travel mug to clarify my question.

She turns a deep shade and mumbles something.

My eyes catch on golden letters that I hadn't noticed before. *That handwriting.* Lifting the mug to eye level, I turn it slowly to read the inscription. *A heart pranck...*

I rush back into the break room and lean my back against the shut door, my heart beating hard against my ribcage.

A heart pranck reign.

Pain twists my inside, tears spring to my eyes. Everything we shared, everything we were, was contained in that phrase, the anagram of our names, a salute to the way love took hold of our hearts and wouldn't let go, playing pranks on us. And how we played pranks of sorts on our friends and families to be together.

A soft knock brings me back to my senses. To the present. "Grace? Are you alright?"

I lunge onto the couch. "Sure!" I call out, my voice raw. I clear my throat. "What's up?"

The door cracks open. "Your next appointment is here," Claudia says softly. "But she's early. I'll tell her to wait." She leans deeper in the door opening. "Oh-oh." She slides inside, closes the door after her, and sits next to me.

I take a comforting sip of the coffee, and Claudia smiles. "Good. For a minute there, we thought we'd made a mistake in letting him leave the mug here."

She strokes my hair, then pats my thigh. "You wanna talk about it?" Claudia is older, just a few years younger than Mom. She has a tough life, with a no-good husband and two teenagers she's raising on her own. My troubles are nothing compared to hers.

"It's really nothing." I shake my head. "I can't wait for him to leave Emerald Creek," I whisper. "It's just too hard. A long time ago, I thought he was the love of my life. And then..." My lip trembles, so

I just stop talking. After a deep breath, I add, "I just don't ever want to see him again."

She shifts uncomfortably on the couch. Clears her throat. "About that—"

"Hello? Anybody here?" Ethan's low rumble messes with my core.

A female voice somewhere in the spa says something, and before I can gather myself, the door to the break room opens after an unceremonious knock on the door. "Oh, sorry," Ethan says to me, then turning to Claudia, "Where d'you want all the stuff?"

Claudia jumps to her feet and they both leave the room as if I wasn't even there, closing the door behind them. There's the sound of cabinets opening and closing, boxes shuffling, stomping. I finish my coffee—it'd be a shame to let a Maple Kiss go to waste just because of Ethan—use the bathroom, and freshen my makeup for the second time today.

There. Whatever Ethan was doing here, he should be gone now. And it's time for my next appointment.

I square my shoulders and step swiftly into the heart of the spa, the vast waiting area connecting the entrance and reception to the treatment rooms. Designed for the female customer in need of me-time, it's a haven from everyday life, with its dimmed lighting, feminine touches, and soft music.

The baby blue, deep couch with fluffy white pillows and the softest throws is typically the seating of choice for anyone. It's more than just inviting or relaxing; it's luxuriously indulgent. At the moment, however, it's empty.

My client is seated in the more rigid but still comfortable velour wingback chair, her bare feet propped on a tiny ottoman covered in faux fur. Next to her, on the smaller of three nesting tables, her organic loose-leaf tea is brewing in an artisan mug. Going by the scent wafting to me, she chose lemongrass. Good choice—though it doesn't seem like she's touched it.

Likewise, she's ignoring the high-end fashion magazines carefully fanned on the higher tier of the nesting table. She's not on her phone either.

She is, however, deeply absorbed by the observation of the built-in ornate bookshelf displaying the products for sale, located directly in front of her. Her arms wrapped around her knees, she watches in rapt attention as Ethan—Ethan!!—unpacks a box of serums.

He places them, per the instructions he's holding in his hand and that I typed myself, two-and-a-half inches apart, staggered on the shelves, so there's a sense of abundance yet airiness. "How does it look?" he asks Fabrizio.

His gaze jumps from Ethan's ass to the display. He stands next to him. "Great but—shouldn't you differentiate by type?"

"What type?"

"Serum Number One, Serum Number Two, etcetera. Then Forever Cream Number Twenty-Four, Forever Cream Number Thirty-Seven, etcetera."

"F—okay. Lemme see." He pours over the sheet again. "Is she gonna notice?"

"I think she already did," Fabrizio whispers while I whip around to Claudia. "What is he doing here?" I hiss.

"He insisted."

"But-but-but... how? Why?"

"Just keeping busy until you're available to talk," Ethan says, his back to me, still carefully lining product on the shelves.

My belly does a little somersault as his voice ripples over me. I turn to Claudia.

She tells me a complicated story about the delivery that got lost somewhere. Fabrizio, Hope, and Shanice being booked, Cheyenne being off, and Ethan insisting he make himself useful.

Ethan hands the last box of products to Fabrizio. "Are you available to talk now?"

The air seems to vibrate with the inquisitive glares of all who are present. It looks like they're taking sides. And it's pretty clear they're Team Ethan. At least Shanice and Fabrizio are, judging by the way they cross their arms as they stare me down.

Well, I'm Team Grace. And nope. No. I am *not* ready to talk.

I glance at my client.

"Mallory, so nice to see you! Right this way. Let's get you settled." I let Mallory step in front of me and dart my eyes at Ethan.

He turns to me with a smile that does nothing to strengthen my resolve. Then he goes back to arranging the display, his stature crowding the place in a way that makes me want to go back to my bedroom, me against the wall, his knee between my...

Ohmygod, what am I doing? This has to stop.

But also? Yeah, we do need to talk.

Just not right now. And not here.

CHAPTER EIGHTEEN

Ethan

"Anything else you need me to do?" The missing packages have been retrieved from two counties over and delivered, the products shelved just like Grace wants them to be (Claudia said so herself), the boxes have been flattened and placed in the recycling dumpster.

But I still haven't been able to talk to Grace. She's been too busy.

"No thank you, young man," Claudia says. "You've been a godsend."

Tell that to Grace.

I glance toward the door to the treatment room.

Claudia smiles kindly at me. "You might want to try her another day."

"Okay. Thank you." I get to the door.

"Oh and Ethan?"

"Yes?"

She hands me a bunch of brochures for A Touch Of Grace, and I take them awkwardly, not sure what I'm supposed to do with that. "For your mother and her friends," she says, then hesitates. "Grace... she might need a little time. Just... don't give up too soon on her."

I nod and get on my bike. Too soon? What is that supposed to mean? She keeps mementos of anything that has to do with us. Yet she doesn't want to talk to me. Doesn't seem interested in me. At least, not the way she used to be.

Okay—maybe not all the time. Sure, she wasn't indifferent when I had her straddling my knee. Fuck, the way her pulse beat in her wrists? The glaze in her eyes? Her panting breaths?

The way her whole body so effortlessly molded against mine, followed my lead—fuck but I wanted to take her. All she needed to do was say the word. Just say my name in that way that used to drive me crazy.

Still does.

But she didn't.

I'll get to the bottom of this. I'll have this conversation with her. Meanwhile, I just need to kill time. So I go to my brother's pub.

Lazy's is crowded, both on the sidewalk and inside. I find a free stool at the bar, close to the register. Perfect. I'll wait 'til it quiets down and see if he knows anything about what's up with Grace. I could start there. It would help to have some context.

"Hey, Justin, when's your next community dinner?" a female voice asks behind me just as Justin storms out of the kitchen, holding two burgers and fries.

"Not 'til after foliage, Kiara. I'll be in touch."

What's a community dinner? It's the first time I'm hearing about that.

Someone taps my shoulder. I turn around to see Colton standing there. "Hey, man, what's up?"

"Hey! Can I buy you a beer?" Returning the favor seems to be the thing to do. Not sure, though, that he's who I should be talking to. Just a beer will do.

"Nah, thanks. Still got a car to deliver to a client tonight." He stands there, though, doesn't go anywhere. "Yo, Haley, any chance Shane can get me something to go? Anything'll do."

"Lemme check," my sister answers and disappears behind the kitchen's swing door.

"You *deliver* cars?" I ask him.

Colton nods. "That kind of car, yes." He takes a deep breath. "Ah, man, it never stops."

He takes the glass of water Haley hands him, then looks at me. "I heard you were a pretty good carpenter."

I shrug. "I'm just handy," I say, thinking he's talking about the bleacher repair I did for the fair.

"So what was wrong with Damian?"

Damian? Grace's cat? Shit. I clear my throat. "I-I think he's gonna be alright."

"Uh-huh? Good. That's good. I take it her door is fixed?"

"Yup."

Haley hands him a paper bag. "Here's Chef's treat, Colt. Don't ask me what it is. Got no time!" Before he can answer, she's at the other side of the bar, filling orders. Justin whips by us, carrying dirty dishes in both hands. He gives us a chin tilt and disappears into the kitchen.

Colton slaps my back. "One day at a time, man. Just don't make it worse for her." Then he leaves, giving Haley a wave on his way out.

I pull out my phone, feeling totally useless. Worse. Feeling like an outsider. I thought the hardest part of my stay here would be resisting feeling at home. Resisting the familiarity. The rut. The old jokes and the stale gossip.

It's not.

It's feeling like I don't belong anymore.

The farm is doing great without me—and why wouldn't it?

My young brother is a pillar of his community and has more work than he can handle.

My sister has two—or is it three—jobs and is rocking each one of them.

My first and only love can barely look me in the eye.

My childhood friend doesn't know if he can trust me with his sister.

I'm just the guy who ran away. The guy they're all watching, in case I mess things up again.

The guy they like better when he's not around.

Instead of ordering another beer and looking like the loser I feel I am, I slide into the kitchen. "What can I do?" I ask Justin as he comes out of the walk-in cooler.

He looks me over top to bottom, seeming to hesitate. "Dishes?"

"You got it."

For two hours straight, it's an endless stream. The minute I have my clean racks stacked away, loads of dirty dishes are dumped almost literally on my lap. Finally the flow slows, and a couple of young guys—twins—come in. "We're taking over from here," they say.

"Hey, guys. Thanks." They look vaguely familiar. Do I know them? But they don't seem to recognize me—it's almost refreshing—so I leave it at that.

I wash and dry my hands and head out to the bar, hoping to catch up with my brother, if only for the heck of it. I don't feel like talking about anything serious anymore, but just a beer at his pub would be nice.

I'd like to tell him how impressed I am at his operation.

But when I walk out, I see Grace sitting at the bar, deep in conversation with Justin. My brother is scribbling on a piece of paper she's intently looking at. I hear the words "liquor license." Someone's name. A dollar amount.

She glances up at me then pores over the paper again. Unfazed. Uninterested.

I pull up a bar stool next to her. "Hey. Got a minute?"

"I'm in the middle of something," she snaps.

"I'll wait." I stand, go behind the bar, and just like I saw Colton do the other day, I grab the gun and fill a tall glass with club soda, then plop a slice of lime in it. Justin cocks an eyebrow at me. His mouth twitches into a repressed smile, but he says nothing. Then I grab a paper coaster, set it in front of Grace, set the glass on top of it, and round the bar to stand next to her.

"It's gonna be a while," she says, staring at the glass but not touching it.

"Then lemme get you somethin' to eat."

She shuts her eyes briefly, and I take it as my cue to go.

By that time I know the lay of the land. Two hours doing dishes didn't happen without noticing how things were run and where stuff was stored. I don't want to bother the chef, Shane, so I grab a plate and make Grace an Ethan special.

"The hell is this?" Justin asks when I set the plate in front of Grace a half-hour later.

I shrug. "Just—proteins and vitamins to keep her going. Nothin' fancy."

"Nothin' fancy my ass," Justin comments. "Let's pick this up later, Grace. Enjoy." He leaves, silent laughter shaking his shoulders.

I sit on the stool Justin just vacated, sideways so I can look at her looking at her food. Or at me. Whatever she chooses.

She clears her throat. "How d'you do that?" she asks, picking a radish delicately carved in the shape of a rose.

I shrug. "Eh. Some people say I'm good with my hands."

At least she graces me with the shadow of a smile. Runs the radish in the hummus that's nested in a carved-out tomato and bites into it. Then her thin fingers pick up a julienned carrot that's been wrapped into the shape of a heart. "That must take forever to make."

"I have all the time in the world for you."

She nods slowly. Dips another radish in the hummus and eats slowly. Wipes her mouth, squeezes the wedge of lime in the club soda, and takes small, ladylike sips, her throat bobbing in the most erotic way. Then she picks up a piece of toasted baguette lathered with olive oil and herbs. "Would you like some?" she asks.

"Not yet. You've worked all day. You're exhausted."

"I don't want to eat alone."

"You're not alone. I'm watching you."

She smiles, a big smile that hits me right in the heart, warms me to the core. She glances at me sideways, just a flash, just a nanosecond of eye connection. She places a piece of prosciutto on the baguette, tops it with a cornichon, and turns to me, our knees brushing briefly.

"Chris and Justin, they have this thing about food bringing people together. Either you're eating with me, or I'm not eating at all." Her smile is soft and confident as she brings the food straight to my mouth, and this time our eyes connect and never let go, and I don't have anything to say. So I close my mouth on her fingers.

She blushes deeply and turns back to face her plate. "Thanks for picking up the delivery today. Claudia told me."

"Was nothin'. Happy to help."

She nods and blinks a few times. "It's been crazy busy at the spa."

I nearly reach over to caress her hair, tell her it'll be alright, cup her cheek. The temptation to touch her is too big, so I turn to face the bar. "Any news on the sale?" I ask her. It has to be the main thing on her mind—it's not like I'm bringing up a topic she's trying to forget.

She shakes her head. "There was a visit. The realtor almost lost it when the girls pretended to be buyers and talked the building down in front of his clients. Apart from that, nothing." She plops an olive in her mouth and chews pensively, her gaze fixed nowhere in particular.

I clear my throat. What can I say or do to make her feel better? Nothing comes to mind. "Do you need something stronger than water?"

She shrugs softly. "Maybe later." Then she takes a deep breath and turns her adorable face to me. "You wanted to talk?"

"It can wait." Right now, I want to see her happy. I want her to finish her food. I want to give her a foot massage. I want to pour her a glass of wine. "You're not finishing your veggies?"

"They're not veggies. They're works of art. I can't."

"You better not put them in your box," I growl.

She laughs softly. "I guess you have a point." She plucks at the carved carrots, the radishes, the thin slices of zucchini, and eats them one by one. "I should have taken a photo."

"I'll make you others." My heart hammers, trying to escape. Trying to reach for her, to hold her, to tell her everything will be alright.

She blinks and stops eating. "Why don't we go for a walk," she whispers.

CHAPTER NINETEEN

Grace

I manage to grab Haley and ask her to box my food and keep it in the fridge for me. I might be out of sorts at the idea of having "the talk" with Ethan, but I don't want his food art to go to waste.

And yes, I might take a photo of whatever is left, print the photo, and put it in my box.

What? I'll delete the photo from my phone after that. Ethan souvenirs belong in the box. Nowhere else. That's where it's safe for me. The rest of the time, Ethan does not exist in my life.

Except right now. For the next few days, maybe. And for now, I need to be a responsible adult who's capable of a grown-up conversation, even if it's going to reopen some of my wounds.

Ethan holds the door open for me, and I almost teeter as I brush against him to enter the warm summer night. He settles me with a light touch between my shoulder blades, then safely plunges his hands into his pockets just as I fold my arms on my chest.

Good.

I take a left, toward the lower part of The Green, instinct guiding me away from the church, and its projection room, and the memory of where I first threw myself at Ethan.

"Place has changed, and at the same time, it hasn't," Ethan says as we walk slowly toward the park and the river.

"M-hm." I take a shaky breath. What does he want to talk about? The box? Why did he leave my house so calmly earlier? What's on his mind? "They added picnic tables to the park."

"That's nice," he says.

"Nathaniel complains it adds work. The trash cans."

"Nathaniel's still here?"

"Oh yeah." The old man is a fixture in town. I can't imagine Emerald Creek without him.

"I guess ten years is a long time, but not *that* long either."

"Not when you're happy. Nathaniel's always happy."

"True. Until the trash cans."

I chuckle. "Until the trash cans."

"Maybe they should come up with a trash can solution? Emerald Creek wouldn't be the same without a happy Nathaniel."

I nod. "You should suggest that at the next Town meeting."

"Ah. I don't think I'm allowed to talk there. Not anymore."

"Good point." Vermont's town hall meeting day, the first Saturday in March, is where all local topics are discussed. In Emerald Creek, it got a little out of hand when second home-owners thought that was the quaintest direct democracy experiment ever, and wouldn't it be cute to participate? With some gentle guidance from the community, and after some discussions went totally out of hand, they were informed that only full-time residents were allowed to speak up. We felt a little arrogant, and then we felt like zoo animals when part of the crowd came just to observe us, but eventually we all got used to this bizarre state of affairs. "You could suggest someone bring it up."

"Would you bring it up for me?"

My answer comes straight out. "Nope."

"Why not?" he chuckles.

"Because I'll be volunteered to pick up trash at the park, that's why."

"Ah, I see. The whole *don't raise a problem if you don't have a solution* approach."

I nod. "Still going strong here."

"Mm," he says softly, as if looking for a segue to the-conversation-he-wants-to-have.

"So—what made you change your mind?" he asks in a low voice.

"About what?"

"An hour ago you couldn't look me in the eye. Now you're taking a walk with me under the moonlight. It better not be the veggies."

"It was totally the veggies."

He chuckles. "Ouch. So—anyone puts a pretty plate in front of you, you go for a walk in the night with them?"

"If they're attractive and kind and make me feel safe, why not?" *Oh god why did I just say all this*? It looks like I'm hitting on him.

He stays silent while I quell the tears threatening to choke me. I've had this little talk with myself earlier, and I'm secure in my decision. I think. "It wasn't the veggies. I realized I was holding onto the past. That's why I was upset with you. And that's no way to live. I'm over all this. I really am. I won't let the past bog me down. Letting the past define your future is a foolproof way to being miserable your whole life. And I've decided to be happy."

By now we've reached a road that runs alongside the river. The moonlight is bright enough to light our footsteps and draw our shadows out. A few more steps and we'll be at the covered bridge, and my heart stutters. Ethan won't remember, but this is where he kissed me, two years after the disaster in the church basement. Where he told me things too beautiful to ever forget.

Where we really began being us. At least for me.

Our steps echo inside the wooden structure, and I instinctively move farther from Ethan, as if I can't trust myself in this place, in his presence.

I've been known to be impulsive, especially where Ethan is concerned. I've managed to keep a handle on myself until now. I'd like to keep it that way.

We exit on the country side of the bridge, and Ethan takes a deep breath, as if he'd been holding it in too. He walks up the hill a bit, then turns around and takes it all in. The village at our feet, softly glowing in the golden hue of the streetlights. The resort way beyond, reflected on the still surface of the lake. Farms dotting the landscape, the large shape of their barns looming dark against the moonlit fields.

"Was there something you wanted to talk to me about?" I finally ask Ethan.

"I uh—yeah. I wanted to know why you kept all the mementos of us, when clearly... you know. There's nothing between us or-or-or rather, you didn't want to talk to me. Plus what you just said about not holding onto the past. Doesn't really all make sense to me."

I huff, grateful that the semi-darkness hides the tears lining my eyes. "Well... I'd argue that it's really my own business, what I choose to safekeep." My words are so low, he may not have heard me. Is this really the conversation I was dreading so much?

He clears his throat. "The tree..."

My heartbeat picks up. I retreat toward the village, and he falls in step next to me. "The tree?"

"When was it hit by lightning?"

How does he know that? I can barely hear myself breathe, the blood in my ears wooshes so strongly. I clench my middle with my folded arms in a piss-poor attempt at comfort. Every nerve in my body is ready to snap. How can I be so sensitive to all of this?

"Grace? You okay?" His hand on my shoulder blades jolts me and warms me at the same time. I want him to leave his hand here, and I want him to go away at the same time. "You're shaking."

I hasten my steps, but he merely takes longer strides. As we reach the covered bridge, I trip on an uneven plank. Ethan catches me, one hand under my folded arms. "Hey-hey-hey."

"It's this stupid bridge." I pretend to laugh. "I'm okay." I try to walk away from him, but his hand trails down my forearm, catches my fingers, and doesn't let go as he stops abruptly.

"I'm not okay." He tugs on my hand, forcing me to face him. "I've been struggling all day trying to figure out what to tell you, and I'm at a loss. You said we were over, we were nearly nothing, and I was going to respect that, even if that's not how I feel, and then this morning... this morning I find out I'm *not* nothing to you. I've *never* been nothin' to you. Just like you've never been nothin' to me, Grace. You've always been everythin' to me, and I need you to know that."

What is he saying? My heart seems to try to escape through my throat. What he's saying doesn't make sense. "Why did you stay away for so long?"

He contemplates our fingers still loosely joined. The corner of his mouth dips, and he briefly shuts his eyes. "It was stupid. I was stupid. I... I didn't feel wanted here anymore." He drops my hand and takes a few steps to the edge of the bridge, leaning over the thick wooden railing, his gaze lost somewhere on the dark river below us. "I know it wasn't true, at least as far as my family was concerned."

His voice is so low, I can barely hear him, so I close the gap between us, and, turning my back to the river, I lean my elbows on the railing, almost facing him. "It took me a while to understand it," he continues. "To understand that just because I hadn't prevented Justin's accident, my presence wasn't going to be a constant reminder of it. But by that time, I found I was more useful in the service than here, so there was that. It's not something I deal well with—not being of service. Not being useful, wherever I am. And then..."

He takes a deep breath and turns his face to me. "Then there was you." He squints at me, like he's expecting me to say something.

"Me?"

Straightening, he faces me, the moon lighting his side. He reaches for my face and caresses my cheek with his knuckles. "Why did you end it between us?"

CHAPTER TWENTY

Ethan

Her eyes widen and her mouth sets in a fine line. She jerks her face away from my hand. "Why are you doing this?"

"Doing what?" For the life of me, I don't understand her.

"Look, Ethan. We're adults. We still have chemistry. I'm not going to deny it. But don't try to gaslight me, okay? Out of respect. I don't resent you for what you did. I know you thought I was too young for you. I know older girls were more interesting to you. That doesn't mean it didn't hurt at the time. It hurt like hell." She takes a shaky breath. "I'm over it, because it's been so long, but it's insulting to me that you—"

I clench my jaw, keeping my anger in check. "Hold it. Hold it right there. I have no fucking idea what you're talking about. Are you insinuating I wasn't faithful to you? Because that's absolute bullshit."

"Ethan. You weren't."

Twelve years ago, Grace and I found ourselves alone in the tiny projection room of the church basement. I was home from college, it was youth night, and whoever was in charge asked me to show Grace how to operate the projector. I was only going to show her how to start and stop a movie, and get out of there in less than a minute. But once in the tiny, cramped room, barely large enough for one person, when I'd leaned over to show her, my body cupping hers, she'd turned around and stood and laced her hands around my neck and then my hands fell naturally on her hips as she pulled herself to me without any hesitation.

She's too young. What are you doing?

Then she'd whispered something that felt very Hollywood-y to me: "What are you waiting for? Just kiss me." And she'd closed her eyes, mouth half-open.

When I hadn't kissed her right away, she'd stood on her toes and molded her open mouth to my closed one, pulling my chest to hers, her heartbeat fast like mine.

Stop right there. Right now. She's too young.

"It's just a kiss, you idiot," she'd whispered sweetly against my mouth. "There's nothing wrong with a kiss. I want it and I know you want it. Right?" This last word was tentative, full of doubt, scared.

Of course I wanted it. And I wanted her kindness, and her spirit, and her soul. I wanted Grace, all of Grace. Yet I had to let her down. "Grace, I'm too old for you. You're only sixteen."

She'd sighed, amused, a small smile painted on her face. "So you're saying your feelings will be different once I'm eighteen?" She'd set a hand on my beating heart, daring me to tell her I didn't feel anything for her.

I pulled my hands off her hips. "My feelings won't be different. But maybe yours will be. I can't do this to you—with you—now."

She'd pulled away from me, her eyes shiny.

It hurt *me* to be hurting her. "A kiss with you will never be just a kiss, Grace. It will always mean more to me. And now... now..."

"I get it. I'm too young." She'd stomped out of the room and slammed the door behind her, leaving me... heartbroken. Why did doing the right thing with Grace need to be so painful?

Two years later, I was home from college for the summer before joining the Air Force. After a night swim in the river with a group of friends, Grace and I found ourselves alone on this very bridge.

"You remembered my birthday," she said to me. Our steps were tentative, teetering on the bridge, the uneven planks pushing us together, our reflexes pulling us apart.

She'd turned eighteen a few months ago, and I'd sent her a card from college. "Of course I remembered your birthday." My voice strangled in my throat. Did she still want me? I felt so vulnerable. She couldn't possibly, right? I mean, I barely ever saw her now. Not one-on-one, for sure. Every time I was in town, I'd see her at the farm with Haley. She'd even worked there the summer before, and again during Spring break, she was there bottling syrup. But she didn't make eye contact with me. She didn't ask for help with math or physics like she used to. She didn't ask me about my college classes like she did before that time in the projection room. I had let her down as softly and gently as I could, yet it seemed I'd broken our connection in an unredeemable way.

Since then, it seemed she had blocked me out.

So yeah, when I sent her a birthday card? I was hoping she'd get that what I was telling her. That I was still thinking of her. That I knew she was no longer sixteen. Or seventeen. That we could be something, if she still wanted to.

I was hoping she was still waiting for me. Because I sure as hell had been waiting for her.

I can't remember who kissed who first on the bridge. But man, did we *kiss*.

And more. That summer was magical. Perfection.

Until it ended brutally, in more than one way.

Ten years later, Grace stating as a cold fact that I wasn't faithful to her is a load of bullcrap that I'm clearing right now. "How can you say that?" Same for all the other bullshit she just said about girls older than her being more interesting to me. "You were everything to me. You were *it*, Grace."

I run my hand in my hair, take a few steps away from her. Yeah, maybe I've been dreading this. Dreading knowing what got her to break things off with me, when I thought we were doing so well. I was wrong, clearly. I'm seeing now I'm not really over the breakup. Not over her.

And I can't say that seeing her now—what she's become? It hurts even more, knowing she should have been mine. Should have stayed mine. I stand back in front of her, fists on my hips. "We had something real, Grace. I never cheated on you." Did someone put that in her head? Who? And how could she believe them? How could she not talk to me, at the time?

She shuts her eyes briefly, tears rimming her lashes, but she stays in control of her voice. I'm going to take a wild guess here: she has a long practice of trying to hide her feelings. "Stop doing this. I *saw* you, Ethan. And I *told* you, I under—"

I crowd her space. I want to feel her body under mine when she answers me. I want to hear her heartbeat. Feel the breath coming out of her mouth. She and I were as good as one, once. What happened? "What do you think you saw?"

She sighs, acting exasperated, but the pain in her eyes is real. The tremble at the corner of her mouth doesn't lie like the rest of her tries to.

Finally she sets her gaze on me. "You know," she starts slowly, "I never told you I was sorry... about Audrey." She crosses her arms and shakes her head.

Fuck. Is she going where I think she's going?

She continues. "I was young and stupid, obviously, but also extremely selfish and self-centered. I mean..." She looks at me sheepishly, then turns around, her back to my front, looking at the water flowing past us instead of straight into my eyes. "I actually believed all that stuff about us being together forever."

My heartbeat picks up.

"So much time has passed, but I'm sure you still miss her. I guess I just wanted to say I was sorry for your loss. And-and-and I should have told you at the time, but, of course, I was too busy being self-center—"

Yep. It's that boatload of crap again. "What the fuck are you talking about?" The power of my voice, the fact I'm stomping away from her, makes her turn around to face me.

She sighs and crosses her arms. "Ethan, look. I know you always meant more to me than I did to you... I mean, look at me with my box of mementos... how stupid is that?" Her eyes turn liquid. "But it doesn't mean that I can't... empathize with..."

Does everyone in this town believe Audrey was my actual girlfriend? And does Grace actually, really think I would be seeing another girl when I had her? Who does she think I am? This is so screwed up.

She narrows her eyes on me. "Ethan? Are you... are you okay?"

"No. No I'm not okay."

She widens her eyes at me.

"What makes you think she and I had something going on?" And what makes her think I loved her less than she did me?

"Ethan, please. I saw you. I saw you *with her*." Her throat bobs as she swallows with difficulty. "It's okay. I was young and... I mean she *had* to be more interesting than me, I get it. I totally get it *now*. I wish, that night, I hadn't lashed out at you the way I did." She gives me a small smile. "I mean, what you did wasn't cool, but hey. I get it."

My blood turns cold as understanding dawns on me. I remember those last moments with Audrey. Looking back, they'd been blurred by Grace's brutal breakup minutes after—and now it all makes sense.

After Audrey ran away from the party with Justin, after they were caught in an accident, after Audrey died and Justin almost died, too, trying to save her, I ran that evening through my mind a million times, seeing every little thing I could have done differently, every opportunity I didn't take to make a difference. I wished I could have been that butterfly wing flap that changed the outcome. That prevents a succession of totally unrelated and seemingly innocuous events from turning into utter tragedy. Turned out, my rejection of Audrey was what had set that chain reaction in motion. "You saw what exactly?"

Grace's eyes mist again. Ten years. Ten fucking years and now I'm finally going to get the truth. And she's been hurting all this time. "Ethan..." she pleads.

"Let me guess. You saw her throw herself at me—"

She turns her head away from me and takes a shaky breath.

I take her chin gently in my fingers and force her to look at me. "You saw her throw herself at me—"

"She kissed you." Her chin wobbles, the pain still fresh after all these years.

"And I told her she couldn't."

Grace shakes her head. "You took her hand and walked into the darkness. With her, Ethan. You kissed and…"

We didn't kiss. "She was a little high and strung out. She came onto me. I didn't want to make a scene, so yeah, I walked her away from the party and told her… I told her I had someone. That…"

"That what?"

I take a deep breath. I don't know how Grace is going to take this. For the little that I know the new Grace, I've noticed she can be very strong, like when she's running her business, but she can also be so fragile. And my inkling is, when it comes to our past, I'm dealing with fragile Grace.

I also don't know what her recollections are. Memory is a strange thing. Constantly alive, evolving. We reconstruct events that did or didn't happen in a way that suits our present needs.

"That I never had real feelings for her." I'd always wondered, to this day, if those were the words that sent her over the edge. If I'd said something different, would she have reacted better? Stayed at the party? "Before you and I were together, before… we started being together…"

"Just spit it out, Ethan. There were other girls," she says, and the way she says it nearly kills me. The defeat in her tone? I hate myself for that.

Reminding myself she was fourteen—a child—when I left for college, I feel a *little* better. "Audrey… was one of them. *But*. I hadn't been with her, or anyone, since you and I… opened up to each other about our feelings."

She gives me a sad smile, but I know she believes me. "I thought—I thought you were doing me… a favor."

A *favor*? "What the fuck, Grace? How could you think that?"

Her mouth distorts and she looks away, pulling her arms tighter against her chest.

"Grace, talk to me."

"No," she whispers. "You talk to me. You tell me the whole truth, Ethan. About how you felt back then. Don't sugar coat it." She wipes her face and looks at me. "I'll feel better once I know I wasn't making it up. That we had something good back then. It would really help me feel better about myself. Not as crazy."

"What do you mean, crazy?"

"After you left, I thought... I'd sort of made you up. I mean, made up who you *really* were. Fantasized something—someone that wasn't real."

I don't know where we're going with this. I need to set the past straight, but I don't know what the future holds for us. Grace is so special and so beautiful and so fragile emotionally. I see now I've wounded her badly.

"I was shattered when you broke up with me. That's who I was. I didn't understand it—I do now. And with Justin's accident—and the part I indirectly played in it—I just needed to get the hell away from it all and stay away.

"I wish I'd come back sooner to Emerald Creek. I wish you and I would've talked. But with Justin in the hospital... my life seemed on hold. I should've talked to you before leaving. I'm sorry I didn't."

Tears are streaming freely down her cheeks. "I ruined everything, didn't I?"

"How can you say that?" I run the back of my hand against her cheek, and this time she lets me. "You've always been the best part of me, Grace. Always will be."

She widens her eyes. "What are you saying?"

"I'm saying a part of me is still that boy on this very bridge hoping you still want him. Another part if me is this grown-ass man wondering how the hell life passed him by and he let the best woman on Earth get away."

"Ethan," she breathes.

"And another part of me is wondering how the hell he got lucky enough to be standing right here again, with this very woman just inches from him, her beautiful eyes on me."

"Ethan." Her voice is barely audible. "What are you saying."

"I'm saying things are different and yet they're the same. I'm saying I'm angry we were too young to see our errors and fix them. I'm saying it's too late for us to have the life we thought we'd have, but fuck me if I'm going to stand here and not tell you how hard I'm falling for you all over again.

"Now before you say it's just the memories this bridge brings about, or the way that the moon lights your beautiful eyes, or whatever other BS excuse you're gonna find to push me away, hear this. If I were to meet you right now for the first time, never seen you before, you'd catch my eye. First time we speak, you have my attention. All of it. Ten minutes with you—I'd be falling for you. Not kidding, Grace."

Her breath stutters, she crosses her arms, her gaze darts right and left like she doesn't know what this is all about.

"What I'm really trying to say is, I want to kiss you."

She shuts her eyes softly, her throat bobbing when she swallows. "Then kiss me. What are you waiting for?"

I cup her face with both my hands and feel her melt under my touch. She opens her eyes and twines her fingers on my nape, pulling herself up to meet my lips. Eyes half closed, we stay like that, suspended in time, our breaths mingling, our mouths not quite touching. I can't believe this moment is real. I'm half expecting it to end here. She's going to change her mind. Someone will drive by, breaking the magic. A phone is going to ring. The bridge is going to collapse.

"What happens after we kiss?" Grace asks, and I feel her retreating already. It's like I can see all the blocks she's coming up with as to why this is not a good idea. The painful past. The future with no place for us.

Fuck it.

This is the present.

Chapter Twenty-One

Grace

What was I thinking, asking him to kiss me? I ruined both our lives with my stupid impulsiveness back then, and now I'm about to do the same. Because I know the moment he kisses me, I'll be lost to him. I can tell already.

Just his voice, rumbling down to my insides. His hands, cupping my face. God... *god!* His hands on my face? The *best* feeling. Always been.

The desire behind his hooded eyelids.

And when he murmured, *"I'm falling for you all over again."*

Oh god, and now his lips are trailing mine, not quite a kiss yet, just the whisper of one, his exhale a caress. My whole body vibrates, my center is a hot mess, my knees barely support me.

But what happens next? How do we pick ourselves up, when our daily adult lives, now set without each other in them, take over? When this kiss on the bridge lives on as a memory, will it carry me through my life?

Or will it destroy me slowly.

"What happens after we kiss?" A kiss with Ethan will never be just a kiss. It will be more than that. It always was. We should talk about that first. Even if we end up just kissing, shouldn't we set reasonable expectations? Limitations? I mean, if the past has taught us anything—

His lips claim mine, shutting my brain off. I whimper under the onslaught of emotions, under the warmth and weight of his body engulfing mine, under the erotic strokes of his tongue, slow and questioning first, now downright domineering, claiming, taking.

I thought I remembered everything about him.

I was right, and I was wrong.

No matter how much I tried, his taste, the *feel* of him was always elusive. But now that he's taking me, greedy, possessive, oh *god*—I remember all of it. The slow sweeps of his tongue, asking for a permission it doesn't need, accessing my mouth tentatively first, then with the intense devotion Ethan always had for me. His hands press my back tighter against him, the fierceness of his rapid heartbeat confirming this is not, will never be, *just* a kiss.

This is ten years of yearning finally coming to an end.

I dig my fingers in his short hair, and he growls against my mouth, presses himself harder against me, claims my mouth with more urgency, as if he's afraid I might leave and he wants to seal us together right here, right now.

I might leave. I *should* leave.

"God, I missed you," he growls as he dips his mouth to my neck and suckles on it. Desire zings through me, and my head falls back, giving him better access.

My whole body caves, gives in, takes him.

I'm not leaving.

Not now that his strong arms close around me, sheltering me from the outside world. From tomorrow. Not now that his hands claim my body, roam up and down my back, caress my ass, hitch my leg up his hip. Press his erection against my belly.

"Ethan..." is all I have the strength to utter. I'm powerless in his arms.

How could I have been so stupidly impulsive, back then, to turn him away just because of what I thought I saw?

He nibbles on my lower lip, kisses my eyelids, then dips down to my mouth again, our teeth clashing as he pulls me tighter against him.

"God, I missed you," he whispers again against my lips, his breath tingling my insides.

How could I have been so infatuated with my own self that I didn't give him a chance to explain himself?

"Missed your smell. Missed how good you feel in my arms. Missed your mouth under mine." He hoists me onto his hips with surprising ease, dips his head in my neck again, and suckles me, sending pleasure rippling through my center. "Fuck, but I want you so bad."

I want you too, Ethan. So. Bad.

Ten years. I gave up ten years of this because I was so impulsive.

But what am I doing, now? I'm being impulsive again. Not thinking about the consequences. I have my life here. He barely ever gets time to visit. This is another disaster in the making.

"What happens now?" I whisper. I knew this kiss would be the best. No question. That's why I dreaded it.

He doesn't answer. Instead, his hooded gaze follows the curve of my neck, falls on my chest. He strokes my breast slowly. Agonizingly slowly. His rugged hand is just the right amount of rough on my sensitive bud.

Ethan was always the best lover. Bar none. After we split, I caught a wild hair in college, and I gathered material. Nothing compared to Ethan. Sometimes, in the years that followed my return from Texas, I'd let myself think that I'd idealized him because he was my first.

I was wrong.

I tighten my legs around his waist and run my hand through his hair. God he feels so good.

I moan and writhe under his touch, the last shreds of my reason fleeing with every stroke of his hand on my body, every place his lips have kissed. Wanting more and knowing I'll regret it, come morning. "I think we just had too much to drink—"

He cups my face with his hands, again. Makes me feel like the center of the universe, again. "Coke. I only had Coke. And you had water."

He runs his lips on my hair, and shivers run down my spine, making me arch my back and press myself even tighter against him. "This is real, Grace. You know it and I know it. I know you're scared, and I am too. And I know I can't give you tomorrow, but I sure as hell can give you tonight."

He glides the ridge of his nose against the tip of mine. The tender, intimate gesture nearly undoes me. "Do you want to give me tonight, Grace? Do you want to be us again? If just for now."

Tears surge and fall onto my cheeks.

"Fuck," he draws out. "Please tell me these are happy tears."

I nod and burrow my face against him.

"Happy tears?" he growls, stomping to the other side of the bridge with my legs tightly wrapped around him, my dress bunched up, my hands fisting his short hair.

I nod against his chest, inhaling his masculine scent.

"Tonight?"

At least we're on the same page. I'd give a lifetime of memories for a night with Ethan. I nod again.

"Your car or my bike?" he growls.

I straighten in his arms and look around. We're on the narrow road leading back to the village. "I-I'm not... having sex on your bike." I wiggle to let him know he can set me down, but he ignores this.

He chuckles. "Now that's an idea..." He flutters kisses on the top of my head. "I meant to get to your place."

"Oh..."

"Did you want to go somewhere else?"

I wiggle again, with no success. We're approaching The Green, the streetlights, the nosy stares. "Um... we could go to Woodbury Knoll."

"All night? The treehouse is gone."

Did he check on the treehouse? And what did he just say—*All night*? Am I spending *the night* with Ethan?

He finally sets me down, and reading my thoughts, he lowers his gaze on me while I adjust my dress. "We're not teenagers anymore, Grace. This isn't some..." His hand waves dismissively, his thought interrupted. "So—your bike or my car?"

The question is not how we get there. The question is that Ethan—Ethan!—will be spending the night, the whole night, at my place. In my house. In my bed. There will be coffee in the morning, and-and-and...

"I mean, nothing wrong with the woods. Just might get a little chilly early morning," he offers, proving once again he's reading my thoughts, my fears.

He might have the same.

"Let's take your bike," I whisper, liking the way his lips curve up. Our hands link together as we hasten up to The Green.

Lazy's is still busy, light and voices pouring out of the open doors onto the sidewalk. Haley comes out holding a tray full of drinks. Her gaze is on her patrons, and I try to keep mine straight on the bike.

Ethan hands me his helmet. The bike revs, and I climb behind him, trying to pull my dress down my thighs in a futile attempt at modesty. My sixth sense tingles, and as I look to Lazy's, I break into a huge smile at Haley's double take. At the happiness on her face. At her happy wink.

Ethan pulls me closer to him and caresses my bare leg, then grabs my hand to place it around his waist, then gives his gawking sister a small wave. I lace my other hand around his torso and lean my head against his back as we lurch off from the curb.

The roar of the engine means we can't talk, only feel. And I can feel everything, down to the tiniest gravel on the road. The bugs hitting my bare arms. The warm air feeling cool on my skin.

His hand, warm against my thigh.

His heartbeat, pounding under my hand.

What am I getting myself into?

Chapter Twenty-Two

Ethan

F uck, what am I doing?

The moment I've been wanting for so long. The moment all previous moments have led to is here, and I'm... paralyzed. Scared shitless.

Should I be doing this? Should we be doing this?

This has happened so fast. What if she doesn't feel for me what I feel for her? What if this is just physical for her? Am I ready to lose her all over again? I know I said I can only give her tonight, but... you never know.

I park the bike and help her down. She takes the helmet off and fixes her hair. She looks a little scared. Taking her face in my hands, I examine her closely. I can't get a read on her, right now. "Talk to me. What's wrong? Were you scared on the bike?" I tried to ride the bike slow and gentle, and the Grace I remember is fearless. But what if I'm wrong? It kills me that I don't know things like that about her anymore.

She frowns. "Scared? On the chick magnet?" She blinks. "Oh no, that—that was cool."

"The what-did-you-call-it?"

"The chick magnet." She gives me a side smile. "I can see the appeal. For girls, you know. Women, whatever." Then her eyes flutter and it hits me. Grace is insecure.

I lower my face to hers and talk against her mouth, just like she used to like me do. "Lemme be clear. I got this bike for fun, and my idea of fun is not chicks. Or girls. Or women."

She swallows loudly, her body trembling against mine, and fuck it, but I'm doing this.

"My idea of fun is being alone on my bike on a desert road, going too fast. My idea of fun is being alone on a mountain, backcountry snowboarding on a powder day. My idea of fun is skydiving, the earth under me, the wind holding my fate in its hands. You wanted to take my bike, we took my bike. I wasn't trying to scare you, and I'm sorry if I did. I wasn't trying to impress you, though I'm not sorry if I did."

Her eyes smile at these words. "The bike was fun."

I take her mouth slowly in mine.

She lets me kiss her, doesn't pull back but doesn't pull me to her like she did earlier. Doesn't really kiss me back. Just... lets me take the lead. I don't like it. Don't like that she's so uncertain. But I get it.

I lean my forehead against hers and whisper. "Look, I know you're scared, and I am too. We don't have to do this if you don't want to, but if we don't... just know... I'll be running this night in my head for the rest of my life. The last time I saw you, I cried for days knowing I'd never see you again. But... god... you're even more... *everything* than you were back then. I've been imagining this moment so many times, but holding you in my arms doesn't even begin to compare to my fantasies.

"I'm sick and tired of the what-ifs. That'll be just one more to add to the list. And, Grace—I'm tired of living with regrets. I'd like to take a real risk for once in my life. And you're the best risk ever."

She still doesn't close the infinitely small space between our lips.

But I do. I kiss her deeper and my hands find their way under her dress again, and she lets me, she even moans a little in my mouth, and her body molds against mine, and her ass tilts up a bit when my hand gets there, and fuck me, but the signs she's giving me?

She's fighting. She's scared.

Pulling my hands outside her dress, I add, "Or we can decide to put an end to whatever this is and just stay friends. Or strangers, if that's what you want." Hell. The thought of that just about kills me.

She pulls my shirt in her fist and kisses me fiercely. I back her to the porch and from a tiny bag she has slung across her, she produces her keys.

CHAPTER TWENTY-THREE

Grace

He shuts the door with his foot and hits the deadbolt while I kick my shoes off, and then we leave a trail of clothes to the bedroom as we tear each other's clothes off. When my fingers hit the bare skin of his torso, I stop a beat to take in the ridges, the definition of his pecs, the bulge of his biceps.

But as my fingers inch down to his jeans, he lifts me in his arms and carries me to the bedroom. Instead of throwing me on the bed and having his way with me like I've been fantasizing, he rounds the bed, pins me against the wall, and says, "Where were we? Oh yeah." And then he raises my wrists over my head with just one hand, spreads my legs with his knee, then lifts me up slowly until we're eye to eye. "I want to make love to you. But first I'm gonna fuck you."

He slides his hand down to my hip, his thumb playing in the crease of my leg, inching under my G-string, then I hear a snap and the G-string sliding off me, and I'm totally naked, straddling Ethan's leg, his mouth at my mouth, my breasts against his chest. He lifts me higher, and his mouth finds my nipple and sucks on it. Ripples of pleasure flow down through my core. Letting go of my wrists, he hoists me even higher, to his face, brings my legs on his shoulders, his face to my center, my back to the wall, and licks my folds, finds my clit and teases it, making me moan. I find purchase by grabbing his hair and leaning against the wall.

When did he get so strong, so assured, so... experienced?

Then I look at us in my bedroom's standing mirror. Ethan's strong back muscles rippling under the effort, his head moving between my legs, his jeans hanging low on his hips.

"Ethan... Ethan! I'm-I'm-I'm... I'm gonna come."

He looks up at me. One long look, a slow smile, then he dips back and laves my clit until I shake, folding on top of his head. He places me on the bed and proceeds to take his jeans off. Slowly. Looking at me the whole time. The metallic sound of his belt buckle, followed by that of sliding leather is an unbearable tease.

My hand goes between my legs.

"That's it," he growls. "Touch yourself. Touch yourself for your man."

Your man. My chin wobbles. "Ethan," I whisper.

He kicks the jeans off slowly. "Right here." His cock beats under his black briefs. He strokes himself through the thin fabric. "You want that?"

"Oh god yes."

"Where do you want it?"

"In my pussy. Now."

He chuckles. "You were always greedy. Where else?"

Take the briefs off already. "In my mouth."

He groans, his eyes heavy with desire. "Fuck. You wanna make me come, don't you?" His large hand strokes his throbbing cock slowly.

"Yes. Come all over me." I run my hands on my breasts, then lift a foot to try and pull his briefs off.

Leaving his cock, he grabs both my feet and pulls me to the edge of the bed and wraps my ankles around his neck. "What did I say earlier?" he asks in a gruff voice.

My naked center is against his cock but those damn briefs are still there. I want to see his cock, touch his cock, have his cock, and I want it now. "I was greedy?" I venture.

"I said I was going to fuck you." Suddenly the briefs are gone, and his cock is at my entrance. "Yeah?"

I pant. Then I reach for his cock, but before I can touch it, he thrusts inside me, and I cry out, "Yes." Ohmygod, it's been so long. So long without sex, but more importantly, so long without Ethan.

Then, abruptly, he pulls out. "Fuck."

"What?" I whine.

"Condom. I forgot."

"I... I'm good. Clean and IUD."

He seems to hesitate for a beat, but then he takes me again, his strokes slow while he nibbles my earlobe. "I'm clean too. Fuck, Grace. You taste so good. You have no idea how much I missed you. Everything about you. How you taste." He breathes heavily against my neck, pulls his cock out just enough to stroke my clit with it, then plunges back in, hitting my spot, making me arch my back. "The sound you make when you come." His cock beats heavily inside me, making me writhe. The pleasure is so intense, I'm ready to snap. "Come for me," he says, and I start to unravel. "That's my Grace," he says again, holding me.

I rake my fingernails down his back and onto his ass, pulling him tight inside me. "You're coming with me. Fuck me harder."

He lifts his head, slightly startled, then pummels me. My orgasm rolls out, my pussy clenches around him, and he grunts my name as he empties himself inside me. His weight on me is so good. The way his cock stretches me, the slickness of our combined sweat, the suction sounds of our reacquainting sexes. Everything is so good and so new and so familiar at the same time.

His body shakes under my hands, then stills. He holds me tight against him, running his hand all over me, until he reaches the slickness between my legs.

He gets off the bed and comes back with a warm, damp cloth. As he cleans me, he drops little kisses along my thighs and over my belly. My center is sensitive, bordering on sore, but god—I want this again.

My breath still heavy, I nudge myself against him, wanting to commit every moment to memory. I run my hand on his torso, reading him like Braille. His heart plays a hard drumbeat. Lifting my face to him, I catch him watching me. I sit up and straddle him, running both my hands on him, my center on his cock already coming back to life. His hands land on my thighs, slowly stroking.

In the ten years since I lost him, Ethan has become a man in full. Larger shoulders. Stronger neck. Hairier chest. "No tats?" I ask him, tracing the blue veins on his forearms, feeling them under the pulp of my fingers as I look him in the eye.

He shakes his head and his gaze leaves my face to start its own exploration. He lifts one hand to cup a breast, then trails down to my belly, making me slightly self-conscious. "Beautiful," he murmurs. He swallows, his Adam's apple bobbing, and for some reason that punches me in the gut. I lean down to kiss him there, softly. His hand comes to the small of my back and I lay my chest on his, wiggling to find the perfect spot where our bodies meld to each other like they were always meant to.

The first time we made love I was eighteen, and that day defined the rest of my life. I'd become a woman under Ethan's caring body, and as had been my wish for as far as I can remember, I would remain his forever and ever. With a love as perfect as ours, sealed by this ultimate act, nothing could keep us apart.

Not the fact that he was way too old for me. Not the fact that I was barely out of high school, and he was graduating college. None of that, in the grand scheme of life, could matter.

"We should keep the heavy stuff for the morning," Ethan says softly.

He even knows what I'm thinking. "M-hm." I wiggle my ass over his cock.

"There's my Grace," he says again, and those words, those three words rock my world and scare me and send me back a decade.

He lifts me off him and turns me over. "On your knees." His commanding voice brings me back to the present. Glancing at him, the hunger in his eyes is all I need to get wet. His cock is long and hard again. He gives it a few strokes, looking down my body with a lust that makes me pant.

Ethan *wants me* like no other man has ever wanted me. "Fuck, you're sexy. You make me crazy, you know that?" He places himself behind me, reaches over and plays with my nipple, his cock beating at my entrance. Then he fucks me like he promised.

When morning comes, whatever hatred I pretended to have is long gone.

All I have left is dread for when this comes to an end, but I've learned to take things one day at a time.

CHAPTER TWENTY-FOUR

Grace

When I wake up, the bed is empty. No Ethan, no Damian. I stretch, knowing from the sounds in the house that I'm not alone. I savor this moment. The smell of sex in the room. My night jersey, rolled in a ball in a corner after Ethan found it under my pillow. The knowledge that this is not over yet.

I know he said he could only give me last night, nothing more—it was a figure of speech. He's not leaving Emerald Creek just yet.

There's more to come. More to enjoy. More good days with Ethan.

I slide into the bathroom, and when I'm done, I grab his jersey, wear it butt naked underneath, and go look for my man.

It doesn't matter that we haven't been together in ten years.

It doesn't matter that I don't know where this is going.

No matter what, Ethan was always my man, and he always will be.

I see him on my little patio, wearing only his jeans, bare chested, bare feet, splayed on the one lounge chair, a coffee cup in one hand, his phone in another, Damian sprawled across his lap.

Glancing opposite him, out the window over the sink, I notice my jeep in my driveway.

On the kitchen counter, another cute travel mug from Easy Monday. This one is deep red with cutouts of white roses all across it. My belly does a little funny dance when I see it. My fingers tingle when I grab it. Sliding the lid open, I take a whiff.

Yesss.

I tiptoe to the patio and place my free hand over Ethan's eyes. Damian looks up and jumps off him.

"Hey," Ethan growls, setting his phone and coffee down and pulling me onto his lap. Before I can say anything, he's kissing me full-on, his stubble deliciously grazing my skin, his tongue making my lady parts come alive again, his cock twitching under my thighs. His fingers tenderly knead my nape, telling a story he's not saying with words.

Telling me how much he missed me.

I know.

I know Ethan.

I can tell.

He pulls out of the kiss and keeps me there, close to him, examining my features while I get lost in his deep blue eyes.

"You always had the most beautiful eyes," he says, echoing my own thoughts. "Deep brown with flecks of gold. And a halo all around. Like an angel." His eyes mist a bit and trail over my hairline, down to my mouth. "You were always my angel," he murmurs.

His words unravel me. For all the time we were apart, who was I really to him? How did he think of me? *Did* he think of me?

I shut him up with a kiss. When we come up for air, I echo what he said last night. "Why don't we keep the heavy stuff for another time. Another day."

He gives me his half smile and tucks my hair behind my ear. "Works for me." Then his gaze drops to the travel mug I set on the floor. "Millie said that'd be an appropriate design for this morning, and that a Sunrise Caramel Macchiato was definitely in order."

I laugh softly. "Millie's always right. She's a little witchy like that."

He pretends to frown. "I thought Cassandra was the witch. Is there competition?"

"More like an underground group."

Amusement flickers in his eye. "Ah. A conspiracy. I see."

I giggle. "Totally. A coven." I take a sip of the coffee and moan. "God, I needed this. So good."

His cock grows under me. "Mm. Better than sex?"

I grin. "Close second."

"Close second, huh? You haven't seen anything yet, Ms. Harper."

I blink several times. My core begs to differ. I saw *a lot* last night. I'm torn between a vague jealousy of all the women Ethan must have practiced with to become so accomplished, and an intense appetite to reap the benefits of his progress. The latter wins over, and I wiggle over him suggestively, feeling his cock harden under my bare butt.

He skims a hand over my thighs and his cock twitches when he reaches my ass. "You're naked under my jersey?" he growls.

"M-hm."

He sweeps his hand up my belly and cups my breast. "And you sleep like that..."

"Every night."

"Fuck." He sits up, lifting me with him. I'm so surprised, my brand-new travel mug whips out of my hand and lands on the floor with a soft thud. He knocks over his coffee cup and kicks his phone as he stands to carry me to the bedroom, shutting the door closed with his foot before Damian has a chance to hop in with us.

He sets me on my knees on the unmade bed, facing him. Rakes his fingers through his hair, looking at me. Leaning over, he ties a knot at the bottom of the jersey, revealing my naked slit. "Fuck, Grace." He grasps his crotch.

My mouth waters and I lift myself on my knees. "Let me."

"Turn around." I know what he wants. I want it too. But I want something else too. I want to pleasure him. I want to be his everything, if only for a few minutes.

Tracing my fingernails on his jeans, I lick my lips. "Me first."

He throws his head back and growls. Then looks down at me with hooded eyes as I unbuckle his belt, unzip his jeans, and free his heavy cock. "Fuck, Grace, your mouth... god I missed your mouth."

I slide to my knees on the floor and take him in, my eyes on his, savoring his taste, his smell, and his look of lust, of utter abandon. If I'd known yesterday that I'd be on my knees pleasuring Ethan this morning, I probably would have panicked over my lack of practice. But here, now, my own lust takes over, and I know, I remember what he likes, and I make up the rest. I take him deep, I lick his shaft, I suck and I tease with barely sheathed teeth, I moan when he's deep down my throat.

His knees buckle and he lifts me, carries me up to him and kisses my neck. "I need to fuck you in my jersey. I want to see my name on you when I come."

He sets me on all fours on the bed, my ass to him. "I wanted you to come in my mouth," I whine and look at him over my shoulder.

"Oh, I'll fuck your mouth alright." He hoists me to him and brushes a finger on my clit. "You're drenched. How come?"

"Your cock. I want your cock."

"Where?"

"In my mouth."

"That's it?"

"In my pussy."

"Take it." He drives into me, making me cry out. The remaining soreness from last night cedes to an intense pleasure I never thought I could experience. "You like that, don't you?"

"Ah."

"You like my cock, huh?" He pummels into me. Places a hand on my back, tracing his own name, *King*, right above where our sexes join. Then he grabs my hips with both hands and starts a punishing and exhilarating pummeling of my pussy. His pants and growls mix with the suckling sound of our joined sexes. "Take it, baby. Take my cock."

"Ethan!" I cry out. He's expertly massaging my G-spot with his cock, and now glides one finger over my clit.

"That's it. Ah fuck, baby, you're so good. So tight."

My inner walls clench at his words.

"Wench," he hisses. "Do that again."

And I do. I clench around his cock, and then I feel the orgasm take a hold of me, building up, so strong I wail and shake, and when his hot come spurts out, I cry out his name again and again. Glancing at the mirror, I see him clenching his jaw as he empties himself inside me, his eyes roll back, and his corded neck tenses. He orgasms for long seconds, his gaze on me, on my back, on us.

When he pulls out, I let out a small whine as his cock grazes on my sensitive center, leaving me with a dull soreness, yet wanting more. "I wanted you to come in my mouth," I pretend to complain as he spoons around me.

He pulls me closer to him. "You will." And his cock twitches again.

I chuckle. "You ever get tired?" I say, wiggling my ass against his cock so he knows I'm talking about sex.

He nuzzles my neck. "Not with you, it seems. He hasn't seen so much action in... forever, to be honest."

I warm at his words. It doesn't really matter, but still. It's nice.

"And he's ready to go again. But you need a break. Besides, we have all day."

I tense in his arms. We don't have all day. "I have an appointment at one."

"But it's Sunday."

"I know."

"You work on Sundays?"

I turn around in his arms to face him. He's so handsome, and I love the way he looks at me. Right now, he's frowning, his blue eyes darkened with concern. "I promised this client I'd fit her in."

"Why can't she come Monday or Tuesday?"

I shrug. "She works. And she has a kid. No dad. Grandma's looking after her kid today. So... She needs this."

His gaze darts between my eyes, but he says nothing.

I boop him. "I'm going to take a shower, then we can go for a ride or brunch somewhere, not too late? Whatever you want. I should be done with her before three."

He lets me leave his arms and settles on his back, gazing at the ceiling.

"Wanna join me in the shower?"

A slow grin spreads across his face as his gaze travels down my body. I slowly take his jersey off, leaving my hands up in the air and wiggling my ass at him as I leave the bedroom.

"Be right there," he calls after me.

CHAPTER TWENTY-FIVE

Ethan

W hat.

The fuck.

Is happening.

My heartbeat won't slow. My mouth is dry. My hands tingle from the absence of Grace.

I force myself to stare at the ceiling and empty my thoughts and ground myself.

I find that I'm not ungrounded, or whatever the word is. I'm not disconnected. There aren't a million different thoughts going through my mind.

I have only one thought.

Grace.

One feeling.

Completeness.

I have no other thoughts or feelings.

And that's a good thing. I'm in the moment. Present. That's all I need right now.

I look to the bathroom where she disappeared.

Seconds later I'm in the shower with her, lathering her luscious breasts. My balls are asking for a little time off, and I know she needs a break too. So my dick will have to sit this one out.

Grace looks down at me and licks her lips, then lathers my torso, slightly scraping her fingernails on my skin, hunger all over her face.

"Do *you* ever get tired?" I growl, echoing her earlier question.

"Not with you."

My dick twitches while my heart pinches at this. That she had others. But that it's better with me. Which, I get it, is probably something she or any woman would say anyway. But let's be honest. In my case? I think it's true. I think I'm the best she's ever had. Why? Not because I'm arrogant. Well, I *am* arrogant. But honestly, I saw the look on her face. She was at times surprised by my moves, always eager to follow, and her moaning? She could make porn stars blush. And one thing I know about Grace: she doesn't fake.

"Mm. Looks like you're not tired either," she says, stroking my now-hard cock under the pretense of lathering it. Looking down, I have a view of my rod in her hand, and her pebbled nipples dripping water. I palm her breast, flick her nipple, and she tilts her head up to me as she moans, water droplets running down her cheeks, the pink tip of her tongue running over her lower lip.

She strokes me hard, bringing the tip of my cock against her belly. Then she gets on her knees and looks at me pleadingly, and fuck me, but her expression right now? I could come all over her face just for that. So when she says, "Can I please suck you off?" and lowers her eyes to my cock, I'm torn. While she waits for my answer, she rinses the soap suds off my cock and licks her lips again.

Despite my earlier protestation of needing a break, I was about to fuck her against the shower wall, a personal fantasy I've yet to fulfill. I know, weird it hasn't happened yet, but I'm not mad I'll get to do that with Grace first. I can just see it, her glistening skin, the slickness of our bodies colliding, me holding her wrists above her head, driving inside her effortlessly.

She looks up at me, the shower hitting her face, making her blink. "Just fuck my face, Ethan," she orders in that small voice that always drove me wild, *"Just take me, Ethan, take what's yours,"* she'd said to me ages ago when she gave me her virginity.

"Do you like it?"

"I *want* it. With you, I want it. I *want you* to take your pleasure with me."

My dick weeps at her words. "But do *you want* it?"

She slides a hand between her legs and her eyelids lower as she nods timidly. This woman is utter. Perfection.

I place myself at her mouth, and good god she's hungry. She reaches over to turn the shower off. Then she sucks me off, checking on me to see if I like it, what I like, until she places both my hands on her head and motions for me to fuck her face.

So I do.

I could do this for hours. And I want to. But I don't want to put Grace through this for too long. So with a little regret and immense thankfulness for how she likes sex with me, I pull her off my cock. "I'm gonna come, babe." I hope she stays on her knees, so I can come on her face, or at least her breasts, but she takes me deep inside her mouth, and I hit her throat. She grabs my ass to pull me tighter, bobbing her head, sucking with her tongue, her cheeks, driving me wild with just a little teeth, and I empty myself in her. And I groan like never before. And I hold her head against my crotch, the tremors of my orgasm shaking my whole body. And when I'm done and she pulls out, she swallows one last time and as she stands, she wipes her mouth with the back of her hand and straddles my thigh.

"Fingers," she whimpers, and my god I can't believe it, but she's drenched, drenched from giving me head. She comes on my hand, on my thigh, and once her shaking subsides, I kiss her, and we both slide down to the shower floor and catch our breaths.

"Do you think I have a problem?" she asks in a small voice after a little time has passed. We're still on the shower floor.

I stroke her back. "What do you mean?"

"I-I just like sucking you off so much. It makes me wet just talking about it." She wiggles in my arms.

Ah fuck. My dick stands at attention. Again. "Yeah, no, I don't think that's a problem," I chuckle.

She nods, then after a few more beats swallows loudly.

"What is it?" I prompt her.

"Are-are all women like that?"

I look down at her. "I don't know about all women. All I know is, you're perfect."

Another loud swallow.

"What?" I ask teasingly.

"Am I? *Perfect* doesn't sound very sexy."

"Ah. I see. Hmm." How can I put it without scaring her away? "You're my dirtiest fantasies come true. How's that?"

"Now *that's* perfect." She seems to think about it. "Fantasies? Name one."

"Fucking against the wall. Fucking in the shower." That's two. I could go on. *Fucking you in my jersey.*

"You never had sex in the shower?"

Ouch. "No. You?"

"No," she says immediately. "But you seem so... experienced, I figured you'd done it all."

I have taken the exploration of the woman's body quite seriously, and especially the foreplay that leads to a woman craving a man. But sex in the shower? "Sex in the shower is... it's just too intimate."

"And yet here we are," she says.

And I don't know what to answer to that. What does she mean? That we're not intimate enough for that, or that we are?

CHAPTER TWENTY-SIX

Grace

"What time is it?" I'd better start getting ready. "Do we have time to go for brunch before my one o'clock?"

Ethan wraps both his arms around me, he gives me a squeeze and a long, soft kiss on my neck. My insides tingle, and my legs threaten to never be able to carry me again. I run my hand over his forearm, relishing the way he holds onto me as if he never wants to let me go. I tilt my head back and welcome his lips on mine. He lifts us effortlessly and wraps me in a thick towel, drying what's left of the drops of water. Then he grabs another towel and plops it on my head. "Show me how to do that," he says.

"Do what?"

"Wrap your hair in a towel. I wanna do that."

I do the top of the head twist and he helps me tuck it in. Then he turns me around and says, "What do you want for brunch?"

"Anything, as long as it's not too far."

"We're having brunch here."

I whip around to see him walk out of the bathroom, a towel wrapped around his hips. I almost lose my train of thoughts at the sight of him, half naked, in my space, like he lives here. *Storing that memory for future use.* "There's nothing in the fridge."

"I brought eggs and bacon from Lazy's. When I picked up your car." Dropping the towel, he pulls on a clean pair of briefs and a T-shirt from a small backpack he definitely didn't have yesterday. Did he stop by the farm this morning?

He definitely picked up my car, one way or another.

"Chris gave me a ride early this morning. Found your keys in your bag," he explains. "I hope that was okay?"

Why is the idea of Ethan rummaging through my bag sexy? I'd be offended if anyone else went through my stuff. "Yeah, sure." I unwrap my hair and pat it down, shaking the water out of my ears.

"And Chris's girlfriend gave me a little container of her pancake batter."

I gasp. I should really be focusing on the fact that everyone knows we spent the night together, but really—"Alex's pancake batter? Ohmygod, it's the best." My mouth waters and my stomach growls.

He pulls the T-shirt over his head, then plucks his jeans from the floor. "I swung by the farm to get a change of clothes. Mom had some fresh-pressed OJ. Dad said you were probably still good on syrup, but just in case, he gave me a jug."

Oh great. *Everyone* knows. I feel a little fuzzy inside, to be honest. Not even remotely embarrassed.

"You get ready." He boops me and strolls his tight ass down the hallway. "I'll cook you breakfast." My belly does a happy somersault while my eyes and my ears sear this memory in my brain forever.

I slide into my standard black slacks and white blouse, do my make-up, and tie my hair in a bun. The sounds and smells coming from the kitchen are positively sinful, and my belly growls.

My small kitchen table has been moved to the deck, two chairs catty-corner looking at the view, plates and napkins and even stem glasses set. Stem glasses!

"Hi, beautiful," Ethan says, setting a spatula next to the range, pulling me to him, his hands around my waist, his face inches from mine. His gaze is all kinds of dangerous—the good kind of dangerous. I set my lips on his, and he kisses me long and deep. Then, with a sigh, he says, "We better go sit down, or your client will never get her facial."

And that sends tingles down to my toes and right back up to my scalp.

"Grab the coffee?" he says as he takes a platter with scrambled eggs, grated cheddar, diced tomatoes, and a plate of pancakes. "And the syrup. It's warming in the microwave."

He serves me a heaping plate, but I feel satiated just looking at him. At his corded forearms while he pours the coffee—"Won't be as good as Millie's, but eh!"—at his frown when he plops a heaping spoon of scrambled eggs on my toast—"I should have asked you if you like them runny or dry. Which is it?"—at his sudden inhale when he takes a forkful of pancake dripping in King Knoll Farm maple syrup—"Oh god. Missed that shit. M-mhm."

His jaw flexes, his eyes open, he looks at the pancake in wonder. Takes a bite with no syrup. "Damn. Damn! That's good stuff right there."

"Yeah, it's her mother's recipe. Good, huh? Did she give you ghee to cook it in?"

He chuckles. "Got a whole list of instructions to go with it."

We eat in silence for a beat, Damian sprawled in the sun.

"Tell me about your spa. How'd you get started?"

I wipe my mouth and take a sip of Lynn's freshly pressed OJ. "When I came back to Emerald Creek, I started working at the resort spa. I'd been doing facials and nails and stuff for a while before that. I already had some certifications and training, and I got a few more while working there. The job at the spa was okay until it wasn't anymore. Too much drama. At that point, I had a steady stream of clients, and a lot of them were encouraging me to open my own place. It was a little scary, but I got with Emma, and she helped me with a business plan and finding financing."

"Who's Emma?"

"Oh right. She's not from around here, so you wouldn't have known her. She's our only CPA here. Most businesses use her. Strong woman. Raises her kid alone. She helped me—helped us—a lot, when Chris first came back home with baby Skye. With, you know, tips and stuff. Skye and her daughter are best friends. Lots of playdates and sleepovers. It helps."

"So she helped you start the spa?" he says, getting me back on track.

"Right. By that time, Colton and Chris were already starting their own businesses, so I knew it could be done. We'd talk a lot about the bottom line, and seed money, you know. And Kiara too. Actually," I pause with my fork midair, trying to remember the facts accurately. There's so much Ethan has missed! "Actually, we met Kiara at a start-up incubator we all attended. That's how we all became friends with her. And then she moved to Emerald Creek."

"She moved here?"

"Yeah." I wink at him. "Dunno if you heard, but we're hard to resist." I smile, but he takes a long sip of his coffee, exhaling loudly. "You okay?"

He sets his hand on mine. "Never been better."

I wave my fork in the air. "What was that, just now?'

He shakes his head slowly, his lips tilting up a little. "Nothin'. Just... you know."

"What?"

He nods slowly. "Feeling like I missed out on a lot of stuff."

"Ts'okay." I shrug. "I'm sure a lot of people who stayed here wish they could have had your career. Greener grass and all that."

"I guess. You only really know what you had when you lose it." His eyes mist a little when his gaze sets on me. His hand still on mine gives me a quick squeeze.

I set my fork on my plate. Take a deep breath to keep my own emotions in check. "We shouldn't do this. This-this-this what-if. It's gonna kill us." Tears well up despite my bravado.

He sits up straighter in his chair. "You're right. Tell me more about your spa. Your staff." His voice is cheery, his smile genuine. "Claudia's a hoot. How did you find her?"

"She's actually my latest recruit. I got her through Chris. One of his apprentices—Isaac—his dad is a real dick. Ended up in prison. His mom was looking for a job. I needed a receptionist. So I hired her."

"Simple as that, huh."

"Simple as that."

"How about the others?"

"Oh. I could write novels about the others. Never-ending drama. Lots of love. Lots to give. Okay so, Fabrizio—not his real name, but don't tell anyone—was trained in Paris—"

"—Really? Why isn't he Fabrice, then?"

"You can ask him that," I laugh. "He has a perfect eye for style and our brides *love* him. Shanice has the magical hands of a healer. Swear to god, some women actually choke up when she gives them a facial. She has some kind of gift. I'm trying to convince her to move onto massage therapy. And then we have Hope, our longest employee—she can do anything—and finally Cheyenne, our nail artist. And when I say artist, I mean it. She'll do your regular mani-pedis, but where she really shines is in her artistic creations."

I stop there, or else I'll bore him to tears. Probably already did.

"So what's with the landlord?"

"Oh." Between Ethan's lovemaking and my focusing on just my staff, I'd almost forgotten about *that* detail. "You know, he wants to sell the building. What can I do? I have a right of first refusal, but there's no way I can afford the house. I don't even want to contemplate that kind of a mortgage. It's too early for me."

"So if he sells to someone who wants to live there, you just have to pack up and leave," he grunts.

"Yup." I take another sip of OJ, but I'm not fooling myself. I just don't want to talk about it. I don't want to ruin this perfect moment.

He turns my hand in his, trailing the inside of my wrist. "What are your dreams for your spa, long term? Wherever it might end up being."

My heart stutters at his question. I love that he gets I don't want to talk about the lease issue, at least not right now. I also love that he refuses to see that bump in the road as the end of my business. "Long term, I want the spa to expand into a sort of... holistic wellness experience. It's still a little fuzzy in my mind, but... I don't know. I could see early morning meditation and yoga, or maybe even sublease one room to an acupuncturist to have that seem to be in-house. Things like that. Down the road, I'd like to organize day-long retreats with a whole range of offerings. But something that would make sense to the needs of each person. Something thought-out for them."

Ethan's gaze roams from my eyes, to my mouth, to my throat. It's official. "I'm boring you to tears."

He frowns. "Not at all, quite the opposite. You want to create a Wellness Sanctuary. Addressing mental and physical needs tailored to each individual. I think it's brilliant."

"Thank you." Now he's making me blush. "But we're only talking about me."

"Not much to say about me," he says, stacking his cutlery on his plate.

I down the last dregs of my coffee. "I'm sure that's not true."

He represses a smile. "Another time. We need to start moving if you want to make your one o'clock."

We clear the table, then carry it back inside. Ethan follows with the chairs while I shoo Damian back in.

"How long have you lived here?" Ethan asks while he does the dishes.

I stand next to him to wipe and put away. He doesn't ask me to stay seated, and I like that he seems to understand I need to move, and I need to put my things back where they belong. And also, I like doing that with him. It warms my heart. Another memory to keep safe for later.

"I bought the house about a year after I moved back. So what—four, five years? Something like that."

He seems to think about things and I expect him to ask me why I chose this house. I know he noticed. What am I going to tell him when he asks? I'll just say it was a coincidence. Total coincidence.

But he doesn't. Instead, he says, "Did you move back... right after your divorce?"

I take a deep breath. It's not as simple as that. "Before, actually. The divorce was final later. A few months after I moved back home."

He keeps his eyes glued to the dishes, scrubs a plate that's already clean. "What—what happened?"

How can I tell him? I'm not ready for this, not right now. Later. "Um... there just—there was nothing left for us to share. It..." I take a break and look at him, at his strong profile, his easy presence. "I'm not really ready to talk about it."

"That's okay." He hesitates. "Was it a bad breakup?" he pushes.

"Not the way you might think. He was a good guy. A real good guy. We just... had nothing. It just fizzled out."

I'm not ready to share with Ethan the deep loss, the wound I still carry around. But maybe, someday, we might get there. Maybe I can let him close enough to share this with him.

"Okay," he says softly, handing me the last plate.

After I put the plate away, he pulls me into his arms and runs his hand over my back. "Is someone's birthday coming up?"

I narrow my eyes at him. "Apart from Lynn's?"

He drops his head and laughs softly. "I'm not gonna live this down, am I? Who else knows about this?"

"Lemme see... the whole town?"

He shakes his head. "Any reason there's a shopping bag with a cute as hell swimsuit in your car?'

"A wh—? Oh!" I frown. "How? Oh right." He picked up my car, and I still have Cassandra's bag in it.

He nods. "So. Swimsuit?"

"A gift from Cassandra."

His lips graze my hair. "I like her taste. After your client, I'm thinking we should get you in that excuse of a bikini and go for a swim."

"Sure. I'll just need to go grocery shopping real quick before that. And then we can go for a swim. That'd be nice."

"And what's that booster seat? Is that for Skye?" he asks as he lets me reluctantly out of his embrace.

"Yeah. I guess, now that Alex is back for good, they won't need me as much. But... yeah. She has her bedroom upstairs too. With Chris's crazy hours as a baker, she used to spend a lot of time here, so we wanted to make her comfortable." It's going to feel awful empty, once summer is over, Ethan is gone, and Skye doesn't need me to take her to school anymore.

He grabs my waist and pulls me to him. "I'm sure they'll be grateful for the babysitting." He kisses my eyelids softly and gives me a squeeze, and I just love, love that he knows how I feel but also knows not to dwell on it.

Chapter Twenty-Seven

Ethan

Being with Grace is just so much more than I ever anticipated. Hoped for. Dreamed about. She was my dream woman when we were just kids, and she's even more so now. Funny, sweet, sexy, strong.

But mostly, she makes me feel... at peace.

My brief freak-out last night? Everything I feared is true. I'm falling hard for her. It's going to hurt like a bitch when I leave. But so what?

No regrets. I have no regrets. I could live a lifetime on the memory of this one night, this one morning with her. I don't need anything else. I've had it all.

This is the present, and I'm going to savor every second of it.

I snap a picture of Grace's shopping list before leaving her house on my bike. Just in case. She's working, I'm on vacation. It seems like the least I could do. I'm going to take a wild guess that she'd say no if I offered to do her shopping. Could be any reason. I just don't see her eagerly accepting.

Once it's done, though? Different story.

Or not. We'll see.

My saddle bags aren't huge, but Grace's shopping list is tiny. Toma-toes, ham, yogurt, basil cleaner—whatever that is.

Seriously. That's all that's on the list. What does she actually *eat*?

I stop at Noah's general store. There's no point going to the small supermarket on the outskirts of town. Noah will have it all. The store hasn't changed. I'm instantly thrown back decades by the slight bend of the wooden planks giving under my weight.

It's a large space, made of several buildings connected together over the decades. A deli corner on one side with produce and cold cuts and salads. Kitchenware on the other. The same seemingly bottomless barrels of candy are still at the very front, near the checkout registers and the greeting cards. There's a sign that says *'More cards at the bookshop.'* My third-grade teacher is sifting through them.

"Hi, Ms. Angela."

The little lady beams at me. "Oh hi, sweetheart." She puts the card back and picks another one up, turning it in her fingers. Louder, she says, "Noah, I'm rearranging your cards, if you don't mind. This doesn't make sense the way it's done. I'm gonna do it the way they have it at Shy Rabit."

Noah's muffled agreement sounds from somewhere in the middle of the store.

Cookies and sweets and canned goods are in the middle. Moving toward the back, three steps on the left lead to a wine cellar in a separate room. The clothing section is still central. Wandering farther inside, I notice a new section—pets. My eye lands on a toy that will be perfect for Damian, so I snatch it.

If nothing else has changed, farther inside will be toys, then hard-ware, construction and garden items, and finally the loading dock, for those heavy bags of seed, the occasional wheelbarrow, shovels, bags of sand. I resist verifying how many changes Noah has made. One thing that hasn't changed, is that this unassuming shop seems endless, and I don't have the required hours at the moment to tour it all. Another thing is the smell. Old wood and dust and burnt coffee. I guess they still have that terrible coffee machine. You could get a coffee for a quarter back in the day, and even that seemed expensive.

Fuck, but that smell brings back so many good memories.

I make my way back to the wine cellar, wondering what Grace likes.

"Heard you been busy."

Turning around, I see Noah, hands on his hips, big smile on his face. My forehead feels warm, just thinking about last night. About Grace's mouth under mine, her hands on my body, my jersey she's been sleeping in for years.

Noah extends his hand and pulls me in a half-bro hug. "Coaching hockey, helping out Thalia and Lucas... and your dad mentioned all the fences and barns you're repairing."

Shit. Now it's my chest feeling warm. What the hell? "Ah, just keeping busy."

"Damn. I missed you, dude." He glances at the bottle I'm holding. "How long you here for?"

"'Nother few days." I've yet to hear from my commanding officer. When I got here, I was anxious to get my orders. Now...

He nods slowly. "I uh... wonder if you'd mind talking to my kids—my coding club kids." He shakes his head. "Still summer, but most of them are around, and matter of fact, we're meeting tomorrow at the high school. They'd love to talk to you 'bout your career. Give'em some ideas."

Noah is tall and muscular, but in a sinewy type of way. His locks of blond hair are now trimmed shorter than they used to be, and between his slightly receding hairline, his glasses, his tan, and his corded forearms, my impression of him the other night at Lazy's is confirmed: he looks like an outdoorsy nerd. I bet the kids in the coding club love him.

"You run the coding club? Course I'll come. Tell me what time tomorrow."

He smiles. "We meet around noon."

"That for Grace or Lynn?" Ms. Angela's voice startles me. She materializes next to Noah, and she's looking at the Chardonnay I'm holding.

"Um…" I huff. Yep, small town.

Noah grabs two bottles. "Lynn is partial to her Finger Lakes Riesling, but if it's for Grace… you can't go wrong with this Russian River Zinfandel."

Ms. Angela nods. "What I was going to say."

I put the Chardonnay back. "I'll take both."

Noah gives me a wink that our retired teacher doesn't see and walks with me toward the front.

On my way out, I take some yogurt and freshly sliced ham from the cooler, then stop at the small produce section and start bagging a few tomatoes. Ms. Angela slides next to me and whispers, "If you could ever show me how to carve fruits, I'd love to. You know, for the bed and breakfast. You know I have a bed and breakfast now, right?" she adds.

"I heard about the bed and breakfast, and yes, I'd be happy to show you. Strawberries would be great for that."

I eye a colorful bouquet of flowers wrapped in a simple kraft paper and tied with twine. Would Grace like that?

"You know, I'm happy for you and Grace."

Well, we're not printing wedding invitations yet.

"You'll find a way," she adds, reading my thoughts, or her own fantasies.

I pluck the bouquet out of the bucket, turn it around.

"You were meant for each other."

I clear my throat.

"You're finally the right age and the right... everything for each other."

I shuffle my feet and can't help but feel the heat creep up my face again.

"She'll like the flowers. Nice and simple. Start small."

I pretend to put them back in the bucket. Getting the hint that she won't get anything from me, Ms. Angela mumbles something and scampers out under Noah's mild frown. I stick the flowers under my arm.

"D'you see Owen yet?" Noah asks as he weighs the tomatoes for me.

"Yeah, I bumped into him."

He smirks. "He's gotten better."

I have to chuckle at that. Owen was a bully when we were growing up. I had to teach him a couple of lessons.

"Believe it or not, he and Colton get along."

"Do they now?"

"Seems like you drilled some sense into him. Shit, I'll never forget that time." He laughs.

Back in the day, Colton was a scraggly boy. He took a while to blossom. Owen, on the other hand, was always big. He took advantage. I never could understand the appeal of being mean to others, but as long as it stayed within certain limits, I let Colton deal with Owen however he could. But one day Owen crossed a line, and I did too.

And I'm glad I did. Owen never bothered Colton again. Colton knew he wasn't alone. And Grace had even more hearts in her eyes when she looked at me.

What a bunch of idiots we were. I smile big at the memory. "His mom seems to like me," I drop.

"I bet she does. Gave him the whipping she couldn't. Hell, turned him into a close-to-decent human being."

"That's all we ever wanted."

"Amen to that."

We make our way slowly toward the front. I stop at a display of chocolates *"Proudly Made in Emerald Creek"*.

"Kiara makes those," Noah informs me. "They're dangerously good."

I snatch a box. "Hey, any idea what basil cleaner is?"

Noah frowns briefly. "If it's for Lynn, I don't know. If it's for Grace, here you go." He hands me an all-natural, all-purpose, organic liquid soap.

I take the soap. And feel that fucking blush again.

"Shit, man," Noah says, smiling, "never thought I'd see the day."

I chuckle slightly, hoping he doesn't elaborate.

But he does. "Ethan King buying groceries for Grace Harper."

"Cute, right?" Ms. Angela pipes up from god knows where.

I stifle a smile. "So—tomorrow, noon at the high school?" I say as I pay.

"Awesome. Thanks, man," Noah answers.

On my way out, I crane my neck to holler goodbye to Ms. Angela and literally bump into Colton coming in. He holds the door open for me and glances at my groceries. "That a Zin you got here?" he asks with half a smile. "You gonna carve the cork into... ah, forget it," he fumbles.

I hear Ms. Angela's cackle all the way to my bike.

As I fire my bike up, Colton pokes his head back out. "I thought you were gonna drop her off. The rattle."

I can't help the smile. "I will."

I meet Grace back at the house. She fusses over the flowers, tries different vases before settling on one. Then she folds the kraft paper carefully, places the twine on top of it, disappears toward her bedroom and reappears empty-handed.

The chocolates, she sets in a cupboard.

"Car or bike?" I ask her, pulling her out of the contemplative mood she seems to be falling in.

"Bike!" Grace answers right away.

"Really? The... the *chick magnet*?" I feign surprise.

She throws a beach towel at me. "How big are your little bags on the side?"

"The saddle bags? Big enough." I roll two towels tight and grab some water bottles, give Damian a scratch between the ears, and we're off.

The feel of Grace on the back of my bike is... more than I thought it would be. She's wearing jeans. *"I flashed enough of Emerald Creek last night"* was her excuse for foregoing a summer dress, and I like to know her better protected, even if the ride is a short one. When the road is straight or we're at a stop sign, I run a hand on her thigh and feel her tighten against my lower back.

God this woman. She's under my skin, always was, always will be. No matter what happens between us, she's the standard I've compared all others to.

It was unfair to them. Being back in Emerald Creek and being with her feels natural, and also a little surreal. As if I'm having a glimpse at what my life could have been, if it hadn't derailed.

Ironically, we reach the intersection where Justin had his accident, ten years ago. I slow down to take the curb, my head turning to where his car was propelled. Of course there's no trace of it, it's been so long. I wasn't even here after the crash, but knowing that's where it happened gives me chills anyway.

Thinking about it darkens my mood.

After a few minutes, Grace points to a carriage trail branching out from the road we're on. "Go as far as you can on that path," she yells over the roar of the engine. After a couple of minutes in a wooded area, I see the blue ribbon of the river below us just as the carriage trail turns into a path. When we can't go any further, I stop the bike and we gather our stuff from the saddle bags.

Grace is quiet, leading the way down to the river, to a flat rock that juts above the water. She lays the towel flat, meticulously pulling on its corners. Then she strips down to her bathing suit, folding her clothes neatly and setting them on the small side of the towel.

"Last one in the water is a chicken!" she cries and runs away from me, from the hug I was going to give her, from the words I was going to say to her.

And now I see it clearly. Now that's she's running away. I wanted that, with her.

This quiet, small-town life. The simple pleasures. The shared friendships.

I jump after her.

CHAPTER TWENTY-EIGHT

Grace

My body hits the water with a punishing slap, the cold seizing me. So many of my memories of Ethan are tied to the water—this very place on the river, and the lake. I need to shake the funk, wash away the tears threatening to spring, the regrets I no longer have any reason to have.

What only matters right now is swimming back up to the surface, taking a deep breath, calming my heart beat, being happy. I open my eyes and look up, to the liquid ceiling, Ethan's silhouette, the sun behind him. In a few strokes, I break to the surface right when he dives at a safe distance from me, then comes up, shaking the water droplets off his hair.

We look at each other and laugh. He swims up to me. "You always liked the water."

I used to, it's true.

Then he cups my head and brings his lips to mine. Pulls my body into his. I wrap my legs around his waist. "You know," he says, "this is the exact spot where I broke up with Amy."

I really don't want to be talking with Ethan about Amy. "Oh yeah?" Especially if he remembers where he broke up with her. Jesus. *TMI.*

"Yeah." He runs his hands along my back. "Because of you."

"Oh please." Really?

"She'd been mean to you... and I didn't like it. At all. You were what? Fourteen? It was the summer before college for me."

Something stirs inside me. I remember that time. She'd been constantly teasing me... Ethan runs a finger on my chin and says, "I couldn't stand to see how she was hurting you."

"I really don't remember that," I lie.

"Yeah, you do. You just don't want to talk about it. And neither do I. But you should know, that's what happened. It was always about you."

"Ethan, I was a baby."

He growls. "Doesn't matter." He nibbles on my lower lip, making me squirm in his arms, and I feel him grow against my center. "You were my person. Always were. Always will be."

"Ethan..."

He kisses my forehead. "That's just the way it is." His eyes go dark, then sunny as he grins wide at me. "Swim to the other side?"

We spend the rest of our time at the river swimming, kissing, exploring the riverbanks. At one point, we let ourselves drift too far downstream. The current is too strong to swim back up, so we resort to hobbling over the river stones.

When we get back to our spot, Ethan pulls me up the flat stone and onto his lap. "You're a tough cookie. Come here." He situates me so he can reach my feet, and starts giving the gentlest foot massage.

"God that feels good."

"Mmm. Better than... other places?"

"Almost." I watch him gently rub my sore soles. "I never gave you a proper massage."

"Um. Excuse me? I think you did."

"That was not a proper massage."

"What was it then?"

"First off, it was a mini massage. Second, it was... a little on the angry side. On my part."

He stops massaging my feet and pulls me to him. His tongue slides into my mouth, his hand under my bikini top, then he rolls on his back, taking me with him. "Fuck, I want you right now. Right here."

I stand and pull him up and show him the way. Under the flat stone is a cavity where shallow water flows in and out. It's the cleanest spot and totally private.

"Was this always here?" he asks.

"Couple of storms created this cavity, maybe two, three years ago."

"And you were keeping this all to yourself?" he groans, setting me gently on my back. "Fuck, Grace, I can't seem to get enough of you."

I close my eyes, keeping this precious confession forever in my heart. "Same," I breathe into his neck. "Take it off," I say, tugging at his swim trunks. He shakes them off and pulls my bikini off. Ethan's face is already between my legs, laving my folds, making me moan, his noises mingling with the lapping of the water under our bodies. He brings himself above me and enters me slowly. "You okay?" he whispers.

"God, you feel so good."

He groans and thrusts himself powerfully inside me.

"Yes! Ethan. Ohmygod. Ethan!"

"You're so wet for me, aren't you? So wet and tight." His torso rubs against my bare skin, pushing me hard against the soft river bed.

"Hold me, please, hold me tight," I beg against his neck, wrapping my legs around him, pulling him into me, my fingernails digging into his back.

"Yeah, baby. Mark your man."

I curl my fingers on his lower back, pulling him closer inside me.

"That's it, sunshine."

I come at his words, clenching around him as he empties himself inside me in forceful thrusts, the sound of his grunts and my wailing making me come even harder.

He rolls to his back and pulls me on top of him. "You gotta stop doing that. My balls hurt."

I go to sit up, but he holds me firmly against him. "Doing what?" I ask, horrified. Ohmygod, I am such a klutz! I feel myself blush in embarrassment.

His fingers trail on my back until he cups my bare ass with a full hand. "Being so fucking sexy. I just... I just wanna have you all the time."

"And that... that *hurts* your balls?"

"Looks like it. Too much sex."

Too much sex? Looks like it? Does he not have sex marathons on the regular? I would have sworn... Mmm... this new bit of information finds a nice little spot in my mind and promises to sit on a shelf where I can see it. Empowered by this knowledge, I wiggle against him and feel him harden under me. *Nice.*

His stomach growls and I lift my face to his. "When it's not you it's me. Hungry?"

"I guess. If I'm not gonna eat you..."

"I thought your balls hurt."

"They do. Come on, lets go."

I lift myself off him and look around. "Ethan?"

"Mm?"

"Where are our swimsuits?"

"Um... didn't you have'em?"

"Ohmygod." I crawl to the downstream side of the grotto. Nothing. Nothing at all. "Um... okay. Bad news."

"Commando?"

Looks like it. I peek out the opening of the cave. "Other bad news."

"That was a nice bikini. I'm gonna miss it."

"No, but really."

"What?"

"There're people on the other side. I can hear them."

"Fuck. Lemme see?" He crouches next to me. "Shit, are these... these the kids from camp?"

"Yeah. Only the boys, though. Looks like you're it."

"I'm it?"

"Yeah. You get to crawl naked up there and get our clothes."

He sighs but lets out an amused chuckle. "Okay then."

Standing upright, he leans his upper body outside the cave. "Yo, guys!"

"Hey, Coach! Everything okay?"

"Everything's fine. I just need you to turn around for a minute."

"Why?"

"Don't want to permanently damage your retinas."

"Coach! Are you naked?"

"Just turn around. Or watch at your own risk. No girls with you?"

"No..."

Ethan hoists himself up the flat stone. Moments later he comes back down with my clothes.

"Coach, you're not alone?"

"Coach, who is it?"

I giggle as I slide inside my shorts and sandals and button up my blouse. "Is it see-through?"

Ethan makes an appreciative face. "It's... very nice. Might wanna keep your back to the peanut gallery across from us, though."

I wrap my towel around my neck and pull up the sides to cover my breasts. "That'll do."

We exit our hiding place under the boys' claps and whistles. "I knew it! I called it!" they shout over the roar of the river.

I blow them a kiss, hurry to the top of the hill, and hop on Ethan's bike.

When we pull up my driveway, he stays on the bike. I have a little pinch in my stomach. But all good things must come to an end. "I had fun..." I start.

He pulls me against him. "Pick me up at the farm in an hour? I hear there's a pub in town, the Lazy something, they make decent burgers." He smiles against my mouth then strokes his tongue inside my lip. "I just need underwear," he chuckles.

Butterflies flutter all the way down my toes and up to my scalp. "You wanna go to Lazy's together?" Going to my favorite place with my favorite person? Things are getting dangerously perfect.

"Unless you want to go somewhere else? Whatever you want." He cups my ass in his hand and growls slightly. "I better go."

When I get to my bedroom, I notice his small backpack still on the floor. He didn't take it back. I shower off the sand from the river, singing the whole time.

Half an hour later, I'm at the farm. Lynn and Craig are sitting on the front porch, sipping iced coffee. They both greet me with warm smiles as I come up the steps.

"Isn't nice not to have to sneak around anymore?" Craig cracks.

Lynn elbows him, and a drop of coffee lands on his shirt.

"What?" he says. "About time these kids know they don't fool no one."

Lynn pats the chair near her. "Come, sit." There's a third glass of coffee on the wicker table. Lynn fills it with ice cubes from an ice bucket and hands me the glass. "Here. This one's for you."

I take a sip in silence, awaiting an interrogation. Jokes. Some sort of expression of whatever mood they are in. Nothing comes. "It's so quiet," Lynn finally whispers. She leans her head on the back of her chair and closes her eyes. "Enjoy the quiet times, darling. Before you know it, you'll be like me. A house full of shouting, fighting boys." With a sweet smile contradicting what she says next, she adds, "If the universe is mean enough, you'll have a girl, too, just to ensure you can never find your clothes or your makeup in the morning. And forget about ever having perfume. That thing'll be gone just like that." She snaps her fingers.

Ethan's silhouette appears in the doorway. He leans on the frame, crosses one bare foot over the other, and looks at me tenderly. "I see you're getting the King Family pregnancy protection talk." His voice does funny things inside me. It's the first time I can look at Ethan the way I always wanted to and not have to hide it. It's the first time I'm at Ethan's place and I'm in a... *situation* with him.

And it definitely is the first time he prowls toward me in front of his parents, lifts me, and sits me on his lap. "Are you drinking my coffee?" he says with a smile.

Lynn's eyes are open and on both of us, wonder in her gaze. She reaches for Craig's hand and pats it.

"Don't get too ahead of yourself, honey," Craig says. "Give the kids some space."

She closes her eyes again. "Alright, alright."

Ethan pulls my back snug against his front and hands me the coffee. We sip from the same glass, watching the cows grazing in the distance, the breeze playing in the maple trees, monarchs fluttering from milkweed to zinnias to coneflowers. Ethan's hand plays in my hair, his breath tickling my neck. I turn my head to the side, where the swing sways slightly. How many times did I sit there, dreams in my head? *Look at me now*, I internally whisper to the little girl from the past. *Look at me now.*

She smiles back at me.

At Lazy's, Ethan picks a booth in the back and slides in next to me. Haley comes to our table to take our order. One look at us, and she's sitting across from us. "Finally. Fucking finally!" Leaning over the table, she grabs my face and loudly kisses my cheek. "Damn it." Then, turning to Ethan, says, "What took you so long?"

Ethan blushes, suppresses a smile but doesn't quite succeed, and looks down at the menu.

Haley reaches over and takes the menu from him. "Regulars don't look at the menu. Either you know what you want or you ask Shane to pick for you."

"Burger."

"Burger," I echo.

Haley frowns. "Huh. You never order the burger. What happened?"

I lift my eyebrows at my friend. "I'm hungry?"

Pink tints her cheeks. "Gotcha." She stands and snaps the menu from Ethan. "Lemme get out of here before you overshare."

"Don't overask," Ethan calls after her.

"Overask what?" Justin asks as he appears at our table, his girlfriend Chloe tucked under his arm.

I've never seen my friend this truly happy, and it sends happy vibes down to my toes. Chloe is beaming. Those two really deserve to be happy together.

"You guys coming tomorrow, right?" Justin asks, his hand playing with Chloe's hair. She turns to him, a dreamy smile on her face. Ethan looks down at me, the same dreamy look in his gaze.

It's scary.

"Going where?" Kiara says as she slides across from me in our booth.

"Barbecue at my parents'," Justin answers. "Mom wants a small family dinner."

My belly clenches. It's everything I've ever dreamed of, but it's way too soon.

"Oh, how cute!" Kiara says, "Family barbecue with the two older King brothers finally hitched."

Chloe blushes while I dip my chin to avoid the stares.

"Oops. Too soon?" Kiara asks.

Ethan places a comforting hand down my back, as if he can read my unease. We haven't talked about the future yet, or about what we are to each other right now. We've covered the past, although barely, and the part that's clear is that we messed up and never should have broken up. But life went on for both of us after that, we went our different paths, and you can't always just retrace your steps. Just because we're loving every second of our time together doesn't mean we can skip some steps.

"You mess up again, Grasshopper?" Colton says as he joins our group.

"Story of my life," Kiara answers, rolling her eyes. "Is my car ready?"

"Are my cupcakes ready?" Colton shoots back.

"Ugh. Okay, gotta go bake, guys. Keep me posted," she says to me as she leaves.

"Kiara, wait up!" Chloe says, following her.

"I'll check on your order," Justin says, leaving the three of us alone.

Colton sits in the spot Kiara vacated. "Wassup," he says, looking at Ethan.

"She's making you cupcakes?" I tease my brother.

He shrugs. "For this girl I'm seeing."

Oh. "Is it serious?"

He frowns at me like I'm crazy. "No."

That's my brother. Few words. Nice. "Wassup, man?" he repeats to Ethan once our burgers are served.

"Not much," Ethan says and tears a bite off his burger. "Want a beer?"

Colton doesn't answer, just stares at Ethan.

"What's up with you?" Ethan finally asks, as confused as me.

"If you're gonna keep taking my sister on your bike," Colton finally says, "I want to check that rattle."

Ethan breaks into a smile. "Gotcha."

"Keys."

"Now?" Ethan takes his keys out. "I'm sure it's nothing."

Colton snaps the keys from him, prowls outside, starts the bike and crouches next to it.

Ethan takes his eyes off Colton and looks at me. "Colton was always super protective of you." He clears his throat, opens his mouth like he's about to say something, then stays silent.

"What?"

"Nah, nothin'."

I set my burger on my plate and stare him down. "What."

He clears his throat again. "Way back then, your dad... went to talk to my dad... about us."

I stiffen. They knew? I kinda got that from Craig, earlier, at the farm. But I certainly never suspected our parents *talked* about us.

"Dennis wasn't happy about it. To say the least. My dad told him he trusted me, and he didn't like to mingle into his children's... lives. Or that aspect of their life, unless something was really wrong. And he didn't see anything wrong with us."

My anger flares up at the idea of Dad going to talk to Craig. "When was that?"

"After I graduated college. You were eighteen. The reason I remember is that..." He takes a long draw on his drink.

"Yes?"

"We hadn't kissed yet. Or rather," he adds with a small smile, "*I* hadn't kissed *you* yet. And... it made me hesitate for maybe... half a second?"

I'm woozy from his last words, but anxiety knots me over what happened with my dad. "Why? What did he tell you?"

"In no uncertain words, to stay away from you."

What?! "That's crazy. When? How?"

"I had just gotten back from college. I came by your house to see you, but you were out. He told me there was no point in me coming to see you. Next day, he showed up at the farm." Ethan pauses, an uneasy look on his face.

"He was drunk," I whisper, stating the obvious to ease him into telling me everything. We've never discussed our parents before. Not like that.

"After my dad told him to cool it, he threatened to file charges."

Blood leaves my face. "What?! Charges for what?"

"Nothing that would have made sense, even less held in court. But your dad... at the time he was..."

He was a mean drunk. I blush in shame at the memories. There's a reason I never talked about it with Ethan. I was too ashamed. Even now, realizing he knew, I don't know how I really feel about it. I'm proud of Dad for going through rehab. For being years sober. But the stigma of who he was, back then, the mean things he would say to Mom, the unfair way he would treat Colton. All this slaps me in the face.

"What did he do?" I whisper.

"He ordered me to stay away from you. And he brought Colton along."

I frown. "Colton?"

"First I thought it was because Dennis still had enough wits about him to not drive drunk, and he wanted Colton behind the wheel. And maybe that was the reason, initially. But then he told Colton, *ordered* him, to report anything suspicious going on between the two of us. He said it in front of me, so I knew my friend was ordered to spy on me."

My heart hammers and my eyes well. That was the sort of manipulation Dad would get into when he was drunk. Which at the time, was... always. He'd threaten. Destroy friendships. Almost destroyed our family, until Mom threatened to walk out on him.

Fun times.

The lump in my throat isn't going anywhere. My heart clenches. Sweet, sweet Colton never said anything to me. "He never would have said a thing."

"I know. I just couldn't risk getting him in trouble, if word got out. And at the time, I knew—well, I *thought* I'd have you all to myself at some point in the near future. That it was just a matter of time and there was nothing Dennis could do. I could wait a little."

I pinch my lips, battling the resentment growing inside me. Dad has fought hard to become a better person. I can't fault him for the sins of a past he's trying to atone for.

"I'm glad he's better, Grace. I really am. I only brought this up because... I guess, seeing Colton so protective of you—it brought back memories."

"I'm glad you told me too... all this time, I really believed you weren't really that much into me. That you were ashamed, hiding me because I was still too young for you."

Ethan looks at me in shock. "I built you a treehouse. You had many boyfriends do that after me?"

I laugh.

Ethan takes my hand softly in his. "Hell, Grace, any boy had you, they'd want to show you off."

I nod quietly. Now it's beginning to make sense. The treehouse, the secret meetings. None of this business of having my dashing date pick me up, come inside the house, have my Dad give him the talk. Does Dad even realize how much he messed up his own life, let alone the lives of his loved ones?

Ethan's hand closes around mine. We've both lost our appetite. "I'm so sorry you had to live through that with your Dad. And I'm so sorry you felt that way about me. I kind of assumed you knew, that he'd told you as well, but I didn't want to rub it in by bringing it up, at the time. I just wanted all of our moments to be happy."

"He's much better, you know," I say to excuse my father. "Night and day."

Ethan nods slowly. "I kind of got that impression at the farm. I'm happy for you."

We both play with our food for a bit, trying to climb back up to happiness, until Colton comes back and slides the keys on the table. "All set, man."

Ethan gestures to the empty seat in front of us. "Lemme buy you dinner."

"Won't say no to that," my brother says.

And now I'm looking at my two favorite men, sitting across from each other, stupid jokes flying, and my appetite is back.

Until Ethan's phone chimes, and his frown is a total mood killer.

CHAPTER TWENTY-NINE

Ethan

My phone chimes with a text message, and I make the mistake of checking the screen.

Shit.

I pocket the phone. I'll answer later.

Grace's gaze on me is questioning but warm. She wants to know, but she'll let me share on my own time.

We go back to talking shit with Colton, which is way more enjoyable.

When we get back to Grace's place, the sky is turning pewter. There's still time to enjoy the day. I open up the bottle of Zin I bought earlier and pull out two stem glasses.

While Grace is in the bathroom I call Damian. "Hey, bud, look what I got for you." The laser light is an immediate winner, and my four-legged friend is running around the living room like crazy, jumping the couch, pounding into the air, crashing into furniture.

"Ohmygod, what did you feed him?" Grace half shrieks, half laughs when she joins us.

I hand her the gadget. "Here. Got that at Noah's store. Isn't it cool?" I pour the wine and slide the porch door open. Damian trots behind us—or rather, behind the red dots bouncing randomly around.

"You spoiled little cat," Grace coos as she sits on my lap in the single lounge chair.

My phone digs into my hip. I pull it out to set it on the floor. Then I take a long draw on the wine and set my eyes on Woodbury Knoll. "That was my commanding officer, earlier. Sent me a message to let me know I should get ready to go back in a couple days." I feel Grace tensing against me, so I add, "It'll just be for a week or two of meetings." Hell, there's no avoiding it. "But after that, I won't have much time left. I'll see where they send me."

She sets her glass on the floor and moves on my lap so she can look at me. "I thought you were going to Brussels?" Her voice is barely audible.

I smile feebly at her, not even asking how or where she got that information. It's true, that was what I was hoping for. "Ultimately, I'll go wherever I'm needed. But yeah, Brussels would be quite the career move."

"What's in Brussels?"

"NATO."

"You deserve the best, Ethan, and if Brussels is your dream post, I hope you get it. I *know* you'll get it." Her eyes are shiny, but her smile is genuine. "Now tell me what you'd be doing."

I take a sip of the wine, let it swirl in my mouth, swallow slowly. "For NATO, it'd be doing anything from cyber defense initiatives to protect communications, to threat analysis, or it could be partnering with countries or other international organizations, training and exercises, incident response... whatever they need. It's part of what we'll be assessing in the next few days. The world is a scary place, Grace. Potentially the most dangerous wars are fought online now. That's where guys—and girls—like me come in. We always need to be one step ahead."

She looks at me with a devious smile and sets one hand on my chest. "Do you spy on the bad guys?"

I grin. "One step ahead, baby."

"Too bad this has to be in Brussels."

"Could be Maryland, or Florida."

"For NATO?"

"No—that would be NSA in Maryland, or the Air Force could want me in Florida, or Texas. We'll see. Like I said, wherever I'm needed."

She plays with the top button of my button-down shirt. "And so—where you're going soon, that's..."

I set my glass on the floor and my hands on her hips. "Undisclosed location. Basically, we gotta talk through shit." I'll be in top-secret meetings where needs and skills will be discussed and evaluated, and then I'll be posted wherever it makes the most sense to the powers that be. I used to find that exciting, rewarding. I felt needed, valued.

I'm not sure I feel that way anymore.

And then there's the fact that when I got here, I couldn't wait to leave.

Now, I'd rather stop time and just stay right here forever. "I'll come back for a few more days. But after that..."

She nods softly, resigned. Sets her hand on my shoulder. "Then you should spend the night at the farm. With your parents."

That catches me by surprise. I thought we'd had a good day. The river was fun, and so was having a dinner at Lazy's. And I feel like we've opened up to each other a lot. We've talked about the past and fixed some misunderstandings. It was good but exhausting. At least to me it was. "Would you rather be alone tonight?"

Her eyes narrow on me. The nerve on the side of her eye is twitching, and I'm not sure what to make of that. "That's not what I said. I just suggested you might want to go home tonight."

"I don't have a home." What I really want to say is, *Home is where you are*. But that'd be crazy, right? I might scare her away.

"Don't ever say that again, Ethan. Your home is here, in Emerald Creek."

"What I mean is—"

"I think I know what you mean. But a house isn't a home. A home is where you're loved no matter how long you stayed away. No matter how far away you are. It's where you live in people's hearts."

My throat tightens and my eyes prickle. "Okay. I'll sleep at the farm tomorrow, after the barbecue." Even though where I feel at home is right here, with Grace.

She cups my face in her hands, just like I love to do with her. "Get used to it. You're loved here."

I pull her into me, tightening my arms around her, burying my head in her hair, inhaling her scent as I try to contain my emotions. How am I going to go about my day-to-day without her by my side now?

"You know," she says softly, her cheek against my chest, "I never understood why you stayed away from Emerald Creek for so long. Why you didn't at least visit your family once a year or something."

"My folks came to visit me," I counter, feeling defensive and trying not to show it. "They said it gave them a reason to travel." My hand goes up and down her back in a gesture that's soothing to me.

"Right." She grabs the laser beam off the floor and plays with it, sending Damian in a frenzy. "It's just... you used to love it here, and then your siblings didn't get to see you that often. Why? What happened?" She straightens on my lap, looking me in the eye.

I shrug.

"You don't want to tell me," she drops, waving the hand that holds the laser in the air, in a gesture of disbelief.

Damian jumps over us to try and keep on top of his perceived task.

I stay silent.

Grace drops the laser beam. "That's not going to work. You need to help me help you." She swings one leg over so she's straddling me, nesting her center against my dick, plunging her gaze into mine. "Talk to me."

I take a deep breath. "I uh... I took Justin's accident personally. Meaning, I felt responsible for it. And... I felt like me being here, healthy, alive, was just pouring salt on a wound."

"I don't understand," she murmurs, a deep frown shadowing her features as she strokes my hair.

I close my eyes and lean my head back against the lounge chair. "I can see now how stupid it was, and maybe I was just scared, unable to face the mess I felt I had created."

"What mess? What are you talking about?"

"I didn't look after Justin. I was dismissive of Audrey. All this wouldn't—shouldn't have happened. The fucking butterfly effect," I add, hoping she won't ask for an explanation. I'm getting exhausted.

"M-hm." She's still stroking my hair. "Did you ever think how it made your parents feel?"

I open my eyes. Can I tell her this? Will she understand? I don't want her to judge my parents poorly. I'm the one who fucked up. "I think at the time, they sorta wanted me gone."

I feel her stiffen on my lap. Her hand stops stroking my hair. "How can you say that? They adore you." Opening my eyes to meet hers, I see compassion, not the disapproval I was expecting.

"They wouldn't let me postpone my departure. It's like they *wanted* me to leave."

"That was your misplaced guilt talking."

"Pretty sure Mom said I owed it to Justin to go live my life the way I had it planned out. I couldn't delay because of him. Although I wanted to. I would have done anything to help him out. I was going through hell after his accident."

Grace's eyes fill with tears, and she tugs at my hair. "Oh, *honey*. You know Lynn. Somewhere between her heart and her mouth stuff gets mumble jumbled and she can say the worst things ever at the worst possible time but with the best intentions. I mean, pretty sure even our sweet Sophie is writing an anthology with all the collected material at this point."

I chuckle at the fair point she's making. "Sophie?"

"Sophie Yarwood. She's our librarian now. And she writes stories. No surprise there."

"Sweet," I say, remembering a nerdy and lovely girl our age who would insist on writing the screenplays for our high school shows so our productions would be original and royalty free.

Grace brings us back on topic. "You need to talk to your mom. There's no way she said it the way you took it. No way."

"I'll talk to her tomorrow. When we go to the barbecue," I add, squeezing her hips in my hands.

Her gaze strays off my face. "About that. I might-I think I'll pass. Tomorrow is just the Kings."

I look at her but only a grunt comes out of my chest as I think of all the arguments against this. That she's mine. That we've always been together. That she's always been family. "Chloe is coming," I counter.

"She and Justin are together. She's as good as a King. Did you see how Justin wouldn't stop touching her?" *I'm always touching you too. Right now you're on my lap. At the bar I was playing with your hair, stroking your back.* "They're so cute together. He really deserves to be happy." *Yes he does. You do too. Me? Debatable.* "And she doesn't take his shit, lemme tell you. She's something else." *And you're in a league of your own.* "Don't you love her?"

"I love you," is what comes out of me, raw. There. I said it. This isn't a fling. An interlude. This is the real deal and I need her to know it.

Her hands clasp around my face. "And I love you too, Ethan. Always have, always will." Her voice is a bit shaky. She doesn't lean down to kiss me. "No matter what happens now."

No matter what happens now? What does she mean? "So what you're saying is... we're not really together."

And are we? Back together? I can't decently think this way until I have my shit together, and that means a plan of action. Next month, next year, next ten years, the rest of our lives.

"What I'm saying is, I don't feel comfortable going to a small family dinner..."

I shut my eyes and clench my jaw. I want that, god I want that so much. I want my name on more than just the jersey she sleeps in.

"...yet," she adds, reading my emotions. "I need a little time. And also, we haven't talked about... us."

"Yet," I counter, pulling her against me. Her lips finally find mine, and her hands get lost in my hair and my grunts are echoed with her moans.

I stroke her neck when she breaks the kiss to nuzzle against my chest. "Would you? Want to..." Fuck, I can't ask her this way. This is no way to propose to anyone, and certainly not to Grace.

"You don't always get what you want, Ethan." She turns to me, eyes shiny but chin firm. "You and I... all this is very new. We can't just pick up where we left off. Even if it sometimes feels like it's what we're doing, there's a lot to... to think about... and consider. I mean..." She makes an all-encompassing gesture. "This is where I live. This is my world. I've got Dad, who's sick. I've got Skye. I've got Mom and even Colton. My spa. My staff. My clients. And you have your ultra-top-secret career. Here one day, gone the next."

I love, love that she's already thinking about all that. She's level-headed, if you exclude the squirreling tendencies—but even those, I can rationalize. I can see her point. And I hate that I'm who made her that way, in a sense. I bring her mouth to mine and kiss her tenderly. "You've always been the one for me, Grace. But you're right, this is going very fast."

She closes her eyes, and I suspect it's to keep the tears in.

"Grace? I love you. You're the love of my life. I... I want to find a way where I stop hurting you. Stop messing it up. I want to find a way for us." I just don't know where it is.

She shuts me up by kissing me again. When she looks up at me, tears are streaking her cheeks. "I love you too. And I'll say it again. Always have. Always will. No matter where your path takes you."

"I know." And she'll always be my home.

CHAPTER THIRTY

Ethan

The next day at noon sharp, I roll into the high school. Noah greets me at the door and lets me in. Just like when I went to the Arena, the familiarity and good memories make me smile like silly.

"They're super excited to see you," Noah says.

"I am too. It's so cool you're their advisor."

"I mean—*super* excited," he emphasizes. "Not all of them could make it, though," he says, pushing a door open to let me in, "but these are the die-hards."

Two boys and two girls, who look as if they range from ages thirteen to eighteen, are standing at a table, in a semi-circle facing the door. On the table there's chips, soda, pizza, paper plates and cups, and colorful paper napkins.

"Welcome to our club," a third boy who's not standing says. He maneuvers his wheelchair to swiftly come greet me, extending a strong hand. "Honored to meet you. I'm Zach."

I shake his hand. "Zach. Wow. I didn't expect lunch. This is... thanks so much. You didn't have to do this," I say as I'm introduced to each one of them.

"It's the least we could do," the youngest one says, a boy who looks barely thirteen. He stiffly grabs a paper cup. "What would you like to drink?"

"Why don't we just sit down," Noah says. We pull up some chairs, start eating, and the ice breaks. These kids impress me with their questions. They don't need me to tell them the difference between cryptography and cryptanalysis. No, they jump right in with questions about cryptographic nonce, elliptic curve cryptography, and P vs NP. One of the girls asks me pointed questions about blockchain technology. The other one wants to know what she should study to work for the NSA. The third boy, the quietest, engages me on the software I use. "What do you think kids our age should look into? Like, since we're the future," he asks.

Good question. "The future is probably in post-quantum cryptography. Uh... one of the challenges we're going to face is that quantum algorithms—like Shor's algorithm—could theoretically break current cryptographic systems. So it wouldn't hurt if sharp minds like yours got a head start on that."

They exchange looks that go from excited to downright worried. "Meanwhile, for fun, look at ethical hacking and CTF competitions." They all nod like this is already what they're doing.

Which they probably are.

"Are all the jobs in big cities or like... underground in Texas?" Zach, the oldest of the group, asks me.

"They're everywhere, but—and you know this—nowadays, with a skillset like that, you can work from anywhere. Remote. Maybe not right away when you get started, but down the line? For sure. So, something to think about."

We talk about different careers, gaming, and growing up in Emerald Creek. I end up staying way longer than I planned, and yet I don't want to leave.

"Thanks so much, man," Noah says when he walks me out. "You can't imagine how much it means to them."

"They're great kids. And thanks for lunch," I add, slapping his shoulder.

"That was all the kids. Their idea, their execution."

"Awesome." I look at him for a beat, envious of his life. I almost tell him as much, but I don't. After all, this could have been my life, if I'd wanted to.

After that, I go to the farm alone.

"No Grace?" Mom asks me as she pecks my cheek tenderly.

I shrug. "We want to take it slow."

"Well that's a refreshing change," Dad says as he walks in.

"Is that what you kids call taking it slow these days?" My younger brother Hunter is holding up a pair of black briefs and a very familiar red bikini.

"What the hell?" I pretend to look shocked, confused, angered.

"You're welcome," he says, wrapping the bikini bottom around my head while I try to swat him away. He holds my briefs at a distance, between two fingers, looking disgusted. "Mom, you need to teach him how to clean his underwear."

"Shut up, you moron," I say as I grab the briefs from him.

"Ah, the river took care of it," Haley says as she joins the fun. "Clean enough for a military guy."

Meanwhile, Logan is walking around, back arched, top of the bikini wrapped around his jutted pecs, lips pursed as he says, "I'm so sexy, look at me Ethan."

Now I'm pissed. *Pissed*. I could break his nose. Make him, literally, swallow his words. But that'd be messy. Instead, I walk casually up to him, and in no time I have him in a choke hold and joint lock.

I know the feeling. I've been there. It's so painful you can't make a single sound. That's the beauty of it. The choke hold makes you almost pass out but not quite.

"I'm going to let you go now, and you will never, ever, make fun of Grace again in any way. Blink once if you got me."

He blinks.

"I didn't hear that."

He blinks furiously.

"That was several times. There is no meaning for several times. Be clearer. One for 'you got me,' two for 'you don't care that much about your life'."

"What's that called?" Dad asks, totally undeterred by his older son exercising interrogation techniques on his younger son.

"Is he okay?" Mom asks. "I think he got it, hon. He blinked."

I whip my face to her, ignoring Logan. "He did? I didn't catch it."

"Fuck, that's wicked," Hunter says while Haley picks up the bikini top and carefully folds it. They're all crowding us.

I think I made my point.

I let Logan go. He takes a few seconds to recoup, get his breath back, get motion in his arms. Then the little fucker turns to me and says, "That was wild, man. You gotta teach me that."

Fuck but I missed that. Missed messing with my brothers. Missed having them mess with me. Yeah, I had a family in the service. But nothing like that. Nothing like blood family, at least this one.

"Yeah, show us," Hunter echoes.

"You sure? I can't show you until you experience it. You have to go through it first to know what you're doing. And even then. You gotta be careful."

"Show us," he insists.

"Jesus," Haley sighs and rolls her eyes.

"Lunch is almost ready," Mom says, trying to deflect her boys from dangerous activities.

"After lunch then?"

I chuckle. "You do *not* want to do that after eating. Trust me."

"Real quick, now."

Mom rolls her eyes. "Take it outside, then."

"I'm coming too," Haley says. "You never know, these days."

"You comin'?" I ask Justin.

He peels himself from Chloe. "What the heck, why not."

Chloe follows him.

After I show them a few moves, and after we eat way too much, and after we lounge outside in the shade, and after we shake the slumber off by walking through the pastures, and after my siblings are all gone, I sit alone with Mom and Dad on the deck. After meaningless chit chat, I say out of the blue, "I can't believe I messed up Mom's birth date. How could that happen, I thought for sure it was July 19."

Dad sets a hand on my thigh. "That was your Grandma's birthday. She passed the day right before."

Grandma? I haven't thought about Grandma in... forever. Literally. My heartbeat pumps up, emotion overcoming me. Tears prickle at my eyes.

"You okay, son?" Dad says.

Mom leans to me. "Oh, honey."

I take a deep breath. Look at my parents, asking for... for what exactly? What the hell is happening to me, in this moment? So many emotions flooding me. A memory I've suppressed pretty much all my life.

"She was... your mom, right?" I ask Dad.

Mom sighs. "Yes. She... your dad and I, we eloped. You know that—right? Our families weren't... happy that we were together and they... wouldn't talk to us. Neither side. Anyhoo, a few years after you were born, my parents died in a plane crash, and I inherited the... proverbial farm. We came to work it. Your dad's parents came around and we reconnected. Your Grandma would come during growing season to help with you and Justin."

I remember. She'd wear a flowery dress. We'd make apple pies. Finger paint outside. She taught me how to read. As the memories flood back, even her sweet violet scent comes back to me.

"One day, the day before her birthday, we came back and she... she was gone."

"Gone?"

Dad nods. "She'd died in her sleep. During her nap."

"You were so good," Mom says, patting my lap. "You don't remember?"

I frown. No, I don't.

"You thought she was cold, so you'd covered her with your blankie. You even changed Justin."

"You were quite the little man," Dad says.

And then it comes back to me, like a gigantic slap in the face.

Justin crying from his crib.

Grandma so cold.

And me. Me. Such an idiot. I knew what you were supposed to do when an accident happened. You called 9-1-1. I knew how to use the phone. I'd even been through it in my head. *If Grandma falls and can't get up, I dial 9-1-1 from any phone. I stay calm and tell them my address and what happened. Same if there's a fire. 9-1-1. Stay calm. Tell them where I am.*

But Grandma was sleeping. And I knew you weren't supposed to wake up adults. Adults need their nap time. Just like babies like Justin.

I remember the smell of baby poop lingering on my fingers, and it remains linked to the shock of understanding I hadn't done what I was supposed to do for Grandma.

It was simple, wasn't it? All I needed to do was call 9-1-1, and they would have taken care of Grandma.

But I didn't.

I failed them.

I remember the shame I felt when they took Grandma away. My toes curling in my shoes. My head slumping between my shoulders. Tears welling in my eyes, that I didn't feel I had the right to shed.

I'd failed my family. I hadn't been good enough for them. I'd failed to protect them.

I was the oldest. There were things that were expected of me. And I didn't meet these expectations.

The years that followed, I'd strive to be the best at everything. I had natural abilities that made certain things easy. But when it came to my family, it seemed that whatever I did, I failed.

Like the time when Justin jumped off the roof into the pool and broke his leg. I'd saved Grace, but my brother? I didn't.

"Best way to go," Dad says. "In your sleep."

"Nightcap?" Mom asks.

It's late. But we've been mindlessly chatting, looking at family albums, and it doesn't feel right to ride back to Grace's house to just crash there, even if it's where I want to be. She hasn't called or texted all day, and I wonder if she's giving me space or if she needs space herself. "Nightcap sounds perfect. Let me just check on Grace real quick." I walk out toward the barn to talk to her in private. Her sleepy voice stirs all kinds of feelings inside me—lust, longing, and more lust. We don't talk long. She sounds tired, and just the rasp of her night voice makes me want to be in bed with her. But that wouldn't be fair to her. She has an early start tomorrow. She needs her sleep.

And I hear the clink of the small glasses Mom pulled out of her cupboard, and Dad's shuffle as he comes back on the porch with two bottles of who knows what.

We hang up, and I feel a little lonely, yet surrounded at the same time. Surrounded by my family, with the ties we're learning to weave again. And by Grace, and how we're finding our way toward each other again.

Loving Grace is the simplest and most complicated thing I've done in my life.

Simple, because it just is. I love her. Always have, always will.

Complicated, because she's fragile and complex. She's not telling me everything—in fact, I feel there's a lot she hasn't told me yet. And how can I love her completely if I don't know inside out what happened to her, how she navigated the past ten years of her life, moving from being a teenager to an adult? And how she's navigating her present life? She seems to have this boring life, alone with her cat, but she doesn't. She takes care of her dad, and her cousin's daughter, and her employees, and her needy clients. She spends time with her mom and checks in on her brother.

"How is Grace doing?" Mom asks as I sit down.

"Good. Tired."

"Mad River?" Dad asks, referring to one of Vermont's bourbons.

"Sure."

"Limoncello please," Mom says. "The poor thing must be driving herself sick with the spa."

Mom is always so dramatic. "Yeah, she's a little worried."

"Did she find a new space yet?"

"I think that's a little premature. He might end up selling to another investor."

Mom sets down her glass. "Oh no. I hear it's that young woman, a friend of yours, who's buying to live there."

"A friend of mine?"

Dad clears his throat and shifts uncomfortably on his seat. "Yeah—what was her name? Never cared much for her. Annie?"

"Wasn't Annie," Mom says. "What was her name? Oh, she wasn't *that* bad. Lessee... Prescott's niece. From Fish and Game?" She turns to Dad like that's going to help. "Amy! That's it. Amy Keller. She's moving back to Emerald Creek. Her mom must be happy."

What the fuck? Grace never said anything about Amy buying the spa. A nervous tick takes control of my cheek. "Grace never said anything."

Mom waves a hand like it's nothing. "And maybe I misunderstood."

"It's probably a rumor," Dad interjects. "Or she just made an offer, and she's getting ahead of herself."

Fucking *Amy* is buying the spa? Over my dead body.

"Grace just doesn't want to worry you, honey," Mom says like that's going to soothe me. My inner caveman is thumping his chest, shouting *Why isn't she coming to me for help? Ethan Protect Grace. Ethan Fix Grace Problems.* Mom sets her hand on my thigh. "She probably didn't want to bore you with work, honey. I wouldn't read too much into it."

I bored her with my work yesterday. Didn't seem to bother her. "Yep." And now that fucking tick in my jaw just won't let go.

We clink our glasses and take small sips in silence for a while, letting the darkness settle around us like a blanket. Dad takes a couple deep sighs.

"Well, next time we have a family reunion like this, Grace has to be here. I'll call her myself."

"Thanks, Ma," I say, taking her hand and squeezing it gently.

"It's so good to have you back, honey," Mom says, teary-eyed. "And I know you have to leave again, but hopefully, now with Grace, you'll come back more often."

Dad grunts.

"I know life isn't exactly exciting around here but... oh well—I'll say it. I was a little hurt you never came back. Sometimes wondered if we said or did something to keep you away, all these years."

My heart bottoms. *"You need to talk to your mom. There's no way she said it the way you took it."* And there it is. Grace was right.

I shift in my seat, uncomfortable about what I'm about to say. The last thing I want is to hurt my mother. "I kinda felt, at the time, that..." How can I put this? "that it'd be better for Justin and-and-and the rest of the family if I stayed away for a while."

Mom sets her glass on the small table to give me her full attention while Dad grunts, "And why is that?"

I rub my hands together, lean my elbows on my knees. "I felt, at the time, that I could have prevented Justin's accident." I raise a pacifying hand toward Mom who's already starting to voice her disagreement. "That's how I *felt*, Mom. Audrey and I had had an argument, and I *felt* that argument had a bearing on the rest of the evening. I actually know for a fact it did." I have their attention now. "And uh... in the hours that followed, I wanted to cancel or at least postpone indefinitely joining the Air Force. The fact that I felt responsible for the accident made me argue this with you more forcefully than if I'd had no impact at all on that evening. But you wouldn't let me."

Mom jumps in. "Of course not! I had one son whose life had been derailed, I didn't want another one to give up on his dreams!"

I smile at her. "I... that's not how I understood it at the time. You said something like I *owed it to Justin* to go live my life, and I thought... I just thought... anyway. That was stupid—"

Dad just grunts again while Mom pales. "Oh, honey, what I meant was..." She turns to Dad. "How can I put this?"

Dad takes Mom's hand in his. "Just like you said before, Lynnie. You didn't want both your sons having their lives on hold."

Mom's teary eyes land on me. "I never ever meant you had any kind of debt to your brother. What I meant was, go and enjoy life while you can. Because you never know what might happen. That's what I meant by *owe it to him*. As in, live and have fun for the two of you."

"I see that now, Mom. It's just... these were messy times for me. I didn't know how to talk and open up."

"You had it too hard, as the first born," Dad states. "I sometimes regret it, and other times, I think this tough upbringing is what made you who you are now. You're reliable. You put others first. That's one reason you're such a good asset to the Air Force—in addition to everything else. I can't say that I entirely regret putting so much on your shoulders, 'cause most of it, we didn't have a choice. Your mom was eighteen when you were born, and both our families had thrown us out. But I can tell you now—it's time to let go and give yourself some grace."

Mom breathes shakily. "Well, I'm glad we got that out of the way." She smiles. "Also, honey," she says to Dad, "good one."

"What'd I say now?" Dad asks gruffly.

"*Give yourself some Grace*."

Dad chuckles. "You're the worst, woman."

Mom takes the last sip of her drink and sets it on the small tray holding the liquor. "Welp," she says, standing, "I'm gonna get myself to bed." She leans over me and kisses my forehead. "Sleep well, honey." Then she waves at Dad and wiggles her eyebrows at him. "You know where to find me!" she sing-songs.

I shake my head but can't stifle the silent laughter shaking my shoulders.

"I'm spending time with my son, woman," Dad pretends to growl, a wide smile contradicting his tone.

I can't bring myself to tell my Dad to go warm up Mom's bed instead of spending time with me. It's just plain icky. But honestly? I wish I could have that, someday.

After Mom leaves, I go to the kitchen to get a glass of water and then head to the bathroom. When I come back out from the light, I can hardly see, but an unmistakable smell is in the air.

I squint at Dad. "I didn't know you smoked." Moonlight contours the white wicker of the chairs and the coffee table, the railing around the porch, Dad's cigar a glowing ember that brightens as he pulls on it. My eyes slowly adjust to the night, until I can make out his facial expression. Contentedness.

"I don't." He eyes me sideways and a silent laughter shakes his whole body. "Siddown."

I sit at an angle from him, and we stay silent for a while. Then he says, "Your mother doesn't like it." Another long silence. "We do a lot of things for the women we love... We *think* we do it for them. But if you think hard enough about it... they have us do it for our own good." He takes a long puff of his cigar, then butts the end off. "Least, that's how I see it."

It's good to be with Dad, just like this. Just staring into the quiet countryside. "Here," he says, pouring from the bottle of Mad River's Revolution Rye he kept on the floor next to him. "Have another."

I swirl the amber liquid in the glass and take a swig. It warms my insides and calms my nerves. I sit back in the chair.

"Tell me about... that thing you'll be going to. This week. What's that all about?"

I told Mom and Dad about being gone for a few days, after my phone chimed several times. Using our encryption app, my C.O. was filling me in on what to expect. It will be a high-level strategy meeting about our cryptanalysis program for NATO. What we can and cannot share with our allies. How we should proceed moving forward. I'm tasked with analyzing the ever-evolving technology and presenting to the brass in Brussels next month. "Some bullshit."

"Uh-huh. Makes sense. They call a Major on leave over the weekend for bullshit." I don't know where Dad stands with regard to our country's military, our foreign policy, or even politics in general. Frankly, I don't care. But I do love serving. Do we make mistakes? Of course we do. But only people who do nothing don't make mistakes. And doing nothing in this world is not an option.

"So... what did they really call you for? Come on, you can tell your old man. Gimme a least a little something."

I take another sip of the whiskey. "That why you're trying to get me drunk?"

He guffaws. "I wouldn't even try to make you say something you shouldn't."

I rub my face. "Some analysis they need."

He grunts. That's all he's going to get from me. "What does that mean for you?"

It means pretty fucking great things. "I dunno yet."

"Might wanna think through it before push comes to shove."

I run my hand over my stubble. "Yeah."

"Would that put you in more danger?"

Danger in this day and age is relative. There's cut and dried frontline danger. And then there's the shit that happens even here, on US territory, where we're supposed to be safe. The real hold up for me is different. "It'd mean living in Europe."

"Which you already are."

"I was. I left Germany. I was hoping for stateside this time."

"Right."

I'm thinking about Grace, lying in bed right now, her fucking key probably back under the stupid rock, and I feel the urge to be by her side and protect *her*.

"Wouldn't you do better work in Europe? Be more of service to your country?"

Probably. "It's more about... the accomplishment." The NATO job would be a huge promotion, especially at my age. There's a reason I'm being considered for it. I'm good at what I do. Really good. "Other guys can do it." And it's true. There are other people as qualified as I am—thank god for that. But they're older, they have families, demands. It's more of a headache to move them around. More expensive. Me? I'm as flexible as they come.

Dad reaches for his glass and finishes it. "'Course they can. The real question is, where are *your* priorities now? What do you want from life?"

A dull pain churns in my stomach. Nights like this remind me of my time in the tree house, with Grace. Life ahead of us. I thought I had it all figured out. We'd be a family someday—soon. I'd be able to provide for everyone.

"Did uh… Did Grace ever tell you why she came back to Emerald Creek?"

I'm surprised that Dad's thoughts are on Grace as well, although I suppose I shouldn't be. He has to know where my hesitation comes from. "She got divorced," I say, as it's the most obvious thing. Isn't that why? Why is he asking me? "Right?"

"You're asking me?"

"No. You're asking."

"Just… just making sure… You know what?" He waves in front of him as if to erase his words. "Forget I even asked."

"What the fuck, Dad? You do know we're adults, right."

"This has nothin' to do with what Dennis… said. Back in the day."

Right. So what does it have to do with? "If there's something I should know, you better tell me."

"Absolutely not. Anything you need to know, you should find out on your own. Innit your job anyway?"

Seriously? "Holy fucking… just hand me the bottle."

CHAPTER THIRTY-ONE

Grace

Earlier that day

*

After my ten o'clock hot stone massage with one of my oldest clients, I review Shanice's training plan, then follow up with a few orders before taking a minute to check the realtor websites for any commercial leases.

No luck. As I tuck my phone back in my pocket and walk back to the reception to check in with Claudia, George Richardson comes in.

"I was just thinking about you." I try to mask the sarcasm in my tone, but judging by his pursed lips, I'd call it a fail.

"A minute of your time?" he asks me.

A slew of snarky comebacks pop into my mind, but I choose to save my breath. I guide him to my small windowless office, which was originally a closet but is ample space for what I need: a computer and a minimal filing system. We sit on each side of my sleek glass desk.

"I wanted to pay you the courtesy of a visit, Ms. Harper."

Seeing as I've learned from the grapevine about his intent to sell, and a realtor already showed the place, he's way too late for a courtesy visit, but I let him talk anyway. It's not in my interest to be confrontational, so I let him dole out his platitudes.

Finally, he gets to the reason he's here. "I have an offer in hand."

Already? My eyebrows shoot to my hairline, but I manage to smile. "Congratulations."

"Sight unseen, if you can believe it." He takes a deep breath. "It's a cash offer, and I'm ready to accept it. I'd like to move quickly on this deal, and I'd appreciate it if you'd help me do so by formally expressing that you don't intend to exercise your right of first refusal."

Well, screw that. "What makes you think I don't want to buy the building?"

He smirks. "I didn't know spas were so profitable. I should look into that line of investment."

Did he just assume I can't afford the building?

Well—he's right. But it's insulting. "And why wouldn't I exercise my right of first refusal?"

The smirk becomes intolerable. "To stay on my good side?"

"Let me recap. You've still not fixed the deck, which is a safety hazard to my clientele. You *just now* have informally informed me that I will be losing my place of business. And you want me to stay on your 'good side'?" I air quote. I resist asking what being on his bad side looks like. I don't have time or patience for rhetorical arguments. Instead, I stand. "I'll have to think on it."

He raps his fingers on my small desk. "How long?"

"I'll have my lawyer look into the lease agreement."

"See, that's where people like you don't understand business. You're going to spend your hard-earned money on a lawyer who'll just end up telling you there's nothing you can do."

I open the door. "Well, it's *my* hard-earned money, isn't it?"

He stands and smirks. "One last thing. The buyer would like a thorough visit. As is her right. And your obligation."

I nod and shrug. "Of course."

"Fine then. Miss Keller?"

I whip around to see Amy in the reception area, phone in hand, snapping pictures of every detail in the spa.

My heartbeat picks up, and I clench my jaw to keep myself from lashing out at her. Really? I take a deep breath. "Amy, so nice to see you again!" I take a few assured steps her way. "Claudia, why don't you show Amy around? I have a few things to tend to."

"I can show her," Richardson says.

Screw *that*. "I'm still running my business from here, so either Claudia or I will be with you. If you don't mind."

Amy waves a dismissive hand at me. "Whatever, Gracie. Get over yourself."

Claudia's jaw drops open at her rudeness, but I shake my head at her. *No need to lose it.*

They take their sweet time visiting the whole place, taking measurements, photos and videos.

It's when they're finally gone that I feel the world closing in on me. It's getting real. And it doesn't matter whether it's Amy or someone sweet buying the house.

I need a new space, stat, or I'm going to have to shut down.

Feeling depressed by this turn of events, my instinct is to inform the Bitch Brigade. But they'll march here and make a fuss. It's the middle of the day, I have clients coming in. I can't deal with this now.

Ethan? He's at the farm, enjoying his family. I don't want to ruin his day. He'll take it even more personally once he knows it's Amy buying the place. I'll tell him later.

Kiara is who I need.

"There's something to be said about starting over," she says when she gets here.

"And here I was hoping for a bitching session." I lick my fingers. Her maple fudge is about to send me into a sugar coma. Exactly what I needed.

"No, but seriously. Do you know that when I left my parents', I slept in my car for two weeks, until I had enough to pay for a motel?"

I tear up at her confession. "I had no idea," I whisper. "What-why...?"

She waves my concern away. "Doesn't matter. Point is, I never, ever would have become a pastry chef without that. Sleeping in my car is what saved me."

I frown, needing a little more than that.

"This big hotel was hiring night shift cooks. They'd give us the title of pastry chefs to make us feel good, but we really didn't know what we were doing. Just blending mixes and trying not to burn the shit and being semi awake when glazing. The point is, I took the job because it was a night job, and I found out you can get away with sleeping in your car during the day. At night is where the trouble starts. Cops, other homeless people, overnight parking bans. So I took the first night job I found. And voila. Ten years later, one thing led to another, best chocolate maple fudge in the state—you're welcome, by the way. Best macarons, best petits fours, best everything."

"Why d'you leave your parents'?" I didn't know this about my friend. From what she's saying, this happened before we met at the incubator.

"Doesn't matter. What are we going to do about you? Where's your beau?" She looks around like Ethan should have been here the whole time.

"Oh—he's with his family. At the farm."

She nods. "I remember. Barbecue at the farm. So why are you here?" She frowns. "Isn't he leaving like... tomorrow or something?"

"Day after tomorrow. It's best this way. I... Ethan has his life with the service. He... we..." I swallow. "I think I need time to myself again."

"I hear you. I couldn't live with a man. Or anyone."

My heart stutters. "See—the thing is, I *can* live with him. I *want* to be with him. So. Bad. It's-it's terrible."

"Sounds like it," she snorts, then looks at me. "Hey, Gracie. Sorry. I didn't mean to... you're a fucking mess, aren't you?" She leans next to me, suddenly grasping that I'm getting way emotional.

"I'm trying not to be a mess. But he's easy to get used to, you know? It's going to feel so empty when he's gone. I'm going to *feel* being alone. His toothbrush is next to mine, his favorite beers are in the fridge, his shoes are in the entrance—"

"He takes his shoes off?"

What? "Well, yeah... I mean..." Doesn't everyone?

"You got him pussy whipped. Sorry if that's not PC." She laughs, hiding her mouth with the back of her hand. "Wait 'til Colton hears that."

Colton? Think of it, Dad and Colton don't take their shoes off. What does it matter? "Why would Colton... what does he have to do with it?" I am so confused with Kiara right now.

"Sorry for going on a tangent there. Back to you. So, bottom line, you're happy he's leaving because you were getting used to him. Makes sense. Makes perfect sense."

"It does?" She makes me feel better. I thought I was being a bad person there, for a while, wishing him gone so I could get back to not dreaming the life I will never have.

"Yeah. You finally have something good. Something scary and big and life changing. Why keep it?"

My heart hammers. "You're just plain cruel, Kiara. I know you don't mean it. But that hurts."

"Butterfly," she says, taking my hand. "You've been through shit, and you found a balance. And I admire you for that. But you can't stay stuck there forever, only taking care of others, never taking what you want. Ethan is your man. I can see how happy you are with him. Don't let his macho speech about how much the country needs him fool you. If he's the one for you, he'll find a way to be with you."

"How did you know he says his country needs him?"

"Just a wild guess," she states. "But more importantly, he's going to want you to tell him you want him. Guys like him, all muscles and big talk, they're softies inside. They want to be wanted. Don't forget that."

"You're so right," I breathe, thinking of my conversation with Ethan about why he'd been gone for so long.

Kiara stands and claps her hands. "Gotta go. I'll put the therapy session on your charge card. As for Amy, I suggest the Bitch Brigade get together and sew little voodoo dolls and we get busy with pins and shit." And just like that, she gets a smile out of me.

That evening, as I'm getting ready to go to bed, my phone rings with a local number that's not in my contacts. It's probably a marketer. I find it so annoying how they trick you with numbers that are local. There should be a law against that. Impersonation or something.

On the other hand, it could be a client who needs to change their appointment for tomorrow. Or a lead on a new building. Everyone in this town seems to have my number, and it's fine by me.

I pick up.

"Did I wake you, sweetheart?" Ethan's low rumble shoots straight to my core.

"Aww, honey, you can wake me anytime you like."

He says sweet little nothings to me.

"How'd you get my number?" I ask.

"Uh—still the same number."

Right. I erased Ethan's number a week after our breakup. Guilt eats at me that he kept it, and I didn't.

Ethan doesn't seem to pick up on that. He tells me he's about to have a nightcap with his dad and he'll be staying the night at the farm, then he tells me sweet little nothings again, and then we hang up.

It's going to be like that, moving forward. We'll be together on the phone more than in person. I should get used to it.

After we hang up, I save his contact, then do my evening routine in the bathroom, taking more time with my lotions, the toner, the serums. It's soothing. I notice he left his toothbrush here and his backpack. I almost call him back to tell him, but it's stupid. Lynn will have a toothbrush for him. Or maybe he just carries spares in his saddle bags, who knows? He's so used to not having a home.

That makes me sad, so I try to think about happy things as I slide into his jersey for the night. About what our life together will look like. About the fact that he kept my number in his phone for all these years.

I wonder what the time difference with Brussels is. And does that mean it'll be morning there when it's evening here? Or the opposite.

I always get confused with that.

We'll have to schedule our calls. Get into a habit, if his job allows it.

It's a good thing I'm my own boss. I can make and receive calls whenever I want. I suspect it won't be the same for Ethan. At least one of us will need to be flexible.

I'm not really tired anymore. I thought I was, and then... my mind started on its own little path. So I pull out my souvenir box, sit on the floor with it, and go back down memory lane.

Just like usual. Life is different, and it's the same in a way. In a way better way, of course.

Just not everything I hoped for.

It never is. For anyone.

Like anybody else, I need to deal with what I can have, and cope however works for me.

CHAPTER THIRTY-TWO

Ethan

It's the middle of the night, Dad has gone to bed, and I can't sleep.

The alcohol has long worn off, so I leave the farm and ride to Grace's. Once on her road, I kill my engine and push the bike up her driveway.

Then I let myself in, leave my shoes at the entrance, tread to the bedroom, strip my clothes off, and slide in next to Grace,

"You came back," she says in her half-asleep voice.

I scoop her in my arms. "Couldn't sleep without you."

She does a little happy sound, her body wiggling against mine. "You smell like an old man."

A silent laugh takes hold of me. "My dad smoked a cigar, and I had whiskey."

She grunts. "And you drove your bike? At night?"

I grunt back. "S'okay. Sleep now."

She turns in my arms so that I spoon her, and nests her ass against my dick. "How'd you get in?" she murmurs.

"Your fucking key was back under the rock," I grunt.

"Mm. Aren't you happy it was?" And on these words, I can tell from the weight of her body and the rhythm of her breathing, that she's asleep in under a minute.

Damian wakes us up before dawn when he jumps on the bed, walking on our faces, tripping on one of my socks he's holding in his jaw.

Grace sits up, squints her puffy eyes, licks her morning swollen lips, and shakes her bedhead, the trifecta an absolute turn-on. My morning wood becomes rock hard just looking at her wake up.

I just want to fuck her.

"Eww, Damian, what's that smell?" she whines.

I clasp the sock Damian is proudly dragging on her face, pull it to my side of the bed, but the cat stays attached to it and lets out a muffled yowl as he lands on the floor.

"The fuck?" Grace whispers, plopping herself on her elbows.

I should have closed the door. Note to self: Damian needs to be contained outside the bedroom. I sit on the edge of the bed, my back to Grace so she doesn't see my hard-on. "I'll get us some coffee."

Before I can stand, her arm snakes around my waist and pulls me to her. Then her hand trails down. "Coffee will wait," she draws out. "Get Damian out of here, and come say a proper good morning."

Yes, ma'am.

I make sweet love to Grace. Her movements are slow and loving and deep. This is almost goodbye, and even though I don't want it to be, this will be our life now. Better get used to it.

There will be time for wild sex, for fucking, later. This morning is not one of those.

This morning is for our bodies to say *I love you* in their own way. For remembering every square inch of her body. For imprinting myself with her smell, her taste, her sounds.

When she comes undone, she clasps me with more fierceness than normally, with something harsh that might look like sadness or resignation if I didn't know better.

"I won't be gone long, I promise."

"I know."

But after that, I will be gone long.

I tack on my jeans strewn on the floor from last night, among some other mess I'll have to address later. "Stay here, I'll make coffee."

I come back with our two cups, mine black, hers with a heart-attack level of sugar and cream—that's the only way she can tolerate house coffee. She's dozing off, and my weight on the bed wakes her.

She snuggles her soft body comfortably against me and takes a few sips in silence.

"How was your day?" I ask her once I assess her brain fog must have lifted. Grace needs a little time in the morning, and just because we made love after Damian woke her up rather brutally today doesn't mean she doesn't need some time with her thoughts first thing in the morning.

"Ugh, you don't wanna know," she sighs, leaning her head against my shoulder in a dramatic fashion.

"I actually do."

"Guess who came to visit the spa that they made an offer on?"

Shit, so it's true. "Amy," I drop.

She jumps and nearly spills her coffee as she cranes her neck to look at me. "You knew?"

"Mom heard a rumor. We were hoping she heard wrong."

Her gaze softens. "Did you talk to Lynn?" The change of topic catches me off guard. But that's Grace right there, more concerned about others than herself.

Balancing her coffee in one hand, she sits cross-legged to face me. "You did, right? What did she say?"

I take a strand of her hair in my free hand. "Like you said. It was never what she meant. Dad said some things too that were... I guess, that shed a light on stuff." I smile at Grace, my heart swelling with gratitude. "You're the best thing that ever happened to me, Grace. And to think you've been in my life from the beginning, it's... pretty fucking awesome."

She smiles big at me. "Agreed."

"What are you going to do about Amy?"

She lifts her shoulders. "It was fifty-fifty until last week. If Richardson—that's the landlord— was going to sell to an investor, I'd have a good chance of keeping it. I always pay on time. and I'm an easy tenant. I haven't even bitched about the broken deck yet. But Amy is buying it to live there, so that means I have to move."

"No leads on other possible locations?"

"Still looking. But it'll be hard to find something as nice. And when I think of all the time and money I put into decorating it just right, it's... heartbreaking. But you know what... I had a talk with Kiara yesterday, and she made me realize... sometimes we have to start from scratch and it ends up being for the best."

I pull her face to mine and lean my forehead on hers. "I just... fuck I just wish I could *do* something."

"I know you do. But don't worry about it, it'll take care of itself."

I'm about to destroy that argument, but it's useless. I know what she means. There's no point ruining our last hours together. We can talk about that on the phone, later.

She finishes her coffee, sets the cup on the nightstand, then comes to cuddle against me.

Then out of the blue she says, "Tell me about Germany."

Ah, fuck.

CHAPTER THIRTY-THREE

Grace

I have so much to catch up on, when it comes to Ethan's life. I used to know everything about him, and now it's like there's this whole void, this universe that his life has become that I know nothing about.

He doesn't want to, or can't tell me about his job. Fine. But I want to know everything else. "Tell me about Germany."

He sighs and arranges himself on the bed so he's holding me tight. "What do you wanna know?"

"How long were you there for?"

"Three years."

"You spent three years in Germany?"

"Yup."

"Wow. *Germany.* For someone who doesn't want to live in the cold? That's not exactly the tropics."

He shrugs.

"Did you like it there? In Germany."

Another shrug.

That can't be classified. "What did you like about it?"

He still doesn't answer.

"The beer? The job?"

He looks down at me and kisses the top of my head.

My heartbeat drops. "Oh. A woman."

He kisses the top of my head again. That's a *yes*.

"What is... was her name?" *Is* there still a woman? No, right?

He huffs. "Uh—Ilse."

My heartbeat picks up, but I force it down. "Ilse. That's a pretty name. What happened?"

He takes a deep breath but doesn't answer.

"We don't need to talk about it if you don't want to."

He strokes my shoulder repeatedly. "It's fine. It's just... I never put it into words, what happened. She uh... we were supposed to get married. I mean we... talked about it. And she wanted to. But I never... I never got around to proposing. And that seemed to be a big deal for her. She wanted me to propose. Not just do the paperwork at Town Hall and be done with it. I—I make it sound like I was a jerk. I don't think I was. But now that I think about it, maybe I was. Anyway... We had a big argument, the day before I was going off base for a month. And I hated that. I hated that I argued with the woman I was going to marry. So I promised myself I'd propose when I came back. And then while I was away, I kind of..." He takes another deep breath, his hand now caressing my arm. "The days went by and I didn't miss her. I realized I'd only think about her when she called. And I had to put a reminder on my phone to call her."

"Well—were you very busy? That could explain it." How awkward is it, that I'm trying to find him excuses.

He leans over me to kiss the top of my head. "No. It was a boring as hell mission. The kind when you just sit, you need to stay awake, and you're just waiting for intel that never comes in. Lots of time to think about shit. And the shit I was thinking about... it wasn't her. The *woman* I was thinking about... it wasn't her." He squeezes me softly, trailing his lips along my hair. "I'd only ever missed one person in my life, Grace. And so, after that, I broke things off with Ilse and decided it was time for a bigger career move."

I take a while to process this. I'd never pictured Ethan with someone else, but of course he would have been. Of course he'd be in a relationship. He's such a good, solid person. How is he going to deal with being alone in Brussels? "Brussels is pretty close to Germany," I venture.

He turns me in his arms, his gaze roaming my face. "So?"

"Nothing," I breathe.

He kisses me softly. "Good."

Then he takes a breath, moves his head around, and I know he's going to ask me about my failed marriage. It's only fair. I owe him the explanation.

"So..." he starts. "What's up with the box?"

The box? Shit. *The box.* It's on the floor. I was making space in it to add... ohmygod, this is so embarrassing. "What box?"

"The hoarder's delight."

"The what now?"

"The crush in a box... The stalker's chest..."

"I'm not a stalker!"

"No? I think your therapist would differ."

"I don't have a therapist." *Liar.*

He guffaws. "Ha! Therein lies the problem." He plops me off him and scissors off the bed. "What do we have here?" He crouches next to the box, then grabs his underwear and throws it on top of his bag. "Don't want that ending up in there," he mumbles.

I can't help but giggle.

"Seriously, Grace, should I be worried?" Damian walks up to him and watches him as if he's just as worried as him.

"Why? I'm just... attached to souvenirs of my..." Love? (too much). Devotion? (too crazy). Crush? (Not deep enough). I settle for, "souvenirs of us."

"Souvenirs of us, huh?" He takes apart all the bits and pieces of my life without him and lays them neatly in order of size.

Afraid he's going to throw them away or destroy them somehow (he did call me a hoarder and a stalker, after all) I stand over him. "What are you doing?"

"Thinking about making something."

I knew it. "Making what?" I try to sound sane and reasonable, but I'm ready to lose it. No one is touching my souvenirs, not even very present, very real, and very sexy Ethan *right here* almost naked in my bedroom.

Which, I get it, is a contradiction. You might think I don't need all these things now that I have Ethan. But here's the thing. I *don't* have him. Not really. He's going to come and go. I'll have his love, always—I know that for a fact—but the tangible reality of him? I won't.

That's what this box is to me.

"Why did you take it down? The box," he asks me suddenly.

Um... "I was going to add to it. I need to make space, or possibly get a new one."

"For what?" He's genuinely confused.

I cross my arms. He's not talking me out of this one. "For the flowers. I'm going to dry them. And the chocolates—or the chocolate box. I'm eating the chocolates. I might keep one or t—"

Still crouching, he twists around to look at me. "What the fuck are you talking about?"

"You heard me." I jut out my hip to show him I'm serious. *My house, my rules.*

He stands slowly until he towers over me. Holds my shoulders and stares me down. I pinch my lips. I am not giving into him.

"Listen to me, babe. This," he says, pointing to my treasures laying on the ground, "is the past. You and I, we have a future together. The flowers, the chocolates? You're going to get a lot of those. So many they won't mean as much."

I open my mouth to protest. But there's no way he can understand. My eyes water.

"I'm going to get you so many flowers and chocolates you'll beg me to stop. You'll be nauseated. You'll open a flower shop. You'll be a Valentine's pop-up store. Not only that, but jewelry, and clothes, and perfume, and whatever else I feel like sending over to you when I'm away."

And that's when my heart breaks. "You don't understand, Ethan."

"No?"

"I only want you."

"Fuck," he growls and pulls me into him. "Then why do you keep all this shit?"

"Because when you're not here, I can touch it, and see it. It's a piece of you."

"Shit," he whispers in my hair, and I don't know if that's a good thing or a bad thing.

CHAPTER THIRTY-FOUR

Grace

"I'm leaving early tomorrow," Ethan thinks necessary to remind me as we get dressed for the day after a quick shower together. "I have a couple of errands to run, and I want to stop by Mom and Dad's to say goodbye." He pulls me to him by my waist. "Tonight is all for you." His eyes go dark as he leans into me for a long kiss. He pulls my face into his chest after breaking the kiss. "You very busy today?" His voice is raw with emotion.

I'm packed. "A little." If only I could get cancellations today.

He kisses the crown of my head. "Why don't you let me get you a proper coffee? What's today's gonna be?"

I smile big at him. "A Maple Kiss in the mug with the kittens. Please."

"You don't want a new mug?"

I giggle. "You already gave me three. Plus, Millie'll give you a discount if you bring your own mug."

"Ah. My Grace is thrifty. Good to know." He takes a deep breath, his gaze doing all sorts of funny things to my insides as it goes through different emotions, until he blinks the shine out of his eyes. "I'll meet you at the spa? Let you get started."

"I'll try to get out early," I whisper as he boops me.

"One Maple Kiss, coming right up!" He grabs the mug from its display shelf as he leaves the house.

It's the mug he personalized in his own hand, and just thinking about it makes me as giddy as a teenager.

It feels good. I'm tired of feeling old and acting reasonable. I know this thing with Ethan is nowhere near my teenage fantasies of a happily ever after, house full of his babies, Ethan's mouth on my body every morning, but hey—it's close enough.

It's better than I had a month ago.

So. Much. Better.

I'll do what life has taught me to do: accept and adapt.

The spa doesn't open for another hour, so I start on my admin work right away, hoping Ethan will take a minute to sit with me and have a coffee before going about his day. I'm close to inbox zero when his bike roars faintly outside. Closing my laptop, I greet him at the door.

He jumps up the steps, holding my travel mug and a disposable mug, and whirls me in his free arm as if we haven't seen each other in forever.

"Hi again, beautiful," he says against my mouth before kissing me. "Just a quick kiss and I'm out of your hair."

"I have time for you."

"I was hoping you'd say that."

I take his hand. "Come outside. We just need to stay away from the rotten planks."

He steps to the deck's damaged area, examining it. "I didn't realize it was that bad," he grunts, irritated.

But me? I'm just realizing how sharing the little things, the daily frustrations, makes everything *right* again. "Yeah, it sucks for the golden girls' wellness session. I'll have to move them inside." Oh well. "Come sit," I say as I pull two cafe chairs next to each other and sit in one.

Ethan takes the other and throws his arm over my shoulders, pulling me inside his warm frame. He plays with my hair absentmindedly, brushing his fingers against my nape occasionally. "You'd let me know if there was anything I could do to help, right?"

What does he mean? "Yeah, sure."

"Good," he says softly, kissing my temple. Then he adds, "What's that tiny piece of twine?"

"What?" I look around but see nothing.

"In your box. There's a little plastic pouch and inside, it looks like twine tied in a loop."

"Oh." I swing my head to look at him. The distant memory collides with today's reality. What will he think? Oh—who cares. "It's a wedding band you made for me. We were playing wedding—Haley's idea. She'd convinced Justin to play with us, probably bargained something. You came up and declared they didn't know what they were doing. That Justin wasn't saying the right words, or that Haley couldn't marry her brother. I don't remember the details—I wasn't paying that much attention until then—until you placed yourself in front of me, looked into my eyes, produced a little ring—it had blue flower buds at the time—took my hand, slipped the ring on it, and said "I thee wed and shall protect you forever and ever." Then you turned to Justin and told him what he was supposed to say. He refused to repeat it, so you leaned over me, kissed the crown of my head, and said 'I now pronounce us husband and wife.' And then you left." I laugh at the memory, but there's a part of me that doesn't think it's laughable.

"And you kept that ring," Ethan says, not making fun of me, not even chuckling a little bit. Even I can see how ridiculous it is that I'm holding onto that. Not just the ring, but all the memories associated with that day. The pebble in my sandal poking under my big toe. The fact that Haley was wearing the white dress and not me. The bees buzzing around us. How Justin had decided to prop us on crates for some reason, and I'd stopped internally complaining about the unsteady situation when that brought me closer to Ethan's height, high enough that I only needed to tilt my head just so to look into his beautiful, soulful, kind eyes.

The way his hands had cupped my head for the briefest moment when he dropped a quick and chaste kiss on my head before leaving to do his big kid stuff with his dad.

"Forget-me-nots" Ethan says, interrupting my daydreaming.

"What?"

"I braided forget-me-nots in the twine."

My breath halts and my heart kabooms. He *remembers*? "I wasn't gonna let you be the maid of honor." His fingers dig softly into my nape as he brings my mouth to his. He kisses me languidly, the blue of his half-closed eyes shining bright in the morning sun. He shifts my thigh on his legs and cups my breast softly, running the pad of his thumb over my nipple. "I'd better go," he groans.

Too stunned to talk, I sit with my feelings, unsure what's happening right now. The door shuts, his bike hums in the distance, and then, after a while, voices inside call me back to reality. To every day. To the present.

After another hour of admin work (writing up a proposal for a bachelorette party, renewing my insurance, answering yet more emails), my first appointment is a massage, and I take that as a good sign. Sign that people are trusting me to bring them deeper wellness.

My client is Wendy, who owns a small hotel in town with her husband. I bring her upstairs, where I've put my treatment room toward the back—out of the hubbub of the first floor, with its large lounge area that lends itself to chatter and laughter. It's still a little bare. I was going to work on the decor before fall, but with a pinch in my heart, I realize it won't be needed anymore.

Wendy growls as I tackle her shoulders. "Too much pressure?"

She groans an unintelligible answer.

"You're very tight up there," I say in a soothing voice. "Try to relax."

She moans softly, and after a few minutes, snores lightly. *Good.* She mainly needs time away from it all. I'm halfway through my routine, ready to gently wake her and have her turn around, when excited whooping wafts from downstairs all the way to us. What is going on? I smile to myself. This is exactly what I wanted. A space for women to come and take care of themselves.

As Wendy turns around, I glance out the window overlooking the deck, wondering how long it will be until the deck is repaired. It'd be nice to... *What is going on?*

Ohmygod.

My mouth gapes.

The three damaged planks are pulled out of the deck and set aside. The deck is turned into a mini woodworking station, complete with trestle, electric saw, and a couple more tools I don't know the name of. Brand new planks—you can tell by their lighter color—are being cut to size.

By Ethan.

By Ethan on my deck.

Under the brutal sun.

T-shirt clinging to his torso, he maneuvers the new planks as if they were as light as twigs. Brings the first to the gaping space on the deck, adjusts it, measures stuff one last time, and drills it in place. Neat, quick drills. He knows what he's doing. Standing, he wipes his brow, then—get this—whips his T-shirt off, wipes his face with it, and throws it on the railing.

The whooping downstairs stopped, and I can fill in the silence: disbelief. Hungry glares. How can I blame them?

"Oh my. He should be in the movies. At least some ads for... beer or somethin'. Ya know?" Wendy is standing next to me, wrapped in the sheet.

"Oh—s-sorry." I clear my throat. "Let's get that massage finished."

"Why don't you bring him a glass of water? He looks thirsty."

"Um... no-no-no. I need to... we need to..."

"I'll be right here waiting. Unless you'd rather someone else bring him water?"

I end up bringing him water—of course I do. And not because I'm worried about *someone else* bringing him water.

By the time I'm out on the deck with him, he's finishing the third plank. "Babe!" he flashes his full-on smile and grabs the water from my hands. "Awww. Thank you. You're the best."

Um... *me*? "Ethan... I... I don't know what to say."

He downs the water in loud gulps, then wipes his mouth with the back of his hand. Handing me the glass back, he pecks my lips, then stays against my mouth and adds, "'bout what? Too loud? Sorry—didn't think the saw and drill situation through. I'll be out of your hair in no time. Promise." He grabs his T-shirt, pulls it back on, gathers his tools, the broken planks and the trestle, and drops everything over the railing. He leans back into me for a longer kiss and an apology

("I'm sweaty"), then hops over the railing, grabs everything, and just disappears.

Brand new deck.

Just like that.

I turn around and look at all the women on the other side of the windows, mouths agape, just like I thought. And at Wendy upstairs, beaming and giving me a thumbs up.

Chapter Thirty-Five

Ethan

Okay, maybe I shouldn't have come during business hours. I can see that Grace is very particular about how she runs her business, and seeing how successful she is—I mean, the place is always packed—she knows what she's doing. And quiet and peacefulness is one of the things I know she wants at A Touch Of Grace.

I caused some disruption this morning. Hopefully she won't get too many complaints. Hopefully the benefit of having her deck back for the enjoyment of her clients will outweigh the nuisance of my unannounced presence there.

But really—the landlord? Bullshit. The damage was not from last night or last week. You could tell from the break. It was fresh, but not *that* fresh. It's taken care of now. Grace can hold her outdoor thing now, whatever that was. It seemed important to her, so it's important to me.

I'm angered and worried that Grace is going to lose her space, though. And to Amy, of all people. Can she just get a break? My stomach is in knots just thinking about how she must feel about the whole situation. There's got to be a way. I just don't know what it is.

I fill up the truck with gas and drop it off at the job site Lucas is currently working. "You sure you don't want a job?" he half jokes.

Last time, I turned him down without hesitation. This time? It takes me a beat. The temptation is real.

But seriously. *No.* The promotion I'm up for? It's huge. Not the money—that's never a factor when you're in the service. The prestige? A little of that. But nothing to brag about. You don't want anyone to know what you're really doing. No—it's the impact I have. The knowledge that I'm really making a difference in keeping the world safe.

That's not something I'm ready to give up.

Fighting my feelings, I gun my bike back into town and stop at the antique shop. There's another project I want to work on for Grace before I leave. This one requires more creativity and no muscle work.

I clench my jaw at the memory of the ring I'd made for her. Not gonna lie, I had forgotten about it. But when she told me the story, it came back to me. Brutally. Raw. In all the pure truth of our childhood feelings. Grace was always special to me. She was. I admired her from afar for how lively and fragile and pure she was, like Mama's flowers. And occasionally, I had to protect her. Help her. Serve her. Like when Haley and Justin thought it was okay to play wedding day and have her stand there holding a makeshift train.

No way.

Not Grace.

Grace, in my eyes, was always meant to be the center of attention. The star. How could they not see that?

"Ethan? Ethan?"

I whip my head to the redhead calling my name in the Antique shop. "Autumn! It's been a minute." If memory serves me well, her parents own the shop. "Do you work here now? Or did you take over?"

A large smile brightens her face and she rolls her eyes. "Not a chance. But I am setting myself up as a decorator, and I shop here... occasionally. Or a lot," she says, laughing, "depending on what my clients want."

"Decorator, huh? That's cool."

"What brings you here?"

I tell her a little about my project, getting more animated as she nods enthusiastically at my words.

"That is *so* sweet. Let me show you a couple of things that I think might help, and then I'll run out of here before Dad convinces me that I am actually working here."

A half-hour later, I'm fastening my purchases to the back of my bike when I spot Amy on the street, strutting up to me on the sidewalk like she owns the place. She flashes a smile at me and places her hand on my chest like she owns *me*. "Ooh, someone's been working out," she purrs. "Wanna go for coffee?"

I want to tell her to go to hell, is what I want. "Sure, let's catch up."

"Hitch a ride?"

"Maybe another time. Let's just walk."

"Easy's not that close."

"What's wrong with the coffee here?" I point my chin to the general store. They still have that god awful juice that tastes like fermented ashtray. If Amy really wants a coffee with me, that's what she'll have to put up with. Once she's done hearing me out, she'll probably just throw it to my face anyway.

"Hey, it's all about the company, right?" she answers, pulling my hand to hers and leading me inside. The woman has no shame.

I pull my hand away from hers, pretending it's just to get the door, and once she's inside, tuck both my hands in my pockets. *There.* That should do it.

Noah walks by us as we're helping ourselves to coffee, does a double take at Amy, and thankfully says nothing as I take a sip from the near-full plastic cup.

The dishwater that passes as coffee is just marginally better than I remember it, or maybe I've gotten less difficult with age. Amy decides we're to drink it on their back patio that is new to me. "You know what, I like this spot better than Easy's. It's more private."

"So, I hear you're buying a new place?"

She purses her lips. "Oh... so that's why you're having coffee with me. You think you can talk me out of it. You know what, Ethan? Yeah, I'm buying a new place. I fucking deserve it. I worked my ass off for the money I'm making, and if I wanna buy the prettiest little house in town and live there, it's my fucking right."

I heard Amy became an actress or something, and good for her for making it. It's not a given. The woman has grit. "It's just... I kinda find it interesting that you don't seem to give a fuck that Grace might lose her business because of that. I'm sure there are other houses that are just as nice, even nicer. Places with land. Where you could raise a family. Have a big back yard. Horses. Whatever."

She smirks. "Tough luck. She can outbid me."

No she can't, and Amy knows that. Grace doesn't have that kind of money. "I'm just surprised someone from Emerald Creek would do that, is all. A tourist? Sure, any day. But us? It's just not... not how we look out for each other."

She sets her paper cup on the table and crosses her arms. "Look who's talking, giving me lessons on small-town life," she snarls.

"Seems to me you left Emerald Creek as well. Looks like you forgot how to be a decent person in the process. I'm trying not to."

Her eyebrows lift. "Seriously? *You're* trying to be a decent person? *You're* trying to do the right thing by Grace, of all people?"

What the fuck is she getting at? Hell yeah, I am.

She snickers. "You roll into town, get in her bed, she's got so many hearts in her eyes it's pathetic to see, really, and then what? What's your plan, Ethan?"

What does she fucking mean?

"Mm? Nothing?"

I crinkle my empty coffee cup, throw it in the overflowing garbage can, and stand.

"Yeah, I didn't think so." She stands too, leaving her still full coffee cup on the table. "See, the way I look at it, I'm doing her a favor. Cause when you get out of Dodge, once again, with her heart broken way beyond repair this time, guess what will keep her mind off your stupid dick? Me. The fact that she needs to fight to keep her business afloat. The fact that she needs to move and start over somewhere else."

The woman is crazy. Positively crazy. I swing the store's back door open and stomp through to the front, Amy on my heels, Noah glancing at us from behind the register. "Next thing you know, you're gonna tell me you're doing this all for Grace," I spit as I march past checkout, ignoring the stares following the two of us.

"Nope. I'm not. I'm doing it for me. Just like you are. Whatever it is you're doing," Amy says, waving dismissively at my saddlebags packed with shit, "it's for you. The difference between me and you is, whatever I'm doing is going to help her get over whatever shit you're pulling on her."

I'm so angry with her I can't even talk.

"Like leaving like the fucking coward you are," she thinks necessary to enlighten me.

"Always a pleasure to catch up with you," I snap as I straddle my bike.

"Pleasure's all mine!" she yells back.

I fasten my helmet and count to three before starting the bike. Wiggle my neck to work out the tension. Then count back down. Three. Two. One.

Okay. Amy Fucking Keller is out of my mind. For real.

But as I ride up to the farm, my thoughts drift back to Justin. Looks like dark thoughts are the theme today, because guilt eats me as I think back to him going through months in the hospital and in rehab after his accident. Guilt for not being there. For having been part of the succession of events that brought this upon him.

A succession of events that also tore Grace away from me.

There's no way for us to repair what was lost. Those ten years apart, resenting each other, longing for each other, missing each other, and eventually building lives without each other.

As I get organized in the small workshop Dad has off the main barn, I wonder what I'm doing here, creating yet other souvenirs of what could have been? Is this what I'm supposed to do to fix it? As I nail and hammer and sand, taking pride in my work, I can't help but ask myself: Does it really fix anything for her? I'm doing stuff that makes *me* feel good—but what about *her*?

Could Amy be right?

When Grace goes on the deck of her spa and sees the off-color planks, is she going to think about me each time? Will that bring her comfort or pain?

Am I being selfish by wanting to do things for her?

Am I forgetting about the most important person here—Grace?

I take a deep breath and look at my handiwork. Not gonna lie, it looks great. I think she's gonna love it. And if she doesn't? She can always throw it in the back of her dressing room. Throw it at me.

She might.

When she comes back from work that evening, her reaction ends up being, "Ohmygod, Ethan." And honest to god, I don't know if it's a good thing or a bad thing.

CHAPTER THIRTY-SIX

Grace

M y belly somersaults when I pull up my driveway and see the chick magnet sitting in my driveway. *Ethan*. Ethan is here. In my house.

I swing the door open and throw myself in his arms. He swirls me around and kisses me. "Hey, beautiful."

"What are you doing here?" I throw my car keys on the kitchen counter.

He gives me a squeeze. "Is it okay I came? I have a surprise for you."

"You're the surprise. Of course it's okay." I grab his nape, wrap my legs around his waist, and hoist myself up with the help of his hand under my butt. "Kiss me first. Real good. Real hard."

He nibbles at my lower lip. "Always so bossy, you."

I smile against his mouth. "Too much?"

His gaze deepens. "Never enough," he murmurs. Then he takes my mouth in slow strokes, his hand in my hair, as he walks us to the bedroom.

"Thank you for the brand-new deck," I whisper when he releases my lips reluctantly.

He seats me softly on the bed and cages me, his fists in the bed on either side of me. "Wasn't too loud?"

I grin. "You mean your cheerleaders?"

He looks utterly confused. Did he not notice all my clients eating him up and whooping? "Never mind," I say.

Damian wedges himself between us, purring. I scratch between his ears. "Were you a goo'boy?"

"He was a very goo'boy. He helped me with a little project." Ethan straightens himself and moves sideways. "What do you think?"

I stare across the space he left empty, to the wall across my bed. Frames of varying sizes adorn the wall, and a sense of panic seizes me.

Two pucks on shallow, framed-in shelves.

A folded Jersey in a glassed-in frame.

A ring of twine in a vintage jewelry box.

A slab of wood with an engraving: *A heart pranck reign.*

And a collage of photos around an old mirror.

My blood buzzes in my ears, and I feel lightheaded. My heart booms in my chest, and my lower lip trembles as wetness pours from my eyes to my cheeks.

Ethan moves to the wall. "I can—I can remove everything if you don't like it. I just... I just..." He starts unhooking the frame with the jersey. "I'll just put everything back the way it was."

I extend a hand. *Nothing can ever be the way it was.* "Don't. It's—it's fine. I mean, it's gorgeous, and thoughtful, and beautifully done... Ethan. Come here." I grab his hand and pull him down to me. He leans over me, pushing me onto my back on the bed, peppering kisses over the tears streaking my cheeks. I'm not sure what's happening to me right now. These mementos up on the wall... it's like a weird museum of lost dreams. "D'you think I'm crazy?" I whisper.

He frowns, then rubs his face with his hand. "I'm so sorry. I—I thought—I wanted to do something sweet for you. I fucked it up, didn't I? I knew I'd fuck it up." He rolls on his back and takes me with him, my head on his chest, his heart beating like crazy, booming through to my core. He strokes my back softly while I try to calm my thoughts. "You didn't fuck anything up," I murmur.

"Grace, d'you think I'm selfish? Be honest."

What? "Where is this coming from?" I lift myself up to look at him.

"Never mind." He flits his gaze to me, boops me, and resumes his observation of the ceiling.

I stroke his arm softly, the ridges of his bicep under my fingers awakening something lower in my body. My gaze settles on the wall. "Why'd you do this for me?"

"I—I didn't want the memory of me to be hiding in a box." He kisses my hair. "I—I wanted you to keep thinking about me... when I'll be gone. But I realize it was selfish." He takes a deep breath.

"Aren't we quite the pair. The crazy bitch and the selfish prick. Perfect for each other."

He laughs and pulls me to him. "You're so romantic." Then he kisses the crown of my head and adds, "You're not crazy, and you're certainly not a bitch."

"Seriously though, why did you build me a shrine to our love?"

"I'm practical. I don't want you to go through that box all the time."

"Admit it. You just want to cockblock the men I'll bring home once you're gone."

He laughs and pinches my waist. "Busted." But when our gazes meet, his smile is forced.

"I'm sorry. That was a stupid joke. You know there will never be anyone else but you."

"Course I do," he says, his voice breaking a little. "Just like there can never be anyone else but you for me." His gaze caresses my face as he adds in a whisper, "Only you can touch my soul, my heart, and my body the way you do."

I kiss the corner of his mouth, and he pulls me in for a full-on kiss, his hands kneading my ass, pulling my whole body to his. "One more thing," I say when he releases my lips. "You and I, we have a future together. It's just on us to design it. It may not look like what we thought it would, but... it's ours to build." I glance to the wall with all our memories. "Our past was just a fumbled, if beautiful, beginning."

"Fuck, Grace," he whispers, "What d'I do to deserve you?'

"Right back atcha." My eyes mist at the thought that these are our last few hours together until Ethan leaves. And even if he'll be coming back for a weekend, for the foreseeable future, our lives will be like this now. Apart.

I roll off him. "How'd you get in?" I ask to change the topic. I swear I locked the door this morning.

He produces a key from his pocket. "I might have kept the key you had under the rock. Here." He puts it in my hand. "Just promise me you won't put it under the rock again."

I don't want the key under the rock. I want it back in his pocket. On his keychain. "Promise." I take the key and shut my eyes and kiss him so we don't talk about the heavy stuff again.

"I'll go grill us some burgers," Ethan whispers against my mouth. "Did you want to change? Or take a shower? I could join you in the shower. What do you want?"

I want you to stop being so nice and attentive. I want you to stop giving me options that are all so overwhelming.

His gaze darkens. "Grace... stop looking at me like that."

My strength leaves me as I inhale his scent, rinse my eyes with the sight of him leaning over me. How did I ever get so lucky to have Ethan King in my life not just once, but twice? "Like what," I manage to whisper, my fingers playing in his short hair.

"Like... like *that*." He shuts his eyes, seeming to be in pain, and lowers his body over mine, running his hands along my sides, then lifts me higher in the bed and kisses me softly. His hands cup my face as if I'm something so fragile and precious to him, and I love—*love*—when he does that. The outside world becomes muffled, and my entire being seems encapsulated in Ethan's strong hands, the object of his sole attention.

He runs his hand under my skirt, caressing my hips, then trails to the inside of my thighs, his thumb rubbing my clit through the thin strip of my G-string. I moan against his mouth, grasping at his strong back. With a soft flick, he moves the fabric aside and exhales loudly as his fingers dip into my folds.

He lifts his head slightly away from me. "I want to watch you come. Let it go. Come for me." He draws circles around my clit then narrows in on the sensitive nub, bringing me to the edge.

"Ethan," I moan, writhing under his touch.

"That's it, baby." His touch intensifies. "God you're so beautiful when you come for me."

My back arches on its own as the orgasm rolls out. He dips two fingers inside me, and I come harder, crying out in agonizing pleasure. He cups my pelvis as the last of the orgasm shakes me, then when I'm calmer and breathless, brings my skirt down and caresses my hair.

"How's that for the end of a stressful day?"

"Better than all the cocktails in the world."

His laughter rumbles softly through my body. "I'll go make us some burgers. *And* a drink if you'd like one."

"That sounds perfect."

CHAPTER THIRTY-SEVEN

Grace

It's the soft click of the door that wakes me, the definitive sound of Ethan leaving before the sun is up. "Good luck," I whisper, although he can't hear me now. I do hope he gets the job in Brussels—*the posting*, whatever he calls it. I really do.

Right after he leaves, although it's still early, I swing my legs out the bed and stretch. There's no way I'm falling back asleep now.

And I have too much on my plate to wallow because Ethan is gone.

I don't even know how long he'll be gone. *He* doesn't even know. One week, two weeks. He couldn't even tell me exactly where he was going, only that he wasn't leaving the country—yet—and that whatever he was going to do would determine his next posting.

I use the bathroom, make the bed, and get dressed. Damian is rubbing against my legs, so I go to the kitchen to refill his water and kibble before finishing up my makeup.

On the kitchen counter is a large Mason jar, filled with little envelopes in different colors, with things written on them.

In Ethan's handwriting.

There's a large card taped to the top of the jar. It says, Open First. So I do.

My one and only,

I will miss you every day that I'm gone, and I don't know how to make up for my absence. Here are some of the thoughts of you that will occupy my mind. Open only one each day, and I promise to be back before the jar is empty.

Yours always,

Ethan

I close my eyes and take a card at random.

WILDEST FANTASY COME TRUE

Kissing you under the covered bridge again

I shut my eyes at the memory, happy tears flooding me.

Day 1 of Ethan being away, and he's already making me happy through time and distance.

My knees give slightly under me, and my palms moisten at the sight of all these cute little envelopes, all different colors.

So many of them, it seems. *How long will he really be gone*?

So many thoughts, I want to read them all. Starting right this minute. All in one sitting.

I rush to the bathroom, finish my makeup, grab my bag, and flee the house before I break a promise I didn't make and read all of Ethan's musings before he's even on the plane.

Since it's early, I head to Mom and Dad's so I can give Dad a massage before I start my day. I haven't seen them much lately.

"What's eating at you, sugar bug?" Dad reads my energy. "You miss Ethan already?" his gruff voice rubs me the wrong way today. But does he even remember what he did, back in the day?

"I do miss him, but in a good way," I answer, focusing my gaze on my dad's legs. "He's a good man."

Dad clears his throat. "I didn't like it, back in the day. This thing going on between the two a'ya. But uh... maybe... well, I might've been a little harsh on him."

Is this Dad apologizing? Does he even know that I know? There's no point having an argument, bringing up past wounds. "Other leg," I tell him, squirting massage oil on my palms and shifting in my seat.

"I just wish..." He interrupts himself, looking past me. "Hey, son."

Colton is standing in the doorway, hands on his hips. "Car is taken care of." He drops the keys on a side table and sits next to Dad, elbows on his knees. "Grace, gimme a ride back when you're done?"

"Course."

Dad grunts.

Colton looks at him. "You were saying something, Dad. You wish what?"

"Ah, heck."

"Want me to leave?" Colton provokes him. I wonder if he heard it was Ethan that Dad was talking about. I glance at my brother. We really don't need this drama now. It's history. I'm not a teenager anymore, and whatever Dad wishes for won't change my romantic life, or my opinion of Dad, for that matter.

"All I'm sayin' is, I wish Gracie Bear had a man to look after her. Not someone who's here one day, gone the rest of the year."

I snap my eyes shut for a beat. "I don't need a man to look after me, Dad." This is a useless conversation. Why am I even engaging? "I can take care of myself. Been doing that for a long time now." I flex Dad's foot, the last part of the treatment I'm giving him today, then pull down the legs of his tracksuit.

"Seems to me Gracie has the best of both worlds," Mom says, appearing out of nowhere, dressed for work. "Thanks for bringing the car back, honey," she says to Colton. Then, looking at Dad, continues, "A sweet, strong man to fix her door and deck and then gets out of the way so she can enjoy her peace and quiet." She cackles, but her pointed look at Dad tells me there might be a smidge of resentment, over a difficult past, that she's not entirely gotten rid of yet. "Lemme get you your juice and stuff before I leave," she adds in an effort to soften her last words.

"And you guys wonder why I don't want to get attached to a woman," Colton mumbles with a smirk. "Bye, Dad," he manages to add with affection as I lean in to give Dad a peck on the cheek.

Dad gives us a tired wave. "Bye, kids."

"Believe it or not, I'm with Dad," Colton says once we're in my car. "I don't like knowing Ethan's not with you. I guess I just don't see the point."

I wave at Ms. Angela watering flowers in front of her bed-and-breakfast. "You have yet to introduce us to anyone... yet you're not exactly celibate, from what I've heard. So what's your point?"

He shrugs. "It's different. I don't care about them. But if I had someone I cared about, I'd tell the Air Force to go fuck themselves."

"It's not that simple," I snap back.

"Yeah, it is."

He doesn't get it. "Ethan can't just up and leave. And what would he do in Emerald Creek anyway? It's not like there's jobs in cyber stuff around here."

Colton bites his fingernails, looking out the window. "He should figure it out."

Now he's making me angry. "I thought he was your friend?"

"Doesn't make him any less of an idiot."

I pull up to his garage. "This is you," I drop and stop the car abruptly.

He winks at me. "Thanks for the ride."

"Thanks for the conversation," I answer sarcastically, then soften my words with a smile and squeeze his arm before he jumps out of the car. I love my brother to death, and what he said rattles me.

Driving back toward the spa, I run through my mind what Ethan said to me about Colton being caught in the middle, back then. Threatened by Dad. Protecting his friend. So why is he saying these things now?

Needing to calm my nerves, I call Kyle from the car.

"Hi, honey."

"Hey."

"Tell me everything."

And I tell Kyle everything. And I end on, "So, what do you think?"

"I think Colton and your dad love you very much. I always knew that. They've always tried to protect you."

"And about..."

"Ethan?"

"Yeah," I breathe out.

He clears his throat. "Knowing you, I don't think you could love an asshole. Give him a little time. He's sorting his shit out. He can't just tell the Air Force to go fuck themselves. That's not how it works."

"Right." He's right. Absolutely. "Thank you. I needed to hear that."

"However, I'm with Colton and Dennis."

What? Why did I think calling Kyle was going to help? Of course he's going to side with the macho men in my family. He just doesn't underst—

"He didn't think he'd fall for you again, hell, he didn't even think he'd see you this time around," he says, interrupting my thoughts. "The guy is figuring things out. Give him... give him a few months, honey."

"For what?"

"To get his life sorted out. Look, and again, I don't know him. But if he's halfway decent, and you guys, you know, went all the way... I mean he must know what this means."

"I don't want Ethan to leave the Air Force for me. You guys are crazy!" There's no way I can expect, or ask, Ethan to let go of his dream job for me. That would be petty of me. Selfish. That would demonstrate utter misunderstanding of the man I love. He's chosen to make the world a safer place, and I'm not expecting him to change that for me. Just because we fell back together doesn't erase the ten years that drew us apart.

"What do you really want, Grace? And you don't have to answer me, but really—answer yourself. Is this what you want? Being with a man who isn't by your side?"

I don't know how to answer this, even to myself. Think about it, there's a part of me that wishes Ethan had never come back. And another part that wishes he hadn't left this morning. But the sane part of me knows I must accept what I can't change. It's the only true path to happiness. "What are you saying?"

"I'm saying, I'm with Colton, but with a little more patience."

I stifle a huff.

Kyle continues. "I don't want to see you alone, Grace. You deserve better."

I swallow my tears.

"You better believe me."

"Thank you, hun," I manage to say.

"Bye, honey. It'll figure itself out. I'll call you 'round Christmas."

I hang up, feeling worse, which was not the outcome I was hoping for. I wanted validation.

Kyle always knew what I needed, and he knew it wasn't him. He knew about Ethan *before* my first date with him. He knew about Ethan the whole time we were together. He knows what I'm going through. Why couldn't he just tell me what I needed to hear?

As I hang up, my phone rings, and I pick up immediately

Ethan's voice fills my car, and instantly my hands get moist, my heartbeat picks up. "Hey darling."

"Heeey." I make my voice as cheery as possible, but it's a stretch.

"I miss you already. I'm at the airport... Uh... Just wanted to say... just wanted to hear your voice." I can hear the smile in his voice.

My smile is so big it hurts my cheeks. "You didn't kiss me good-bye."

"Did too. Didn't wake you, though. You're a deep sleeper."

I'm not, I'm really not. Except in Ethan's arms. Anything could go down when I'm in Ethan's arms, and I wouldn't wake up.

"It's because I know you're here, taking care of me." It's true, but also—really?

"Ah, babe, don't say that, or I might not get on that plane."

Then don't, I almost want to say.

Reading my mind, he says, "I'm still technically Air Force. You don't want to be with a deserter. Not a fun life."

Be with? Life? This is *real*. We have something *real*. No matter what the other men in my life might think. "That bad, huh?" I answer, pretending like he didn't just rock my world.

"Oh yeah."

I stay on the line, listening to his breathing. I don't want to hang up. "I got your... all your little letters."

"You didn't read them already, did you?" he growls, a smile in his voice.

My inside warms at his tone, at our intimacy. "No. Just one a day, I promise."

"Did you open one this morning?" His words make me all sorts of soft.

"The covered bridge," I whisper.

"Ah damn. You have no idea how many times I hoped for... a second chance. Going back and-and-and... things turning out differently. I couldn't believe it when... Ah shit, they're boarding my flight. I gotta go. I'll be in touch. I promise."

"Okay," I whisper. With a steadier voice, I add, "Good luck with the interview... and all the other stuff."

"Yeah." He clears his throat. "Thanks."

My heart does its little dance again: I want him to go, and I want him to stay. I want him to have the success he deserves. I want him to have a fulfilling life. And it's within his reach.

But I also want to wake up next to him every morning. "Lemme know how it goes, okay?" I ask, just to hear his voice once more.

"Of course. I'll call you."

Chapter Thirty-Eight

Grace

After I hang up with Ethan, I feel much better. By the sound of his voice, I could tell he's conflicted too, and not the asshole Dad and Colton and Kyle suggest he might be. He sends a quick text when he lands, but I only see it an hour later. I answer him, wanting but not daring to call him. I don't know what his schedule is. I don't want to interfere.

During my lunch break, I walk to the general store to get some kibble for Damian. At the register, keychains and cute charms catch my eye. I choose a few and set them on the wooden checkout counter. "Solid choices," Noah says with a small smile.

My cheeks burn. "Yeah, thanks."

After work I go straight home. I'm still vaguely pissed at Dad and Colton, and I don't want to go to Lazy's and just wallow with my girlfriends over Ethan's departure. I check my phone every five minutes, but there's no message from him.

I'm tempted to open one of the little envelopes now, so I move the jar to my nightstand.

I'm about to sit in front of a movie when my door opens.

Kiara, Alex, Chloe, and Haley barge in. Kiara has a box of pastries, Alex some fresh baked bread still warm from the oven, Chloe brought takeout from the restaurant she manages, and Haley has not one, but two bottles of wine.

"Your house is so cute!" Chloe exclaims.

Haley sighs. "Dude, still no deck furniture?"

"You sound just like your brother," I say, smiling.

"Awww, look at that smile," Haley teases, while Kiara sets her boxes on the couch, opens the sliding doors, and lifts one side of my kitchen table. "We're still bringing the party outside. I need another pair of hands."

"You should ask Autumn," Chloe says as she carries chairs outside while Alex and Kiara bring the kitchen table out. "She set me up with great stuff for a really good price."

"Yeah, you better. I'm not doing that again," Alex says. "No wonder you're always eating out. Your place is cute, but it's not... entertainment-level ready."

I shrug. "No one ever really comes over, except Skye." And although I told Ethan this was his home, it's not like he's going to be spending any time in it.

"Shit," Haley says. "Now that I think about it, it's true. Why not?"

Because I put all my energy into my business, and when I come home, all I want to do is sleep? "I dunno."

"Well, now that Ethan has pretty much moved in, you might wanna, you know, zhuzh it up a bit," Kiara says as we all move to the deck, each of us carrying a mismatched chair.

Zhuzh it up? What's wrong with my house? It's cute, and neat, and clean. "He hasn't moved in. Although…"

Haley stops what she's doing. "Although what?"

"Well, when he comes back, I'm giving him a key."

"You go, girl," Kiara says.

"Umm… To be honest, I think I kinda got ahead of myself. I already told him… I said…"

"You said what?" they all ask.

"I told him this was his *home*. Well, I said *Emerald Creek* was his home, but he read between the lines." *At least I think he did.*

They gape at me. *Crap. I knew it.* "I'm crazy, right? I'm so… so out of practice. Why did I tell him that? He must think I'm so desperate."

"What!? What is wrong with you?" my friends exclaim.

Haley takes both my hands in hers. "Honey, listen. You are not desperate. You are a strong, kind, loving woman who gave her heart to a strong, kind, loving man. What are you scared of?"

I widen my eyes at her. What is she talking about? "He's never gonna be here. Can't you see? I'm not thinking straight." Dad's and Colton's and even Kyle's words resonate as words of wisdom, now that I've had a few hours to process.

"You're giving him an anchor. A place to call home. A place to visualize as his when he's all alone doing god knows what. A place for the two of you. That's huge. That's everything. God he's so lucky to have you," Haley says.

I'm lucky to have him, too, even if I miss him so much it physically hurts.

"On a scale of one to ten, how sad are you?" Alex asks.

"About what?"

While Chloe and Kiara set the table outside, Haley pours us an orange-y, bubbly drink in rocks glasses. "Drop the act, sister. About my idiot brother."

"I..." Words escape me. I shouldn't really be thinking about this now. Measuring how sad I am isn't how I'll protect my happy. All I can say is, this morning I got out of bed after Ethan left, didn't lose it when Hope, who does the waxes in addition to facials, called out and I had to do Mrs. Summer's Brazilian bikini wax. And I did not panic when I failed to find any commercial rentals online should I lose my space. So on a scale of one to ten functioning? I'm at a ten. The takeaway? "I'm doing fine."

Alex rolls her eyes. "She's doing *fine*. We know what *that* means." She takes a sip of her drink and stifles a grimace.

"Have some Wiener Schnitzel," Chloe says, pushing the serving platter toward me.

"I'm really not hungry."

My friends exchange *the look*.

"You don't like it?" Haley says, looking around the table, then at our glasses. I take a sip. Ouch. It's very sour, and really... "What is it?" I ask.

I'm saved from Haley's murderous look by my phone's ringtone. I jump out of my chair and check the display. *Ethan.* I pick up and go find privacy in my bedroom.

His voice rumbles like a welcomed storm after a hot summer day. "Hey, darling. Sorry I didn't call earlier. There's poor service here, believe it or not."

"See?" I giggle like a giddy teenager. "It's not just Vermont."

"Mmm. God I love your voice. What are you doing right now?"

"Sitting at the foot of my bed, talking to you."

"And before that?"

"The Bitch Brigade came over for dinner."

"The who?"

"The Bitch Brigade." I tell him how that moniker came about just last week.

"I didn't know you were the entertaining kind. But I'm not surprised."

"There's a lot you don't know about me," I say coyly, "but to be honest, they think I need to buy deck furniture. Pretty much they lectured me on my poor hostess skills."

"I don't know about the hostessing, but the deck could use a little more... actually, forget it. I like having you on my lap."

"A-ha. Now you see my point."

"Are they still there?"

"Yeah, they got here not too long ago."

"Call me when they're gone? I want to hear all about your day, minute by minute. But I don't want them to continue bashing your hostessing skills."

His sweetness goes straight to my heart. "Including the minute-by-minute account of Mrs. Summers's Brazilian bikini wax?"

"I'm not sure what that is, but it sounds painful and not something I need to hear. Unless it caused you some trauma you need to offload on me."

I laugh out loud and hang up with the promise of calling him the minute the Bitch Brigade is gone.

"Ohmygod, look at that smile!!" Alex gushes.

Haley shakes her head. "I can't believe my brother is responsible for that." Then she looks at me seriously and squeezes my hand as I sit down. "I love you," she whispers softly, tears in her eyes. "And swear to god, he might be my brother, but I will kill him if he hurts you."

Kiara pops a piece of bread in her mouth. "Fuck. What was that about?"

"We're the Bitch Brigade. You said it yourself. We look after each other. And this one," Haley says, taking my hand again, "has been my soul sister since we were born. So... my blood brother better not mess it up."

"Haley, it's fine. We... Ethan and I, we have an unconventional relationship. First off, this is all very new, and we need time to figure out how we want to be together."

Although I can't help but wonder... are you truly together if you don't spend each and every night together? In each other's arms, breathing the same air? Making love?

"You're doing good, keep going," Haley prompts me.

"Yeah, spill it," Kiara says.

"At the beginning, I thought it'd be better if he were away. This way, I wouldn't fall for him too much." My friends give me encouraging looks. "But now... now, he's all I can think about. He's all I want, and how pathetic is that?"

"It's not pathetic at all!" Alex exclaims.

"It's like, I had this great, stable life as a single woman, a successful business owner, and now suddenly, the carpet is pulled out from under me. I'm struggling to keep my business together and the world feels... empty without Ethan in it." I don't even have Skye to take care of, now that Alex is in Chris's life. So much is going to be different, and everything happened so fast.

"It's called being in love," Alex says, taking my hand. "You caught the bug."

"That's bullshit," Kiara declares. "Butterfly, I thought we talked about this. Change and shit. Nothing you can do about it. Note to self, though: this is why I don't do relationships." She looks around the room, seeming satisfied.

Haley takes my other hand. "I think what Kiara is trying to say is, nothing lasts forever. This is just a transition. You'll figure out your spa situation one way or another, and Ethan won't be in the Air Force forever. You'll figure it out."

"You're right." It's just the in-between that's so hard. "I'm so grateful for you guys." I clear my throat and decide to let it all out. "I just think that... it's just that... we've had so little time together. And I worry. I worry that we may not be as solid as I think we are. I worry about him being alone. About needing someone by his side. You know?"

Haley squeezes my hand. "He would never. *Ever*. Sweetheart, you're worried over nothing."

"You're right. You're right." God, where did my mind go just now? Is this how it's going to be, moving forward? Constantly missing him? Constantly wondering if my voice on the phone is enough? Waiting for the other shoe to drop? This is pure horror. I need to focus back on my friends.

I take a sip from the glass Haley poured us. It hits my taste buds in an indescribable way, so I set it on the table. "Though I think there's studies about how spending the whole night with someone brings people closer. Something about breathing the same air and how your bodies communicate with each other when you're sleeping?"

Kiara guffaws. "What's in that—whatever beverage you're serving us? Grace is hallucinating."

Haley seems offended. "It's sumac and pear cider. Can't you tell?"

"Yeah!" Alex says. "You know how your bellies talk to each other when you're in bed?"

Kiara looks at Alex with a disgusted look. "Um—no, I don't. And ew—gross."

"My cider's gross?" Haley says, but I know it's to take the conversation in a different direction.

"No! Your cider is... it needs a little more work."

Haley sighs. "Can we deconstruct the tastes?"

Kiara and Chloe swirl the drink in their mouths, sniffing, talking about acidity and fruit and roots.

Finally, my mind is off its dangerous path as an idea strikes me. "Guys! I just had an idea." They all look at me. "What if I had my own line of products, at the spa? Locally made with all this stuff," I say, waving my hand at the chocolate and cider on the table.

They're all quiet, until Haley breaks the silence. "That's a great idea. When you or we have the money to fund the research and the place to make it and—"

"I'll look into it," Alex says. All eyes turn to her. "We're looking to support local initiatives in the food sector. I'm sure we can... interpret our mission statement liberally." She recently inherited a baking empire from her grandmother, and she's in the process of turning it into a co-op and moving the headquarters to Emerald Creek.

We end up brainstorming my project and discussing Haley's latest creation over a bottle of my store-bought wine.

They leave late, and I call Ethan right away, hoping I don't wake him.

"Darling," he drawls lovingly.

I tell him about my evening, and he listens attentively. "Your friends are awesome, sweetheart. So happy you have that in your life."

"How did your day go?" I ask, suddenly self-conscious I've been talking only about myself.

He sighs deeply. "Okay, I guess. I just miss you. Are you in bed?"

"Not yet. I have to brush my teeth."

"Get ready and call me from bed? I want your voice to be the last thing I hear tonight. And I'm not sleepy yet."

"Okay," I breathe against my better judgment. How can I say no to Ethan asking me to be the last thing he hears?

See? We can make it work. We can have a long-distance relationship.

CHAPTER THIRTY-NINE

Grace

D AY 2 LOVE NOTE:
SENSORY IMPRINTING
The smell of your skin: honey with a hint of lavender and jasmine

Proving my point, the next morning, Randy, Emerald Creek's florist, delivers a gorgeous bouquet in tones of blues and golds to the spa. The envelope says *Grace*, and the note reads, *Always thinking about you*. It's in Ethan's handwriting, which means he planned this before leaving. And how sweet is that? Would I have gotten a gorgeous bouquet if he hadn't left? I don't think so.

It's the silver lining of a long-distance relationship.

The proof that we can be unconventional. That our love is stronger than our geographical separation. Last night's angst is flying out the window.

Randy and Claudia move a side table so we can set the bouquet at the entrance. "It elevates the whole place," Randy points out.

I want it there so I can see it every time I come through the main room, which has to be a hundred times a day. I'm tempted to take it home, but I still have the smaller bouquet Ethan got me before leaving.

Randy clasps his hands together. "Oh gosh, Grace, I'm so happy for you. He's such a catch!"

My heart swells. "Hey, he sure knows how to make his absence worthwhile. Your arrangements are gorgeous."

Randy blushes. "Oh, thank you."

After Randy leaves, I take a selfie in front of the bouquet to send to Ethan.

"Let me see?" Claudia says over my shoulder. "Let me get a better one." She takes the phone from my hands and directs me to stand in front of the flowers.

Ethan hearts my message with the photo but doesn't text back. He doesn't call in the evening either.

That night, I Google *How to dry a bouquet.*

DAY 3 LOVE NOTE:

FUNNY-NOT FUNNY
Your face when you rushed to your house thinking Damian was sick, and instead found me and your box of souvenirs

That day, I finally text the Bitch Brigade about Amy visiting the space. With Ethan having just left, I didn't have it in me to talk about that, too, with my friends. But it's time.

And now I have to fend off a slew of angry texts and plots for vengeance.

Which is exactly why I didn't text them right after the fact. They might have been able to convince me to get on the warpath. And the truth is? There's nothing I can do but move and start somewhere new. Richardson was right about not spending my money on a lost cause.

Even assholes are right sometimes.

Finally, Alex chimes in with something constructive.

Alex

> Let's take a look at the Mill. You might like it.

The Mill is a stone building alongside the river, three levels high if you count the basement level. It's hosted artists co-ops, pop-up events, a yoga studio for a while. My theory was that none of these businesses survived there because the vibe wasn't right for anything wellness centered. Add to that there is little light. But maybe it's time I set my woo woo theories aside and be realistic about my future. Yeah, just like for my personal relationship. *Be realistic, Grace.*

Me

> You're right.

Ten minutes later, Alex texts me back.

Alex

> We're on for this afternoon.

"Anybody free to join?" I ask my staff while we're sharing a quick lunch on the now-repaired deck, enjoying a rare moment when almost all of us are free at the same time. Only Hope is giving someone a facial.

"I'll come, if I must," Fabrizio sighs.

Shanice has been aimlessly running her fork in her quinoa salad since I started talking about moving. "Me too."

"Anybody else?"

"I'll hold down the fort," Claudia says.

"I don't want to manifest moving," Cheyenne declares. "I'll stay right here with Hope. She feels the same."

That evening, Ethan calls me. "I'm sorry about last night, baby. It went on for hours. I didn't want to wake you."

I'm sprawled on the one lounge chair, drinking club soda. Damian is at my feet, squinting at the great outdoors, dying to explore it but too chicken to do anything about it. "You should've. You know you can call me anytime, day or night." I don't want to tell him how much I missed hearing his voice, but he needs to know there's nothing I want more than to hear him.

"How was your day?" he asks me.

I tell him about the visit to the Mill. "Worst case, I'll take it." The Mill is like I remembered it, except that empty, it looked even more uninviting.

"Is it that bad?"

"No, but it's just not... not anything like what I'm offering now."

"What's it like?"

"A large empty space, very high ceilings, cool stone walls, dark cement floors. It screams tech company, not luxurious, pampering spa."

"Gotcha," he grunts. "Nothing else on the market?'

"A couple houses that are too small. But I'll find something. Don't worry about me."

"I *want* to worry about you, Grace. In fact, it's the only kind of worry I'm interested in, these days. Get used to it," he grumbles in his low voice.

I want to touch him, see him, smell him. I switch the call to video. His face appears, grayish and vaguely distorted. "Hey, babe."

"Wanted to share the sunset with you," I say, pretending, switching away from the selfie view, taking in his features as he looks at his screen.

"I wish I was there. How's my boy Damian?"

Damian pricks his ears at his name, and I angle the phone so Ethan can see him. "You taking care of my woman, cat?" he says, and why does him talking macho like that make me all mushy coming from him but all prickly when it's Dad or Colton, or even Kyle? I wiggle in my chair, becoming bothered, in a good way, at all this sexiness.

I switch back to selfie view, we talk about nothing for a little bit, and then Ethan stifles a yawn. "You get some rest, sweetie," I say, not allowing him to protest. "We'll talk tomorrow."

I switch the phone off after he tells me again how sexy I am and how much he misses me, then I stay on the lounge chair for a while, staring mindlessly at Woodbury Knoll.

When it's past midnight I open an envelope.

Day 4 Love Note:

My Proudest Moment
Holding you against your bedroom wall and managing not to fuck you
although I wanted it so bad and I could tell you did too.
But you said otherwise, so I complied.

God that memory is hot. *So* hot.

Seared into my brain. I still feel his hand clasping my wrists over my head, his hard thigh under my clit, his breath teasing me.

That night, I fall asleep with my hand between my thighs.

The next morning he texts that he'll be out of reach for the next few days, and day after day, all I have are his loves notes.

Day 5 Love Note:

WTF

Your box of souvenirs. Freak out on so many levels.

Day 6 Love Note:

AND THE GOLDEN GLOBE GOES TO...
Grace Harper for best actress, pretending she doesn't give two shits about
Ethan King in the feature film Five Nights At The Arena, where she
broke his heart one mug at a time.

Day 7 Love Note:

BEST AND STRONGEST MEMORY FROM THE PAST
You in our treehouse, after our first time.

This one brings tears to my eyes, which in turn makes me pause. I realize I've not yet given myself the time and grace to look back into the past and acknowledge all the good I had with Ethan, years ago. After my initial rejection of him, I've been too focused on making sure we were still right for each other *in this moment*. Then, that it was okay to have a long-distance relationship.

We may seem to be different people because of our life experiences, but fundamentally we're still the same. I'll always remember Ethan's loving attention when I gave myself to him—or more in fashion with eighteen-year-old Grace, bossed him around to have me. He was entirely focused on me, on my pleasure and comfort, from the way he aroused me with his kisses and caresses, to how he checked in on me, making sure I was still on board. To the way he cared for me, after.

At the time, I was solely focused on the way Ethan King came undone inside me, the magic of seeing his features transcended by his own orgasm.

I felt powerful. Invincible. Unique. I loved him fiercely, but failed to see how much he too loved me. I was insecure.

Now, I know. I know how he loved me then, and how he loves me now.

This kind of love resisted the test of time. It'll stand the test of distance.

That day, I walk home to find a gorgeous bouquet of red and white roses waiting for me. There's a card signed Ethan, but it's not in his handwriting. Four simple words, "*Miss you so much*," echo my sentiment exactly.

There's another card, this one simple and white, with my spare key on it. The handwriting is identical to the one signed Ethan, and the message reads, "*Ethan said I'd probably find your key under a fake rock next to your door, and if I did, to let myself in, lock myself out, and remind you this might be Emerald Creek, but danger lurks everywhere.*

No key under the fake rock.

Randy

PS: Don't kill the messenger

᪥

Day 8 Love Note:

WTF # 2 – However
The fact you kept the twine ring I made you a quarter of a century ago just blows my mind. You're the most loving and faithful person I know.

᪥

DAY 9 LOVE NOTE:

LEAST PROUD MOMENT
You telling me Emerald Creek was my home, and me not daring to answer that you're *my home.*

Oh, Ethan. My chin wobbles while I'm smiling at his admission. What a pair of fools we are, holding back on saying how much we love each other.

That day, I keep my phone with me at the spa, in case Ethan calls. The week is up. Surely he'll call.

It's nighttime when he finally does. "Hey, beautiful." His voice is like a magical balm on a burn. It makes everything go away.

"Ethan," I breathe. "I missed you. So much."

"Sorry, babe," he growls.

And then it hits me. I can't be telling him that. Not when I'm sorta agreeing to a long-distance relationship. I can't guilt-trip him. "I missed you in a good way," I correct.

"Yeah well, I missed you in a real bad way." Ohmygod, the growl in his voice makes my insides pulse. "Fuck, but I want to be with you right now. Wanna be inside you, if I'm honest."

"Baby," I whisper.

"Are you in bed?"

"On my couch."

"Whatcha doin?"

"Stuffing my face with the chocolates you sent me." Yesterday, Kiara came to the spa to deliver the box herself. "Good news is, Ethan'll be happy to know there's no key under the fake rock," she said. "But I didn't want to leave these outside in the sun." Whispering, she added, "His instructions were they're for you only." So I brought the chocolates home (I did offer one to each of my staff), and now I'm indulging.

Ethan grunts. "You alone?"

"Yeah, why?"

"Your voice is making me so hard right now. You're using your horny voice. Am I right? You horny?"

"Fuck yeah," I whisper.

"What are you wearing?"

"Um. Yoga pants and your jersey."

"And under that?"

"Like a... a thong."

"No bra?"

"N-no."

"Fuck," he growls.

My hand goes between my legs, and I wriggle on the couch. Feeling self-conscious, I run to the bedroom.

"Babe, say my name."

"Ethan," I whine.

"Are you touching yourself? Fuck, babe, you're touching yourself, aren't you."

"Um..."

His breathing is labored on the phone, and the sound of fabric comes through. "My cock is beating for you, babe. It's full and hard."

I slide my yoga pants to my knees and push the thin strip of my G-string aside. "I'm so wet for you," I whine.

"Fuck, babe. Now touch your breasts."

"O-Okay." I put the phone on loudspeaker and pinch my nipple with my other hand. "It's not the same when it's not you," I complain.

"Shit. Tell me something. Anything."

"I want to suck your cock."

He grunts.

"And then I want you to have your way with me. What will you do to me when you see me, Ethan?"

"I'm gonna fuck you so hard, you won't be able to walk for days. I'm gonna make you come so loud, the church ladies will sign themselves when they see you in town. I'm gonna mark you, Grace. I'm gonna make you mine."

I buck under his words, my fingers working my clit. "I'm coming, Ethan. I'm coming for you."

He grunts softly, then lets out a long "fuuuck."

We're silent for a while. "You still there?" I ask, slightly out of breath.

"Yeah. Shit that wasn't bad, but nothing like the real thing."

"No." The house is quiet. There's no after sex cuddle. It feels a little... sad.

I stand and move back to the living room.

"Where you going?"

"To the living room."

"I thought you were there already?"

I blush. "I moved to the bedroom when... when it started heating up."

He growls. "No living room sex?"

I fill a glass of water. "It feels... it feels weird."

He laughs softly. "We'll work on that."

Ohmygod. "Okay."

"Okay," he repeats in a chuckle. "God you're cute. How was your week?"

"Nothing new with the lease yet. Waiting to get some sort of official notification. It's a little nerve-wracking." Then I tell him about Fabrizio freaking out after a client insisted on him giving her what he calls a Karen haircut. About Cheyenne finally entering a graphic arts competition. About the idea I had the other day, with the girls, that I just can't let go of, of having my own line of products.

"I think that's a great idea. Fuck Richardson and Amy. You're gonna crush it no matter what. I just know it."

That evening, after hanging up, I sort through my clothes and free up almost half my closet and a portion of my drawers.

DAY 10 LOVE NOTE:

A FREAK-OUT MOMENT—AND I WANT THIS TOO
Skye looks so much like you, I thought she was your daughter.

Yeah, a lot of people think—*Ohmygod!! What is he saying now?* I reread the title, and then the note.

Am I understanding this correctly?

Ohmygod.

I think I am.

But I don't think I want a child with a long-distance father. That doesn't seem... on the other hand...

The next day, after dropping my clothes in the donation bin at the church, I text the girls.

Me

who's down for a trip to the Grange?

Alex

> Yup

Haley

> Finally

Chloe

> What's the Grange again?

Kiara

> Who's buying

Autumn

> I have a discount there

Chloe

> I remember now. LOVE THAT PLACE

Me:

> Kay we'll need 2 cars. Sunday work for everyone?

My last message gets varied emojis and no protests. It's a date.

The Grange is a large consignment barn that doesn't accept people's crap, but rather serves as an outlet for furniture stores, high-end hotels revamping their still-good furniture, and the occasional treasure from an estate. The day we meet up is hot as hell, and we're all in shorts and tank tops. Alex brought Skye with her, and she jumps into my arms. "Alek-zandra said I could have a princess bed. Will you help me look for one?'

"If you'll help me look for a dining room table and chairs and stuff for the deck."

Skye wiggles out of my arms, grabs my hand, and drags me inside. Stopping in her tracks, she frowns. "What kinda stuff?"

Heck if I know. "I'll know it when I see it."

"Well, I know exactly what my princess bed needs to look like."

But Skye is just like the rest of us females, and she gets sucked in, forgetting her initial goal. Going to the Grange is like stepping inside a time warp. We go from find to treasure, calling each other out, taking photos, sneezing in the dust. At least it's cool inside.

"Okay, what do we got?" Autumn calls out at some point. "I have two contenders for a dining room table and chairs, and options for the deck."

"I found twelve cute as hell old school tables."

"I found five vintage sinks."

"How about this century-old pile of bricks for a built-in barbecue?"

"I like this for the deck," I say. It's a wide wicker couch with an ottoman just as wide.

"Nice," Autumn says. "It can double as a lounge chair for two." She writes something down on a notepad and mumbles, "Let's see if they'll throw in the two matching armchairs. Now, what we came for in the first place. Outdoor dining." Autumn points out several large metallic tables. "They're foldable. You could store it somewhere in the winter, so it doesn't age too fast. They have matching chairs and pillows in perfect condition. If you don't like the patterns they have, we can have new ones made." These tables seem huge, like they could fit eight people easy. Soft excitement courses through my veins as I choose one of the patterns among the three or four they have—a bayadere stripe in tones of red and orange that just screams happy summer.

Autumn scribbles in her notepad, then says, "Now lemme show you what I found for the dining room."

We clear the tables so we can examine them properly. To my great embarrassment, Autumn points out every sign of wear to the two sales people now following us like their next paycheck depends on us (which might be the case). Turns out, they're not offended, and we get a good price.

I set my choice on an English-style farmhouse table in natural pine and distressed white, with four matching chairs and two armchairs. The Grange employees throw in an area rug and a cute tray with heart-shaped cutouts.

While they haul my purchases to the front under Autumn's watchful eyes, the other girls roam the aisles some more. No princess bed for Skye here, but everyone still has a thing or two they couldn't possibly live without. When we're all paid for and gathered in the parking lot, we're stuck with a problem.

"That'll never fit in any of the cars."

Haley calls Justin. "Our future sister-in-law needs a moving truck," she says, laughing into the phone. My belly does a full flip. What did she just call me?

Skye squeaks. "Did Uncle Ethan propose?"

"No, honey, he did not. Haley is just being... facetious."

"Fashy...?"

"Silly."

Haley hangs up. "The guys are on their way. They said to leave everything here."

"Can we go for ice cream?" Skye squeaks.

"This one's got her priorities right," Kiara says. "Come on, sunshine."

"Let's go to that place down by the river. Remember?" Chloe says.

A half hour later, we're all holding ice creams, our feet in the cool stream. "Can we go and set up Aunt Grace's house now?" Skye asks.

"We have to wait," Alex says.

"For what?"

"For the guys to have everything delivered to Grace's. If we get there and help, they're gonna say we're in the way," Haley explains.

"What Haley means is, let the guys do the heavy lifting," Kiara says.

"Shoot," I say.

"What?"

"My key. It's no longer under the rock. They won't be able to get in." I should have left it there. "I'll go. You guys stay here and relax."

"Can I come with you?" Skye asks.

"Course!"

She runs to my car and sits in her bolster seat. "This is exciting," she declares as she wiggles her little body so I can fasten her seatbelt. "Is this a surprise for Uncle Ethan?"

"Not really, but kinda."

"I like him. He's big."

I have to laugh at that.

"I hope he proposes. Daddy is going to propose to Alex."

Warmth and excitement courses through my veins. "Oh, honey! Are you happy?"

"Sooo happy. But you can't tell Alex. I'm helping him organize it."

"Of course not." My smile won't go away.

After we pull into my driveway, I open the door to the guys who are unloading my new furniture. Then I give my cousin a big hug. "I'm so happy for you," I whisper. He deserves this happiness so much. He never gave up on Alex.

He squeezes me back. "Happy for you, too, Gracie. You'll get there too."

We all forge our paths our own way. One step at a time.

Two hours later, my house looks fantastic. Colton, Justin, and Chris brought everything in, in no time, set it up, and moved everything around until I was satisfied. Now the girls are showing up with food, and we're setting up to have a proper barbecue. Skye and Alex give me a set of linen napkins. Autumn brings yet another vase 'for all the flowers you're going to get.'

Haley hugs me when she sees the house and says, "I had the feeling you might want to wait until Ethan's back to throw a housewarming party. So the gifts'll wait."

I look at Justin throwing flank steaks on the barbecue and Chris slicing breads. Chloe sets a salad in the center of the outdoor table. Alex lights a few candles to keep the mosquitos away, then helps Autumn arrange a string of bistro lights on the deck's perimeter. Colton is setting the table under Skye's directions, while Kiara is arranging a display of mini cakes on a three-tiered dish she bought at the Grange. "This turned into way more than I expected," I whisper, moved to tears.

CHAPTER FORTY

Ethan

I t's been twenty-four hours since I've touched my phone. Twenty-four hours of non-stop work with just a handful of stolen minutes to doze off in a chair, no phones allowed.

The first thing I do when I'm done isn't going out into the sun and drinking a beer with the other guys before collapsing on my bed. It's retrieving my phone and turning it on.

Grace

> I love you

Grace

> Thinking of you

Grace

> He misses you!

> <photo of Damian with a sock wedged between his paws>

Did I leave my dirty laundry at Grace's?

Grace

> Good morning my love <heart emoji>

Justin

> Looking after Grace for you. Get your ass
> back here.

I click on the right-pointing arrow to start the video he's sending, sick in my stomach that something might have happened to Grace.

Instead, I see a close-up of her laughing. The video pans out and swipes to the right. She's on her deck, sitting at a table that's new to me, Colton next to her with Skye on his lap. Next to him is Autumn, then Chloe, an empty chair (presumably Justin's), Haley, and Kiara. They're laughing and talking together, oblivious to the fact that Justin is filming them. The video finishes on Justin's face, and a "Miss you, asshole" that punches me hard.

Miss you too. All of you. So damn much.

I start the video again and stop it on Grace. There's a soft glow about her, a strong happiness, when she's surrounded by her friends and family. It's not just the way she's smiling wide at something Colton is telling Skye. Not just her rust-colored T-shirt and how it flatters her complexion. Not just the way her gold earrings reflect the flickering candlelight. It's something deep, and profound, and stable, that emanates from her.

A sense of home.

I want to be there. I want to be part of those who make her so happy. So fulfilled. And I want to be on the receiving end of her happy too.

I'm jealous. Fuck yeah, I'm jealous of this.

I hit the call button.

Chapter Forty-One

Grace

D AY 11 LOVE NOTE:

Sexiest thing you do #2

The way you purr—like a kitten, but softer

I'm at the spa when my phone rings with Ethan's ringtone. Specifically, on the deck with Ms. Angela who wants a repeat of the wellness day I organized for the Golden Girls. She cocks an eyebrow and starts saying, "You should get that," but I'm already back inside, ducking for the break room.

"Ethan!" I half screech, half whisper. My heartbeat is out of control, my palms sweaty. "Are you okay?"

"Yeah, babe. Just sort of... out of it. Been stuck inside for days, working on shit."

I look out the window, at the lush green trees swaying in the breeze, the birds hopping from branch to branch, the thin stripes of clouds gently marring the deep blue sky. "That doesn't sound healthy. I'm sorry."

"How are you?"

I miss you like crazy. When are you coming home? "I'm doing good. Nothing much new over here. Daisy was in town a couple of days ago, eating the flower baskets in front of the library. Logan and Hunter managed to wrangle her and take her back home."

His strangled laugh makes me smile. "Wrangle her?"

"Like two legit cowboys. Rope and all. Logan was riding Sunshine, Hunter was on a BMX. You should have seen them." I laugh at the memory of Ethan's two younger brothers coaxing their runaway cow to come back to the farm. "Honestly, I think it was Sunshine who convinced Daisy it wasn't worth the trouble." The horse was whinnying softly, and you could tell Daisy was paying attention. It was the cutest thing to see, but I don't want to lay it too thick on Ethan that he's missing so much of life's daily pleasures by dealing with the world's bigger problems.

Someone has to deal with those big problems so the rest of us can continue leading our simple, almost worry-free lives.

We talk for a bit, but I can tell he's exhausted. "I'm going to catch some shut-eye, beautiful. Not sure when I'll be calling again."

I don't ask him when he's coming back.

DAY 12 LOVE NOTE:

SEXIEST THING YOU DO #1
Sleeping naked in my jersey

As of now, there are only two envelopes left in the jar. One green and one pink.

⋰⋰

DAY 13 LOVE NOTE:

MIXED EMOTIONS

You and Justin discussing your business made me feel so happy for the both of you, and excluded at the same time.

What is he talking about? When did I discuss my business with Justin? I can't remember. Could have been anytime. My heart pinches knowing Ethan feels excluded now.

⋰⋰

DAY 14 LOVE NOTE:

FEELING COMPLETE AGAIN

You having coffee with Mom and Dad on the porch, waiting for me. Been wanting this my whole life.

There are no envelopes left, and Ethan is not back yet.

But he calls that night.

"Hey, beautiful."

"Ethan!" The sound of his voice never fails to excite me. There's background noise I can't really make out, but I don't dare ask him where he is or what he's doing. Top-secret stuff and all that. But he sounds tired. Worn out. "What's wrong, baby?"

"Nothing. Just wanted to hear your voice. God I missed you. Tell me what happened. Just tell me anything. I need to hear your voice. How's work? Any news on the lease?"

I'm not ruining a phone call with Ethan with my work problems. Especially since they now involve *Amy Keller.* "I've had better."

"Tell me everything. Every single thing."

So I do. I pop a gold-flecked chocolate in my mouth, not really caring about the shit that was my day anymore, and I tell him I got officially notified about the impending sale, and that I had a certain time to let the owner know if I wanted to buy the house. I tell him I decided not to answer, just to scrape a few days or weeks. I told him that according to Ms. Angela, Cassandra and other women did some kind of woo-woo chanting around the house at night. She knows because someone called it in and Declan took his sweet time so as not to interrupt the ceremony, according to one of Ms. Angela's friends who has insomnia. Also, he flashed his lights so everyone had time to scatter before he got out of the car.

Ethan's low chuckle on the phone makes everything right.

There's a sound of an engine, muffled, and his voice is a little tinny when he asks, "And how's my boy?"

Damian stretches on the deck and looks at me as if he knows Ethan is asking about him. "He's been trying to unhook all your little love letters."

"Unhook?"

"Yeah.... They had the cutest little thing at the general store, to hang pictures? It's like a thin black cable, and there's little pins in the shape of birds, to hold the cute little envelopes? It's been driving him nuts. *Nuts!* He managed to snatch some, but he didn't damage them."

The low rumble of his soft laughter is about to undo me. "Did you like my little notes?"

"Oh, honey. They're the best. *You*'re the best." I sigh and pluck another chocolate from the box. Looks like chocolate and a sexy voice are good for the mood. Just like Kiara said. Well, the chocolate part at least.

"Are you eating?"

"Chocolates," I answer, my mouth full.

"Keep some for me."

"I don't know if I can. They're so good. Kiara is a magician."

He sighs. "How many chocolates in there?"

"I dunno."

"Babe."

"Mm?"

"I'll be home soon."

"What?" I screech. And also: *home*. He said *home*. "When?"

Chapter Forty-Two

Ethan

Maybe I should have told her I was on my way from the airport, but I didn't want her to get all crazy about fixing her hair or running to the store or whatever else she would have thought was necessary. Now I'm kind of rethinking that—too late—because it feels like I just lied to her.

Truth is, I want to see her reaction when I ring the doorbell.

But shit—I should have killed the engine to keep this a surprise. The door swings open as I pull up to her house. She's in my jersey, nothing else that I can see, and she's running to me barefoot on her gravel driveway.

I swing off the bike and catch her flinging herself at me. "Ethan, oh Ethan—you're back!"

I lift her to me so she's off the harsh ground, so she's entirely in my arms, so she can wrap herself around me, so her eyes are almost level with mine, and her mouth caresses my lips.

She cups my face softly in both her hands. Her gaze roams my features, as if she's checking if I'm alright. For a beat that feels like an eternity, we just look at each other, our heartbeats echoing into each other's chests, our eyes saying things we both understand. *I missed you so much. I never want to be away from you again.*

But this is our life, now.

I run one hand down her back and confirm my suspicion. She's butt naked. Fuck. Reading me, she kisses me hard as I carry us inside the house, her taste of chocolate lingering on my tongue.

I kick the front door closed, carry us to the bedroom, remember to close that door as well, due to Damian.

Grace tears my windbreaker off while I fumble us to the bed, then pulls my T-shirt over my head, trailing her hands down my torso to my abs and below. "I missed you," she says, unhooking my belt.

I run a hand over her naked thighs, "You missed *me*... or my cock?"

She smiles deviously. "Okay, you win. I missed your cock."

But her eyes are on mine and nowhere else, searching my soul, her lips tentative when they meet mine again as she pulls herself up to kiss me. Her eyelashes flutter closed as she wraps herself around me again.

God, but I missed her. Missed her warmth and her surrender, missed how she gives herself entirely to me, missed how she makes me feel whole again.

She runs her hand in my hair, down my nape, her breathing uncertain, her legs tighter around me. "Take me," she says. "Take me like I'm yours."

I rear my head back. "You *are* mine."

"Always were," she whispers and my throat tightens at her words. Thank god my dick is not the emotional kind because my woman wants me to take her, and I'm not sure she'd be too pleased if I went limp right now. But that's how moved I am. I don't care whether I fuck her brains out right this minute or not. I just want to hold her and make the world right for her.

But then she adds, "Always will be... yours."

And Jesus Fucking Christ. My brain shuts down, and my whole body takes over. I make quick work of the rest of my clothes. As I enter her, her whimpers drive me wilder and wilder. The headboard bangs against the wall, her nails dig into my back, her perfect little pussy sucks me in. "S-sorry, I'm coming," she whispers as she clenches around me.

I lean down to suck her nipple, and she cries out, her features beautifully transformed, her eyes rolling back as she cries out my name. "Ethan, don't stop, don't stop, don't stop."

Fuck. I did this. She's so beautiful, I hold it, focusing on staying hard for her, on putting her first, on giving her whatever she needs, even if there's nothing more I want right now than to come inside her.

As she comes down from her orgasm, she repeats, "I love you, love you so much," holding my head to hers, caressing my back, kissing my face.

I watch with utter awe, too stricken to say anything back. The power of Grace's love unlocks something deep inside me.

She settles in the bed, eyes closed, a small tear pearling at the corner of her eye. Still maddeningly hard, I slowly get out of her. "What's wrong, babe?"

Her eyes softly open on me. "I'm so happy." A small smile forms on her face.

I wipe the back of my hand where the tear is hesitating to fall. "You're crying."

She shakes her head. "Tears of joy."

"Really?" I kiss her lips softly, looking for a sign that she's lying. A trembling. A set in her mouth. I don't find anything, but that doesn't mean she's not hiding something.

Her hand sets on my chest, and she pushes me slightly. Getting the hint, I flip us so she's sitting on me. She slides down to my legs and looks up at me, my cock beating between her breasts.

Then she goes down and licks my shaft, her eyes on mine. Takes me deep until my cock hits the back of her throat, darts her tongue and sucks on me and fuck. Fuck, she's hot. And fuck, she knows how to please me.

I pull her head off my cock before she decides to suck me dry.

"I'm coming inside you first. Then you can do whatever you want to me. But first you need a little break."

"I don't need a break." She whimpers and climbs on me. "Ethan," she sighs in that little voice that drives me wild. Straddling me, she lowers herself on me, her breasts bouncing just so. "Ethan? Did you miss me?" she teases.

"What do you think?" I growl. "Fuck you're so wet. How did you get so drenched again so fast?"

Her eyelids drop. "One look at you."

I place my hands on her hips, pistoning her up and down on me. She whimpers at my bossiness and brings her hands to cup her breasts. My cock twitches inside her in response.

"Tell me. Do you get wet for me all the time?"

Her eyes roll back in pleasure. "All the time."

"Anywhere?"

"Everywhere," she breathes.

"Fuck." I sit up and turn us around. I want her pinned under me. I want her at my mercy. I want to control her orgasm again.

She bites her bottom lip.

"Let it out, babe. Tell me."

She wraps her legs around my back and moans. "You feel so good. Fuck me harder. Harder."

And so I let it out, the sound of our juices and her noises and the smell of sex taking over.

"Do you like my cunt?" she whispers in my ear. "It's all yours. Take it. Take it hard."

As she clenches around my dick, I empty myself into her in long, uncontrollable spurts, her aftershocks sucking me dry.

"I do like your cunt, you dirty little girl."

At my words, her inner walls clench around my dick again. "Fuck, you like my dirty talk?"

She pulls me harder inside her with her legs. "Before the sun is up, I'm giving you the blow job of your life."

We end up falling asleep, tangled in each other. When I wake up, Grace is lying mostly on me, emitting rhythmic, soft hums, Grace's adorable version of a snore.

How much more perfect can she be? She's always had my heart, but now I'm finding out she likes my dirty talk, maintains she gets wet just looking at me, and is planning on giving me the blow job of my life. And her snores are lighter than a cat's purrs.

The need to possess her again and right now coils deep in my lower stomach. Breathing deeply into her hair, I run a light hand across her back.

With one hip movement, her pussy is against my dick, and she's grinding against me. "Take me again."

I take her lying on her side, leg thrown over my torso, her eyes on mine. She comes with a soft wail, fingernails digging into my shoulder, and when I follow, my orgasm is so powerful I grunt harder than I ever have.

After I clean us, she tucks herself against me. "Why didn't you tell me you were coming tonight? I would have made food, and changed the sheets, and—"

"I didn't want you to fuss like that. And also, I was scheduled to fly in tomorrow, but there's a hurricane going up the coast. My C.O. gave me the go-ahead to fly home earlier so I wouldn't be stranded down there."

"I like your C.O."

I like him too, and not just because of the extra time. He's got this sense of humor that just makes the hardest things easier to handle. "Don't get too excited. He wants me back in a couple days."

She goes stone cold in my arms, then takes a breath and says, "Yeah, I kinda expected that." Then she lifts her beautiful face to me and kisses the corner of my mouth. "Are you hungry? I have some leftover lasagna Mom made, and a bottle of wine, and a slice of apple pie your mom dropped off yesterday."

"Boy, aren't you the hostess," I tease her.

She gives me a big smile. "I know! Working on it, with both our mothers' help." Then she turns serious. "You know, I make a mean quiche."

Now my stomach is rumbling. "I did not know that."

She nods. "Chris taught me."

"Must be pretty good, then."

"It's the bomb."

"Will you make me one?"

"Sure. Not tonight, though. Tomorrow, since you're leaving soon. Wait—you'll be going to the farm, right? And—"

"Wherever I'm going, you're going," I say, nipping in the bud that nonsense about "*taking things slow.*" Then I scissor upright on the bed. "And right now, I'm going to heat up that lasagna. You coming?"

I nearly trip on Damian as I come out of the bedroom. He jumps at me like he's a puppy and follows me around in the kitchen, Grace right behind us. "What's with the yoga pants?" I ask her as I take two plates out of the cupboard.

Pulling the lasagna from the fridge, she plucks a small piece of cold crust and nibbles on it. "I don't eat with my butt naked."

"I seem to recall very differently."

She gives me a shy smile, the same memories flooding the two of us. "Breakfast doesn't count."

"I see. You have standards." Looking outside to the deck and seeing the new furniture, I add, "Oh wow. Totally hostessing. The whole yoga pant getup makes perfect sense now."

She slaps me playfully on the chest, then proceeds to nuke the lasagna.

Minutes later we're outside on a large, low sofa, our feet on a matching ottoman. Grace wasn't hungry, but she's still nibbling from my plate with her fingers, her head on my shoulder.

I tell her what I can about work, which isn't much.

What I don't tell her, is that my enthusiasm to go to Brussels has all but vanished. Problem is, this is what I'm good at. And I'm too unsure of how I feel about my future to even bring this up with Grace.

I'm sitting there with too many thoughts on my mind, and Grace's light weight on my body, when I feel her jerk slightly as she falls asleep against me. Setting my plate on the floor, I lift her in my arms.

"I can walk," she says, popping her eyes open.

"I know you can. Been dying to carry you to bed, though. Okay?"

She perks up in my arms, her hair tickling my face. "Okay."

"I'm gonna put the food away and get my stuff from the bike," I say while I set her on the bed.

"I made you some space," she says cryptically as she nests deep under the covers, her big fat yawn calling me to sleep.

I tidy the kitchen and get my stuff. Then I turn the lights off, close and lock all the doors, throw my bag on the bedroom floor, and crash in bed, scooping Grace against me.

Chapter Forty-Three

Grace

That morning, before I even get out of bed, I call Claudia to have her reschedule my appointments. Ethan growls and throws his arm my way, pulling me into him. Into his heat, into his kisses, into the weight of his thigh across my waist.

His hard cock now beating against my belly, I wiggle down his length, parting my thighs to take him.

"Fuck you look good under me," he growls. "I'm crazy 'bout you, Grace. Totally crazy."

"Fuck me," I whisper.

His eyes narrow. "Careful what you ask for."

"Fuck me," I repeat, louder, stretching my arms over my head.

He snatches both my wrists in one hand, pinning me under him, and enters me in long, deep strokes that take me over the edge in stupidly little time.

I need to learn how to control myself. I need to make this last longer. Ethan is only here for two days, for fuck's sakes.

"What's wrong, babe?" he stops mid-stroke, his hard dick beating inside me.

"I need to... never mind."

He pulls out. "You need to what?"

I clasp my thighs around his waist, trying to pull him back into me. "Come back inside," I whisper with a smile, "where it's warm and wet."

"You need to what?" he repeats, his brow furrowing. "You wanna go to the bathroom?" He pulls himself higher above me on his elbows.

I can't help but laugh softly at his question. "No! No-no-no. Come back in, seriously." This time I drag my fingernails down his back, to tell him I mean business.

"Grace. You need to what?"

I roll my eyes. He's not going to let go, is he? "I need to learn how to hold it."

He frowns.

"I already *came*!"

His eyes widen on me, understanding hitting him. "I'm sorry. Fuck. Shoulda..." He licks his way down my neck, starts a trail of kisses that take him to my nipple, which he sucks with a fervor that makes me arch my back.

My center pulses already. "Babe," I whisper, "that's not what I meant. I-you-you-you don't need to do that."

He grunts, licking his way down from my nipple to my belly button.

"Babe, honey," I insist. "I want you back inside me. I just meant I—"

His tongue darts lazily down my center, parting my folds.

Trying to pull his head up to me is useless. He hits my clit, and I lose all willpower, bucking under his mouth. "Ethan…" is all I manage to whimper.

He lifts his head. "Yeah, babe?"

"Nothin'… Ohmygod, Ethan!"

In one swift movement he's back over me, his cock is inside me, and we lock gazes as he sets a powerful rhythm. "Take your time or come right now, sweet Grace. Whatever you want. Whatever you need." He runs callused fingers over my nipple.

"Oh…"

"You like that?" He pinches the nipple with exactly the right pressure, making me arch my back.

"Oh, honey."

"What?" he grunts.

"I love how you… and what you… and everything," I babble.

"You're the sexiest thing alive, you know that?" He punctuates his words with a thrust that almost brings me to the edge.

I knead his nape, committing to memory the feel of his muscles rolling under my eager fingers. "You like me? In bed?"

He grunts, picking up his rhythm. "Fuck, babe. Did you hear what I said about you driving me crazy? No joke, you're all I can think about. You're the only air I want to breathe. The only battle I want to fight. The only life I want to live. I just wanna stay in this bedroom for the rest of my life, making you come 'til the end of time."

I come from his words more than from his magnificent cock, pulling him to me with all my strength, feeling him empty himself inside me as he holds me tighter.

After, we stay tangled, our breaths mingled, our heartbeats loud.

CHAPTER FORTY-FOUR

Ethan

I already knew showering with Grace was up there in the top most sensuous experiences. Now I'm discovering it's also highly entertaining.

Grace sings in the shower. Loud. Totally off key. And totally hilarious.

There's a theme to her repertoire, and I'm not sure if I should be worried. She wrapped up "Hit the Road, Jack" while I was shampooing her hair, and now she's on her knees, lathering my balls to some song about a girl carving her name in the leather of some dude's car, and not as a sweet memento of their undying love.

"You sure 'bout that song?" I ask.

"It's Carrie Underwood!" She looks at me like that should settle it. "It's a classic!"

Oh well, if it's a classic, then...

We rinse, then she trots out the bathroom, bellowing the lyrics while doing some sort of line dancing routine.

Fucking adorable.

I follow her and tag my jeans from the floor. "Coffee?"

"Sure." She eyes me top to bottom. "'s long as you don't wear anything other than those... sinfully-hugging jeans."

I grab her by the waist and pull her to me. "Sinfully-hugging?"

She smirks and blushes, then shrugs my question away. "It's in a book I read. Made me think of you."

I kiss her forehead and let her go, or else we'll end up in bed again. Not that I mind, but I promised Mom and Dad we'd come spend time with them today. "What kinda books you read, beautiful?"

Another shrug. "Uh, you know, nothin' serious."

"Like, what's the title."

Her throat bobs and her eyes dart to her night table for a fraction of a second, then she starts making the bed. "I dunno, it's on my Kindle."

Taking the other side, I follow her cue of smoothing the fitted sheet, then pulling her fancy duvet up. "So what if it's on your Kindle?"

"Once you start the book, you don't see the title. I never know what I'm reading."

We fluff way too many pillows on top of the bed, then pull up a cute throw. "Well, let's find out." I stomp to her side and open the nightstand. "Oh. I didn't know Kindles came with actual flip pages made of actual paper and glossy thick covers and shit."

She raises her eyebrows. "Yeah, they call it the Krinkle. It just came out."

I flip through the pages of the paperback, then zoom in on the cover, a slow smile taking a hold of me.

She continues, "People are over the digital stuff. They want to touch the paper, smell it... ya know."

"Krinkle it."

"Exactly, krinkle it." She swats the paperback from my hands and goes to put it back in the drawer.

The model is bare chested, leaning on the door jamb, looking at the camera with sex on his mind. I frown. "This the guy with jeans that hug him?"

"I guess so." Her eyes don't stop to look at his abs or the V revealed by jeans that are clearly lacking in the hugging department, seeing as they're about to fall off him. She closes the drawer and turns her back to me, lifting her hair off her neck. "Can you tie this up please?"

I fumble with the ribbons holding her summer dress, a part of my brain registering that this dress needs to stay up all day but also come off real quick tonight. "You think of me when you read that book?" I'm not sure how I feel about that, and I don't say this in a way that suggests I don't approve. I'm just... at a loss. Is this a good thing? A bad thing? A neutral thing? An I-don't-give-a-fuck thing? Probably the latter. The truth is, I have to admit, I feel fucking jealous of this paper guy because he gets to stay next to Grace while I'm gone.

Fucking shit. I'm pathetic.

"Yeah, I do think of you." Dress tied up, she goes to her closet.

Okay. Shoulda kept my mouth shut. I don't want to hear how she makes up for my absence.

Or maybe I need to grow a pair and listen—understand—what her pain is like because of me.

She comes back with a hamper. "I think about how lucky I am." Stopping in her tracks, her eyes darken as they set on me. "That I have my own happy ever after now. That I won't ever be without you again."

Emotion floods me and I pull her against me. She lifts her face. "What kind of books do you read?" she asks me.

"Second World War. Spy books. That kinda stuff."

She makes a little sound in the back of her throat, boops me, then bends over to the floor. I catch her wrist in my hand. "What are you doing?"

"Just... picking stuff up," she says, dropping my dirty sock in the hamper.

Fuck. I'm a pig. But no way is Grace picking my dirty socks off the floor. I take the hamper from her and go about picking up the rest of my clothes. I am missing one sock, though.

"I cleared some space for you." She opens the closet door wide again to reveal half the shelves and rods empty now, her clothes packed tight on the other side. Before I can say anything, she's opening up drawers that are all empty.

Even with all my stuff that's somewhere in transit until I know where I'll end up, I don't own one-tenth of the clothes needed to fill all this. But that's not why my vision is getting blurry.

"I'll go make coffee while you settle in," she says, fleeing the bedroom like maybe she did something wrong.

I clear my throat, set the hamper in the closet, unpack my duffel bag. I only have a couple of days here before I leave. I don't *need* to unpack. But I *want* to.

She's talking nervously to Damian, singing some other country song that just about rips my heart out. Something about tomorrow maybe never coming.

Fuck this shit.

I'll find the other sock later. I need us to be happy for the short time I'm here. "Babe," I say as I come into the kitchen where she's fighting with the coffee machine. "Lemme handle this."

She seems happy to let me take over, and then her sad face lights up. "Oooh! I have something for you." She dashes away, then returns holding a small packet all wrapped up with curly ribbons and bows.

"Let's go outside first," she says as she pours cream and maple syrup in two cups, then fills us up with coffee.

I start tearing the gift open once I'm settled on the outdoor sofa. "I like this little couch, babe. Perfect size for the two of us."

She wiggles against me, careful not to spill any coffee. "I know. That's why I got it." She blows on her coffee and slurps her first sip. "You like it?" she says, smiling huge at the gift sitting on my lap.

I unwrap it clumsily, letting it fall on my lap. It's a mumble jumble of little things hooked together.

The outline of the state of Vermont.

A heart.

The name Grace.

A key.

And a ring to hold it all together.

Her key.

She gave me her key.

"Grace," I start, speechless. It's the most thoughtful gift she could have gotten me.

"It's kinda girlish, I'm sorry. But it's not like you're going to be using it when you're in Brussels. Matter of fact, you should just tuck it in your travel bag and leave it there, so you have it when you come back. So you don't lose it."

"I'm not gonna lose it." My eyes water. "You gave me your key."

She sets her coffee on the floor and turns to face me. "I didn't give you my key. I gave you *your* key."

I wrap her in my arms and kiss her softly, then deeper.

She straddles me, then breaks the kiss, her puffy lips and hooded eyelids making me re-consider my plans for the day. "Aren't we going to the farm in a few minutes?"

"Yeah..." I drawl as she wiggles off me and snatches her coffee from the floor.

I look at the key nestled in the palm of my hand. "No one ever got me a keychain. It'll be in my pocket all the time."

"But it's... goofy."

"No it's not. It's sweet. And caring. And loving. It's everything you." I turn the name **Grace** in my fingers, running my thumb over each block letter in a soft pink. Sweet like her lips, her kiss, her love.

Then the heart. It's black. Like death and mourning. Surely they had red hearts. Why did she choose black? Reading my thoughts, she says, "I thought that'd be less girly, but you know what..." She huffs. "You can just... You don't have to... I'm sorry."

The outline of the state is a predictable green, but it's also the color of our town, and it means something to me, now.

"What are you sorry about?"

"It seemed like a good idea. It seemed funny. It's really nothing. I don't know why you keep looking at it like that. It's really nothing."

"It's everything to me."

"Ugh!" she pretends to mock moan. "I should have gotten you something nicer."

"Come here," I say, pulling her back into me. "It's the nicest thing you could have gotten me. Seriously. You gave me the key to your house."

"I didn't give you the key to my house, Ethan."

"Oh." Now I'm embarrassed. "Sorry," I chuckle awkwardly. "I just—I assumed..." It does look like her front door key, though. "So...?"

"I gave you the key to your home."

My heart stops beating as I crush her against me. I'm so over-whelmed, words refuse to form in my brain. I'm just a mess of feelings right now. This is all I ever wanted. Just because it didn't happen the way I planned or wanted or hoped for, doesn't mean it's not happening.

We're happening, and that's all that counts.

This time, she doesn't protest about going to the farm with me. We take her car and not the bike, because there's a chance of rain—that hurricane coming up the coast that bought me a few extra hours with her.

Grace stays tucked against me the whole time we're at the farm. Logan and Hunter hug her tight when they come in for a quick lunch, their smiles huge. I get a slap on the back but no stupid jokes, and I don't even need to scowl at them or issue death threats.

In the kitchen, we help ourselves to Mom's chicken salad. Grace knows her way around here better than me, and she's who pulls out our glasses for lemonade. We sit on the porch, bowls in hand, no set table, taking in the peaceful scenery. A sudden burst of wind runs through the woods. A shutter clatters somewhere.

"Good thing you took the car," Mom says. "They're saying we might get an inch of rain, starting this evening."

Dad looks at his radar app on his phone and grunts. "Not looking good."

Then he asks about my next steps, and I feel Grace's hand snake tighter around my waist, and her face lifts to me.

"I need to report back in forty-eight hours," I say. "Actually, thirty-six now. Waiting to hear what my posting will be."

Grace leans her head against my shoulder and squeezes me tight. "Fingers crossed he gets Brussels."

Looking down at her, I see only pride and true happiness. No doubts, no fear, no regrets. She's all in with me, and she supports me no matter what. My free hand goes straight to my pocket where her keychain is—correction: where *my* key to *our* home is.

When we leave, Mom's eyes get a little wet, but I know it's happiness.

"I talked to my C.O. about potentially staying stateside. There could be opportunities in D.C. or Florida," I say once we're in the car. We've been too busy pawing at each other to talk about the future—or maybe we've avoided that conversation.

"I thought you wanted Brussels?"

"I did. I changed my mind."

She takes her foot off the gas to look at me. "Please tell me that doesn't have anything to do with me."

"And what if it did?"

"I don't want you giving up your career because of me," she says.

We pull up to her house. Our home, I should say. Once we're done with this conversation, I need to talk to her about sharing costs. Why do I think this isn't going to go easy? But one thing at a time.

Right now, she's ranting about Brussels as we walk up to the front door. "Brussels was your dream posting. Your career goal. Like, just *weeks* ago. I don't want you giving up on that because of me." Her fists are on her hips.

I pull out my key, a stupid grin locking in place while my heart drums a crazy, wild beat. I unlock the door and step aside to let her in while she's going on about me making rash decisions or potentially resenting her for god knows what. "Your career is everything to you," she insists.

I stop, key in the lock. "No, it's not. Not anymore," I say with enough force to make her stop in her tracks and look at me. She's already inside the house, kicking her shoes off. I point to the key in the door, to Damian greeting her. To her bare feet that'll hook behind my hips in the next few hours if I have anything to say about it. "This. This is everything to me. You and me."

"Ethan," she whispers, setting her soft hand against my chest. "I understand that. It's the same for me. But-but-but your job, your career, is important too."

"Not as important as you."

She shuts her eyes for a brief moment. "You can have both. You can have Brussels and me."

I need to tell her. Brussels? Not a lot of off time. And it's close to impossible to just visit for the couple of free days I'll have here and there.

"I been thinking," she says, pulling me inside. "I can plan to take a week off from the spa each month. You know once… once the dust settles with the building, and I'm relocated somewhere, and everything is smooth sailing again. I could totally block off a week each month to visit you in Brussels. My staff can handle themselves for a week without me. And I looked at miles and stuff for the airfare. It's doable."

I shut the door and put the key back in my pocket. She stays against me, snaking her hands up to my neck, pulling my mouth against hers. "You can have it all," she whispers against my lips.

"I already have it all." I burrow my face in her neck. "You gotta understand. Brussels meant somethin' to me before, because that was all I had. Now I have you, and my family, and my friends. Everything I thought I'd lost was just waiting for me to get my head out of my ass. So if I tell you I don't give a shit about Brussels, you better believe it. Now, I still need to make a living, and I'm good at what I do, and that can't happen here, but believe me when I tell you, I'd drop the Air Force in an instant if I had a solid plan B *here*." Matter of fact, I've been toying with ideas about said plan B, but I'm not sharing those with her yet.

"Ethan King, don't you dare leave the Air Force because of me or even Emerald Creek," she declares, leaving my arms.

Yup. Not sharing plan B just yet. Especially given that the only clear part about Plan B is '*I wanna stay here,*' and that's not a fucking plan at all. "I'm not leaving the Air Force."

"Good. Now let's kick back and sit outside before the rain starts."

CHAPTER FORTY-FIVE

Grace

We left the farm with enough meat and vegetables to feed a whole family, and Ethan helps me store it away.

"That's making me hungry," I say.

Ethan pulls out a butcher block I never use. "I'm cooking." He starts chopping onions, the sound making Damian appear out of nowhere, then pulls chicken thighs out of the fridge. Looking at Damian, he takes a pack of ham out and throws him a piece.

"I'll catch up on emails." I bring my laptop to the kitchen counter and start working, getting lost in work while Ethan does whatever he set out to do. There's a lead from Alex for a building *in another town*. I decide to leave that aggravation for another day, and switch to the notifications of our latest reviews, all five stars. I take a few fulfilling moments answering them, then send congratulations to my staff. I flag invoices for tomorrow, then focus my attention on Ethan.

The chicken thighs are marinating in a mixture of olive oil, finely chopped onions, and spices from small glass containers I almost forgot

I had. In a frenzy of nesting, I let Chris convince me to buy those, but never used them. It's a good thing spices have a long shelf life.

I nudge myself behind Ethan and grab two plates. "Want me to start the grill?"

He pulls me into him. "Let me do this." He plucks the plates from my hand, sets them on the countertop, and softly rubs his nose against mine and, god, why does this feel so erotic? "I want to take care of you. You go sit down before it starts raining."

I turn around to the deck. The table is set, candles and all, all the way to a sweaty jug of margarita.

"Hurry up," he growls in my ear. "Weather's gonna start any moment, and I been meaning to serve you a drink, rub your feet, and grill for you all day. Don't want a couple rain drops ruining it." He peels himself away from me.

"All day?"

He narrows his eyes on me. "Way more than all day," he mutters. Grabbing the chicken and a colorful salad I'm only now seeing, he swats my butt gently. "Go."

Fifteen minutes later, I'm biting into the most tender, tastiest chicken I've ever had. I have a nice little buzz going from the margarita I drank way too fast. "I mean, you ever get tired of being a super, secret whatever-it-is-you-do, you could definitely work with your brother."

Ethan stops with his fork midair. "That the alcohol talking?" he asks with that adorable smile.

I'm not tipsy enough to forget our earlier conversation. "Yesh. Drank the margarita too fast. The chicken's great though. Like I said, something to fall back on if... never mind." I don't want him thinking I changed my mind about him not leaving the Air Force. I didn't. "I was just paying you a compliment."

He smiles at me. "Thank you." His eyes dance on my face, like he's thinking something good but doesn't want to share with me.

"You'd be bored here. Don't you dare."

"You're right. I'd be bored grilling all day for strangers. Wouldn't mind cooking for you every night, though." Those mischievous eyes again. What is he up to? I can't say that his talk about cooking for me isn't making me melt at some very intimate level.

I frown at him. "*That's* the alcohol talking."

"No, it's not."

"Ethan," I warn him.

"I said I wouldn't *mind it*."

You said you wouldn't mind it like it was the only thing on your mind. Like it was a lifetime goal. Like cooking for me every night was the end-all, be-all. "Okay."

"Okay." Those damn eyes dancing on me again. "Now eat."

We eat in silence for a while, looking at Woodbury Knoll seemingly swerving as the trees sway under the wind. It's warm out, with that sense of foreboding and release that precedes the rain.

Then fat drops start hitting us, and we scramble to our feet.

"Shit," Ethan growls and picks up both our plates and cutlery. I follow with the margaritas and the candle, then we both run back out to grab the pillows as the rain intensifies.

I can't believe how quickly and forcefully the storm is hitting us. "I'll check the windows," I say as Ethan runs back out to deal with the barbecue and the umbrella. As I shut the bathroom window, I see him on the other side of the house, closing my car windows. By the time he's back inside, he's soaked. "They weren't kidding," he says, looking at the weather radar on his phone screen. "Shoulda paid closer attention."

He strips to his underwear and throws his shorts and T-shirt in the dryer.

Rain is now pummeling my little house, the barreling sound on the roof so loud it's almost scary. I glance at his bike, outside in the pouring rain. "Is it going to be alright?"

"We'll find out. No big deal."

I should build a garage.

"Come on." He squeezes my shoulder and guides me to the living room.

We sit on the couch facing the deck, watching as the howling wind bends the trees. I instinctively nest myself inside Ethan's embrace when the dreadful crack of branches sounds. Lightning strikes in the distance, Woodbury Knoll strobing eerily.

"It's kinda beautiful," I say. Ethan wraps me tighter against his warm, hard, and almost naked body when thunder rolls. "I watched it go down. Our tree house," I add in a whisper. "Two summers ago."

Ethan stays silent. It's possible he didn't hear me, the noise from the storm is so loud. But he pulls me against him and kisses my hair tenderly. So maybe he did hear me. Maybe he did and he's just like me. There's nothing really to say.

Lights flicker and the power goes out.

"Shit," Ethan says, pulling himself gently from me to stand. I hear him open and close the dryer.

"Are they dry?" I ask.

A deafening crack tears through, the house seems to shake, and Ethan stomps up the staircase. "Fuck."

As he barrels back down, I jump off the couch to meet him at the bottom of the stairs.

"What is it?"

"There's water coming through the ceiling. Probably a tree. I'm gonna check. Try to find Damian," he orders, then steps outside. If trees are falling, shouldn't he stay inside? As he steps out, another tree falls with a murderous roar, taking the limbs of other trees with it as it lands with a bounce on the side of my front yard.

"Ethan!" I shriek. "Come back here!"

"Shit," he says as he steps back inside. The wind recedes as quickly as it had picked up, but the rain persists, long, steady sheets of water coming down. "D'you have a bucket? Or three," Ethan says, looking up. The telltale plop-plop-plop of a water leak is unmistakable.

"Under the kitchen sink," I say as I go to the bathroom to take another one.

We both run up the stairs. There's a mostly empty room at the end of the hallway, but of course that's not where the leak is. No, it's where Skye's bedroom is. Right next to her bed. Ethan starts pushing the furniture away from the water, and I roll the area rug and hoist it out of the room. The first bucket is almost half full already.

Ethan frowns when he sees me. "It's not safe here. Wait for me downstairs."

I empty the bucket in the small upstairs bathroom and return to find him leaning out the window.

"Ethan!" I screech.

He pulls back in, shuts the window, and shakes the water off his hair. "Yeah, babe?"

"What are you doing?"

"A huge branch fell through your roof. It's not safe here. Pack a change of clothes. Soon's the front is gone, I'm taking you out of here." He takes my hand and pulls me down the stairs. "Call your parents, see how they're doing. See if I can drop you off there. The roads to the farm might be cut off by fallen trees." He stomps to my bedroom and looks under the bed. "Come here kitty-kitty. Come on!" He pulls a trembling Damian out. "Got a bag for him?"

The protective streak is sweet. "I'd rather stay here and look after my house."

Ethan turns around, Damian cuddled in his arms. "*I'll* look after your house. I'm gonna go find tarp. I'll see what needs to be done to the roof. But I can't do that if I'm worried about you."

Seriously, how can I resist that? The vision of my little cat protected by his muscular arms. The idea that he's putting me out of danger so he can take care of my house.

The wind is receding, but the rain keeps falling steadily, with no sign of letting up. There's an ominous crack upstairs.

"Let's go," he says, seeing my resistance weaken.

When we get to Mom and Dad's, they've lost power too. To top it off, their basement is flooding. There's a small brook behind their property that's generally dried out in the summer. With the sudden rain, that seems to have hit the whole state, it overflowed with a rage, and water quickly seeped inside the house. "There's a washer and dryer, plus a freezer down there," Dad says, standing uncertainly at the top of the basement stairs.

"Where's the breaker box?" Ethan asks.

"Over there," Dad answers.

Ethan shuts the power off. "Safer this way, when the power returns." Then he asks, "You have a generator?"

"Shed," Mom says, wringing her hands. "There should be a fuel container next to it. Dennis keeps it full."

"I'll help you," I say, setting a frightened Damian on Dad's lap. "You two look after each other," I add with a playful wink toward Dad.

As we step outside to the shed, Colton drives up. Ethan quickly fills him in, and the two of them get the generator started and hooked up to the refrigerator and a couple of extension cords. "I'm gonna go with Ethan," Colton tells me. "Get a pump for Mom and Dad and see what's up with your roof."

And just like that, the two of them are gone.

CHAPTER FORTY-SIX

Ethan

"Come with me," Colton says.

I send a group text to my siblings and parents to find out if everyone is okay. The answers come in: Everyone's fine. I update them on the situation at Grace's and her parents' and get offers of help.

> Me
>
> Thx. I'll let you know. Stay where you are for now, roads are unsafe.

I jump in Colton's truck while he places a call. It's late in the evening, so I'm not sure where he thinks he's going. Or if he expects to get a call back. "Hey, man," he says in his phone. "I'm gonna need a pump, some tarp, plywood, shingles. 'Spect I won't be the only one to ask, but this is for my family. Can you set that aside for me? Yep... Nah, me and my friend can handle it. But thanks... yeah. Gotcha."

"Got something?"

"Yeah, guy owes me. He owns a lumber yard and construction material."

"He has a pump too?"

"Yup." He swerves around dead branches littering the road. "Pretty bad."

"That happen often?"

"More and more. I think the whole state's getting hit this time. I'll bring the pump back soon's we're done at my parents'. Other people're gonna need it."

"First time they're flooded?"

"Yeah. I'll have to ask Lucas about some drainage options. What happened at Grace's?"

"Huge branch went through her roof. Or might have been a tree. I didn't have time to check from the outside. I wanted to get her out of there before anything worse happened."

"She give you a hard time?"

I shrug. Grace's face materializes in my mind's eye, her stubborn frown, the cute set of her mouth. "Not really."

He lifts his chin. "You know how to talk to her." He takes a turn toward Grace's house. "Let's check it out, see if we'll need anything else."

We round her house and it's like I thought. Although it's getting dark, we can see that a thick tree limb fell, nicking the roof in the process. "Good news," Colton says. "Tree's on the ground."

There's a gaping hole in the roof, the pelting rain punishing, damaging the house with every passing minute. "Let's get that tarp."

Colton nods. "Tarp first."

At the lumber yard, I add two-by-fours, nails, and roof cement to my order while Colton loads the pump in the back of his truck. Colton's guy throws in two harnesses and ropes. We borrow a ladder and head back to Grace's house. Colton pulls headlamps from the back of his truck, and we get to work. The roof isn't too steep, but it's slippery in the rain, and the work is tricky. "Wouldn't have risked it without the harnesses," Colton yells over the falling rain, and I agree. We wrap one side of the tarp around the two-by-fours, nail it to the roof, pull it tight, then move to the next side.

"Can't do the sealant now," I say, wiping the water from my eyes. "It's still raining."

"Let's get outta here," Colton agrees.

We gather our tools, unhook our harnesses, and get back down. "Why don't you check the inside while I pack up," Colton says. "I'll leave the harnesses and rope in the house, and the ladder right here."

The power is back in Grace's quiet house, and I'm reassured to see the leak is now a trickle. There must be accumulated water in the ceiling, plus some water still coming in through the tarp, that I couldn't seal. I empty the largest of the buckets and place it back under the leak. Taking a quick look around, I'm moved to see how well decorated the bedroom is. Three of the walls are a warm cream color with pastel stencil, and the third wall is a deep pink. The twin bed, which I pushed to the side, has cute pink throw pillows, several layers of blankets and sheets folded like only women would know how to, just to make it look cute. It's touching to see the care and love Grace has for her young cousin.

As I peel myself from the bedroom, something bugs me that I can't quite put my finger on. But there's no time for self-reflection, or reflection of any kind. From the kitchen window, I see Colton climb into the truck. I hurry around the house to shut off the lights we didn't know were on when we lost power, then join him.

"Let's head to your parents'." On our way, we stop at a gas station to fill up several cans for the generator.

Colton and I end up digging a trench to run the water away from the house. With how soggy the soil is, it goes faster than we'd anticipated. Still, by the time we're done, we're soaked from the rain coming down and the brook rushing up around our legs, and muddy from head to toe. Literally. So much so I don't even dare enter the house.

Colton goes in alone while I stand outside the basement's hopper window to grab the hose and direct it away from the house and downhill, then connect the pump to the generator.

"Ready!" I call out to Colton. A low hum comes from the basement, and the hose vibrates gently under my hand.

"All good!" he answers.

"Good here too." I turn around and see Grace, eyes wide.

"You okay, babe?" I ask her, worried.

She eyes me from top to bottom. "Ohmygod, what happened to you?"

I look down at the mud caking me and walk toward her, my shoes squeaking with water. "Just another day at the ranch." I laugh, opening my arms and bending down to pretend kissing her, expecting her to shriek and run away.

Instead, she throws her arms around me and kisses me full on, molding her body to mine, darting her sweet tongue inside my mouth. With a growl, I cup her ass to get her closer to me. "What do you say we go check on your house now?"

She pulls herself from me to look at me like it's the first time she sees me. "You have to stop doing stuff like that."

"What kinda stuff?"

"Sweet stuff."

Sweet stuff? Climbing on roofs, digging trenches at night under the rain is considered sweet now? "Not sure I follow, babe."

She takes my hand and honest to god, it looks like there're tears on her cheeks. Can't be. It's gotta be the rain.

She pops back inside, picks up Damian, we holler goodbye, and she drives us back home.

Home.

That's what her house feels like to me.

Fuck.

"Me and Colt did a pretty good job, considering." I update her on the roof situation, what needs to be done long term, and what her brother and I did earlier. "But I'll have to finish up tomorrow and seal it real good. Soon's it stops raining. Meanwhile, we'll have to keep an eye on the bucket and empty it."

"God Ethan, I didn't know you knew how to do all that stuff." She glances at me, her beautiful face radiating something deep and moving in the night.

I shrug off her compliment. "Ruined your car, babe," I say as I exit the Jeep. I go to take the floor mat and the cute little piece of fabric she has wrapped around her seats, but she shushes me.

"You leave that to me and get yourself in a hot shower." Then she swipes up Damian and we step inside. "Strip here," she orders me, pointing to the floor. "I'll take care of it tomorrow. Get in the shower while I empty the bucket."

"Yes, ma'am." I smile as I walk naked to the bathroom. A minute later, Grace slips inside the shower with me, needy and tempting, her nipples perky, her tongue darting out to lick her lips. She lathers me with soap and proceeds to scrub me, and I can't help but laugh.

"What's so funny?"

"How serious you are."

"You're seriously dirty."

"That why you came in the shower with me?" I ask, pulling her to me. "To make sure I was clean?"

"Well, that and..." She trails a hand between us and gives my dick a stroke.

"I see. Your motives aren't entirely pure."

"When it comes to you, my motives are always pure... and dirty."

I throb at her words. "That so?"

"You know it," she says, her smile small, her eyes pleading.

Fuck, but her look of uncertainty kills me each time. It's like she's unsure of my feelings when it comes to her. "Yeah, I know it, beautiful." I kiss her tenderly. "Babe?"

"M-hm?" she says, moving her hips against me.

"How 'bout I clean up, we dry off, and we take this to bed? I seen enough water for today. Wanna make love to you but wanna make it while I'm nice and dry."

She pretends to whine, and her little noise goes straight to my groin.

"Can I please get a rain check on sex in the shower?"

She giggles. "You're funny. *Rain* check." She steps out the shower and wraps herself in a towel while I bring the temperature to piping hot. "You could also be a comedian if this whole army thing doesn't pan out," she says as she leaves the bathroom.

Army thing. Now who's funny? But it's the second time today Grace mentions alternative careers for me, and even if it's a joke—her serious insistence that I go to Brussels, proof enough—it strikes a chord with me.

I finish scrubbing the mud away, and when I step out, she's back in the bathroom, waiting for me with a thick, plush towel.

And she's wearing my jersey.

I towel off, follow her to bed, and lay on top of her warm, soft body, making quick work of the jersey. She wraps her legs around my hips. "Just take me," she whispers in my ear. "I can't wait."

Fuck. I get lost in the deliciousness that is Grace's body. Grace's kisses. Grace's caresses. Grace's moans. Grace's love. How did I go ten years without her? No wonder I felt like a zombie, going day by day without any taste for life.

I flip us so that she rides me. I love seeing her take control of our lovemaking. Seeing her breasts bounce above me. Seeing her fall apart around me, her arms trembling, her knees barely carrying her, holding herself up by the sheer power of her orgasm, tensing up as I empty myself into her, then folding onto me and laying her sweet head on my chest.

I fall asleep still inside her, holding her snug against me, the physical exertion of the day feeling fucking great.

When I wake up the next day, my first thought is for the roof. I gently nudge Grace aside—we're spooning—and go swap the buckets. The rain has stopped, and the sun is shining bright. On my way down, I get the coffee machine started and find Grace sitting up in bed, stretching. We take turns in the bathroom, and as I'm getting dressed, her phone rings. And rings again.

I ignore it and make the bed. The phone rings a third time, and I glance at the display, wondering if I should bring it to her in the bathroom. Maybe it's her parents? Maybe there's an emergency?

But the display reads *Kyle*.

Who's Kyle? Maybe something to do with work?

Then the phone chimes again with a text message.

Kyle

> **Hey, honey, everything ok?**

CHAPTER FORTY-SEVEN

Grace

"Kyle keeps calling you," Ethan says, emphasizing the name as he hands me my phone.

Shit. Shitshitshit.

"Um… oh yeah?" I sound breezy enough, right?

The phone rings again.

"Aren't you gonna pick up?"

I swallow with difficulty, hit the green button on my phone, and turn my back to Ethan. "Hi, hon—Kyle."

"Hey. I was getting worried."

"Worried? Oh. About the storm?"

"Yeah. Everything okay with you?"

"I-I'm fine. I mean part of the roof is gone, and my deck is a mess, but other'n that, no physical damage. Everyone in Emerald Creek is safe and sound, thank god. Nothin' we can't handle."

"Is Ethan still here?"

"Yeah, he's..." I turn around and face Ethan, watching me with his hands on his hips. He might as well have a question mark tattooed on his forehead. "He's already working on the roof."

"Oh good. Thank god for Ethan."

I giggle. "You got that right."

"Alright then, I'll let you go. Tell him I said hi."

"Uh."

"Or not. Whatever." I hear the smile in his voice. "Love you, sweetheart. Take care."

"Love you too." I hang up and look at Ethan and set the phone slowly on the bathroom vanity.

"And that was Kyle," Ethan states.

"And that was Kyle. My ex-husband."

A muscle ticks around his eye, and god I *hate* myself right now. "Anything you wanna share about *honey-Kyle, I love you-Kyle*, 'fore I go back up there and risk breaking my neck by fixing your roof?"

I exhale. "Yeah, maybe I should have told you about Kyle before. But, really, it's nothing." I walk past him into the bedroom and grab a pair of jeans and a T-shirt.

"'*Honey*' and '*I love you*' doesn't sound like nothing to me."

"I can see how that sounds but..." I can't avoid this conversation now, can I? "Why don't we... why don't we sit down?" I move to the kitchen, pull two cups out of the cupboard, and pour us some coffee.

"Is this a sit-down conversation? Not sure I'm gonna like it."

"Okay then—let's not sit down. We can do this standing up." Forgetting the coffees for now, I pull up a barstool and prop half a butt cheek on it for support. "Kyle and I... we... we were fooling around during college. On and off. He..." I blush and go for it. "He knew about you."

"During your college years? He knew about me?" He says it as a question, but also a disbelief. My college years were after Ethan and I broke up.

"Yeah. I might have told him about you during a drunken party. Or two. And sober late-night confessions."

Ethan grunts but doesn't ask for dates or content, and thank god for that because that might have taken a long time to recap.

"Long story short, since we're not sitting down." I take a deep breath and let it all out. "I got pregnant end of senior year in college, and that's why we got married."

Ethan goes pale, and I can see the internal back-and-forth he's having. But I guess he can't or doesn't want to draw conclusions, because he simply repeats, "You got pregnant."

"Yes."

He runs a hand across his face. His eyes are wet. He takes two steps away and turns around and then faces me again. Then he pulls me off the stool and into his arms. "Fuck, baby. What happened?"

And that's Ethan. My Ethan. No need to tell him more, he understands. Understands why I got married in a rush to someone who wasn't meant for me. Also understands why I'm no longer married to him. And maybe even understands why I'm still talking to him, although that may be a different conversation. Hopefully, a later conversation.

"I lost the baby," I say, my voice muffled against his chest.

His heartbeat increases under my cheek and his hand strokes my back. "Got that part, babe. What happened?"

"These things happen. There was no particular reason. It... it just didn't..." Make it? Take? Want to be my baby? To this day I still can't put words on it. On what happened. I used to constantly oscillate between fate and guilt. I knew the statistics and these helped. But sometimes, on my darker days, I couldn't help but think that maybe my baby didn't want *me*. And that was the hardest. I knew it not to be true, and I knew it didn't make sense, but how could I help how I felt? How my twisted mind needed to make it my fault? To make everything bad that happened to me *my fault*?

Sometimes I feel these thoughts creeping back, and I fight hard to keep them at bay.

"It just didn't happen," I end up telling Ethan.

He closes his arms tighter around me and says nothing for a while, and then he whispers softly, "That explains Skye's bedroom."

I pull my face off his chest to look at him. "What?"

He gently brings me back against his quickened heartbeat. "Skye. She would have been your baby's age?"

Bile rises in my throat. "It's not like that." Chris and I always talked openly about Skye needing a female presence in her life, but also not blurring the lines for her. Despite our physical resemblance, I always set people straight when they mistook Skye for my daughter. For her sake *and* mine. Now, did I go a little overboard by decorating her bedroom here? The jury might be out on that. Me, I don't think so.

"Course not." He strokes my back. "I just think... It's almost like..."

"Just say what you need to say."

"With Alex now... you know." What he's saying is, Alex is taking my place and more in Skye's life, leaving me empty again. And there's some truth to that.

I'm immensely grateful to the universe for sending Alex to Chris and Skye. To us. To me. She's become a close friend. She brought balance to my cousin, and she'll be a wonderful mother to Skye. But Ethan is right. She'll be the one taking her to school now, and going to parent meetings, and looking after her when she has a fever. Reading her stories and helping her become a woman. I'll still be in her life, but it won't be the same. "I'll be fine."

"You deserve this, Grace. I know you want it, and you deserve it."

"What are you talking about?"

"You'll be a wonderful mother someday."

I nod frantically, though I'm not sure I do see that in my future. Not with the way life keeps throwing me curve balls.

We stay quiet for a while. I don't know what's going through his mind. I'm trying to find the right words. "I... I felt dead inside. Not just literally. It was hard, and coming back here saved me. Literally. I felt alive again."

I close my mind and go back to these days. Everything I'd built my new life on—a surprise baby, a new husband I was trying to learn to love as a spouse, a new state, a new environment, a new family. For a few short months, these had been my new reality. I'd worked hard on making them good for me, all for the little bundle of life taking form in my womb.

And then he or she was gone.

Everything was gone.

I couldn't get out of bed. I didn't want anything from life. Kyle got worried, and sent me to Emerald Creek to be with Mom, seeing as she couldn't take time away from work to visit me in Texas.

"I came back to Emerald Creek a couple of weeks later. Just to get better, in my head. And then I never left. There was no reason."

"How did Kyle feel about that?" Ethan asks softly, trying not to push me, but I feel the insecurity in his voice, and I owe him that. I owe him the truth. "He was fine with me staying in Emerald Creek. Probably relieved."

Ethan grunts. "But he keeps calling you."

I look up at Ethan. "We didn't love each other the way a husband and wife should." Then I add, "I call him, too, occasionally."

His jaw tightens but he says nothing. What is he thinking?

"Although he said we should stop talking. Since you came back into my life."

Ethan looks surprised. "He did?"

"Yeah." I shrug. "Not that we're doing anything wrong."

A small smile plays on his face. "How would you feel if I talked to Ilse every now and then?"

Something like jealousy, possessiveness, stirs in my stomach. "Not great."

"See?"

"But you were going to marry her."

He cocks his head. "And you weren't married?"

It's not the same. "I guess I see your point."

He rocks me softly in his arms. "Anything else I need to know about you that you're not volunteering yet?"

"No," I whisper.

Then, "Why didn't you tell me?"

"About Kyle or about the baby?

"About both. Don't they go together?"

"They don't. Kyle... it didn't feel important. I mean, you would have found out eventually." More like, *I was too chicken to tell you I was talking to another man about my feelings for you.* "And the baby... it was... it was too much."

"Too much for me?"

"No. Too much for *me*. I didn't even know where to start. I don't-don't really talk about it. Ever."

"Not even to the Bitch Brigade?"

I scooch deeper into his hold and shake my head. "Not anymore. It's in the past."

He strokes my back, saying nothing for a while. "I'm gonna go finish that roof for you, and then I'll take a shower. And then we're gonna talk about what you need from me."

I raise my face to meet his gaze. "What do you mean?"

He cups my nape with his hand, kneading the back of my head, and his gaze darkens. "I want to be the man you can talk to about everything and anything."

My heart booms so hard, there's no way he doesn't hear it.

His gaze caresses the frame of my face, and he pads his thumb across my lips. "I get that some of the stuff is hard to unpack just like that, but I'm your best friend on top of being your... everything else. I wish I'd be the man you could talk to about your miscarriage without being forced into it." He kisses a tear off my cheek. "I want you to be comfortable telling me you're still talking to Kyle if that's what you need to. I don't want you to feel like you need to hide stuff from me." He kisses the crown of my head. "I want you to feel comfortable telling me you miss Skye like hell even if you're over the moon happy for her."

I hug him tighter.

"If the time comes, I want you to feel free to tell me that's what you want with me."

"What do you mean?" I whisper.

He lowers his forehead to meet mine and whispers, "You and I—this is all going very fast. But it's going in one direction. And we both know which direction that is. So if at any time you need from me more than what I'm giving you, you need to tell me. Because sometimes I'm a little thick, a little slow to get with the program. And I'm going to count on you to keep us on track."

He stands, lifting me with him, sets me on the floor, then gently slaps my ass. "That roof isn't gonna fix itself," he says.

Like he didn't just rock my world.

CHAPTER FORTY-EIGHT

Ethan

Before I start on the roof, I call Colton's guy to order some material. I'll need help to fix the roof, but a couple of guys will be easier to secure than supplies, after the storm that hit the whole state. Then I hoist myself up there and seal the tarp. Once I'm done, I sit on top of the roof, savoring the vision of a work well done, the feeling of accomplishment. My eyes drift to Woodbury Knoll and an idea forms in my mind. By the time Grace comes around to check in on me, I have a whole plan that excites me.

"You sure look happy," Grace comments.

"Good as new!" I say, motioning to the tarp.

"Come down here. You're scaring me."

"Help me out." I lower the roofing cement to the ground using a spare rope and let Grace catch it, then I put my tools in an empty bucket she catches as well.

When I jump off the ladder next to her, she laces her arms around me. "Do you get a rush from being in danger?" She looks straight into my eyes, the gravity of her gaze unsettling.

Was it fun up there? Yeah—for a minute. "I was just fixing the roof." Was it dangerous? Maybe a tiny bit risky. "I have no intention of dying." As the words leave my mouth, I register a tiny narrowing of her pupils, like an assessment. I pull her closer to me. "I was careful, Grace. Trust me. Not many guys go on a roof with a harness."

She gives me a quick nod. "Okay." She moves away from me, and I throw an arm around her shoulders as she walks us to the front of the house. Her footsteps are resolute, her body taut. Like she's weighed the pros and the cons of a situation, and made a choice. Like she knows life is never a given, and shit happens. All the fucking time. She's been there before. She made plans, she changed her life, and life changed its plans on her.

And it made her so fucking strong.

"Hey." I stop us on the side of the house. "I'm being careful. On your—" I correct myself "on the roof. On my bike. Everywhere. You think I'm gonna let something happen to me, now that I found you? Not a fucking chance." And she better believe *she'll* have me in her life for the rest of her days. I don't say as much, but I hope that's what she hears.

"Okay," she whispers, lifting her face to meet my lips.

As I take her mouth in mine, snake my tongue to meet hers, feel the little whimper in the back of her throat, anxiety knots itself in my stomach as I think about our future. How the hell are we going to navigate the next few years? We're only young-ish. How many years until we can start a family? This could turn into a fucking nightmare.

"Come on," she says, breaking our kiss. "There's a community meeting at Lazy's in half an hour. I'll load this in the Jeep while you shower and change." She looks me up and down, her tongue darting out like she could lick me up right now, but also—she appraises me and... did she just tell me to shower and change? No woman except my own mother has ever done that, and if I'm not mistaken, it's the second time in less than twenty-four hours Grace has done that, and it feels... kinda great.

"Are you gonna fix me a PB&J?" I ask on a chuckle.

"Nope," she answers airily. "There's a reason community meetings are held at Lazy's. Justin and Shane provide food. Guarantees optimal attendance, 'specially days like today."

"So what's this meeting for?" I ask once we're in the Jeep. Grace cleaned the floor mat and cute fabric I all but ruined yesterday, and her car smells like laundry day.

"Assess who needs what. Make teams to help out those in need." She drives slowly but confidently, swerving through the debris still littering the streets, waving through her open window at people I don't know anymore. My gaze falls on her soft hands, her short but manicured nails, the thin chain bracelet that jingles softly. It matches her earrings, and I wonder who got her the set.

"What?" she asks with a smile.

"Nothin'."

She smiles. "Really."

"Where'd you get the bracelet and earrings?" I ask her, giving into some primal possessiveness. I should know better.

She wiggles her wrist. "Oh! From Gems in town. Aren't they cute? They were having a Fourth of July sale."

I trail my hand to her earlobe, run the pad of my thumb over the delicate shape of a sparrow. Something warm grows inside me. *I want to give her jewelry.* "I like it. That a nice shop?"

She glances at me, amusement in her gaze. "Very nice. They have reasonable prices and also, they do custom requests. Why? You looking for something for your Mom's birthday?" She giggles.

"Ha-ha." That is *never* going away. I laugh with her. "Maybe."

Grace parallel parks on The Green and we head to Lazy's. My brother's pub is packed. There's a food buffet set on the bar and on a couple of tables in the back, and people are filling plates and soup bowls and huddling together. The chatter is loud yet somber.

Colton walks in right behind us with Dennis and Shannon, so we fill a couple of plates with sandwiches to share and squeeze together around a small table.

Cassandra calls the meeting by standing on a chair and ringing a cowbell. Noah stands next to her and takes notes. They're tallying up the needs in generators, pumps, furniture, food, clothing. Autumn's parents write stuff down, and so do Justin and Chris, Lucas and Thalia, and a couple of other people.

"I wish I could donate something," Grace whispers in my ear, "but mani-pedis and massages aren't top of list right now."

I lean into her. "You could donate to those who are donating," I whisper back.

She elbows me and nods, visibly happy.

"Did you close today?" Shannon asks her.

She shakes her head. "We were going to be open, but everyone canceled." A worry frown appears between her eyebrows.

I wrap my arm around her shoulders and pull her into me, stroking her arm. Then I lean in and kiss her hair. Shit. I wish there was something I could do about that. More importantly, I wish there was something I could do about her losing her lease. I feel her relax under my touch, and right now? That's all I can ask for, and all I need.

"Why don't you run a special?" I say under my breath. "Discount your services for the next couple of days. Or the week."

She nods. "Good idea. I'll post it on Echoes. Shoulda thought about it myself. I just..."

She's in panic mode, unable to think clearly. There's just been too much on her mind lately.

"Just relax. It'll figure itself out," Dennis says.

"It will," I say.

She gives us a small smile, but I know she doesn't believe it.

Toward the end of the meeting, I get a text message from my C.O. checking in on me.

> Me

> Everyone safe and sound, but a lot of damage to houses

> Wish I could stick around to help out.

That second message was a little ballsy, but hey. You never know until you try.

My phone rings. "King. 'Sup," my C.O. says.

I excuse myself from the table, step out of the crowd, and tell him the situation.

"Take four extra days. Then pack your shit and get your ass here." Before hanging up, he adds, "We'll chalk that up to Air Force community outreach, so do me a favor, wear your fucking Air Force T-shirts, and post some selfies like a true millennial. Brass'll be happy to know we're doin' something to counterbalance the pushback on the F-35."

Okay then. Paperwork will follow. I know his word is golden, and I don't need to worry. I just bought myself four more days with Grace.

I get back to Grace right as the meeting ends. She looks at me, a question in her eyes. "Gonna stick around a few more days," I whisper in her ear, squeezing her against me. "My C.O. cleared me to help out with the recovery effort." She holds me tighter against her, as we walk through the crowd to find Lucas. "Hey, man. You're gonna need help. I'm not qualified, but I'm free."

Lucas gives me a friendly slap on the bicep. "You're more than qualified. Appreciate it. When you say free...?"

"Available for the next few days and not charging a dime."

He nods and smiles. "Cool. Come by tomorrow at seven?" He looks at Grace. "How's the roof?"

She tilts her head to me. "You have to ask him. It's not leaking anymore, but it has blue plastic on it."

"It'll hold for now," I say, rubbing Grace's arm to reassure her.

Lucas lifts his chin. "A'right. We'll get to you eventually."

"See you tomorrow," we both say as we part ways with Lucas.

We say goodbye to the Harpers, then stop to catch up with Chris and Alex. Grace tells Skye about her bedroom, and the child listens with wide eyes.

"We'll be sure to cut some of the trees around the house so this never happens again," I tell Chris. The thought that Skye could have been asleep in that bedroom and that the tree could have fallen at a different angle is chilling. I can't imagine what Chris is thinking right now. He nods and pulls Alex into him like I'm holding Grace. In times of trial, the need to feel our loved ones close by is heightened.

I scan the room, see Kiara passing around trays of tiny pastries, and stop Justin as he whisks by me, carrying empty dishes to the kitchen. "D'you see Mom and Dad?"

"In the kitchen," he says.

Grace leads the way. We find my parents at the dishwashing station, taking sips of wine in between loads. Mom wipes her hands and hugs me, then embraces Grace. Dad wants to know everything about the

Harpers' basement and Grace's roof, complete with square footage of damage, wattage and power of the underwater pump. I end up putting dishes away with Dad while Grace and Mom load the racks, talking about colors for ceiling paint.

When the crowd thins, and the kitchen looks under control and my parents are gone, Grace wraps her arm around me and says, "Ready to go home?"

It hits me like a bullet. Knocks me out and settles in my chest and hurts real good.

Yeah.

I'm ready to go home.

I love how it kinda fell naturally from her lips, and now here we are, in bed, the jersey flying off her back, our bodies finding each other, playing off of each other in ways both familiar and new, until we climax together and fall asleep in each other's arms, our breaths and heartbeats seeming to sync.

At some point during the night, we shift, and in the morning, I wake up spooning Grace.

Having her safely nested against me is the absolute fucking best feeling ever. I stay awake for a few moments without moving, savoring the moment, until my dick asks for more, and I slip out of bed to let her sleep.

When I get to Lucas's, he meets me with a concerned frown. "We need to get to the Richardson's house first. They lost part of a wall, and his mother lives there right now. That gonna be a problem for you?"

The name doesn't register right away, but then I get it. He's Grace's landlord. The guy who's selling and doesn't care that means she might lose her business.

I clench my jaw but shake my head. "You're the boss."

As I grab an old Air Force T-shirt from my saddle bag to change into, my fingers touch a glossy stack of brochures. Pulling them out, my eyes fall on A Touch Of Grace.

Perfect. I slide them inside the pocket of my windbreaker and get to work.

The people of Emerald Creek are going to get swift repairs *and* a not-so-subtle nudge to support local businesses by taking care of themselves. Triple win.

Starting with the unsuspecting asshole's mother.

CHAPTER FORTY-NINE

Grace

I spend the morning helping Mom clean up the basement. Ethan went to Lucas and Thalia's early, and Colton had some work. Ethan's idea to advertise a special storm discount was brilliant, and a few hours after posting it on Echoes, I see our online bookings pick up. That afternoon, I clean up the backyard, sweep the deck, tidy up the front yard and rake the driveway.

Two days after, I open the spa early, happy to be back at it. My first client is someone I don't know, and she's booked a whole day of treatments for herself.

"I'm staying with my son for the summer, but half the wall went down when the storm created a water pocket under the foundation, and it's a mess out there. A real mess. Some very nice—and I should add, handsome—young men came to make repairs, but you wouldn't *believe* the amount of dust and noise I've had to put up with. Anyhoo. I told my son, I said, *Darling, Momma needs her me time*. Oh I forgot to tell you, one of the men doing the repairs highly recommended your place. He even handed me a brochure. So I said to my son, I said, *Arrivederci, I shall see you tonight.* Thank god the temperature is divinely perfect this time of year, because what with the walls being down, I would have had to move to the inn or the resort, and I don't want to do that. I only see my son every so often, you see?..."

I mentally shut off her incessant chatter and let my instinct take over the massage, let my hands follow the path that her body needs. Soon after, she's snoring, and when I wake her up gently, she stretches and greets me with a wide smile. "You know what would make my day, dear?"

"Tell me," I say, smiling to myself. "I don't have Champagne, but I do have a locally made bubbly, if that's what you're thinking."

He mouth rounds in a surprised O. "Why not? But I was hoping you'd do my nails for me."

"Cheyenne does a wonderful job. We don't call her a nail artist lightly."

"Pretty please? I promise I'll book with Cheyenne next time. But I just need some pampering, nothing fancy, and you have magical hands, and I want to hear alllll about *you* now."

My next massage is scheduled with Alex, so I shoot her quick text to move her later—I know she won't mind—and smile to my new fan. "It would be my pleasure." When someone books a whole day with you, you give them what they want.

We continue chatting as I lead her downstairs, and I learn that her son from a previous marriage lives here. Her name doesn't ring a bell, and I don't ask her her son's name, because she talks nonstop without prompting, so I just let her follow her own flow while she chooses her nail polish color.

"I'm not familiar with this brand, what is it?"

"It's free of a lot of harmful products, cruelty-free, and made in New England. Not in Vermont, but close."

"I love those colors," she says, picking a bright pink and a turquoise.

"Aren't they awesome? I'm trying to convince the maker to design an emerald green just for us. Private label sort of thing." Or I was, because with the spa's future so uncertain, all my plans are on hold right now.

She clasps her hands together. "You're so creative!" she cries.

I'm not, I'm really not. I just like what I do, and I like people to feel special, and I like my little town.

As I get her settled in for her pedicure, Alex materializes in front of me. "Talk to you for a sec?" she asks.

"Alex! Sorry, did you not get my message?"

She waves my concern away. "Yeah-yeah, don't worry about that. It's... it's about your lease. I might have a temporary solution."

I go to stop the flow of water mid-fill in the pedicure basin.

"You can talk in front of me, I don't care," my client says. "The water's divine." She closes her eyes to give us a semblance of privacy, but I know she'll be listening. No harm in that, and I have nothing to hide.

I turn to Alex, who gets the hint to make it quick and to the point. "There's some space at the old firehouse you could rent. I just visited it, and it's too small for our offices. But I thought of you. I mean, it's not half as nice as here, but... it's something. I was going to show you photos, but I'll just text them to you."

"Sure, thanks." I give Alex a small smile and pinch my lips as she leaves, then force myself to smile at my client. The old firehouse is really not my vibe. It has no outdoor space. And super tall ceilings that will make it hard to heat in the winter. Overall, with its cement floors and rusted metal beams, it has an edgy vibe that's just not fit for a cozy, plush spa.

"Are you looking to expand?" the woman asks me.

"I wish," I tell her, and then proceed to explain in as few words as possible my current predicament, without making it sound like it's the end. In other words, without showing her how I feel.

"My son is in real estate!" she exclaims as if that's the most brilliant idea. "I'm sure he'd love to buy the house as an investment."

Oh, her son is going to be psyched about his mom's meddling, I'm sure. Feeling slightly guilty, I play into her hand. "Well, my understanding is that there's already an offer on the table, but they might be taking backups. I'll give you the listing agent's contact." There's nothing wrong with messing with Richardson and Amy, right?

"Oh, there's no need. He'll have it. Matter-of-fact, let me text him right now. He'll look it up." Her thumbs fly on her phone's screen with the dexterity of a teenager. "Whoopty-doo!" The phone wooshes with the sound of an outgoing message. Then it dings. "Ha! He says he's aware."

There you go. He knows, he's not interested. What else is new?

The phone wooshes again with her reply, but there's no sound indicating a response.

She frowns.

Welcome to my world.

When I close up the spa hours later, my heart clenches at the sight of the sign in the window. A Touch Of Grace. My eyes well up, thinking my dream is about to be shattered.

Like so many things. What's the saying? The only constant is change itself? Something like that. Taking a deep breath to clear my mind, I think about what lies ahead. Dad hopefully getting better. Maybe a steady job at the resort spa for me—less headache and a steady income. And Ethan's career really taking off. Brussels. NATO Headquarters. Wow. Pride swells inside me, for him and also for me, for being happy for him.

Ethan comes back late, as he has the previous nights. We have a quick dinner, and I get to bed while he's in the shower.

"Lucas is working you to the bone," I say as I wrap my arms around him after he's made me come.

He pulls me tighter into his arms. "I'm working on a little side project after hours."

What could he possibly be up to? "A side project?!" I try to hide my disappointment. While I'm proud of Ethan for volunteering to make emergency repairs in people's homes after the storm, I was hoping he'd keep most of his free time for me. Or his family. Not for side projects.

He pulls me back into his fold, spooning around me. God his body feels so good. So protective. How will I ever sleep again once he's gone? "I'm almost done. I'll show you soon."

Now he's gotten me excited. "What is it?"

"It's a surprise," he says sleepily.

"Pretty please?"

He squeezes my hip. "Tomorrow."

"Tomorrow? Really?"

Well, it'll have to be tomorrow, right. Isn't he supposed to leave now-ish?

"When are you leaving?" I ask.

He groans and pulls me against him but doesn't give me an answer.

CHAPTER FIFTY

Ethan

A little while ago, Justin asked for my help building something in the fields, a frame of a house. That's when it hit me.

The need to rebuild the past, to erase my mistakes. No matter what Grace said. I want to forget the ten years that just went by, go back, and start new.

So every evening, after working on Lucas's projects, I head to Woodbury Knoll.

I have a clear idea of what I need and how I want it, and in a few days, it'll be done.

Yesterday I stopped at the antique shop and met with Autumn. After swearing her to secrecy, I had her help me pick out a cute rug, a few lanterns, a kilim-covered futon, wide throw pillows, and colorful blankets. I bought local pottery and pink drinking glasses at Noah's general store. I picked up the finishing touch tonight and dropped it off right before getting home to pick up Grace.

"Close your eyes!" I call out from the front of the bike.

Yeah, she's taken a liking to the 'chick magnet.' So much so, that when I wanted to drive her blindfolded to see the 'surprise,' she still didn't want to get in the car.

I didn't think it'd be safe to have her blindfolded on the bike, so she promised she'd shut her eyes. When I kill the engine and kick out the stand, I turn around to see her with her eyes shut and nose adorably frowned.

"Can I open now?"

"Nope!"

"Ugh!" She swings a leg over the bike and trips on the uneven terrain. "Where are we? I nearly fell."

I swoop her into my arms. Problem solved. "Almost there," I say as she holds onto my neck with both hands.

"It smells like forest," she says.

"Nice try." The sound of my boots crunching twigs and leaves is enough of a tell. The narrow path climbs steadily, but my breathing stays even.

"Just put me down, Ethan. You're struggling. I can tell. I'm too heavy."

"I can barely feel you. We're just... going uphill." A rock rolls down the path. "Just a little more." After a couple more minutes, I set her down and hold her hand. "Duck," I say, moving aside the underbrush that hides the surprise. "You can open your eyes now."

She looks around. "Where are we?" Then she squints. "Is that...? Are we on Woodbury Knoll?"

I swing her around so she's looking in the right direction now. In the direction of the new treehouse I built for her. For us.

She clasps her hands to her mouth. "Ohmygod, Ethan! What did you do?!" The hours spent busting my ass, the extra callouses on my hands, the ache in my lower back are all worth it when I see the wonder in her gaze as she runs to the rope ladder and caresses its rungs before stepping up. She looks at me, stars in her eyes, and fuck me, but it's a throwback to our younger years. To our carelessness. To the way we just wanted to enjoy each day together.

To the way a tree house away from everyone was all we needed. Hell, it was a castle to us.

And it sure looks the same today.

I close the gap between us and nudge her up, following right behind her, my nose right up her cute ass so she'll get there sooner. "Ethan!" she giggle-shrieks, hurrying up to the platform.

She moves the heavy curtain aside and gasps. Prodding her to step in, I join her inside.

"It's huge!" she says. "And look at all this... furniture! It's so much nicer than our first one!"

"I picked up a few skills over the years... And I figured you'd want a little more comfort."

"Comfort? What for?"

"You don't like it?" I say, spreading on the futon, tapping next to me for her to lie by my side.

She remains standing and twirls around to take in all the details. "I love it, but for the record, I'd like to state that I don't *need* comfort."

"Duly noted. I'll just remove the pillows, the curtains, the throws." I lean over to switch on battery-operated twinkling lights that illuminate the whole ceiling of the tree house.

"Ohmygod, look at that."

It does look awesome. "Nah, I'll just take it all out."

"Don't you dare," she says playfully. "What I meant is, being with you is enough."

But I see them. I see the tears in her eyes. I see the way she crosses her arms, hands clasping her opposite elbows. "Come here," I say, my voice lower. When she finally lies next to me, I twirl a strand of her hair in my hand. "It's going to be okay. We're going to be okay."

I haven't heard from my C.O. yet, but at any moment I'll be summoned to report in.

She sighs and shuts her eyes. I cup her hip, loving the feel of her body, warm and strong in its own soft way, just like her. She relaxes under my touch, sinking deeper into the mattress, and a tiny sigh escapes her mouth. I run a finger up her T-shirt, goosebumps forming under my touch. She looks at me through half-closed eyelids and brings a hand to my chest, then up to my neck, bringing me down to her.

My heartbeat picks up as the flow of memories mingle with the present. She hasn't changed, and yet she has. She's matured. She's wiser. Braver. More complex. More patient.

The emotional fire she's been through toughened her and brightened her like a diamond.

She intimidates me.

My fingers reach the lace of her bra, and her breath becomes uneven. Under my hand, the beating of her heart accelerates. She lifts herself off the mattress and removes her T-shirt. I unfasten her bra, then take her perky nipple in my mouth, her moan zinging straight to my dick.

Her fingers fumble with my zipper, and with tiny little cries of want, she gets rid of the fabric between us, wraps her legs around my hips, and pulls me inside her, hungry, wanting, demanding. She nips at my bottom lip, digs her nails in my back, thrusts her hips up, then plants one foot on the mattress, wanting to be on top.

She claims me. Fuck I've wanted that. Wanted that for so long, since she'd rejected me and I had no idea why. I wanted to be first for her. First for everything.

I wanted to *be* her everything.

I wanted to *give* her everything.

"Ethan," she moans as she pumps herself up and down my shaft.

"What, beautiful?"

"Ethan..."

"Yeah?"

"Take me harder." Her eyes roll back as I do what I'm told.

When her walls clench around me, and her nails dig into my flesh, and her moans get louder, and her thighs shake around mine, she grabs my nape and starts tilting us. We roll onto the hard floor of the tree house. "Fuck me right here," she mumbles when I'm on top of her. I empty myself into her, cupping her back in my arms, pushing her hips into the hard floor. "Yessss," she sighs, out of breath, her legs wrapped tightly around my waist, absorbing my cum, keeping us joined.

I roll us back onto the mattress and pull her into my chest, stroking her hair. Then as my dick becomes limp, I reach under the mattress and pull out a wad of tissues.

"You sure come prepared," she says with a lazy smile as I clean her up.

"Next stage is a shower."

She laughs softly.

"Oh right. You don't need comfort. I forgot."

She smiles at me tenderly. "I love the comfort you provide for me," she says, and for real, my dick stands at attention. "I just don't want you to think you need to do anything special for me."

I cup her face with both my hands. "I want to do these things for you. I always did. I always will. And no matter what you say, yeah, I do want to catch up with the past. Erase it. Make up for it. You deserve it. And I want it."

"Okay then," she says, caressing my face dreamily.

"Good." We stay like that for a while, looking at each other. She asks me where I got the stuff, if anyone helped me with the build. "Nope. I wanted to do this alone. It was... I guess it was cathartic for me. The physical labor. The quiet. Being alone." Being close to her in my thoughts. I let this sink in a bit. It does feel like I've rebuilt a bridge, in a way.

Grace moves on the mattress, and her belly rumbles.

"Hungry?"

"Starving."

I reach over to the cooler hidden in a vintage travel trunk—the last item I brought this morning—and pull out a chilled gazpacho soup and a fresh white wine. From a side compartment, I produce a baguette freshly baked by Chris. "There's apples and nuts for dessert," I say, suddenly self-conscious that this is a frugal and simple meal.

"Ohmygod, Ethan, this is perfect. Look at those little bowls!" she says, talking about the pottery. "Where did you get the soup? It's delicious."

I shrug. "I made it."

She stops with her spoon midair. "You what?"

"I used Justin's kitchen to make it without you knowing. If I'd done it at the farm, someone would have told you, so—"

"Hold on. You made this?"

I nod.

"From scratch?"

"Eh, just some veggies and seasoning. Throw it in a blender and voila!"

She looks dreamily at me. "Yeah right. Where'd you learn how to—never mind. I don't want to know her name."

I laugh. "From Justin's chef, Shane. They had it at the fair, and it was pretty good. I asked him for his recipe and made it myself."

She blinks. "I'm sure he would have made it for you. If you'd asked."

"Yeah. I'm sure he would have. Wouldn't be the same, though."

She falls silent for a spell, and I wonder where her mind went. "You okay?"

She answers with a question. "When did you decide to do this? The treehouse, I mean."

"I saw how easy it was to build that cute frame for Justin, using fallen tree branches." His project was a surprise for Chloe. "I figured..."

"You figured you could one-up him," she laughs.

"Nah," I say, trailing the soft skin of her belly. "Those days are over. I'm happy he's happy."

She tilts her face to me. "Ours is a place to hide our relationship. *Was* a place to hide our relationship." She finishes on a whisper, and although her tone is soft and mingles with the humming of the forest in the most peaceful way, it pierces me like a dagger.

"I know I shouldn't, and I know it's impossible, but there's a part of me that wants to fix the past. Erase our mistakes. Start over and get it right this time."

Her eyebrows knit. "We'll get it right. As long as we don't expect to have it all."

But that's the thing.

I want it all with Grace.

CHAPTER FIFTY-ONE

Grace

I feel stupid young this morning. Young and loved and carefree. Everything is right. Everything will work out. Even the impending move of my business is just a bump in the road.

I swing by Easy Monday, the mug with the red roses cutouts in hand. "Chilled Maple Craze, please!" I ask Millie.

"Mmm, mixing it up? I like it," Millie says. "Your fan group is outside," she tells me as she hands me my drink.

I join Haley and Alex on the garden that slopes gently down to the river. I'm surprised to see Emma there as well, and even more surprised to see the three of them smiling and seeming to laugh together.

"Hey," I say, sliding in the empty chair next to the hedge of hydrangeas.

"Hey, yourself," Alex says. "I hear someone's been looking out for you."

Ohmygod, can they tell I've been getting so many orgasms? I feel myself blushing.

"Yeah, looks like my brother finally amounted to something," Haley says, and I know there's no way she's talking about what I'm thinking.

I dip my lips to my cup to hide my confusion and look at Emma. I wonder why she's here, with Alex, when she did things that were not cool at all and almost caused a final breakup between Alex and Chris. But hey, all the more power to Alex for forgiving her.

In small towns, you can't hold a grudge for too long. You never know who you'll need, who will be driving by when your car breaks down, or who's going to give you advice or useful information. The pool of potential friends is just that big, and deep down, I know Emma had Chris's best interest at heart. Even if she messed up big time. She was looking out for one of us, as she should have been.

And the fact that Alex is here, talking with her as if nothing happened, proves that she understands that about our small town.

We forgive each other. We're bound to mess up, and holding grudges never helps.

"So I have this client..." Emma starts.

"Ohmygod, Ems, don't tell me you're about to break the client confidentiality rule again," I warn her.

"Hear her out," Alex says.

Well, if Alex is saying that, then... "Go ahead."

"Let's say I have a client who's in real estate, and his mom is a big fan of your spa. Which she discovered, may I add, through a certain hot volunteer carpenter, if you get my drift."

"Yeah, he's not interested."

Emma tilts her head.

"She texted her son in front of me, and it went nowhere. He knows about the sale and isn't interested in buying the place."

Emma has a sly smile. She leans closer to me. "He's not interested in buying it because he already owns it. George Richardson is your new client's son."

I almost spit my coffee out. "Ohmygod, that's too funny."

Emma's smile widens. "You think that's funny? You should have seen the scene she made when she learned he was the one selling your building."

"What? How do you know?"

"I was in his office, doing his books. She was shrieking so loud, I couldn't not hear. Lemme tell you, little Georgie got quite an earful. She threatened to buy the building herself if he didn't pull it off the market, and she dared him to reject her offer. I was right there in his office when he called his realtor and told him to reject Amy's offer and pull the listing."

My mouth hangs open. I don't even know what to say, or think.

It's over? Just like that?

I take a deep breath. "Wow. That was almost... too easy."

"Yeah," Alex says, "who knew what a hot carpenter and a bossy mom could accomplish?"

"Couldn't have done it if I tried."

"I think this calls for a celebration," Alex declares. "Everyone, Growler tonight."

"Oh yeah," Haley says.

To be on the safe side, I check the realtor's website before calling Ethan. And just like Emma said, the listing is gone.

I call Ethan before even thinking of letting Mom know.

That evening, I wear a cute little sparkly dress, strap on my high-heel sandals, and make my eyes extra smoky. Tonight I'm letting go. My life is perfect, or as perfect as it can be, at least for now.

Tomorrow will come soon enough.

Ethan holds me tight the whole evening, and while he's as happy as I am about the spa situation, I can tell he's not entirely here with me. Something's on his mind, and I think I know what it is.

His time in Emerald Creek is coming to an end, and we'll soon be saying goodbye.

I don't want to think about that, so I grind myself against him. Anything to make him forget.

"Babe, what are you doing?" he growls, half laughing into my neck when I pull his hand over my boob while my ass works his front. All of our friends could see us, if they cared to watch. Turns out, they have better things to do.

"Just enjoy tonight," I yell over my shoulder, trying to cover the music.

He cups his body over mine, taking over our dirty dance. God he's soooo good. I just want to dry hump him right now.

"We're gonna go easy on the drinks, yeah?" he says when we take a break, before I can order another shot.

I pretend to pout and let him order a mocktail. "I want a little umbrella!" I cry out to the bartender.

"Is she drunk?" Colton frowns.

"Working on that," Ethan confirms.

Colton's body shakes with soft laughter. "Dude, never saw my sister wasted. She's funny."

"See? Even my brother says I'm funny. Lemme have a real drink," I whine.

"Listen to your man, sister."

"*Listen to your man, sister,*" I mock. "God you're such a party pooper. And Fuck The Patriarchy!" I yell, lifting my mocktail in unsteady hands, my wobbly knees dangerously tilting on my heels.

"You okay?" Kiara says, frowning at me.

"Did you hear him?" I ask her, pointing my glass at Colton. "*Listen to your man, sister.*"

"Dude, not cool," she says to Colton, but with a smile, and what's up with that?

"Whose side are you on?"

"Babe," Ethan's deep voice in my ear instantly calms me down. "Everyone's on your side. You just don't... handle your liquor too well, is all. You're a lightweight, and I love you like that. Yeah?"

"Yeah," I whisper back. *He loves me like that.*

"Wanna go outside, get some fresh air?"

"Sure," I say, leaning on Ethan. The night air picks me up like a cool shower. Shit. I really did have too much to drink, didn't I? Was I yelling in there? But why did Colton... ohmygod, I *yelled* at Colton. My sweet brother. "I yelled at Colton," I say.

"He can handle it."

I'm turning back to go inside when my phone rings with Mom's ringtone. I let it go to voicemail. I'm in no state to talk to my mother. The phone rings again.

"Want me to get it for you?"

I shake my head softly. I want to stay here, in silence with Ethan, for another minute. Or two. Or two million. He dips his face to mine and kisses me, then brings me against his chest and caresses my back.

My phone rings again.

Then the voicemail chimes.

Then it rings again.

"I'll get it for you," he says and digs into my tiny cross-body purse, picks up, and holds the phone to my ear.

"Gracie—it's Daddy. He's—they're—he's going to the hospital." My heart constricts and I look up to Ethan. He frowns and cups my shoulders with his hand while Mom gives me some info. When I hang up, he says, "I'll drive."

"We need to tell Colton."

"Stay right here." He rushes inside and comes right out, talking to Colton. Colton bolts to his car as we get in the Jeep, Ethan driving.

Ethan cups my thigh with his hand. "Breathe, baby," he says as we get on the highway. "What did Shannon say?"

All sign of intoxication has suddenly left me. "She came home and found him on the floor."

"Shit." He strokes my thigh. "I'm sorry, baby. Did she—did she say if he...?"

I look at him. *If he what?* He looks so worried; I almost feel sorry for him too. "She found him unconscious, so she called 9-1-1. I don't know what she did then—I didn't ask. She called me from the car. She was following the ambulance."

"Did she sound okay?" He lifts his hand from my thigh to my nape and kneads it, then pulls me against him. "I wish we'd driven her."

"She'll be alright," I say in a small voice. That Ethan is worried for Mom is just so... so touching and overwhelming and sweet. And it makes sense but... I guess I'm not used to a man sharing my daily troubles with me. Why did Dad fall? I should have gone to see him. The last time I did, was... I straighten from Ethan's embrace to look through the passenger window. "The last real conversation I had with Dad, we argued." The dark landscape whizzes by while I fight the tears but keep the guilt right where it belongs. Front and center.

Ethan's hand lands on my thigh again. He gives me a squeeze. "Don't go there," he says. Then, stroking me, he adds, "Your dad and your family need you strong. Guilt isn't gonna do that for you, or for them. Trust me on that."

I turn my eyes to him and catch his concerned gaze on me. "Whatever you argued about has nothing to do with what happened to him. Trust me on that too. Don't beat yourself up. Save yourself for where you can help. Just be there for them."

I nod. "Thanks. You're right," I say as we pull into the hospital entrance in record time.

"I'll drop you off at the entrance and park the car," Ethan says as he slows under the carport.

I lean over to kiss him. "You're coming, right?"

"I'll wait for you downstairs."

"No. I want you to come. I *need* you, Ethan. I'll text you where we are."

CHAPTER FIFTY-TWO

Ethan

The hospital is brand new and nicer than what I've gotten used to on base. Its appearance is closer to a mall. I suppose that helps with morale.

My phone buzzes—Grace telling me where they are. When I get there it's just her and Shannon, huddled next to each other on a hard couch. Shannon stands to greet me, and I hug her. Peeling herself from me, she looks into my eyes. "Thanks for being here," she says just as Colton stomps in.

He takes his mom in his arms. "What happened?"

Before Shannon can answer, a nurse enters. "The family can see him now, but no more than two at a time."

I step back and sit on a chair in the corner. Shannon and Grace go first, leaving me alone with Colton.

His broody vibe permeates the whole room. "He was an asshole," he says to the floor, his elbows on his knees, hands clasped in front of him. "Still is, sometimes. There's only so much you can blame on the alcohol. Fucked up a lot of people. Honest to god, I don't know how or *why* Mom put up with him." He glances at me, maybe to make sure I get it that it's me he's talking to, then looks back down to the floor. "I won't be that kinda of man, or that kinda father." He lifts his head and looks at me. "But he's our father," he shrugs. "Sucks."

I step next to him, pull a chair and slump onto it. "I'm sorry, man. Wish there was something I could do."

He shrugs again. "You're here," he says after a few beats. "That's somethin'." He looks at me with a small smile. "That'll mean everythin' to Grace."

We exchange a long look, no doubt thinking about but not wanting to talk about what Dennis did, back in the day. It's irrelevant now. The man is trying to change. Has changed. My heart aches at the thought of all the missed moments in the past ten years. At the thought of everything that I still need to catch up on.

Now's not the time to talk about myself with Colton. I'm happy to be here, with him, right now.

Shannon and Grace come back after what feels like a long time and no time at all. "You can go in," the nurse tells Colton and me.

I stay in my chair. She said family.

"You comin' or what?" Colton says.

"Go, honey," Shannon tells me.

I glance at Grace, and she nods. Alright then, I guess we're doing this.

Dennis is hooked up to an IV and to various monitoring devices. The room feels stuffy yet cold.

"Hey, Dad," Colton says. "You alright?" His voice is warm and low, with a touch of worry. There's nothing left from his bitter confession in the waiting room.

Dennis turns glassy eyes to his son. He looks everything except alright. "I will be. Eventually." If you ask me, Dennis looks like death.

"You better be," Colton answers.

I stay next to the door. Although I've helped at the Harpers' house after the storm, and we sat at the same table at Lazy's a few days ago, Dennis and I have yet to say a single word to each other. I didn't mean it to be that way. It just didn't happen. And now, here we are.

Colton wobbles from one foot to the other, clearly not knowing what to say or even do with himself. "They treat you right?"

"Yeah-yeah-yeah. Son, do me a favor. Get yourself outta here. You hate hospitals as much as I do, and you're not making things easier with all this fidgeting."

Colton squints, his gaze darting between Dennis and me. "You sure?"

"Get the hell out." A small smile plays on Dennis's lips. "Please. Love ya."

Colton seems taken aback by his father's expression of affection. He ends up shrugging and says, "A'right, then. Take care... love you too."

He doesn't see the soft chuckle that shakes Dennis as his gaze follows Colton. I turn on my heel, mumbling goodbye.

"Ethan, stay here a minute," Dennis croaks.

Colton glances at me but leaves quickly. Clearly he does hate hospitals, like Dennis said.

"I been meaning to talk to you, since you came back. Just didn't... didn't have the time or... ya know. Ability." He waves down at the body that is failing him.

"I should have come by and paid you a visit," I say, not sure how to address him now. Mr. Harper sounds a little formal, but I'm pretty sure that's what he used to be to me.

"And why would you have done that? I didn't treat you well, back in the day. I didn't deserve your respect."

I straighten my posture. "You have my respect," I counter.

He waves the argument away. "Point is, I made a mistake, back then. I didn't think." He points to his head with the hand that's not attached to tubes. "I didn't feel how what I was doin' was hurtin' others."

I stay silent to let him catch his breath.

"You hafta understand. I just didn't want to see her grow up. But meanwhile, I pushed a good man away from her. I'll die knowing I messed up, son, and that's the worst that can happen to a man on his deathbed. Knowing he's leaving his daughter alone and knowing it was his fault she's alone."

"She's not alone. And you're not dying, Dennis."

"Grace loves you. She always did. Always will. Take that love she has for you and return it a thousand-fold to her. It'll be worth it, I promise. There's nothing like a life with a woman who loves you." He stops for a bit, exhausted by the effort.

"Maybe we can pick up this conversation when you're out of the hospital," I suggest, getting worried about him.

He ignores me. "I know I'm the one who got between you and her, back in the day. But believe me when I tell you, you were too young. Would have messed it up. Now you're both older, you've seen combat, and she has, too, in a way. You'll know what's important." He stops again, breath leaving him.

It doesn't escape me that he's doubling down on being fundamentally right at the time. And maybe he *was* right about us being too young. We'll never know. "You should really get some rest. Don't work yourself up with all that stuff. It's water under the bridge," I assure him.

"Just promise a man on his deathbed that you'll do right by her."

"You're way too young to die. You need to see your grandbabies."

Color graces the cheeks that were a worrisome gray, and his eyes focus on me. "Grandbabies, huh? How many?"

"As many as she wants."

The twinkle in his eye tells me I talked him over the edge. Sometimes when life is in the balance, people just need a purpose, something to look forward to. I might have given him just that.

And I've given myself that as well.

Suddenly, I want those babies. I want grumpy old Dennis as my father-in-law and Colton as another brother. And Shannon as more than Mom's friend.

I don't want to 'make it work' with Grace. I don't want long distance.

Fuck that.

I wish I could have my life back. All of it.

CHAPTER FIFTY-THREE

Ethan

Shannon and I convince Grace to go home and get some sleep. Even though the main threat to her business is now gone, she's not canceling her clients tomorrow. Not after the loss the spa took when people canceled right after the storm, plus the day she just took off when I got back.

She needs her rest, and I'm making sure she gets it.

The next morning, we get good news from the hospital. They're keeping Dennis under observation one more day, then sending him home. Grace is relieved, and although the dark marks under her eyes say a different story, she maintains she wants to get to the spa early.

I follow her into town on my bike. While she's at work, I'll make my rounds of goodbyes so I'm not rushed when the time comes. I'm bound to leave anytime now.

Someone tied balloons on the front porch pillars like it's a birthday party. I pull up behind Grace's car to kiss her goodbye, and Randy comes out, having just dropped off a bouquet, "compliments of Alex and Chris."

It's only eight in the morning, and clients won't start coming in before nine or ten, so I walk Grace up the stairs. There's a vibrancy in the air, and I'm curious about it.

Shanice, Fabrizio, and Cheyenne are dancing to loud, fun music coming from the hidden loudspeakers—not the spa kind of music. Grace hugs Hope and Claudia, who are beaming. While they're all aware that Dennis is in the hospital and they express their get-well wishes to Grace, I've never seen all of them so happy.

This business is *truly* their life. And it's all because of Grace. Shanice grabs Grace's hand to dance with her just as the phone rings.

Claudia picks up, cheer in her tone. "Now is great!" she says, then hangs up and announces, "Chris is bringing croissants and doughnuts."

I pull out my phone and ask Millie to whip up an order for... twelve people, and manage to kiss Grace on the temple as I snatch her car keys. "Be right back."

At Easy Monday, Ms. Angela calls out to me from her couch. "Good job keeping her spa, Ethan!"

Several people agree, one person even hoots. I put my hands up. "I didn't do anything." I really didn't. "Collective effort," I concede.

"Hear there's grandbabies on the way for Dennis?" someone else calls out.

I have to laugh at that. And maybe blush a bit. I raise my hands. "Not that I know of."

"Yet!" someone else hollers.

"Give the guy a break!" a third person cries out.

Millie hands me a large, heavy bag. "On the house today. Tell them congrats. I have everyone's favorite with their name on it, and some specials for whoever else I forgot. Did you bring one of Grace's mugs?"

"I forgot," I confess. "Didn't plan this."

"Good," she beams. "Now go."

I don't have time to ask her what's good about that. I rush back to the spa. Chris is there with Alex and Skye, delivering breakfast for everyone. "Oh look, there's even a hot chocolate for you!" I tell Skye as I'm unpacking Millie's order.

"Thank you, Ethan. Millie makes the best hot cho-colate. She adds ci-na-mum to it."

"Oh yeah?" I store that info for when Skye will come over. *She likes cinnamon.* I pull out a pink and gold mug with A Touch Of Grace engraved on it. "Oh my god, that's beautiful," Grace gushes. "Did you order this?" Her eyes shine even brighter.

"I wish, but no. It's from Millie." Shit, Millie did good. Real good. Even I can tell the mug looks awesome, and if I couldn't, all I would need would be to look at Grace's reaction.

Alex glances at me. "Millie's smart," she says under her breath. "These would look awesome in those display cases. I wonder how long it's gonna take Grace to—"

"We should totally sell these!" Grace shrieks. "D'you think she'd be offended if I ask her to bulk order some for the spa?"

Alex smiles. "I don't think she'll be offended," she tells Grace. "That *may* have been her idea all along."

Grace's eyes widen. "We should do a joint mug! *An Easy Monday Starts With A Touch Of Grace*. Something along those lines."

"I love it," several people exclaim.

Chris sidles up next to me. "You think you're ever gonna be able to leave?"

I peel my eyes from the group to look at him. He has a content smile, watching Alex and Skye chat and twirl around with Fabrizio and Shanice, who are still going to the beat. "Fuck, it's gonna be hard." I look back at Grace, who's across the room, her dreamy smile on me.

I can't believe how lucky I am. My heart shatters at the idea of leaving all this in maybe just a few hours.

That evening, when my phone chimes and it's my C.O., I put the phone back in my pocket. I know what's on the text. It's time to go.

But Grace just got back home, and I'm not ruining this moment just yet. We get in the shower together, and after some sexy lathering that I'm going to fucking miss like hell when I'm gone, she tells me all about the new mugs she and Millie will be designing. They're even going to sell them at the general store, and Noah is going to contact other businesses to come up with other designs and tag lines.

"What's up with the bookstore name? The Shy Rabit with one b?"

"It's 'Shy Rabit', no 'The,' and it's anyone's guess why it's misspelled."

"Really."

"Yup, really."

She tells me all this while we're toweling off and putting on minimal clothing to just hang out on the deck with our drinks. "Seltzer and lime, honey. Too much has been happening lately. My liver can't handle all the excitement. Dad is better, by the way. The hospital confirmed he's being discharged tomorrow."

I swung by the hospital today to say goodbye to Dennis, on my way back from the farm where I hung out with Dad. And I finally got to visit with Coach Randall. Funny, he hasn't changed a bit. He actually looked younger to me. "You're just getting older, while he's stuck in time," Colton and Justin pointed out when I grabbed what might be the last beer in months with them.

Grace and I sit on the deck, and she pulls her phone out. "I'll post an update on Echoes about Dad. People have been asking." Her thumbs fly across the screen.

"What's that Echoes everyone keeps talking about?" I pull her feet on my lap so I can give her a foot massage.

"Oh—that's good," she moans. "It's our social media. Noah and his club started it a few years ago. It's just for us in Emerald Creek. You should install it! Stay in the loop when you're—oh wow!"

"What?"

She frowns. "The high school—" she begins, then moans as I increase the pressure on the ball of her foot.

"What happened at the high school?" If I let her moans guide my instincts, I'm bringing her to bed right this minute. But I want to hear her talk first, want her to tell me all about her day, all about those little things that'll be so hard to hang onto once I'm gone.

"They got hacked! Noah seems beside himself."

My blood freezes. "Hacked how?"

"Admin can't access the system, all the grades are gone, and the students are getting weird messages. You know, through their portals? It's awful."

"Did they call the FBI?"

Her frown deepens as she reads through the post. "I dunno... apparently, they don't have the resources to figure out the hack. Like—for real? The state needs to help out, and from what Noah is posting, it's not looking good." She raises her eyes to me. "He didn't call you, did he?"

I check my phone, just in case. My C.O.'s message is still there, unopened. Nothing else. "No."

"He won't want to bother you. D'you think you could, like, take a look?"

You don't *take a look* at a hack like you would under the hood of car that's stalling. Also, you don't exactly walk into a high school that's been hacked and say, *Move aside, lemme fix this.*

I certainly can't fix it. The only thing I'd be qualified to do, is probably assess the threat, and then recruit and organize the team who would be able to fix it.

"I'm sure they're working on it."

"Yeah but—not like you could."

"Of course they are!"

Grace tilts her head like she's talking to a stubborn child. "Honey. There're less than six hundred and fifty thousand people in the *whole state*. Do you think they have the kind of cyber-thingy wiz like you on the school payroll? They don't."

"They'll find people."

"And why not you?"

I smile at her perseverance. "No one's asked me."

She pulls her feet from my hands. "So—I'm no one?" she says, looking downright offended.

"I mean, no one at the high school."

"Babe, I didn't ask anyone to give my brochures to Richardson's mom. I didn't ask anyone to look for another location for me. I didn't ask anyone to bring croissants and coffee this morning. And I didn't ask anyone to design a cup for the spa."

Yep. I get her point. I rub the sore spot between my eyebrows. "Lemme call Noah."

"He'll be at the school." She looks up at me hopefully. "He might be too busy to answer his phone."

I pull my phone back out. "I'm gonna text him I'm on my way."

My thumb hovers over my C.O.'s message again. If he wanted an immediate response, or this was an emergency, he'd be blowing up my phone. Plus, everybody knows coverage sucks in Vermont, right? I leave his message unread for now and text Noah.

Grace walks me to the door and grabs my arm. "You know I'd rather spend the evening with you, right, especially since…"

Since I'm going to leave. We both know it; we just don't want to talk about it.

"I know." I cup her face in my hands. "Thanks for telling me about the hack. They probably need me right now, you're right."

She gives me a small nod and kisses my lips.

"You better be sleeping when I get back," I whisper, trailing the dark circles under her eyes.

"Going to bed right now," she whispers back.

I give her one last kiss, then text Noah, give Damian a scratch behind the ears, check that my keys are in my pocket, and I'm out the door.

At the high school, Zach, one of the kids I met in Noah's Coding Club, is waiting for me at the entrance, under the awning. He whips his wheelchair around to open the door for me. "We're working on quarantining the infected endpoints," he fills me in as we swiftly move to the admin offices.

"Do we know what the attack vector was?"

"Not sure yet. Could have been a phishing email. Admins here aren't really up to speed on those kinds of things—no offense."

"How did they first find out?"

He coughs. "I saw some weird activity on the network."

That doesn't sound right. I'm going to play stupid for half a second, but not more. "Was your portal hacked?'

"Um—no. Not exactly."

"So you were in the system, and you saw you had company."

"I'm so fucked," he mumbles.

"Ah, I wouldn't worry too much about it at this point. They'll be able to identify what you did and didn't do. And if all you did was hack the system just to see if you could, and that helped catch a cyberattack before it could do too much damage... Who knows." I can't speak for the school administration, or Zach's parents. "How long did it take you to speak up?"

"I texted Mister N. soon's I found out."

Good kid. "What'd he say?"

"To leave it with him."

"Those guys in there know what you did?" I whisper as we approach a windowed office where Noah is huddled with a man and a woman over two monitors.

He shrugs as he swerves into the office. "Mister K. is here."

They turn their faces to me, then back to the screens.

We keep the introductions to a minimum, then I get to work.

Five hours and a gallon of Coke later, I summarize it for them. "It's gonna take an A-team a few weeks to fix this."

"We're fudged," the woman says.

"Lemme see if I can do something more. Give me a couple-three hours."

We leave before the sunrise, and I get home quietly, remembering to kill the engine so I don't wake up Grace.

I settle on the deck, elbows on the railing, facing Woodbury Knoll, and finally open my C.O.'s message, which is, in essence, that I need to report in tomorrow. Not too bad. That explains the no follow-up phone call when I ghosted him.

I open the secure, encrypted app we use for sensitive information.

Me

> I identified an opportunity for the Air Force to gain more points with the local community.

CO

> What now?

I start typing, *The local high school is under a Cipherstorm ransomware,* but another text comes in.

> Sasquatch on the loose?

... system is contained for now but threat extended to students via portal...

> Maple syrup laced with poison by the Russians?

... TTPs point to foreign intrusion, rollbacks DOA as of now...

> Cheddar cheese pirated by the Chinese?

... Advising FBI be brought in but would strongly advise Joint Task Force...

> Canadians illegally crossing the border?

... Suspect this might be a test for broader attack. While this might be for CISA, would suggest we keep a finger on it

> Emerald ash borer attacking the covered bridges?

Shit, how does he even know about the emerald ash borer?

I hit send on my long-ass text message.

The app dings. *Incoming call.*

"Sir," I answer smartly.

"What the *fucking fuck* did you get the *fuck* into?"

"Just helping out the community. Totally fine if the Air Force doesn't see it as their problem."

His silence is more concerning than his abusive usage of a perfectly satisfying expletive. "Looks like we're missing paperwork in your file."

Yup. That would be the Confirmation Orders. Still unsigned by me. I would never have done that a few months ago. Always had all my i's dotted and my t's crossed. In fact, it's been my plan to get that done... I just never got around to it. And now? Looks like it's giving me options. Leverage.

God, I am becoming a piece of shit.

"Don't hate yourself," my C.O. says as if he's reading my mind. "You're hitting a milestone. It's understandable you're thinking things through."

I don't answer. I don't know *what* to answer.

"I'm gonna get some heat if I don't staff Brussels."

I stay quiet.

"Fuck. That bad, huh?"

I did talk about Grace to my C.O. And about Emerald Creek. "I just can't watch my life pass me by, sir."

"Oh—I know the feeling. I'm twice divorced. Believe me, I know."

When Grace offered to come visit me a week out of the month in Brussels, I was faced with the practicality of what a long-distance relationship was going to look like.

And I didn't like it.

Not one minute.

Sure, it was fun, that first time, organizing those little surprises. The flowers. The cards. The chocolates in case I wasn't back yet.

That's not a life plan, though.

Not to mention, I missed her like *hell*.

"The Air Force needs you, and that's not a recruiting campaign, King." I feel movement behind me. Probably Damian, but this conversation I'm having with my C.O. is too important to let a cat distract me. "I put my neck on the line for you to get Brussels."

"I'm sorry, sir."

"You're not quitting the Air Force on me, King."

"With all due respect, sir, I think I can do whatever the hell I want at this point."

"You fucking serious?"

I'm kind of bluffing. "I do want to serve my country, sir."

"Are you sure?"

"Did you read my message?"

"Why'd you think I called?"

"We might be dealing with a foreign entity testing shit out." I look at the sky turning pink over the hill. "The folks here are gonna contact the FBI first thing in the morning. I believe it's in our interest to be involved. It's in everyone's interest. But hey, what do I know." Sarcasm won't get me anywhere, but my C.O. is getting on my nerves right now. There's a real situation at hand, and every minute counts.

"Is Brussels a yes or a no?" is his answer.

At least he's giving me a choice, and I appreciate that. "Brussel's gonna be a no, sir. If at all possible." I may not have all my paperwork in order, but I'm still Air Force. I follow orders. He knows, however, that there's no point sending someone to a sensitive posting who doesn't see it as their life mission. A few months ago, I would have done *anything* to get that posting. But I've lost that commitment. My priorities are elsewhere now.

"Fucking fuck," he mumbles.

"Lots of other qualified guys—and women—for that posting."

"You think I don't know this?" he barks. "You're making me look like an asshole."

Oh, that's what it is. Who the fuck cares. "I'm sorry, sir. I really am. Now, about the situation here—"

"I stuck my neck out for you," he yells.

And I said I'm sorry. Jesus, look at the bigger picture. "We might have uncovered a new type of attack, sir. There's a good chance this was a test on an unsuspecting victim. If we play this right, we could be three steps ahead of the next major cyberattack."

"That's not exactly your expertise," he reminds me. At least he's calmed down and listening.

"Correct. But with the right team in place, this could be a big win for us. And we could learn a few things about what's brewing."

"What makes you think you're the right person to lead the effort?"

Seriously, now he's suggesting someone else take the lead? Fuck that. "Locals are a little on the weird side, sir. They won't trust anyone that's not from here."

"What the hell do we care?"

"Like you pointed out earlier, we have no jurisdiction." He didn't point that out, but he should have.

He grunts. "What makes you think they'll let you take over?"

"They came to me for help, sir. They didn't need to."

"Alright. I'll see what I can do."

"Thank you, sir."

Another grunt.

"And sir, like you said, the F-35s are unpopular with some folks here," I say, referring to the stealth fighter jets based in Vermont. He knows about that—he mentioned it a few days ago. It can't hurt to remind him everything that's at stake. "The Air Force could use some goodwill around here."

"I said I'll see what I can do," he barks again before cutting the connection.

I take a deep breath and pocket my phone.

"What's that about you not going to Brussels?"

I whip around to see Grace in my jersey, arms wrapped around herself, eyes flaring with... is that anger?

"Babe," I start, all mushy inside at the sight of her. I close the distance between us and take her in my arms, but she stays stone cold.

"Did I hear you say no to Brussels?" she clips.

I squeeze her. "You did." I don't elaborate, wondering why she's acting like this. She should be happy, right?

"Why?"

Why? "Lots of other people can do it." I run my nose down the side of her face. "And this way, I'll be closer to you."

She huffs. "Ethan—" she starts.

"I had this lightbulb moment, and it's all because of you. I can do good anywhere. I don't need to be in Brussels. Other very competent people can do just as well as I would do. But there's only one place where I want to be."

She pulls out of my embrace. "I never should have asked you to go to the high school."

"Why not?" I'm truly puzzled now.

"It... gave you ideas."

Ideas?

"I heard you on the phone," she continues. "You're-you're-you're trying to find a reason to stay here, and you think the high school hack might be that—but it isn't, Ethan. It isn't. You're not seeing straight. You're jeopardizing your career over one little thing I said. God I'm so stupid! I should have seen it coming."

"I'm not jeopardizing anything!"

She stomps her foot. "You are! Okay. So you're gonna fix their system. And then what? Brussels will have gone to another guy, they'll ship you to Florida, and you'll be miserable there. You'll have lost *everything*." She points to the phone in my pocket. "Call him back. Tell him you thought about it. Or-or-or that you were kidding. Lack of sleep. Anything."

I take her hand in mine. "Babe, calm down."

"I'm calm! I am *very* calm!" she shouts, shaking my hand away. "Don't you see what you're doing? You're acting on impulse, and in six months you'll resent me and Emerald Creek, and you'll leave again and never-*ever* come back." She's so worked up, her cheeks are blotchy.

"That's not what I'm doing. Seriously, listen to me."

She folds her arms again, and I just want to kiss her worry frown away.

"Can we just sit down? I need to brainstorm this with you."

"Brainstorm what?"

"Our future. My career."

She narrows her eyes on me, but when I turn to the couch, she says, "This sounds like a coffee moment."

"It totally is a coffee moment."

We both go back into the kitchen. While I make coffee, she fills Damian's bowl. "What did you find at the high school?" she asks.

I tell her, basically, what I told my C.O. I wasn't lying when I said I'm strongly suspecting there's a foreign entity behind the hack, and they're just testing our defenses on soft targets. "I'd like to have the high school start an entirely new system, on new machines, while we play cat and mouse with these fuckers. Give us some time to figure out what they're up to."

"Are you supposed to be telling me this?'

I shrug. "No." I don't need to tell her I trust her.

She nods, pensive.

Back on the deck, we sit on the couch, slurping our coffees while I continue. "Remember when I first visited Noah's coding club?"

"M-hm?"

"I started thinking. There's a lot of work I could do remote, with the proper security in place. The right infrastructure."

She frowns.

"Hear me out. Most of the work I do, I'm alone, analyzing shit. More and more guys are retiring and setting themselves up as consultants for the Air Force. The Air Force likes the flexibility. The guys like the flexibility."

"But you… the Air Force…"

I know what she's thinking. "The Air Force gave me a structure when I was lost. This is not who I am now. And prestige doesn't mean that much to me anymore." I take both her hands in mine. "Think about it, Grace. I could have it all. *We* could have it all. I love my job, and I can keep doing it from here. I could help Coach Randall with hockey and Noah with the coding club."

"You're not thinking straight," she interjects.

I continue. "For a living, I would still do nerdy stuff to protect my country. And I'd be home every night. We could even have our lunch breaks together."

"Honey, you're just sleep-deprived. Don't you see?"

I have to smile at that. "I'm used to sleep deprivation. I'm actually seeing very clearly."

She sighs and shakes her head. "You'd work as a consultant?"

Finally. I got her on board. I need her with me so she can help me brainstorm logistics, like office space and shit. "Yes. I'd need to get myself set up as a business and go through all the security clearance shit again, probably. But it's all red tape and nothing more." Well, and a hefty dollar amount in equipment, if I'm an independent contractor.

She shakes her head slowly. "I never should have told you about the hack. It gave you ideas. *Bad* ideas. This is never gonna work out. I could tell your C.O. was pissed. He's not gonna back you on this. What if you don't get the security clearance? And the contracts?"

"I'll work for the private sector." Fuck, think about it, the high school hack could just help launch my private services, if it comes to that.

"And now you've lost Brussels," Grace continues, on her entirely different track. "Which is the only thing you ever really wanted. I never should have told you. It's all my fault. I asked you. Ohmygod, it's all my fault. I never should have." She flails her arms with genuine desperation.

"Of course you should have. Thank god you did. Don't stop doing that."

"What if it doesn't work?"

"There's no scenario in which it doesn't work. Look, babe, I want us to make these kinds of decisions together."

"Really? It doesn't look like it."

"Are you gonna tell me you don't want me staying in Emerald Creek?" Suddenly, the possibility hits me. Maybe Grace is comfortable in her single life. Maybe she was looking forward to the one-week-a-month thing. Maybe she's not crazy about my stinky socks the way Damian is. Maybe she was generous with calling her house my home and giving me her key because she never thought I'd be a permanent, year-round fixture.

Now she's the one taking my hands. "Of course I want you staying in Emerald Creek. Just not at the cost of your career." Her eyes shine, and I can see how wrong I've been. She only wants the best for me. Always did.

I lean over to kiss her. "I love you for looking out for me. Don't ever regret insisting I go to the high school. It set things in motion. It made me see what was possible."

I run my tongue lightly on her lips. "We look out for each other. Just like me giving Richardson's mother your brochure set in motion a chain of events I never could have planned."

She pulls her mouth away from mine. "Oh—that was *you*?"

"Well, yeah—who else?"

She frowns. "I thought for sure she said it was a handsome carpenter."

I chuckle.

"No, seriously, she said it was a *very hot* carpenter. Not a cyber geek rebelling against the United States Air Force."

"You know, Lucas keeps asking me to go work for them. I could do that, if that turns you on more than the whole geek thing."

She swats my chest playfully. "Ethan King, don't you dare."

"What, you don't want me fixing your house?"

She runs her gaze down my chest, licks her lips, and sets her coffee mug on the floor.

"Our house," she corrects me, sending a zing down my cock.

Right. We need to have the money talk now, but with me living here for good, I don't foresee any trouble.

She leans into me, sex in her gaze. "I guess if you only work for me... and without your shirt on... we could work something out. But what shall we fix?" she adds in a little voice.

I wrap my arm around her waist and pull her to me, then run my fingers over her hardening nipple. "We could start by adding a garage. A three-car garage."

She chuckles. "Oh, you *have* thought this through, haven't you?"

I pull her onto my lap. "Maybe."

Chapter Fifty-Four

Grace

One month later

*

"Everything okay, Claudia?' I lean over the reservation system to find out what's making her frown so profoundly. Even her lips are tilted down, like she just drank something sour.

"Why is she booked with Cheyenne?" she asks, pointing at a name on our nail artist's column of reservations. *Amy Keller.*

"Hey, even Cruella deserves awesome nails." We are the only game in town, after all.

Cheyenne, having heard her name, pops her head between the two of us to glance at the computer. "Oh yeah, I ran into her at Lazy's the other night, and she wouldn't stop raving about my nails. I told her to book online." She shrugs. "That's okay, right? We don't hate her anymore. Right, boss?"

"We don't hate *anyone*," I confirm. "Especially not someone who wants to give us their business."

"I suppose," Claudia says. "I heard she's buying a house up in the hills."

"Really? Good for her," I say. As far as I'm concerned, I have nothing against Amy, and I'm choosing to forget her not-so-glorious, mean girl episode. Carrying a grudge in a small town is unhealthy.

"From Richardson too," Claudia continues. "You know, I never could figure out why he wanted to sell this house. It's an investment property for him. D'you think he needs money?"

I shrug. Not my problem, but certainly a valid question.

"Usual spot?" Randy interrupts us, carrying a large bouquet of flowers.

"Awww," everyone coos.

Ethan has been ordering flowers for the spa and our home ever since he decided to stay in Emerald Creek for good. "*Just because I'm here doesn't mean you don't deserve all the attentions,*" he said.

I blush, thinking at the little notes in colorful envelopes he hides in my handbag for me to find when I'm at work. They're way more explicit than the ones he first made for me. They're actually *so* explicit that I've started putting those new ones back in the jar, and I have him take one randomly every night and demonstrate exactly what he meant.

Most times, it ends in real hot sex. Sometimes, in a fit of laughter.

Of the two outcomes, I can't tell which I prefer.

"How is the high school project coming along?" Randy asks.

"I think they're about to wrap up," I answer. I heard more than I should have, that night on the deck, when Ethan was summarizing the situation to his C.O. I know not to share anything. No one suspects it was ever anything more than a real bad virus, and we should keep it this way. "He's about to move his operation into the Mill, actually."

Ethan snatched the space as soon as he was approved by the higher-ups to become a private consultant.

"I'm so happy for you," Randy says, clutching his hands. Turning to our display of mugs, he adds, "I'm getting one too. Still thinking on what it should say."

Alex comes in for her massage with Shanice, who I've finally convinced to expand beyond facials. Alex was the first person I practiced massages with, back when she had just moved into Emerald Creek, and she's volunteered to be Shanice's test client now. "Happy to brainstorm with you, Randy. We should make it catchy for socials."

At lunch, sitting out on the deck for a quick break, I open the note Ethan slipped into my handbag. It reads, *Is It Friday Yet?*

I smile. Not a kinky note today, but certainly a promise. Fridays are for just the two of us now, to unwind at home. Saturdays are for our friends, and Sundays our families—although there's a lot of overlap between the two.

"Are you coming to Game Nights tonight?" Kiara asks after her pedicure. She never gets fancy manicures, because of her being a pastry chef, but she goes all out on her feet.

Tonight is Thursday. "Wouldn't miss it."

That evening, in the back of Cassandra's lingerie, Ms. Angela is all wound up. She wants to create a new Mystery Board Game. She calls it mystery, but it's really gossip. "We have a lot of new material," she explains.

"Such as?" her friend Cheryl asks.

"Don't you wonder why Georgie is selling property? It doesn't fit his profile."

"I wanna know why the bookshop is called Shy Rabit," Chloe interjects.

Ms. Angela takes out a notebook and writes in it. "That's another one."

Cassandra sips from Haley's latest concoction—something deep blue. "What I'd like to know, is why we have so many beautiful young women who are still single. Emma, Autumn, Kiara..."

"You need to work your magic!" Ms. Angela says. "That's not a mystery."

"Hmm." Cassandra looks around the room, eyes narrowed on my single friends, but tonight, she doesn't call anyone into her boutique.

When I get home that night, my heartbeat picks up as it always does when I come home now. Ethan installed twinkling lights around the frame of the house, that turn on as soon as it's dusk, making the house super welcoming. Lucas and Thalia just finished our three-car garage, and we decided to have an upper level framed in above it. When we can afford it, we'll easily be able to add two bedrooms or an office and a bedroom. Ample space to grow our family.

Right now, I'm content pressing on my garage door opener and sliding into my parking spot between the chick magnet (that nickname stuck) and Ethan's new SUV, and going home to my man and my cat.

"What was that note about Friday?" I ask Ethan as he greets me with a kiss.

"Officially done with the high school project tomorrow, and starting on Monday, I'll be at the Mill."

"That's awesome." I knew this was the timeline he had in mind, but there was always the possibility of last-minute delays. "Do you want to go celebrate? Lazy's? Growler?"

"Not tomorrow. Tomorrow is for us. We can go celebrate Saturday."

"Okay."

"Okay," he repeats, booping me and smiling adorably at me.

The next day, I make sure to get home early. The deck is all sparkling with twinkly lights, the table adorned with candles. It's a little cool out but there are blankets on the couch.

Ethan pulls me to him and lays a big kiss on my mouth. "Take a shower, get comfy, and join me outside."

After a quick shower (why didn't Ethan join me? I need to set that straight), I grab one of the hoodies Ethan got me "for the cold weather" with his name on it. The walk-in closet is filling with his clothes now, thick sweaters and thermals and jeans and snowboarding gear. His smell is everywhere and ohmygod... it's the best. Winter with Ethan is going to be so cozy.

As I walk out to the deck, I'm surprised to see a glow coming from a brand-new gas firepit I hadn't noticed earlier. "What's that?" I lean over it to warm my hands, then plop on the couch, pulling a blanket over me.

"Not as spectacular as a real firepit, but hey," Ethan says, setting a small tray with hot toddies on the ottoman.

"I love it. It's..." It's *ours*. Cozy and all. It's all we need. I reach out for the drink, but Ethan takes my hand. "Hold on, there's something I need to tell you."

I turn to him. Is he going to propose? Eyes bright, I smile at him.

"Damian, where are you, buddy?" he calls out.

I guess not. That's okay. Next time.

Ethan pulls out the laser beam that still drives Damian crazy, and whistles softly. A little jingle sounds behind me. "Who's a gooboy," Ethan says under his breath, playing with the laser beam.

Turning around to see what's up with Damian, I see he's wearing a collar with a bunch of little bells all around it. I laugh. "That's going to drive him crazy! Come here. Come to Mommy."

Ethan directs the laser beam to my lap. "Yeah, come to Mommy."

Damian jumps on me in a mess of jingles. The poor thing is shaking his head to try and get rid of this new gadget. "Come here you poor thing. What did Daddy do now? We'll keep this for Christmas only." I go to take the collar off him, then notice a small pouch attached to it. "What is this?"

"I dunno," Ethan says, as he glides off the couch and drops to his knee.

Not both knees.

One.

My palms get moist.

This is it.

My Ethan *is* proposing. Forgetting all about Damian, I straighten as he takes my hands and starts talking. "Do you know how long I've loved you, Grace?"

I shake my head softly, tears pooling in my eyes.

"So long I don't remember ever *not* loving you. Even as children, you captured my heart in the purest way. You made me better. You made me stronger. You made me braver. I was who I was because of you. Because I knew you were watching me, and I didn't want to disappoint you. Because I loved you. And it's just as true today." He drops his head down for a beat, then looks back up. "Somewhere along the way I messed up. I failed you—"

I shake my head. "It wasn't y—"

He gives my hands a soft tug and smiles softly. "Lemme finish, beautiful."

"Okay," I whisper.

"Somewhere along the way, I messed up. I failed you, and we both suffered for ten long years. Three thousand six hundred and some days, wasted living without you. Three thousand six hundred and some nights, sleeping without you by my side. Ten unnecessary years apart from each other. Now that I found you again, each day and each night is a blessing."

His jaw trembles and his eyes mist. I know what's coming. I know it and I'm prepared and I want it, and yet it's the most emotional moment of my life. Tears flow freely down my cheeks, and I fall on my knees in front of Ethan.

"Grace, you've always been mine. In secret. But you've always intimidated me too. And so it's no surprise that I'm freaking scared right now, right here, asking you to be my wife. Will you?" Uncertainty paints his features. My strong, brave Ethan is unsure.

"I've always been yours, you know it. You make my life complete. Of course I want to be your wife," I whisper, too emotional to speak in a normal voice.

He takes my face in his hands and kisses me softly. Then his eyes dart to the couch. "Damian, buddy, where are you?"

I pull him back to me. "Kiss me more." And he does, but his heart isn't in it. "What's wrong?"

"Damian."

I bunch his shirt in my fist and pull him to me. "Leave him be and kiss your future wife." He kisses me, but his eyes are darting everywhere. "Honey, what's wrong?"

"The ring."

The ring? Oh, *right*. He got me a ring. *Ethan King got me a ring*! The teenager in me is going crazy. Present me is trying to rail her in. So... where is the ring? Suddenly, understanding hits me. "Damian? The pouch around his neck?"

Ethan shuts his eyes briefly. "I knew I shouldn't trust him with that. But I can't believe he's messing up *the proposal*!"

I start laughing. "I know! After everything he's done for us!"

Ethan cups my face again. "Do you have any idea of how perfect you are? Sorry—of how you fit my dirtiest fantasy? You naked in my sweatshirt..." he briefly sweeps a hand up my hips to confirm the statement "laughing because me and Damian messed up the proposal?"

"*That*'s your dirtiest fantasy?"

"You naked under something with my name on it will always be my go-to dirty fantasy. You happy as can be because the ring that should be on your finger is who knows where—guarantee that means a happy-as-hell marriage, Grace."

"Is that a thing? Like rain on your wedding day?"

"It is now."

"I'm sure it was a beautiful ring."

"It's more than beautiful." He lifts me back on the couch, then hands me my hot toddy. "You keep warm while I hunt down the feral thief." Then he stomps into the house, threatening Damian with all sorts of terrible things if he doesn't appear "right this fucking second."

As his voice dims into the house, I take a small sip, trying to rein in all the emotions battling inside me. I knew this day would come... and yet, it's so *big*. And so *strong*. I can't even describe it. It's like—

I'm pulled from my inner contemplation by the sound of tiny little bells chiming under the couch. "Sneaky little guy!" I coo Damian out. He jumps on the couch, sits on his rear end, and slits his eyes at me. Then with one paw, he claws the pouch open, and a small ring lands on my lap. I pick it up and blink, emotion choking me as I take in the tiny blue flowers linked together by a gold twig. I barely register as Damian jingles back into the house, and Ethan surges back on the deck.

"Thank god," Ethan grunts. "D'you like it?" He's standing above me, hands on his hips. "I had it made at Gems. They said they had your size... Hey, what's wrong?" He runs his knuckles softly on my cheek. "Babe? You okay?"

I hand him the ring, my fingers shaking. He drops back to his knees—*both* knees this time—and slides the band on my finger.

"You like it?" he repeats, running his thumb on the intricately carved gold band and small blue stones.

"You-you-you got me... forget-me-nots?" I can't believe Ethan had a custom-made replica of a ring he made for me a quarter of a century ago.

He nods. "Well, sapphires, but the design is... yeah, it came really—"

I shut him up with a kiss, and this time he takes it slow and deep and thoughtful, until I lean into him, and we topple onto the floor and end up making love on the deck, under the cool moonlight.

Chapter Fifty-Five

Grace

A few months later

*

"Your daughter is going to be the most beautiful bride," Mom tells Dad, pecking him on the cheek as Mom and I walk into their house. Ethan is already here, sipping an Arnold Palmer with Dad, a nice fire roaring in their chimney. He stands to greet us, and after a side hug to Mom, gives me a full-on kiss on the mouth.

Sometimes I think he just does it to see how far he can rile up Dad, or maybe as a revenge on the past.

"Missed you," he whispers in my ear.

Or maybe he just really missed me and that's his way of telling me. He wasn't even in Dad's line of sight.

Mom, Haley, and I spent the day in Burlington shopping for a wedding gown, and I found *the one*. I never thought I'd be that person, but here I am. Preparing to marry the man of my dreams—Ethan King.

Over lunch at Leunig's—the best French bistro in Burlington in my opinion—Haley asked about the design of the engagement ring. After I told her, she confessed she had no recollection of playing wedding with her brothers. Ever. Me? I would have said it was her favorite game, at one time. Funny how we really do hold onto the memories that matter most to us, and possibly mold them to suit our personality.

On our way back, Mom and I dropped Haley off at the farm, stopped for tea with Lynn, and showed her pictures of the winning dress. Now I'm at my parents' for Mom's lasagna and some quiet time with my parents and fiancé.

Ethan resumes the conversation he was having with Dad when Mom and I came in. He's catching him up on his latest hire, someone from out of state, and letting him know how the others are doing, whether they're married or not, and how they're liking life in Emerald Creek.

The table is already set for four, and I recognize Ethan's touch in the small tealight candles at each end.

"No Colton?" I ask as we take our seats.

"He had a date," Dad supplies. "Came to grab some suit or something this morning."

"His suit?" Something's off. "Why would he go on a date in a suit?" Come to think about it, I saw him on the schedule with Cheyenne, to get his nails scrubbed free of grease.

"Did he tell you anything?" I ask Ethan.

Ethan shrugs. "Uh... he might have mentioned some girl he met online. Not sure."

"Online?" Mom exclaims. "Why on earth would he do that?"

"It's hard to meet people these days," I suggest, not really sure myself why Colton would need to look online for dates.

"That's ridiculous," Mom responds. "All he needs to do is start repairing his cars bare chested, and you'll see all these cute tourists line up to get their..." She interrupts herself, blushing slightly. "Sorry. That was out of line. Also, it's winter," she adds with a giggle.

Dad chuckles, and Ethan makes a funny face. "Sounds like something my mom would say."

"I'm with you, Mom," I chime in. "I don't know what's up with him. Seriously. Nothing wrong with the women around here. Autumn is single. And Willow. And Sophie. And-and-and..."

"Kiara," Dad says. "She makes good cakes."

"Kiara's not interested," I interrupt him before he gets ahead of himself. "Oh god, we gotta stop."

"Stop what?" Ethan asks.

"This gossiping! It's not right." I take a mouthful of lasagna, so I keep quiet for a beat.

"It's not gossiping if it's not on Echoes," Mom interjects.

"Or said out loud at Lazy's," Dad adds.

Seeing their point, I add, "Or at Easy Monday. That counts as gossiping too."

"For sure," Mom adds. "By that token, what's said at Game Nights is gossiping too."

I roll my eyes. "Oh totally. That's like, gossip central. More so than Echoes. No traceability," I add, having picked up a concept or two from Ethan's work (the little he shares with me) over the past few months.

Ethan moves his fork in a circle. "So... what's this?"

"It's caring!" Mom and I exclaim together.

"Lotsa caring going around in this household," Dad chuckles. "Get used to it, son," he adds naturally.

Ethan does a double take on Dad, his forehead coloring a little, his eyes warming up. It's the first time Dad calls him son, and the way it came out makes me all kinds of mushy. But Dad doesn't show any particular emotion, and even Mom doesn't seem to notice, as if it's a given. Ethan promptly focuses back on his lasagna.

"Haley found her dress too," Mom says to Ethan, then turns to me. "And they had the cutest flower girl dresses, right? Skye is going to be over-the-moon happy."

I give Ethan's hand a quick squeeze. Our wedding is bringing so much happiness to so many people, we've decided to have it at the church, with the reception being on The Green, so that literally everyone in Emerald Creek will feel comfortable attending. Lazy's and Clover's Nook (Chloe's new restaurant) will be catering, but I've made Justin and Chloe promise that they would hire extras from out of town so that they and their staff could have fun as well.

I pull out my phone and show Ethan the pictures of Haley's and Skye's dresses.

He takes the phone in his hands and zooms on the selection of dresses for Skye. "She's gonna love the one with the butterflies," he says, a smile curving his lips up. "Oh wait... does this one have little Ivy leaves?"

I giggle at my future husband's interest in flower girl dresses.

"When are you giving me grandbabies?" Dad asks gruffly.

I act offended. "Dad!"

"You made me a promise on my death bed," he says to Ethan, ignoring me.

"Your what?!" Mom cries.

"You know what I mean," Dad waves dismissively.

Ethan smiles softly and takes my hand. "That's up to Grace."

Dad raises his eyebrows. "A promise is a promise."

Ethan nods. "And I promised you as many as she wanted."

Dad grunts.

"What—When did this happen?" I ask, mildly amused and intrigued at the same time. Dad and Ethan talking about grandbabies on a supposed deathbed? That's news to me.

"Never mind," Dad and Ethan say at the same time.

Okay, then. My dad and my fiancé have their side conversations. That's rather sweet, considering where we came from. "We have a wedding to plan," I state. "We'll talk babies later." I sound way more assured than I feel. Just thinking about having Ethan's babies fills me with something indescribable. And very desirable.

"Well, I would hope so," Mom says. "You have a dress to fit into."

"The voice of reason," I say.

Ethan frowns and grunts. I feel like grunting too. Six more months to go, give or take.

"You've waited ten years. What's a few more months?" Mom says.

Now it's Dad's turn to grunt.

"Who wants more lasagna?" Mom asks, dipping the serving spoon in the dish.

We all hand our plates.

Dad frowns. "Oh—now she doesn't have a dress to fit into?" he asks playfully.

"It's lasagna, honey. It's nice and light," Mom says with a straight face.

Dad laughs heartily at that. "Okay then, since it's nice and light, double serving for me," he says, making us all laugh.

Ethan reaches under the table and strokes my thigh, then looks at me with a sweet smile.

Later, after we say our goodbyes, we settle in the SUV that Ethan started a good ten minutes before leaving so it would warm up. "You know," he says, not driving away just yet, "I had a vague idea of what I wanted in life. Something ideal. With you in the center of it all. But it turned out so much better than I thought. This is all so much more *everything*... So much more love, and fun, and fulfillment. And there's so much more to look forward to." He takes my hand softly in his. "I can't believe this is just the beginning."

I lean across the center console to kiss him. His hands come to my nape, pulling me gently to him, cradling me. "You're the best part of me, Grace," he says, choking a bit on his words.

He clears his throat, and I sit back in my seat. "Home or nightcap at Lazy's?" he asks as he pulls out of my parents' driveway.

I really want to go home, but we haven't seen our friends in a few days. And it's still relatively early. "Quick nightcap at Lazy's?"

His smile tells me this is where his mind was too. We can't wait to get our hands on each other, but we have all night, and all day tomorrow. Even if we decide to go snowboarding, or skating.

With how it's been snowing all day today, Lazy's is less busy than a usual Saturday night. We order hot toddies and chat with Haley, Alex and Chris.

As we're thinking about heading home, the door opens on Kiara carrying one of her pastry boxes, but this one is so tall you can't see her behind it—only her legs in fishnet stockings. Which is totally not Kiara's style. And totally not weather appropriate.

Right behind her, holding the door, Colton comes in, wearing dress pants and a shirt under his coat.

I turn to Ethan for an explanation. He shakes his head at me, just as puzzled as I am.

Kiara sets the cake on the bar and Colton opens the box. It turns out to be the leftover half of a cake, showing several layers that I can already tell will taste decadent. But what renders me speechless for a beat is the décor of the cake. Entirely white—white roses, white twirly things on the sides, some gold accents.

This is a wedding cake.

Now. Why would Kiara have half a wedding cake?

Why would Kiara be all dressed up (granted, not in white)?

Why would Colton be dressed up at all?

I mean, if they'd been to a wedding together, we'd know, right? There would be a good chance we'd know the couple, so we'd know of the wedding, even if for some bizarre reason none of us were invited.

The strangest, yet most obvious answer pops into my mind, and I'm about to ask for confirmation when Haley beats me to it, laughing. "Did you guys get *married*?"

Kiara rolls her eyes and blurts, "Ugh. Even *that* sounds better than what happened," while Colton looks at me like a deer caught in the headlights.

Oh-oh.

"What the hell is going on between those two?" Ethan whispers in my ear.

My thoughts exactly.

Didn't get enough of Grace and Ethan? Click here (bellarivers.com /bonus-scene-rty) for an extra scene showing them in the future, or scan the QR code below:

Are you as curious as Grace and Ethan about Kiara and Colton? Click here to read their story or scan the QR code below.and continue reading for a sneak preview.

Chapter Fifty-Six

Friends Don't Kiss

Sneak preview (Chapter 1)

KIARA

"Why are you so nervous?"

Willow watches as I pipe the final swirl of white chocolate ganache onto my grandmother's birthday cake. She turns the plate so I can finish, then steps back, phone in hand, snapping photos while I arrange petal-shaped curls around the white chocolate roses. Grams will appreciate the extra touch.

I take a slow breath, trying to ease the tightness in my stomach. "I'm not nervous." *Just bracing myself for the family reunion.*

"Uh-huh." Willow tilts her head. "You're biting the inside of your cheeks, and your place is serial-killer-level clean."

I grunt.

"It's super weird to see the Fearless Leader of the Bitch Brigade rattled," she says.

Willow and I became friends not long after I moved to Emerald Creek a few years ago. She works at the bakery that hired me, so we're constantly crossing paths—during shifts, at Lazy's, the town bar, or at one of the girls' nights out someone inevitably organizes. I'm the part-time pastry chef, and whenever I'm on the schedule, she gets bumped from the register to help me bake macarons and chocolate soufflés.

But today, she came to my place to help me bake for the family reunion. We've been at it since morning and through lunch, yet there's not a fleck of flour on the floor, no stray utensils, not a dish soaking in the sink. The couch is pristine, books aligned, throw pillows fluffed, candles angled just right on the white coffee table.

My private space is the only thing I can control today, and I'm hanging onto that with desperation.

"I like my place under control. It's more comfy that way." Even I can hear the sarcasm in my tone.

Willow sees through my lie. "I'm sorry it has to be that way with your folks," she says softly as she ties a ribbon around the boxes of petits fours we made together.

I shrug. "Eh, family. You know how it is."

She gives a small chuckle. We both come from homes that are broken in different ways and understand there's no fixing these things—just learning how to live with them, distance ourselves from them if we can, and build lives for ourselves that don't feel like a constant struggle.

The cake is done. I step back to admire it, satisfaction settling in my chest. It's everything I wanted for my grams' birthday. Everything *she'd* want. The seven-layer torte is cloaked in snow-white fondant, an elaborate arrangement of royal-icing roses artfully spilling down its sides, the most intricate piping I've ever done circling its base.

"Grams is going to love it," I say as much for myself as for Willow.

"It's gorgeous," Willow whispers, awe in her voice. "Let's take pictures and post it on socials. It looks like a wedding cake." She pulls out her phone again. "And wait 'til she tastes it."

The layers of dacquoise—maple, vanilla cream, and hazelnut crunch—are interspersed with dark chocolate ganache and fresh raspberries, all this on a base of Italian meringue. Just the thought of how my creation will bring her the joy she deserves is enough to chase away my family reunion-induced anxiety, at least for now.

"I was gonna say you outdid yourself, but that wouldn't be fair. Everything you make is above and beyond," Willow says as she turns the phone around the cake to capture the variations in the decor.

"Thanks." The word comes out quieter than I intend, my thoughts drifting to the one thing that keeps me going now: establishing myself as a legit pastry chef. I'm almost there. Almost. But true success keeps eluding me.

I still don't have my own shop. I still haven't made a name for myself. No matter how hard I push, how many hours I put into my craft, I can't seem to break through.

Glancing at this cake again, I can't figure it out. What bride wouldn't want something this beautiful, something that tastes as exquisite as it looks?

"How 'bout you make more of these," Willow says, switching to pictures. "Different designs, different flavors, so you have more to show?"

I thought about that. About the flavor combos, too. "M-hm. Orange blossom, pistachio, and Meyer lemon. Pear, white chocolate, and chai. Mint, dark chocolate, and walnut." I grab my notebook and write these ideas down, before something else takes over my brain and I forget. "I could make those next week. Pretend I'm swamped with orders. Fake-it-'til-you-make-it type of thing," I mumble.

That means spending hours baking cakes no one ordered with supplies I can barely afford. I could eat them. Wouldn't hurt to put on a few pounds.

"Tell me when, and I'll come help. Hey, we should post it on socials, saying we're prepping tastings for next season's brides?"

Wow. Why didn't I think about that? "That's brilliant!" I'm moved by the dimples forming on her cheeks, by the way her deep brown eyes are dancing with true happiness. Willow doesn't have an easy life, yet she finds happiness in the smallest things. *I need to be more like her.*

"Okay, let's put this baby away for now. Open the fridge for me?" she says, snapping me out of my thoughts.

Once the cake is cooling, I make us some coffee and we both plop on the kitchen chairs. For the first time today, I let myself relax.

"What did you call me earlier?" I ask.

She shrugs like she has no clue what I'm talking about.

"The fearful bitch?" I nudge her.

She laughs so hard she almost chokes on her coffee. "The Fearless Leader of the Bitch Brigade," she finally manages to say.

That gets me laughing too.

"After, you know..." she adds.

"Yeah-yeah-yeah." Last summer, when our friend Grace nearly lost her spa, we rallied the troops. The name Bitch Brigade came organically to me. Being called their fearless leader is a stretch, but it's still nice. "Thanks for today. I owe you one."

"It's nothing." She takes a long sip of her coffee, her eyes on me. "You'll have your own place one day, I promise. The world is gonna find out what a great pastry chef you are, and you'll have more work than you can handle." She smiles deviously. "Then I'll guilt-trip you into paying me an insane salary with benefits. I'll remind you how I saved your sorry ass more than once."

I tip my coffee mug toward her. "Fair enough. In that case, I need one more thing before you go. If you have time," I add.

"It's Saturday. Chris gave me the day off to help you, and I don't have a life." She shrugs. "What do you need?"

"Help me figure out an outfit."

Willow squeaks with excitement, downs her coffee, and dashes to my bedroom.

I finish my coffee to the sound of the closet door opening and closing and Willow humming to herself, then rinse our mugs and join her.

Any sense of order and control I thought I had is completely obliterated. Half my wardrobe is piled up on my bed, tops on one side and bottoms on the other. "What you got for me?" I say, faking enthusiasm as I stretch my mouth into a smile.

Willow doesn't catch onto my near state of despair. "How about this?" She thrusts a pair of black skinny jeans and a bright green tube top my way.

"Yeah, nope."

"Oh." She blinks, seeming surprised. "More conventional?" She offers a pair of gray slacks and the white blouse I only wear when I have a meeting at the bank.

I scratch my head. Willow isn't making it easier, but at least I'm not doing this alone.

She tilts her head. "With your body type, you can wear whatever you want." She flings the clothes on the bed and finds an empty spot to sit on. "Why don't you tell me what this is about?" she asks with a kindness that is worrisome.

"Just my grams' birthday party. Eighty years old."

"Yup. We just spent all day baking for her, 'member? Try again." She nudges me with her elbow in an attempt to perk me up.

"Alright. *Fine.*" I lean against the closet door, cross my arms, and try to gather my feelings into something that makes sense. "I haven't seen my mom and my sister in a long time."

Willow's facial expression shifts. "Oh. And... are we happy about seeing them?"

I let out a humorless laugh. "Well... They still think I'm a loser who tore the family apart."

After my falling out with them, we went two, maybe three years without speaking. Then Grams forced us to patch things up, and I thought all the ugliness was behind us. That we were a family again.

I was wrong.

Whenever we see each other now, it seems their only purpose is to remind me of how inadequate I am. Of how unlike them I am. Of how I don't belong. Mom calls and texts me, acting like a normal yet distant mother might, but her efforts don't fool me. There's something broken beyond repair in our relationship.

I've learned to shove my feelings down into the pit of my stomach, where no one can see them and they can hurt only me. I've learned to toughen up. I've learned to accept that I don't have a family, that it was ripped from me when I was a teenager. That any so-called family reunion is just another reminder that I fucked up in a major way that will never be forgiven. That no matter how much Mom pretends otherwise, I will never really be back in the fold.

Willow knows the gist of it, but not the details. I've also learned to pretend that I don't care about these things. It's called adapting, and I like to think I've become pretty adept at that survival skill.

She stands and wraps me in a quick hug. "Fuck them!" she whispers.

"Maybe the blouse but with black pants," I say.

She shakes her head. "You'd look like a server." Turning to the pile of clothes, she asks, "Do you want to give them a big fat Eff You or do you want to try and blend in?"

Both.

Since the events that got me banned from the family, I've come a long way. I moved out of my car and into a legit apartment. I made friends that feel more like family than the one I was born into. And I've become a pastry chef—at least, in my mind I am.

But today isn't about me. It's about making Grams happy. Removing any point of friction between us would be the first step. "Blend in," I concede.

"Okay, so traditional, bordering on uppity," Willow says as she extracts a plaid skirt I didn't even remember owning, and pairs it with a black sweater that might be cashmere.

Ditching my yoga pants, I slip into the skirt. "How d'you figure that?"

She shrugs. "The stuff you had when you got here wasn't exactly homeless gear. You had designer jeans and brand-name handbags."

I look at her in surprise as I zip up the skirt, which hangs a little loose on my hips. I always viewed myself as the broke, messed-up black sheep. Did Willow see me as a bougie runaway?

"You were cool though," she says, handing me the sweater.

She totally saw me as a bougie runaway. Which, to be fair, I kind of was.

"Tuck it in, she instructs. Her eyes widen as I do. "Oh wow—that looks great on you."

I turn to examine my reflection in the mirror. "I look like a sixth-grader entering boarding school."

"No you don't." Willow says, tossing a pair of fishnet stockings in my direction. "Where are your booties? The ones with the mile-high spike heels and the gold buckle?"

Once I'm all decked to Willow's instructions and standing six inches taller, I bite my lip. I look like a K-drama heroine. "I think that'll work. Thanks!"

Willow gives an exaggerated sigh. "You look hot, Boss. You forgot the feeling. Tits out!"

"What tits?" I smirk.

She pinches my left boob. "Shoulders back, chin high, ass out. You remember how to walk in those?"

I nod. "Like riding a bike." I lean over to give her a hug. "You're a lifesaver."

"That's me." She smirks. "Now go kick ass and have fun with your grams."

"I will," I lie.

After the door shuts on her, I turn to the mess on my bed and smile. Then, as I start hanging and folding my clothes, I belt out Bejeweled at full volume.

The last step is to style my short blonde hair in its usual spiky, edgy look, which has the distinct advantage of adding another half inch or so to my height. *Perfect.* Just to be on the safe side, I give it one more spritz of hairspray.

Good.

I go back to the kitchen, take the cake out of the fridge, and check my list.

~~Cake.~~

~~Petits fours.~~

~~Candles.~~

Shit. Candles. Where did I put them? There's a strike through the word, so I must have packed them, but now I can't remember where. And just because I checked them off the list doesn't mean I actually did what I was supposed to do with them.

Wouldn't be the first time.

I look around. *Eighty candles.* Can't really misplace eighty fucking candles. Did I even buy them? Yeah, yeah, I did. I remember buying them. I remember deciding they would ruin the aesthetic of the cake—so seventy-nine would go on the petits fours and only one on the cake itself.

Petits fours! Yes. There they are. And inside one of the pastry boxes—candles.

Found them! Crisis averted.

I exhale and let my shoulders drop. I can relax now.

Then my phone dings, and the name on the display makes me think the relaxing might not happen after all.

Mother: Are you still bringing someone?

Fuck. I forgot about that. *No, Mother, I'm not bringing anyone. Who the fuck would I bring?*

Me: That's the plan.

Mother: Is that a yes or a no?

Does it really matter? Of course not.

Me: It's 90% yes. He had a last-minute thing at work and is trying to get out of it.

Mother: What's his name again?

Ugh. I better not answer that, because I'm guaranteed to forget what I told her and then I won't be able to keep my story straight when I'm interrogated—at this point, it's fair to say that I will be.

I exit the chat.

Sighing, I glance out the window, my tension easing incrementally as I let my gaze wander past the small apartment complex where I live—Sunrise Farms—down toward Emerald Creek. The village sits nestled in a bend of the river, huddled around a green. The golden numbers on the church clock gleam in the setting sun, its white steeple sharp against the winter sky. Thick snow blankets the roofs, and plumes of smoke billow softly from chimneys—maybe from Ms. Angela's bed-and-breakfast, or my friends Chris and Alex's Victorian house-slash-bakery.

I could say I made my home in Emerald Creek, and it'd be true. But it's more than that.

Emerald Creek took me in when I was at my lowest and built me up. This place and the people that live here are my true family.

Taking a deep breath, I count to three. It's only one evening. And it's for Grams.

My gaze drops to the small parking lot below, and I grimace. There are many advantages to living at Sunrise Farms. Lockers for skis, snowboards, and bikes. Management clears the access for us.

But the downside? No covered parking. And winters in Northern Vermont can last six months.

Luckily, my first friend in Emerald Creek—and incidentally responsible for me moving here in the first place—Colton, the town mechanic, installed a remote starter for my Corolla.

Which isn't working this morning. I stab the fucker again. Open my window, bracing against the cold.

Nope.

Great. I'll tell Colton—eventually. Not now for sure, or even this weekend. Knowing him, he'd want to fix it immediately. And since he also lives at Sunrise Farms, it would literally be a right now situation.

He already does so much for me, no way am I asking him for anything on a weekend.

The falling snow already added a fresh layer on my car, even though I cleared it before Willow got here. I shove my heeled booties in my bag, swap them for my snow boots, and haul my cakes and pastries outside. After securing all the boxes so they don't slide around in my trunk, I climb into the driver's seat and recheck my list.

~~One cake~~

~~Petits fours~~ *9 boxes*

~~Candles~~ *1 box*

All good.

I turn the ignition.

Click. Nothing.

"Fuck."

Turn. Click. Click. Nothing.

"Come on, you little shit."

Turn. Click.

Fuck me.

I glance around the parking lot. Good. Colton's truck is here. He's home. I guess I'm asking for his help. *Again.* This really needs to stop.

Me

> Yo Colton

Colt

Wassup

> Can you jump-start my car?

Now?

<Thumbs up emoji>

Now?

Duh.

<Thumbs up emoji>

Is that a yes?

<Thumbs up emoji>

Read Kiara and Colton's story in Friends Don't Kiss!

Acknowledgements

J ust as for Never Let You Go and The Promise Of You, this book wouldn't exist without the support of the indie writing community. The knowledge and encouragement shared online, through chat rooms, and at writing conferences, testifies to the generosity of an amazingly creative group.

Thank you as always to my Redbirds tribe of writers, Teresa Beeman, Ariana Clark, Diana Divine, Michele Ingrid, and Kenna Rey. This book wouldn't be here without your weekly cheer, our constructive discussions, and the friendships of fellow writers who understand each other's struggles and insecurities. Teresa, I am particularly grateful for your sense of logic and eagle eye in re-reading Return To You days before its release to try and catch those pesky typos and help me give readers the best experience possible.

As always, I would like to thank my truly amazing developmental editor, Angela James, for her stellar feedback and guidance, and Grace Wynter, for her wonderful copyedits.

I chose to release my first three books in rapid succession, and in doing so, over just a few weeks I met amazing readers and supporters of my work. I cannot begin to tell you how much your words of praise for *Never Let You Go* and *The Promise Of You* made every sleepless night worrying over my stories, rewarding. Even as I'm writing these words, having yet not yet received advance reviews for *Return To You*, I want to say how you've made the countless hours re-writing, re-plotting, re-considering, so worthwhile.

And now maybe I've jinxed myself and you won't like this book!! :)

About the author

Bella Rivers writes steamy small town romances with a guaranteed happily ever after, and themes of found family and forgiveness. Expect hot scenes, fierce love, and strong language!

A hopeless romantic, Bella is living her own second chance romance in the rolling hills of Vermont. When she's not telling the stories of the characters populating her dreams, you can find her baking, hiking, skiing, or just hanging around her small town to soak in the happiness.

Her newsletter is where Bella shares progress on her writing as well as sneak peeks into upcoming books, the occasional recipe from her characters, and books from other writers she thinks her readers might like. You can also find her and interact with her on social media. To subscribe, browse her books, follow along on social, or get in touch, visit www.bellarivers.com

Printed in Dunstable, United Kingdom